"The dead must speak truth," Gellana said softly, "and in life or in death, Bentley Mirrorshade would tell no direct lie. Tell us, my husband, who is responsible for this death."

The specter's eyes swept the assemblage. His stubby, translucent finger lifted, swept to the left, and leveled at Elaith Craulnober with a sharp, accusing stab. . . .

* * * * *

Alone in the darkness, the radiance silently returned, and with it what Rhauligan had been too slow to turn and see: a disembodied head, its face pinched and white, the plumes of the long helm it wore dancing gently in an unseen breeze. It was smiling broadly as it looked at the closed door—and abruptly started to fade away. A breath later, the room was dark and empty once more. . . .

* * * * *

Death was in the air that night—real death and real blood—I could smell it. Murder was only moments away. I edged closer to the stage. The two fat men there were my responsibility. Usually a person doesn't become my responsibility until he's lying facedown in an alley puddle. But these two stuffed sausages were still very much alive, and it was my job to keep them that way. . . .

* * * * *

That night I awoke, startled. The scraping noise was back. It sounded a little like a dog scratching at the door of his master's house, hoping to get in—a big dog. I lit my bedside lamp and when I opened my door, I could see that the door to Pheslan's room was already ~~open~~. I looked in to find it emp~~ty~~ perhaps awakened by t~~he~~

Then I heard the scre~~am~~

FANTASY ADVENTURE

FORGOTTEN REALMS

FANTASY ADVENTURE

Realms of Mystery

Edited by
Philip Athans

REALMS OF MYSTERY

©1998 TSR, Inc.
All Rights Reserved.

Distributed to the book trade in the United States by Random House, Inc. and in Canada by Random House of Canada Ltd.

Distributed to the hobby, toy, and comic trade in the United States and Canada by regional distributors.

Distributed worldwide by Wizards of the Coast, Inc. and regional distributors.

Cover art by Alan Pollack

First Printing: June 1998
All rights reserved. Made in the U.S.A.
Library of Congress Catalog Card Number: 97-062369

9 8 7 6 5 4 3 2 1

ISBN: 0-7869-1171-9
8582XXX1501

U.S., CANADA, ASIA,
PACIFIC, & LATIN AMERICA
Wizards of the Coast, Inc.
P.O. Box 707
Renton, WA 98057-0707
+1-206-624-0933

EUROPEAN HEADQUARTERS
Wizards of the Coast, Belgium
P.B. 34
2300 Turnhout
Belgium
+32-14-44-30-44

Visit our web site at **www.tsr.com**

CONTENTS

Editor's Acknowledgments

The original idea for *Realms of Mystery* came from former TSR Executive Editor Brian Thomsen. The anthology was meant to coincide with our line of "fantasy mystery" novels and was likewise meant to be released around the same time as Chet Williamson's *Murder in Cormyr* and Richard Meyers's *Murder in Halruaa*.

Unfortunately the events that lead to the eventual acquisition of TSR by our new friends at Wizards of the Coast put everything on hold, including the book you're now holding in your hands. We thought long and hard about a mystery anthology, now that it wasn't part of a larger "program," and in the end we just couldn't think of a single reason why all those unconnected events should spoil a terrific idea.

So, thanks to Brian and thirteen other outstanding authors, some of whom appear for the first time in a TSR book, here it is, a look into the darker corners of the FORGOTTEN REALMS . . . where both murder and investigation take on a magical air. . . .

Speaking with the Dead

Elaine Cunningham

The sun began to disappear behind the tall, dense pines of the Cloak Wood, and the colors of an autumn sunset—deep, smoky purples and rose-tinted gold—stained the sky over the Coast Way.

Tired though they were from a long day's travel, every member of the south-bound caravan quickened his pace. While splendidly mounted merchants urged their steeds on and drovers cracked whips over the backs of the stolid dray horses hitched to the wagons, the mercenary guards loosened their weapons and peered intently into the lengthening shadows. The trade route was dangerous at any time, but doubly so at night. Truth be told, however, most of the caravan members lived in greater fear of their own captain than of any chance-met monster or band of brigands. Elaith Craulnober was not an elf to be trifled with, and he had bid them make the fortress by nightfall.

"Last hill! Fortress straight ahead!" shouted one of the scouts. The news rippled through the company in a murmur of relief.

From his position near the rear of the caravan, Danilo Thann leaned forward to whisper words of encouragement into his tired horse's back-turned ears. The ears were a bad sign, for the horse could be as balky as a cart mule. Once they crested the last hill, all would be well. The sight of a potential stable would spur the horse on as little else could, for he was a comfort-loving beast. He was also a beauty, with a sleek, glossy coat the color of ripe wheat. Danilo had turned down several offers from merchants who coveted the showy beast, and had shrugged off a good deal of jesting from the other guards. Dan felt a special affinity for this horse. The "pretty pony," as the sneering mercenaries called him, had more going for him than met the eye. He was beyond doubt the most intelligent steed Danilo had ever encountered, and utterly fearless in battle. His mincing gait could change in a heartbeat to a fearsome battle charge. In Dan's opinion, the horse would have been a worthy paladin's mount, if not for its pleasure-loving nature and its implacable stubborn streak—both traits that Dan understood well.

He patted his horse's neck and turned to his companion of nearly four years, a tall, rangy figure who was wrapped in a dark cloak such as a peasant might wear, and riding a raw-boned, gray-dappled mare. The rider's height and seat and well-worn boots suggested a young man of humble means, well accustomed to the road. This, Dan knew, was a carefully cultivated illusion. This illusion was a needed thing, perhaps, but he was growing tired of it.

Danilo reached out and tugged back the hood of his partner's cloak. The dying light fell upon a delicate elven face, framed by a chin-length tumble of black curls and dominated by large blue eyes, almond-shaped and flecked with gold. These marvelous eyes narrowed dangerously as they settled on him. Arilyn was half-elven and all his—or so Danilo liked to think. She was also furious with his latest foolishness. Danilo, well accustomed to such response, smiled fondly.

Arilyn jerked her hood back up into place. "What in the Nine bloody Hells was that about?" she demanded, her voice low and musical despite her irritation.

"It seems like days since I've had a good look at you. We' re almost at the Friendly Arm," Danilo said. His smile broadened suggestively. "The name suggests possibilities, does it not?"

The half-elf sniffed. "You keep forgetting the differences between us. A bard from a noble merchant clan can travel wherever he pleases, drawing attention but not suspicion. But I am known in these parts for what I am!"

He dismissed this with a quick, casual flip of one bejeweled hand. "In Baldur's Gate, certain precautions were in order. But I hear the gnomes who hold this fortress are admirable little fellows—easygoing folk who set a fine table and mind their own affairs. And the Friendly Arm is perhaps the only truly neutral spot within a tenday's ride. Nothing much ever happens within the fortress walls, so why should we not relax and enjoy ourselves?"

"We have business to attend," she reminded him.

"I'm honored that you take your responsibilities to the caravan so seriously," said a new voice, one slightly lower and even more musical than Arilyn's and rich with dark, wry humor. The companions turned to face a silver-haired elf, just as he reined his cantering horse into step with Arilyn's mare. Neither of them had heard his approach.

Enchanted horseshoes, no doubt, Danilo mused. Elaith Craulnober was known to have a fondness for magical items, and a wicked delight in keeping those around him off guard. The elf also valued information. Though Elaith would probably have given Arilyn anything she asked of him, Danilo suspected that the elf had another motive for allowing a representative of the Thann merchant clan to ride along with his caravan. Elaith knew that both Danilo and Arilyn were Harpers, and that members of this secret organization usually had duties far more pressing than acting as caravan guards.

Arilyn mirrored the elf's faint smile and bantering tone. "I take all my responsibilities seriously," she said.

"Too seriously, if Danilo is to be believed."

In response to that, Elaith lifted one brow and murmured an Elvish phrase, a highly uncomplimentary remark that defied precise translation into the Common trade tongue. His jaw dropped in astonishment when both Arilyn and Danilo burst into laughter. After a moment, he smiled ruefully and shrugged. "So, bard, you understand High Elvish. I suppose that shouldn't have surprised me."

"And had you known, would you have chosen your words with more tact?" Danilo asked, grinning.

Elaith shrugged again. "Probably not."

The three of them rode in silence for several minutes. Something that for lack of a better term could be called friendship had grown between the elf and the Harpers, but Danilo never lost sight of the fact that theirs was a tenuous friendship. They were too different for it to be otherwise. Elaith Craulnober was a Moon elf adventurer, landowner, and merchant. He had far-flung interests, few of which were entirely legal, and a well-earned reputation for cruelty, treachery, and deadly prowess in battle. Arilyn was half-elven, the daughter of Elaith's lost elven love. She was as focused upon duty as a paladin, and Danilo suspected that she would not allow a shared history and a common heritage to stay her hand should Elaith step beyond the bounds of law and honor. Danilo was, on the whole, a bit more flexible about such things. He had traveled with Elaith when circumstances had enforced a partnership between them, and they had developed a cautious, mutual respect. But Danilo did not trust the elf. There were too many dangerous secrets between them, too many deadly insults exchanged, treacheries barely avoided.

At that moment, they crested the hill and the fortress came suddenly into sight. Nestled in a broad valley just to the east of the trade route, it was a sturdy and defensible holdfast of solid granite. A tall, thick curtain wall enclosed an austere castle and a bailey big enough to house perhaps a score of other buildings. This holdfast, once a wizard's keep, was now a wayside inn held and operated by a clan of gnomes.

The massive portcullis rose with a whirring of gears—a sure sign of a gnomish devise, noted Danilo. Most of the holdfast's inhabitants were simple folk mostly occupied with the maintenance of the castle, and in recent years a few gnomes from the island of Lantan had settled at the Friendly Arm, bringing with them the worship of Gond the Wonderbringer and a corresponding fondness for mechanical devices that were often entertaining and occasionally useful.

At that moment the chain raising the portcullis slipped, and the pointed iron bars plunged downward. One of the men approaching the gate shrieked and lunged from his horse. He hit the dirt and rolled aside just as the portcullis came to an abrupt stop, mere inches from its highest point. This brought much laughter and many rough jests from the other members of the caravan, but Danilo noticed that they all rode through the gate with more alacrity than usual.

Inside the fortress wall, chaos reigned. The holdfast was home to perhaps three- or four-score gnomes, hill-loving folk small enough to walk comfortably under the belly of Danilo's tall horse. Most of the gnomes seemed to be out and about, busily loading goods into the warehouses, tending horses in a long, low stable, directing the wagons into covered sheds, or bustling in and out of the many small buildings, clustered around several narrow alleys, that filled the Friendly Arm's grass-covered bailey.

Danilo took the opportunity to observe this unusual clan closely. They looked a bit like dwarves, although somewhat shorter and considerably less broad than their mountain-dwelling relatives. The male gnomes wore their beards short and neatly trimmed, and the females' faces, unlike those of bearded dwarf women, were smooth and rosy-cheeked. All the gnomes had small blue eyes, pointed ears, extremely long noses, and skin that echoed all the browns of the forest, from the gray-brown of the duskwood tree to the deeply weathered hue of old cedar. They favored forest shades in their clothing as well, and the lot of them were dressed in browns and greens—with an adventurous few adding a hint of autumn color.

They were certainly industrious folk. Nearly every pace of the courtyard was occupied by horse or wagon, but the gnomes directed the seeming chaos with the ease of long practice. A northbound caravan had arrived shortly before Elaith's, and the southerners were still busily securing their goods for the night. Merchants shouted instructions to their servants in a half dozen southern dialects. A few swarthy guards loitered about, leaning against the walls and sizing up the newcomers with an eye toward the evening's entertainment. In Danilo's experience, it was always so. The road was long, and travelers were ever on the lookout for a new tale or tune, some competition at darts or dice or weapons, or a bit of dalliance. Most of the guards from both caravans had already gone into the castle's great-hall-turned-tavern, if the din coming from the open doors was any indication.

"Shall we join the festivities?" Danilo asked his companion. He handed the reins of his horse to a gnomish lad—along with a handful of coppers—and then slipped an arm around Arilyn's waist.

She side-stepped his casual embrace and sent him a warning look from beneath her hood. "I am supposed to be your servant, remember?" she warned him. "You learn what you can in the great hall, while I talk to the stable hands."

The young bard sighed in frustration, but he had no argument to counter Arilyn's logic. He nodded and turned aside, only to step right into the unsteady path of a stocky, dark-haired man. There was no time to dodge: they collided with a heavy thud.

The dark, smoky scent of some unfamiliar liqueur rolled off the man in waves. Danilo caught him by the shoulders to steady him, then pushed him out at arm's length—after all, one could never be too careful. The man was unfamiliar to him: a southerner, certainly, with a beak of a nose under what appeared to be a single long eyebrow, a vast mustache, and skin nearly as brown as a gnome's. He appeared harmless enough. He carried no apparent weapons, and his rich clothing suggested a bored merchant whose only thought was to wash away the dust of a long road with an abundance of strong spirits.

"Are you quite all right?" Danilo inquired politely. "Shall I summon your manservant to help you to your room?"

The man mumbled something unintelligible and wrenched himself free. Dan watched him stagger off, then glanced back for a final look at Arilyn and did an astonished double take. She had fallen back into the shadows between two small buildings and dropped to one knee. There was a throwing knife in her gloved hand, held by the tip and ready to hurl.

"I know that man," she said by way of explanation as she tucked the knife back into her boot. "Worse yet, he knows me. He was in the assassin's guild with me, in Zazesspur."

Danilo swore fervently and joined Arilyn in the shadows. Together they squeezed back into a narrow, gnome-sized alley. "Well, at least this confirms that we are on the right path," he said in a low, grim tone. "I suppose it could be mere happenstance that a hired sword from Zazesspur shows up at this particular time, but it's my observation that true coincidence is a rare thing—except in Selgauntan opera, of course. . ."

Arilyn nodded her agreement and said, "I'll find out who sent him."

Danilo swallowed the protest that was his first instinct. As Harpers, they played very different roles and they worked together well. He might hate the idea of Arilyn going up against a trained killer, but he saw no way around it. She had spent many months posing as an assassin in Tethyr. The competition among those ranks was fierce and deadly at the best of times, and she had not left the guild under good terms. It would be to Arilyn's advantage to chose the time and place for the inevitable battle. And she was right: they needed to know what had prompted an assassin's presence in this neutral holdfast. Even if the assassin's purpose was not the same as the Harpers', no one would risk violating the peace of the Friendly Arm unless the need was dire, or the potential gain great. To do so would bar the doors of the fortress against the wrongdoers for a gnome's centuries-long memory. This was a severe penalty in these troubled lands, which for so many years could claim few truly neutral places.

But as to that, change was in the air. The seemingly endless civil war within Tethyr was winding to a close. Zaranda Star had been acclaimed queen in the city of Zazesspur, and was on the way to solidifying her hold on the entire country. To this end, she was preparing for a marriage of convenience to the last known heir to the royal House of Tethyr. There were factions, however, who used controlled chaos to their benefit, and who were not inclined to see peace come to their land. When the Harpers learned that there was a potential challenger to Zaranda's throne, a distant relative of the soon-to-be-king and thus a potential bride, they foresaw trouble. Danilo and Arilyn had been sent to find the young woman and bring her to safety in the Northlands before someone else made her a pawn in a renewed struggle . . . someone who might send an assassin to retrieve—or do away with—the unsuspecting girl.

Yes, concluded Dan glumly, Arilyn had no choice but to face the assassin.

"Be careful," he murmured. Before she could protest, he framed her face in his hands and tipped back her head for a long and thorough kiss.

"You know better than to distract me before battle,"

she said in a tone that tried for severity, but did not quite succeed.

Danilo chuckled. "I shall take that as a compliment."

He turned and strode into the castle, his manner far more insouciant than his mood. The prospect of an evening's comfort and conversation held little appeal, but this was his role to play and he would attend to his part no less faithfully than did Arilyn.

Since this was his first visit to the Friendly Arm, he looked around with interest. The great hall had been set up as a tavern. Long tables and sturdy wooden chairs were scattered about, some of them gnome-sized, others intended for the comfort of taller travelers. A wild boar roasted on a spit in the enormous hearth, and kettles of steaming, herb-scented vegetable stews kept warm in the embers along either side. The air was thick with the fragrance of fresh bread and good, sour ale. Several young women moved slowly about the room carrying trays and tankards.

Prompted more by habit than inclination, Danilo slid an appraising eye over the nearest barmaid. She was young, not much past twenty, and blessed with an abundance of black hair and truly impressive curves. The former was left gloriously unbound, and the later were displayed by a tightly-laced scarlet bodice over a chemise pulled down over her shoulders. Her skirts ended several flirtatious inches above her ankles, and her black eyes scanned the room. They lit up with an avaricious gleam when they settled upon the richly-dressed newcomer.

The barmaid eased her way through the crowd to Danilo's side. A passing merchant jostled her at a highly opportune moment, sending her bumping into the Harper. She made a laughing apology, then tilted her head and slanted a look at him through lowered lashes. "And what can I get you, my lord?"

"Killed, most likely," he said mildly, thinking of the response this flirtation would earn from the half-elf who was prowling the shadows beyond the brightly-lit hall.

"Or severely wounded, at the very least."

The barmaid's dumbfounded expression brought a smile to his lips. "Wine, if you please," he amended. "A bottle of your best Halruaan red, and several goblets."

As she wandered off to relay this order to another barmaid, Danilo scanned the tables for the captains of the northbound caravan. Before he could make his way over, he found his path barred by a stout, stern-faced, white-bearded gnome whose crimson jerkin was nearly matched in hue by an exceedingly red and bulbous nose.

"Bentley Mirrorshade," the gnome announced.

Danilo nodded. "Ah, yes—the proprietor of this fine establishment. Allow me to intro—"

"I know who ya are," Bentley interrupted in a gruff tone. "Word gets around. There'll be no fighting and no spellcasting. Leave yer weapons at the door. Sophie here will peace bind yer left thumb to yer belt."

Danilo winced. "It appears I will never live down that incident in the Stalwart Club."

"Never heard about that one." The gnome nodded to the barmaid who had greeted Danilo earlier. She fished a thin strip of leather from her pocket and deftly secured the bard's hand. As she worked, Danilo scanned the room and noticed that he was not the only one subjected to such precautions: all known mages were peace bound, and everyone was required to leave weapons at the door.

Danilo made his way to the merchant captains' table. After the introductions were made, he poured out the first of several bottles of well-aged wine, and listened as the conversation flowed. Although the merchants talked a great deal, they said little that informed his cause.

As the night wore on, Danilo found his eyes returning with increasing frequency to the door. His fellow travelers trickled in as their duties were completed and the caravan and its goods secured. Elaith was one of the latecomers. Danilo noted with interest that the elf was subjected to peace binding. Few people knew of the Moon elf's considerable magical abilities. These gnomes apparently didn't miss much—although Dan suspected that Elaith managed to retain a good many of his hidden weapons. The gnome's insight was not too surprising. Dan had heard that Bentley Mirrorshade was a highly gifted mage, specializing in the illusionist's art.

The evening passed and the hall began to empty as the gnomes and their guests sought their beds. When Danilo's patience reached the end of its tether, he left the hall in search of his partner.

He found Arilyn in the stable, currying her mare. She looked up when he came into the stall. Her face was pale and grim beneath its hood. Fighting came easily to the half-elf—Danilo had never seen anyone who could handle a sword as well—but killing did not. Even so, Danilo sensed at once that something else weighed heavily on her mind.

"That took quite a long time," he prompted.

"I had to wait until Yoseff was alone," Arilyn said in a low, furious tone. "He had a meeting. With Elaith Craulnober."

Danilo hissed a curse from between clenched teeth. "Why am I not surprised? Did you hear what was said?"

"No, nothing. He must have cast a spell of silence, or some such thing."

"Undoubtedly. Now what?" mused Dan, running one hand through his hair in a gesture of pure frustration. He had investigated Elaith's purpose in this trip, which was allegedly to acquire exotic goods from faraway Maztica in the markets of Amn. The elf would make a fine profit selling coffee, cocoa, and dried vegetables to the merchants of Waterdeep, but he had also arranged to acquire goods that were restricted or forbidden outright: feather magic, enspelled gems, possibly even slaves. Danilo had considered this the extent of Elaith's planned mischief; apparently, he had been wrong.

"And the assassin? What had he to say for himself?"

"Yoseff was never one for conversation," Arilyn said shortly.

"Ah. And he is dead, I suppose?"

"Very. He carried a few things that might help, though."

Arilyn reached into the bag that hung from her belt and took several glittering objects from it. The first to catch Danilo's eye was a finely wrought gold locket on a heavy gold chain. A very nice amethyst—brilliant cut, thumb-sized, and deep purple in hue—was set into the front of the locket and a wisp of fine, black hair was nestled within.

"An amulet of seeking," he surmised, fingering the soft curl. "Hair so soft could only have belonged to an elf or a baby. I'm guessing the latter. So we not only have a fair idea who the assassin came to find, but also who sent him—may all the gods damn the woman who would so use her own child!"

Before he could elaborate, a female voice, raised in a keening wail, cut through the night. It was a chilling sound, an ages old, wordless song of mourning. It spoke of death more clearly than any cleric's eulogy, and far more poignantly.

Arilyn bolted from the stable with Danilo close behind her. They dashed through the nearly empty hall, toward the babble of gnomish voices in a side chamber. A thick-chested gnome barred their way. He was an odd-looking fellow with hair and skin of nearly matching shades of slate gray. Danilo recognized him from descriptions as Garith Hunterstock, Bentley's second-in-command. Though the gnomish commander was determined to keep them out, the Harpers were tall enough to see over the heads of the crowd.

In the room beyond, Bentley Mirrorshade lay in a spreading pool of blood. The hilt of a jeweled dagger rose from his chest.

"No one in, no one out," the gnome gritted out. He raised his voice and began to bellow orders. "Lower the portcullis and bar the gates! Archers, to the walls! Shoot down anyone who tries to leave the fortress before the murderer is found."

* * * * *

Later that night, Danilo and his "servant" attended a grim gathering in the castle's hall. The body of Bentley Mirrorshade lay in state upon a black-draped table. Candles lined the walls, casting a somber, golden light.

The crowd parted to allow a green-robed gnome woman to pass. Respectful silence filled the room as Gellana Mirrorshade, the high priestess of Garl Glittergold and the widow of Bentley Mirrorshade, made her way to her husband's bier. She carried herself with admirable dignity. Her pale brown face was set in rigid lines, but her eyes were steady and dry.

The priestess spoke into the silence. "You are gathered here to see justice done. It is no small thing to speak with the dead, but an evil deed must not go unpunished."

Gellana began the words and gestures of a complicated ritual. Danilo watched closely; nothing about the spell was familiar to him. He had studied magic since his twelfth year with no less a teacher than the archmage Khelben Arunsun, but the magic of a wizard and that of a priest were very different things. Apparently, the priestess was skilled and devout, for a translucent image of Bentley Mirrorshade slowly took form in the air above the pall.

"The dead must speak truth," Gellana said softly, "and in life or in death, Bentley Mirrorshade would tell no direct lie. Tell us, my husband, who is responsible for this death."

The specter's eyes swept the assemblage. His stubby, translucent finger lifted, swept to the left, and leveled at Elaith Craulnober with a sharp, accusing stab.

For the first time in their acquaintance, Danilo saw the elf's composure utterly forsake him. Elaith's face went slack and ashen, and his amber-hued eyes widened in stunned disbelief.

"What nonsense is this?" the elf protested as soon as he could gather enough of his wits to fuel speech. "I am innocent of this thing!"

"Silence!" Gellana demanded. She held a jeweled dagger up for the ghostly gnome's inspection. "Was this the weapon used?"

The spectral head rose and fell once, slowly, in a nod of confirmation. Despite the gravity of the occasion, Danilo could not help but observe that the gnome's spirit had a remarkable flair for drama.

"And whose dagger is this?" persisted Gellana.

"It belongs to the elf," proclaimed the spirit. "It is Elaith Craulnober's dagger."

Gellana Mirrorshade's eyes were hard as they swept the gathering. "Have you heard enough? May I release my husband, and in his name order the death of this treacherous elf?"

A murmur arose, gathering power and fury. The accused elf stood alone in an angry circle of gnomes, buffeted by a storm of accusation and demands for immediate retribution. Elaith's eyes went flat and cool, and his chin lifted with elven hauteur as he faced his death.

That gesture, that purely elven mixture of pride and courage and disdain, was to be his salvation. Danilo had always been a fool for all things elven, and this moment proved no exception. He sighed and quickly cast a cantrip that would add power and persuasion to his voice.

"Wait," he demanded.

The single word thrummed through the great hall like a clarion blast, and the gnomes fell suddenly silent. Garith Hunterstock froze, his sword poised to cut the elf down. Danilo reached out and gently eased the gnome's blade away from Elaith Craulnober's throat. "The elf claims innocence," the Harper said. "We should at least hear him out, and consider the possibility that he speaks truth."

"Bentley Mirrorshade himself accused the elf!" shouted a high-pitched gnomish voice from the crowd.

"The dead do not lie!" another small voice added.

"That is true enough," Dan agreed in a conciliatory tone, "but perhaps there is some other explanation that will serve both truths." Inspiration struck, and he glanced at Arilyn. She stood near the back of the room, nearly indistinguishable from the shadows. "Earlier this evening, Elaith Craulnober was seen meeting with a known thief and assassin. Perhaps this man stole the dagger, and used it to kill the gnome?"

"That is not possible," Arilyn said flatly. "The assassin was dead before Bentley Mirrorshade's murder."

"Dead?" Garith Hunterstock said, turning a fierce glare in her direction. "By whose hand?"

The Harper didn't flinch. "Mine." she said simply. "He attacked me; I defended myself. You will find his body behind the smokehouse."

"And who might you be?" demanded the gnome.

The half-elf slipped down her cowl and stepped into the firelight. Before she could speak, a young gnome clad in forest green let out a startled exclamation. "I know her! She's the Harper who fought alongside the elves of Tethyr's forest. If she says the stiff behind the smoke-house needed killing, that's good enough for me. If she speaks for yonder elf, I say that's call to think things over real careful."

Dozens of expectant faces turned in Arilyn's direction. Danilo saw the flicker of regret in her eyes as she met Elaith's stare, and he knew what her answer would be.

"I cannot," she said bluntly. "On the other hand, it never hurts to think things over. Lord Thann has apparently appointed himself Elaith Craulnober's advocate. Give them time—two days, perhaps—to prove the elf's claim of innocence. I know of Bentley Mirrorshade, and nothing I've heard suggests that he would want anyone denied a fair hearing."

A soft, angry mutter greeted her words, but no one could think of a way to refute them. Garith Hunterstock ordered the elf taken away and imprisoned. The others left, too, slipping away in silence to leave Gellana Mirror-shade alone with her dead.

* * * * *

As the sun edged over the eastern battlements of the fortress, Danilo made his way down the tightly spiraling stairs that led to the dungeon. It was a dank, gloomy place, lit only by an occasional sputtering torch thrust into a rusted sconce.

Since Elaith was the only prisoner, his cell was not hard to find. Danilo followed the faint light to the far corner of the dungeon. The elf's cell was small, the ceiling too low for him to stand upright. The only furniture was a straw pallet. Elaith wore only his leggings and shirt, and his thumbs were entrapped in opposite ends of a metal tube, a gnomish device of some sort designed to make spellcasting impossible. He had been stripped of weapons, armor, and magical items. These lay heaped in an impressive pile, well beyond reach of the cell.

Danilo eyed the glittering hoard. "Did you actually wear all that steel? It's a wonder you could walk without clanking," he marveled.

The elf's furious, amber-eyed glare reminded Danilo of a trapped hawk. "Come to gloat?"

"Perhaps later," he said mildly. "At the moment, though, I would rather hear what you have to say."

"And you would believe me, I suppose?"

"I would listen. That seems a reasonable place to start."

The elf was silent for a long moment. "I did not kill the gnome."

"You know, of course, how difficult it is for the dead to lie," Danilo pointed out. "The spirit of Bentley Mirrorshade named you as his killer. The weapon that dealt the killing stroke is yours. The proof against you is formidable."

"Nevertheless, I am innocent," Elaith maintained. A sudden, fierce light went on in his eyes. "I am innocent, and you must find proof!"

"Really, now!" Dan protested, lifting one eyebrow in a

wry expression. "Since I have a full two days, shouldn't I warm up with an easier task? Pilfering Elminster's favorite pipe maybe, or bluffing an illithid at cards, or persuading Arilyn to dance upon a tavern table?"

The elf ignored the obvious irony. "When you signed on to travel with my caravan you promised your support and aid to the expedition."

"Insofar as its purpose was lawful and just," Danilo specified.

"What better way to fulfill this pledge than to clear an innocent person, unjustly accused? And why would you speak for me in the tavern, if you had no intention of following through?"

The Harper thought this over. "Those are both excellent points. Very well, then, let's assume for argument's sake that I will take on this task. Consider my dilemma. Even under the best of circumstances, 'innocent' is not the first word that comes to mind when your name is mentioned."

"Perhaps the gnome priestess erred."

"An unlikely possibility, but one I have already considered. Gellana Mirrorshade permitted me to test the murder weapon myself," the Harper said. "I cast the needed spell not once, but three times. Each time the result was the same. The dagger is indisputably yours, and it was indeed responsible for the killing stroke. Now, I understand that most people would hardly consider my command of magic sufficient to such a task—"

"Save your breath," Elaith said curtly. "I have seen what you can do. Your command of magic exceeds my own. If it suits you to play the fool and muck about with minstrels, that is your affair."

"Enough said, then. Let's consider the murder weapon. Was the dagger ever out of your keeping? Did you entrust it to another? Loose it in a game of dice? Anything?"

Elaith hesitated, then shook his head. "I didn't even notice it was missing," he said ruefully. With a grim smile, he nodded to the pile of weapons outside his cell. "I carry several, you see."

The Harper folded his arms. "The situation is bleak, make no mistake about it. But it might interest you to learn that I, too, seem to be without an item or two. It would appear that there is a very talented pickpocket at work here. I was jostled by the assassin Arilyn dispatched, and you were seen meeting with. And speaking of which, is there anything you would like to tell me about that?"

"No."

"I had to ask," Danilo commented. "As I was saying, this assassin would be my first suspect. It is possible that he had a partner."

"That is a place to start," the elf allowed. "Then you will do it? You will honor your pledge?"

"Well, since you put it that way. . . ." Danilo said dryly. "But don' t get your hopes too high. Arilyn has bought us some time, but not much."

Elaith's gaze faltered. "She believes that I am responsible."

The Harper didn't deny it. Arilyn had had a great deal to say about Danilo's defense of the rogue elf. Dan's ears still burned from the heat of their argument. "My lady is occasionally more elven than she realizes," he said dryly.

This earned a small, wry smile from Elaith. "If she could not be supportive, at least she has been fair. More than fair. I don' t suppose my other employees have followed her example."

"The caravan guards have already drawn their pay from the quartermaster, and plan to scatter once the gates of the city are opened. Forgive me, but the prevailing attitude seems to be that this is a long overdue justice."

The elf was silent for a moment. "I am not unaware of the irony in my situation," he said finally, "but I maintain that I am innocent of this murder. Go now, and prove it!"

* * * * *

That morning, over a breakfast of bread, cheese, and newly-pressed cider, Danilo related the conversation to Arilyn. "And I have but two days to accomplish this miracle," he lamented in conclusion. "You couldn't have asked for a tenday?"

The half-elf sighed and stabbed a piece of cheese with her table knife. "I doubt it would help. You know Elaith as well as anyone, and you know he could have killed that gnome. He nearly killed you once."

"Three times, actually, but why quibble?"

Arilyn cast her eyes toward the ceiling. "Why do you persist in this?"

"Two things keep me from giving up: my promise to help Elaith, and the task that brought us here," he said quietly.

His partner nodded, accepting this reasoning. "What do you propose to do?"

"You' re not going to like this," Danilo cautioned, "but we could ask the priestess to speak to the spirit of the dead assassin. We need to know who he was working for, and who he was working with."

Arilyn's lips thinned. "You know elves do not believe in disturbing the dead."

"But gnomes do. Gellana Mirrorshade can hardly deny us this, considering that she called back her own husband's spirit. And what other course could we take?"

"Nearly any would be preferable," the half-elf grumbled, but Danilo read the surrender in her eyes and tone. He tossed several silver coins on the table to pay for the meal and followed Arilyn out of the tavern. One of the dark-haired barmaids glided forward to clear the table and pocket the coins. The barmaids were hardworking girls, Danilo noted, recognizing several faces familiar from the night before.

Retrieving the assassin's body was an easy matter. The gnomes had simply tossed it into the midden wagon along with the remnants of the wild boar they had roasted for their guests the night before, some chicken bones, and an over-ripe haunch of venison. The gnomes regularly removed any leftovers to the forest to feed the animals who lived there, and to return their bounty to the land. They gave the dead assassin no less respect, and no more.

Danilo wrinkled his nose as he shouldered the dead man. "I can see why Gellana didn't want to do the ritual on site. That venison should have been buried long ago."

"The same could be said of Yoseff," retorted Arilyn, "but that's another matter. Don't you think it odd that Gellana Mirrorshade told us to bring his body to the temple?"

Her partner immediately seized her meaning. "Come to think of it, yes," he agreed as he fell into step beside her. "Gellana Mirrorshade summons her own husband's spirit in a tavern. Why would she afford greater honor to a human assassin? Perhaps she feared that the curious tall folk who gathered at last night's summoning would ill fit the Shrine of the Short."

Arilyn's lips twitched. "The gnomes call it the Temple of Wisdom. But perhaps the size of the temple explains the matter."

It did not. The Temple of Wisdom was undoubtedly a gnomish work—a curious, asymmetric building fashioned of forest-hued stone and marble and filled with odd statues and embellished with gems—but the vaulted ceilings made concession for human supplicants. In fact, the shrine was large enough to accommodate all those who had witnessed the solemn ritual in the tavern the night before. This puzzled Danilo. He watched the gnomish priestess carefully as she spoke the words of the spell.

A dank gray mist gathered in the hall and coalesced into the shape of the man who has jostled Danilo the night before.

"Go ahead," Gellana said tersely. "Word your questions carefully, for the dead will tell you no more than they must."

Danilo nodded and turned to the specter. "Who were you sent to find?"

"A young woman," the spirit said grudgingly.

"What name was she given at birth, and by what name is she now known?"

"She was named Isabeau Thione; I know not what she is called now."

Arilyn and Danilo exchanged a look of mingled triumph and concern. This was indeed the woman they had been sent to find, and their competitors were also close on her trail. "Who sent you?" Danilo asked. "If you do not know names, describe the person or people."

"There were two: a fat man who smiles too much, and a small woman. She had the look of the old nobility of Tethyr; fine features, dark eyes, and a curve to her nose. She wore purple, in the old style."

Danilo recognized Lucia Thione, an agent for the Knights of the Shield, recently exiled from Waterdeep for treachery against the secret lords who ruled that city. She had never come to trial; hers was a private justice. She was given over to Lord Hhune, her rival. The man apparently kept her alive for his own purposes. Lady Thione, ever a survivor, had apparently found a way to earn her keep. She had birthed a daughter in secrecy and given her away into fosterage. Apparently she now planned to reclaim the girl and present her as a more suitable bride to the royal heir than Zaranda Star, a common-born mercenary with a purchased title. Danilo forwarded two possible results: the girl would be accepted and crowned queen, thereby increasing Lucia Thione's influence and status in Tethyr, or she would be rejected, but in the process providing a focal point to rally the anti-Zaranda sentiment and foment rebellion.

"Thione and Hhune," Danilo commented in an aside to Arilyn. "The Harpers erred when they made that match."

She nodded and turned with obvious reluctance to the spirit of the man she had killed. "What was the purpose of your meeting with Elaith Craulnober?"

The spirit's sneer widened. "Business. No, don' t bother asking a better question—this one I will answer with pleasure. The elf's purpose was the same as mine, the same as your own! Oh, yes, he knew you sought the Thione heiress. He agreed to take you with him for that reason. He is using Harper hounds to sniff out his quarry."

"Elaith has spies among the Harpers?" Danilo demanded, appalled by the thought.

The spirit snorted derisively. "Everyone has spies among the Harpers."

Arilyn turned away. "I have heard enough," she said shortly. "Send him away."

The priestess murmured a few words, and the figure of the assassin faded away. Danilo thanked her, and led his grim-faced partner out of the temple.

"We need to talk to Elaith," he said.

"You talk to him. Yoseff was all I can stomach for one day."

"At least come and listen," he cajoled. "You might hear something that I miss. The answer lies right before us—I am certain of that!"

"Finally, you're making sense," the half-elf said. "Elaith is guilty of murder and more. He planned to find that girl, sell her to the highest bidder. He used us to that end. What more answer do you need?"

When they reached the dungeon, Danilo repeated most of these sentiments to Elaith while Arilyn looked on in stony silence. "None of this endears us to your cause, you know," he concluded. "Frankly, I'm disposed to let the matter stand."

"I have your pledge," Elaith insisted. "You must press on."

Danilo sighed and rubbed his hands over his face. "Somehow I knew you'd say that. But what more can I do?"

"Find the girl," the elf insisted. "Find her, and learn who else seeks her. Who would have better reason to see me condemned to death?"

"Had I more time, I would write you a list," Danilo said dryly. He took the amethyst locket from his bag and held it up. "This is an amulet of seeking, taken from your erstwhile friend Yoseff. The girl is not here, and we cannot leave to seek her elsewhere until the matter of Bentley's death is settled."

"Nor would we expect to find her here," Arilyn said, speaking for the first time. "Bentley Mirrorshade kept the peace for over twenty years. He could never have done that if he got caught up in the endless local fighting, so he swore never to admit anyone to the stronghold who claimed to be of the Tethyrian royal family. We can assume that the girl was never at the Friendly Arm."

"Can we, indeed?" mused Danilo. "Now that I think on it, wouldn't this be a perfect cover for the girl's presence?"

"Possibly," the half-elf countered. "But Bentley is known as an honorable gnome. What purpose would he have in breaking his sworn word?"

"Saving the life of an infant seems purpose enough. For that matter, he could have kept to the letter of his word: he swore not to admit anyone who claimed ties to the royal family. An infant could hardly make such a claim. If indeed Lady Thione's child was brought here, it is possible that the gnome did not know at the time who the child was."

"But he learned," Arilyn surmised. "He probably died to protect that knowledge."

"Undoubtedly," Dan agreed, his tone even. He nodded a farewell to Elaith, and he and Arilyn walked toward the stairs.

"You didn't sound convinced back there," she said.

"I was thinking. Did you notice the barmaids at the inn? Any one of them could be the woman we seek—they are all about the right age, and by the look of them, any one of them could be kin to Lucia Thione."

Arilyn considered this. "Their presence in the gnomish stronghold is difficult to explain otherwise. Do you want to take a closer look at them?"

Her partner responded with a smirk. Arilyn bit back a chuckle and tried to glare. "I'll come looking for you in an hour."

"I shall bear that in mind," Danilo murmured.

He made his way back into the tavern and tried to strike up a conversation with the gnome barkeep. All the inhabitants of the fortress were stunned by their leader's murder, and none of the small folk were inclined to share information with the human who had defended the accused elf. But Dan stringed together a series of grudging, one-word answers and eventually learned that there were a total of eight barmaids, six of whom were on duty.

Since Danilo was more interested in a woman who was not there, he left the castle and went to the barmaid's house, a stone structure built right against one of the curtain walls. Danilo knocked softly on the wooden door. When there was no answer, he tried the door and found it unlocked.

There was but one large room, simply furnished with straw pallets softened by down-filled mattresses. Two women lay sleeping. Danilo recognized one of them as Sophie, the girl who had administered the peace bonds the night before. A shadow of suspicion edged into his mind. He stooped by her bed and softly called her name. When still she slept, he tapped her shoulder, then shook her. Nothing woke her.

Danilo rose and took a couple of odd items from the bag at his waist, then cast a spell that would dispel any magic in the room. The result was only half what he expected.

"Sophie" was not a woman at all, but a pile of laundry. The other barmaid was not a woman either but an iron golem, a magically-animated construction enspelled to look enough like Sophie to be her cousin. One apparently solid stone wall was breached by a wooden door that was closed but not barred.

The Harper crept closer for a better look. The golem was curled up in mock slumber, but when it stood it would be nearly twice the height of a tall man. The body, shaped roughly like that of a human woman, probably outweighed Danilo's horse six or seven times over. No wonder so few gnomes held the fortress, Dan realized. An iron golem could stop a war-horse's charge without getting knocked back on its heels, crush an ogre's skull with one fist, and shrug off blows from all but the most powerful magical weapons. This golem was in need of repair. There was a considerable amount of rust along some of the joints, requiring filing and oils at the very least, and possibly the ministrations of a blacksmith. Danilo guessed that the golem could still do considerable damage in its current condition. He backed out of the room, grateful that the stone floor, which had no doubt been built to support the construct's great weight, did not creak.

He bumped into Arilyn at the door. "The barkeep thought I might find you here," she said.

"Keep your voice down," he implored, nodding toward the golem.

But his spell had faded, and the figure that rose from the pallet appeared to be nothing more than an angry girl. The illusion-draped construct rushed forward, fist raised for a blow.

Arilyn stepped forward, her forearm raise to block the attack. There was no time for explanation, so Danilo did the only thing he could; he leaped at Arilyn and knocked her out of the golem's path. Her angry retort was swallowed by the sound of an iron fist smashing into the wall. Jagged fissures raced along the stone, carving a spider-like portrait on the wall.

The half-elf's eyes widened. "Iron golem," Danilo said tersely. "Rust on the elbow joints."

Arilyn nodded in understanding. In one swift movement, she rolled to her feet and drew her sword. Danilo reached for his, then remembered that only magic-rich swords could have any impact. After a moment's hesitation, he reached for a thin, ornamental blade he wore on his right hip—a singing sword with a ringing baritone voice and an extremely bawdy repertoire.

"Softly," he admonished the sword as he tugged it free of its sheath. "There might be more of these things waiting tables in the castle." Obligingly, the sword launched into a whispered rendition of "Sune and the Satyr."

Arilyn shot him an exasperated, sidelong glance, and then turned her attention to the golem. The woman-shaped construct turned slowly to face the half-elf, spewing a cloud of roiling gray smoke from its mouth. The golem balled one fist into a deceptively dainty weapon. Arilyn sidestepped the attack, holding her breath and squeezing her eyes shut against the stinging gas. She brought her sword up high and delivered a powerful two-handed blow that would have cleaved an orc's skull in two. A harsh clang resounded through the room, and Arilyn's elven sword vibrated visibly in her hands. There was not so much as a scratch on the illusionary barmaid, and as the gas cleared, the golem wrapped its arms around one of the beams that supported the building and began to rock.

As dust and straw showered down from the thatch roof, Danilo remembered his glimpse of the golem, recalled how the iron plates of the arms were arranged. He lunged forward and thrust his weapon into the arm. The magic sword slid between the plates and out the other side. The blade bit deeply into the wooden beam the golem was holding, pinning one arm fast.

Arilyn stepped in and swung again, hitting the golem's other arm once, then a second time. The elven sword severed the arm at the elbow. The limb fell to the stone floor with a clatter, the illusion dispelled. Its iron fingers flexed and groped, seeking to dig deep into an unwary foot. Arilyn tried to kick the arm aside and swore when her boot met unyielding iron. She sidestepped the twitching limb and struck again and again, chopping at the construct like a deranged woodsman determined to fell a tree one limb at a time. With each piece she knocked or pried loose the construct's struggle weakened.

But not soon enough. The golem, now plainly visible for what it was, managed to work its impaled arm free. Danilo's singing sword went skidding across the floor.

At once the half-elf struck, thrusting her own blade back into the same place. She leaned into the sword to hold it in place and shot a look over her shoulder at Danilo. "Melt it," she commanded.

Danilo hesitated, quickly considering his options. Fire would only restore the golem. Lighting, then. He lifted both hands and deftly summoned the force, holding it between his hands in a crackling ball as he shouted for Arilyn to stand clear.

Magic flowed from his fingertips like white-hot arrows and Arilyn's hands fell away from her sword. His aim was true, and an arc of blue-white lightning crashed between his hands and what remained of the golem. The construct wilted like a candle left out in the sun. Arilyn grabbed her sword and, the muscles in her arms corded so tightly they seemed about to snap, pulled the enchanted blade through the golem's iron flesh.

The construct sank to the stone floor and the severed arm ceased its twitching.

Arilyn was white-faced, weaving on her feet. Danilo suspected that only an act of will kept her standing. He went to her and brushed a stray curl off her damp forehead. When he gathered her close, her arms went around him instinctively.

"This battle reminds me of something else," he murmured. "There was a powerful illusion cast on this golem, and Bentley Mirrorshade was a powerful illusionist."

Arilyn lifted her head from his shoulder. "And?"

"One of the main tenants of the illusionist's craft is to make people overlook the obvious. What is the most obvious question, and the one that no one thought to ask?"

The half-elf pondered this. A small, wry smile lifted the corner of her lips when the answer came to her, and she eased out of Danilo's arms. "Give me the amulet of seeking," she said. "I'll go after the girl."

* * * * *

Later that morning, Danilo again stood in the Temple of Wisdom. The body of Bentley Mirrorshade had made it there at last, and it was laid out in the enclosed courtyard in the center of the temple, upon a bier of stacked wood well-soaked with fragrant oil. It was no coincidence, thought Danilo, that the gnomes were preparing so hasty a funeral. Another hour more, and nothing he could do would save Elaith.

He explained his intentions to Gellana Mirrorshade. The gnomish priestess was not happy with his request, but she had pledged her aid to his quest for justice. She sent Garith Hunterstock to the dungeon to retrieve Elaith.

"The accused elf has a right to tell his story," Danilo said, "but he does not wish to do so before witnesses."

Gellana shrugged and spoke a few gnomish words to her fellow clerics. All left the temple. When the only sound was the steady dripping of the large Neveren water clock that stood like a monument in the courtyard, Danilo bid the priestess to summon Bentley Mirrorshade. When the ghostly gnome stood before them, Danilo turned to Elaith.

"You were late to the tavern last night. Did you have dinner?"

The elf looked at Danilo as if he had lost his mind. "I ordered, but did not eat. The gnome's murder was discovered before my meal arrived, and the tavern closed."

"Ah. And what did you order?"

"Medallions of veal, I believe, with capers and cream. Why?"

Danilo ignored the question. "You were also subjected to a peace bond, of the sort given to mages. Is your magical skill widely known?"

"It is not," the elf replied. "The best weapon is often a hidden one."

"Well said. So it would appear that the gnomes knew

more of you than is common. Who tied your thumb in a peace bond?"

The elf shrugged. "A human wench, overblown and under-clad. Dark hair. I did not ask her name."

"That sounds like Sophie. Is peace bonding her task?" Danilo asked Gellana. The gnomish priestess responded with a cautious nod. The Harper held up a small sack of green-dyed leather. "Is it also her task to relieve guests of their valuables? This coin purse is mine. I lost it in the tavern and found it this morning in Sophie's chest. But Sophie herself, I could not find. A marvel, considering that the fortress is sealed."

Gellana scowled. "You had me summon my husband to listen to this nonsense? If you have questions for Bentley Mirrorshade, ask them!"

Danilo nodded agreeably and turned to the specter. "Is Bentley Mirrorshade dead?"

"What kind of question is that?" snapped Gellana.

"A very good one, I should think," the Harper replied. "It is the one question that no one thought to ask. When presented with a body, everyone's instinct was to look for the killer. But Bentley Mirrorshade is an illusionist of some skill, and considerable sophistry. Looking back, it strikes me that your questions at the summoning, dear lady, were rather oddly worded. You referred to the spirit by name, but never the body. The elf was responsible for 'the death,' and his weapon struck the killing blow—that is all that was said. Elaith would be responsible indeed, if the death in question was that of the veal calf he ordered for his dinner."

Danilo held out his hands, his palms open and empty. "Shall I cast the needed spell?" he asked the priestess. "One that can dispel the effects of others' spells?"

"Don't bother," said a gruff voice from the vicinity of the clock. A door on the pedestal cabinet flew open, and Bentley Mirrorshade, very much alive, strode toward his bier. He snatched the illusionary specter from the air and crumpled it as a frustrated scribe might treat a sheet of blotched parchment. On the bier, as Danilo expected, lay the body of a brindle calf.

The gnome illusionist folded his stubby arms and glared up at the Harper. "All right, then, you got me. What now?"

"That depends upon you." Dan said. "Tell me, why did you stage your own death?"

Bentley rolled his shoulders in a shrug. "Had a responsibility to the girl. She's trouble—and make no mistake about that—but she don't deserve the likes of this elf sniffing around. I got no use for those who would use the girl to stir up rebellion—and less for those who would hunt her down to enrich themselves." He glared at the elf.

"And by leaving behind your own illusionary corpse, you created a diversion that allowed the girl to escape unnoticed, and that condemned Elaith Craulnober to death. Masterfully done," Danilo complemented him. "But how did you intend to explain your eventual return from the grave? I have my suspicions, mind you, but I'd like to hear you tell the tale."

The gnome had the grace to look sheepish. "I've been known to go off fishing now and again. Gives me time alone, time to think. I thought to come back when this was over, act surprised by this rogue's fate. And yer right in what yer thinking, Harper; I thought to pin the blame for the illusion on you. Yer known for pranks, and for spells gone awry."

Danilo took note of the remarkable change which came over Elaith during this confession. Understanding, then profound relief, then chilling anger played over his elven features. Danilo sent him a warning look.

"I must say, this leaves me with something of a dilemma," the Harper said. "Elaith has been found to be without guilt in this case, but to make public your scheme would upset the balance in the Friendly Arm, and would alert those who are seeking the Thione heiress."

"True enough," the gnome agreed. "So what yer gonna do, then?"

Danilo sighed. "I see no real choice. I shall take the blame for the illusion, as you intended. If asked, I can cite old and very real enmities between myself and Elaith." He turned to the elf. "In return for this, I expect your word that you will not hinder Arilyn and me in our task. We intend on taking Isabeau Thione—better known as Sophie the pickpocket—to safety in the north."

Bentley snorted. "Yer gonna take the word of such a one as this?"

"In your position, I would not be too quick to cast aspersions on the honesty of another," Elaith said, his voice bubbling with barely controlled wrath. "I am what I am, but the Harper knows that my word, once given, is as good as that of any elf alive, and better than that of any gnome. And so you may believe me when I swear that if ever I meet you beyond these walls, I will kill you in the slowest and most painful manner known to me."

The gnome shrugged. "Sounds fair enough. But mind you, take care who yer calling a liar. I never said a single thing wasn't Garl's honest truth. An illusion ain't never a lie—people just got a bad habit of believing what they see."

Danilo took Elaith's arm and led the furious elf from the temple. "I will keep my oath to you, bard," the elf hissed from between clenched teeth, "but there is another I long to break! Like any other elf I believe that disturbing the dead is a terrible thing. But I would give fifty years off my life to continue this discussion—with that wretched gnome's real spirit!"

The Harper shrugged. "We are neither of us quite what we seem, are we? Why, then, should you expect anything else to be what it seems?"

Elaith glared at him. After a moment a smile, slow and rueful, softened the elf's face. "If a Moon elf of noble family commands half the illegal trade in Waterdeep, and if a foolish minstrel from that same city displays insight that an elven sage might envy, why should we make foolish assumptions about speaking with the dead?"

"Exactly," Danilo agreed, his expression somber. "There is some comfort in having at least one thing proven true."

"Oh?"

"The dead are every bit as dreary as I have been led to believe. A small thing, to be sure, but in this life we should take our absolutes where we can find them."

Elaith gave the Harper an odd look. After a moment, a wry chuckle trickled from his lips. He stopped and extended his hand, and his amber eyes were utterly devoid of mockery or disdain.

The gesture was all the apology, and all the thanks, that Danilo would ever receive. For once, the Harper felt no need to seek for hidden meanings or illusionary truths. He knew the proud, complex elf for what he was, but there were some absolutes that Danilo took when and where he found them. Friendship was one of them.

Without hesitation, he clasped Elaith's wrist in a comrade's salute.

A Walk in the Snow

Dave Gross

Ogden smiled. This was his favorite task.

It had been better when Maere was still alive to share the chores of the White Hart, the inn they'd built together. Then the kitchen would be filled with the aroma of baking bread and stewing meat as well as the sweet odor of cooling malt.

The chore was better even when his old friend Robert had lent a hand, at least with the hopping and fermenting. Rob had visited mainly to keep the widower from despair in the first few months of his solitude. When Rob's first son was born, he showed only every other time. After the second son, Ogden was on his own.

Even in solitude, years past any useful company, brewing the ale for the Hart was still one of his few pleasures.

A breathless voice from the common room cut through the innkeeper's pleasant reverie. "Ogden!"

Startled, Ogden let the steaming brew kettle slip onto his round belly. With a pained hiss he shifted it back over the lip of the oaken tun before him. Cloudy amber liquid resumed its course into the barrel, splashing some foam into life.

"Not now, lad," shouted Ogden. "I'm sparging the wort. It's a delicate part of the proc—"

A bear-sized bulk crashed through the kitchen's bolt-less door. It turned toward the innkeeper, tiny eyes round on a pink face. His pug nose was wide and runny. The first foliage of a beard was evident upon the young man's face. "But Ogden, it's—"

"Whatever it is, it can wait until I've emptied the kettle." The happy smile that had warmed his face faded into Ogden's day-old whiskers. He never shaved on brew day; that was one of his other small pleasures, though when he saw a mirror, he fretted at the conquest of the gray stubble over the familiar brown.

"But—"

Ogden caught the big boy's mouth with his free hand. The kettle shifted again, and Ogden stepped around the tun, keeping his palm firmly pressed over Portnoy's lips.

"Count to twenty," said Ogden. He felt Portnoy's lips move beneath his palm and added, "Silently!"

Portnoy's deep brow creased with the effort, but his tiny eyes set in determination as he struggled to obey. That should take him a while, thought Ogden with a smile of relief. His sister's son was not quite an idiot, but he was often mistaken for one.

The innkeeper wiped his hand on his heavy apron before regaining a grip on the kettle.

"Here, hold the tun steady," said Ogden. Portnoy hesitated, perhaps wondering whether it was a trick to interrupt his counting. Deciding that obedience was the better course, he gripped the oak tun.

"I was trying to tell you that—"

"Uh, uh! There," said Ogden. "Now tilt it back. Careful, it's a bit warm, still. . . ."

Portnoy was far better with his hands than with his brain. His thick fingers were clamps, holding the tun at just the right angle to let Ogden pour the remaining malt with the least splashing. When the kettle was empty at last, Ogden favored Portnoy with a smile. Maybe he should show the lad the whole process soon. Surely it was simple enough.

"Good." Ogden set a lid atop the tun. The malt would need a few more hours to cool, and then he could hop and cask it. A few months later, he'd have another batch of rich ale to serve the villagers of Myrloch. "That's the last one."

He turned to his young charge. The boy was only fifteen years old, but already he stood taller than the war veteran and outweighed him by four stone. Nonetheless, Ogden managed to look down at the boy with fatherly condescension while looking up to see the lad's broad face. "Now what is it that has you carrying on so madly?"

"It's Cole," replied Portnoy. "The wizard."

"Aye?"

"He's dead."

* * * * *

"Mind the village while I'm gone, old friend."

Lord Donnell always said the same thing when he left Cantrev Myrloch. It had become something of a joke between the two veterans of the Darkwalker war. It had carried them through the years of rebuilding after the defeat of Kazgoroth, and it lived on into the reign of Alicia, Tristan's daughter and their new queen.

"Who d'ye think minds it when you're here?" That was always Ogden's reply.

A hundred times had Donnell left the village in Ogden's charge, and it had always been a quiet jest. Donnell would return and say, "What have you been doing all this time? I had hoped for some improvement, a new tower or two, at least. You've grown lazy as well as fat."

"It's the baldness that slows me, my lord," Ogden would apologize. Then he would invite Lord Donnell to supper.

They would spend the rest of the day in Ogden's inn, the White Hart. Inside, the lord would tell his friend everything that had happened on his travels, and the innkeeper would tell his friend what he made of it. After some hours, Lord Donnell would emerge and invite the crowd that had invariably gathered to listen at the door to enter.

"Let the gossip begin!" And he would walk, unsteadily more often than not, up to his stately manor. The villagers would swarm into the inn, where Ogden would share the gossip he and Donnell had agreed should spread. And he would sell a barrel of ale.

Ogden valued that relationship, and he wanted to keep it. That was why he took it so badly that someone should die while Lord Donnell was away at Caer Callidyr, in audience with Queen Alicia. He was due to return today, and Ogden had better have some answers for him when he arrived. He placed one big hand on each of Portnoy's expansive shoulders and fixed his eyes on the lad's own.

"He's what?"

"He's dead, Uncle Ogden."

"You're sure of this, are you?"

"They said he's dead as a stone."

"Well, I suppose they know what it is they're talking about." Ogden gave Portnoy a dubious frown. "Who's 'they.'"

"Dare and Eowan. They says Enid saw 'im this morning, as she was bringing 'is milk and eggs around."

"Did you see him yourself?"

"No, I ran right home."

"Good lad," said Ogden. Portnoy was not a fool, despite appearances. He untied his apron. "Now, you clean up this kitchen while I have a look myself."

* * * * *

By the time he reached Cole's cottage, Ogden wished he had brought his walking stick. The first snow had fallen last night. It paled the low mountains that sheltered Myrloch Vale from eastern Gwynneth. Even so far from the sea, the winds blew unhindered before reaching those rugged hills. They brought the northeastern chill with them, planting it deep within Ogden's old wound. The scar left by a northman's axe still creased his shin from knee to ankle. Each winter it grew a little stronger, the only child of his youth.

Fortunately, the wizard's home was less than a mile north, and the snow was only two or three inches deep, not yet deep enough to obscure the furrows of the barley fields through which Ogden walked. He passed the white-capped houses of the nearest farmers, close enough to wave but far enough to avoid prying questions about his destination and his unusual task.

The snow began to fall again, light enough to leave the boot prints of those who had preceded Ogden to the wizard's home. All of the trails came from the center of the village, where gossip always traveled first. Ogden followed the converging paths until they became a single trail. Soon, he saw a cluster of villagers standing a cautious distance from Cole's door, craning their necks to look through the small front window.

Most of the crowd were Cole's neighbors, but some had walked all the way from the village center to see for themselves. Cole was not exactly hated among the Ffolk of Myrloch, but he was always a curiosity to be observed from a distance. He had come across the sea at the behest of Keane, the queen's wizard and—if Donnell's court gossip were true—the man soon to be the high king himself. Since King Tristan's abdication, town wizards had become something of a fashion among the towns and cities of the Moonshaes. Every petty lord tried to adopt one, granting him a parcel of land in return for ambiguous promises of protection and advice.

The people of Myrloch were astonished when their sensible lord Donnell announced that he was granting a hundred acres to a spindly foreign sorcerer. The grayer heads of Myrloch speculated that Keane had set Cole the task of keeping an eye on Myrloch Vale, just over the western hills. It was to Myrloch that old King Tristan and his druid wife Robyn had retired. That theory was enough to satisfy the people that Donnell had not become frivolous or, worse yet, fashionable. Eventually, the gossip died away.

Still, no one warmed to the wizard. He wasn't particularly aloof, though he visited the Hart only twice or thrice a month. When he added his voice to the gossip, it was only on the most innocuous of subjects. At fairs he never danced nor courted, though the eyes of most village girls had been seen to linger on his slim figure from time to time—which fact surely did not endear him the more to the village men. Cole's dark figure haunted the edges of the crowds. He was never apart from the Ffolk, but he was never fully a part of them.

Death makes all men more interesting to their neighbors, thought Ogden as he joined the silent cluster of Ffolk. He stood with them for a moment, watching their breaths expand and fade. Even in the late morning the sun was too weak to burn the frost completely from the air.

Ogden spied Enid's blond head among the gathering. The slender girl was the only child of Conn and Branwen, who raised cattle and kept chickens. She was a familiar sight to all villagers, for she delivered fresh eggs and milk each morning to those who traded with her father. By the wizard's door stood a covered pail and basket. An empty pail lay by Enid's feet, nestled in the snow. Her eyes met Ogden's as soon as he spied her.

"So you found him, did you, Enid?"

"Aye, constable."

Ogden winced. He'd forgotten that Donnell had bequeathed him with that title officially some years ago. They had both been drunk at fair, and Ogden could never quite remember whether it had been a joke or an honor. This was the first time anyone had called him "constable" in anything but jest.

"How long ago was that?"

"A little more than an hour. His was my last delivery."

"Do you deliver to him every day?"

"Every other."

Ogden nodded, trying to look wise and thoughtful before the other villagers. Some of them nodded at him, expressing their confidence in this line of questioning. Others remained stone-faced, reserving their judgment. Ogden was of a mind with them. He had no idea whether Enid's answers were of any use, but he suspected not.

Ogden nodded. "Well, let's have a look."

"Door's locked, constable." Mane Ferguson was the speaker. He was a dark-eyed boy of Enid's age. In one callused hand, Mane clutched a long branch, recently trimmed. Ogden suspected that the boy had been trying to poke the wizard's body through the window. Mane glanced briefly at Enid before facing the innkeeper. Ogden knew that he wanted to make sure that the girl was watching.

"Back door, too?" asked Ogden.

"Aye, and the back windows're latched," the boy said. "But you can see him plain enough through the front window."

"I don't suppose you tried slipping down the chimney?"

"Ah, no sir. You don't want me to try, do you?" Mane looked very much as though he hoped Ogden would not want him to climb into the wizard's home, but he had to make a good show of it before Enid. Who knew what one might find in a wizard's chimney? Enid hid a smile behind one slender hand, but Mane remained oblivious to her amusement.

"Not at the moment, but stay handy."

"Aye, constable." Mane turned proudly to Enid and mistook her smile for approval. Or perhaps he wasn't mistaken, thought Ogden. And maybe Portnoy isn't the dullest lad in town.

The little crowd parted for Ogden as he walked to the window. Peering in, he spied the wizard's body sprawled upon the floor beside a fine padded chair and a cluttered table. Ogden saw no blood, but he watched long enough to see that Cole was not breathing.

Ogden turned back to the expectant villagers. "Let's have a look inside."

"You won't want to blunder through a wizard's door," cautioned Old Angus. The ancient farmer was likely the first on the scene after Enid. Since his sons took over his land for him, he spent his days walking the perimeter of the village, visiting anyone who would spend an hour's conversation with him.

"Aye," added Mane with a tone of great authority. "You'll likely be hexed or transformed or reduced to—"

"Likely so," interrupted Ogden. He gave Mane a solemn look. Cole had never demonstrated any such spectacular powers, but none doubted he was in fact a wizard. Cole always seemed to know secrets, usually petty stories about his neighbors. Fortunately, he wasn't himself a gossip. But his knowing smile or nod or shake of the head whenever he overheard such tales was enough to convince the village that he observed all indiscretions through his magical mirror, or crystal, or pool, or something.

Ogden smiled at Mane then. "That's why I'll need you to slip through the window, here, and open the door for me."

Mane's eyes grew wide and pale as fried eggs. "But what if—"

Mane didn't have a chance to finish before Enid interrupted, "Oh, I'll do it." She had set the empty milk pail on its end and clambered up to the windowsill before anyone could say a word.

"Enid!" sputtered Mane. When the girl turned to arch a single golden eyebrow at him, he said only, "You be careful, now."

With an exasperated sigh, Enid wriggled through the open window, graceful as a selkie. A few moments later, the front door opened, and the girl stepped back outside.

Ogden nodded his appreciation to the young woman, then entered the cottage. The other villagers pressed forward, and he waved them back. "I'll need the light, now.

Stand away until I've had my look around." They mostly obeyed.

Sunlight streamed through the door, illuminating Cole's body and the table where he had died.

On the table rested a book, a tumble of parchment, and three fresh tapers in a candelabra. The rest of the room was comfortably furnished with several chairs, another low table, and a few shelves, one devoted entirely to books and scrolls. Ogden was one of the few people in Myrloch cantrev who had his letters, but even he owned no books. Lord Donnell had a few—chronicles of the first kings, and histories of the Ffolk—which Ogden had read and re-read. The innkeeper was canny enough to suspect where history ended and legend began, but of the realm of magic, Ogden knew blessedly little. He was not eager to open the wizard's librams.

Ogden knelt beside the dead wizard. Placing a hand on Cole's chest, Ogden felt the dying warmth there. The man could not have died last night. He must have been alive not long before Enid's visit this morning.

There were no violent marks on the body, though black ink stained the mage's once fine blue tunic. It pooled on the floor beside the corpse, and a gleaming black trail ran under the table. Ogden followed the trail to find the tumbled ink pot resting against the foot of the table. He left it where it lay and finished examining the body.

Cole's face had frozen in a faint grimace. His black mustache looked crooked against his final expression, and his eyes were closed. His arms and legs were bent as from a fall, but none seemed broken. Ogden noticed a dark smudge on Cole's right hand. He rose to look at the desktop once more.

Cole had been writing letters before he died. At first glance they appeared innocuous, friendly missives to friends or relatives. Ogden noticed that all of them were finished; none ended suddenly, as he had expected. One must be missing.

Someone cleared his throat at the door. Ogden looked up

to see the villagers looking back impatiently.

"Find anything?" asked Old Angus.

"Hmm," replied Ogden. It was a sound to make when he didn't have an answer. He turned his attention back to the body. He would have one more look at it before summoning Megan to wash and prepare the corpse for burial.

Ogden's eyes scanned the room for any clues. He spied a wide blue bowl half-filled with milk near the window. Enid must have tipped it with her landing as she slipped into the cottage, for her small white footprint puddled the wooden floor. The mage's cat would be needing a new home, he thought.

Nothing else was amiss, so Ogden turned back to the body. Gently, he rolled the dead wizard onto his back. There was the missing letter. The lone page had been pinned under the wizard's arm when he fell. It was also written in the wizard's hand, but this one ended in large, crude letters, smeared but still legible. Ogden stared at the message, not believing his good luck.

The last clumsy line read: "Niall Ericson kille—"

* * * * *

Ogden didn't have to summon Megan after all. Word of Cole's death had reached her soon after Portnoy brought the news to Ogden, and she knew when she was needed. Crafty and wise, Megan was something betwixt the ordinary Ffolk and the druids. She knew the tricks of herb and root, and she had a cunning for sewing wounds. When all cures failed, she was the one to wash and bind the corpse before stitching shut the last wound of all: the funeral shroud.

She was also Niall Ericson's wife.

Ericson was Cole's nearest neighbor, living alone since Megan had left him some six years earlier. She had walked out of their cottage the day after their daughter married a herder from a northern cantrev and left Myrloch village behind. Megan's sons struck out on their own soon after, seeking their fortunes in Callidyr and leaving Niall alone on the farm, bitter and angry. No one asked Megan why she left the man, but everyone had a speculation. He beat her, some said. He was cruel to the animals she sometimes kept as pets. He thought her a witch for her healing lore, for the Northmen were a superstitious lot. The jovial suggested that Niall's colossal snoring was the answer to their separation. There was darker gossip concerning the daughter. No matter what one believed, none knew Niall's side of it, for he seldom walked among the Ffolk himself, and they feared him somewhat.

Megan lived nearer town these days, in a small cottage left vacant by its owners' deaths some years ago. Lord Donnell granted her ownership without delay, for he knew the value of a healer. From her own home, now, she exchanged her craft for enough food to subsist and a little more for trade. The other Ffolk brought her something of each harvest whether they had need of her help or not. It was the nature of the Ffolk to put up a little extra yield against the winter.

Megan's hands were brown and freckled against the dead wizard's wan face. Ogden had helped her lift the body to the wizard's kitchen table, where now she finished her examination of the body. She lifted each eyelid and peered at the dead orbs. She pried open his stiff jaw to peek inside his mouth.

"No mark of poison," she said at last. "None of my kenning, at least." Megan brushed a strand of auburn hair away from her eyes. Time had been gentle with her. While she was nearly Ogden's age, the snow had yet to dust her hair.

Ogden grunted in disappointment. He had hoped that Megan would tell him she knew of a poison that would leave no sign, one that she had long ago taught Niall Ericson. From the moment he saw the wizard's last note, he was all but certain of Ericson's guilt. The problem remained the proof, which he hoped to find before Lord Donnell's return.

"What do you make of the message?" Ogden expected some reaction from Megan when he read her the words. She had no letters herself, though she was likely the most learned person in the village, in her way.

Megan didn't answer at first. Instead, she walked to the window. Hugging her arms, she looked out at the villagers, who were making a poor show of not peering back at her. As she turned back to face Ogden, her foot caught the cat's milk bowl and set it spinning on the wooden floor. Milk sloshed over its rim and splashed upon her shoes.

"Where's the cat?" she asked.

"It must be outside," he said. He realized then that whatever harm Niall had done her, Megan still cared for the man. This business must be a hardness to her.

"Poor thing," she said. "I'll take it in when it's found." She picked up the bowl and took it to the dish pail. There she rinsed the bowl and dried it with a rag. Ogden waited silently, patiently.

"If you mean do I think Niall might have killed him, then yes. He might have." Megan looked directly into Ogden's eyes. "With his fists, perhaps. Or maybe with a blade. But there's no guile in Niall Ericson."

Ogden nodded. Subtlety was not unknown among the Northmen, but it was as scarce as kindness in the likes of Ericson.

"Would he have had a reason?" asked Ogden.

"It's no secret that Niall had his eye upon these fields before Lord Donnell granted it to Cole. If the boys had stayed with him another two or three seasons, Niall reckoned he could buy the tract outright."

"But they left."

"Aye," agreed Megan. "We all left."

"So, you think he had cause," suggested Ogden.

"Cause enough for him. But only in a rage, I think. Niall couldn't murder this man without a violent hand."

Ogden believed it was true, and so the problem remained. What was the proof?

* * * * *

Ericson wanted Cole's land, so he murdered the wizard. That remained Ogden's theory.

"But why would Niall kill Cole? He could never farm that much land by himself." Portnoy asked the obvious questions whenever Ogden failed to ask them of himself. In his more patient moments, Ogden could appreciate that quality. More importantly, he would appreciate having Portnoy's hulking presence beside him when he confronted Ericson. It was well worth the trip back to the inn to fetch the lad.

"Some men can't own to their own failings," said Ogden.

"But Cole didn't take that land away from Niall."

"No, but Niall might still see it that way. Some Northmen have ice in their hearts, and there's no telling what they'll think is fair."

"That's stupid," replied Portnoy plainly.

"Aye," agreed Ogden. "That it is."

They walked a while in silence, and then Ogden said, "Enid was the one who slipped in to open the door."

"Aye?" Portnoy feigned indifference, but Ogden knew better. Portnoy had been smitten with the lass since childhood. Unfortunately for him, Mane was the most active in courting her attention. Portnoy could never work up the nerve.

"Aye. I'd asked Mane to do it, but he balked."

"Aye?"

"Aye. I think he shrank a bit in Enid's eyes."

Portnoy didn't say anything to that, but Ogden watched him from the corner of his eye. The lad smiled to himself, and Ogden saw his lips silently trace the word "good." He let it lie at that.

As they approached Niall's farm, the first serious doubts began to form in Ogden's mind. If Niall had killed Cole, how had he managed to bar the doors from the inside as he left? And how had he killed the wizard without leaving a mark? Niall wasn't the sort to poison a man he could break across his knee.

By the time Ogden and Portnoy came within a hundred yards of Niall's house, Ogden was sure he had been misled. He turned away from the cottage and began circling the farm. Portnoy followed obediently, without asking why they'd turned. Eventually, they reached the pond behind Niall's farmstead. It was frozen over. The light breeze swept the snow from its face, revealing its smooth, hard surface.

Ogden turned around, and he and Portnoy retraced their steps. Then they walked all the way around the other side, once more reaching the pond. On this side, nearer the house, Ogden saw where Niall had chopped out a block of ice. The flat chunk lay on the ground. The blue shadows of Niall's boot prints lead a winding path from the house to the water's edge, then back.

Ogden winced at the pain in his foot, and Portnoy was puffing with exertion. The boy could stand to lose some of that weight, thought Ogden. Together, they stopped to catch their breaths and observe the snowy field.

"What do you see, lad?"

"Uh . . . Niall's house? The barn? The well? Those trees?" Portnoy's eyes scanned the field for other guesses.

"Right, but what don't you see?"

Portnoy frowned and stared at the land they'd circumscribed with their path. Ogden studied the lad—for so he still considered Portnoy, even though the youth had grown taller than his uncle—watching for some glimmer of deductive reasoning. Portnoy would never be a village sage, but there was something more than moss growing between his ears.

Or so Ogden always hoped.

"Boot prints!" the boy exclaimed. "They don't leave!"

"Aye," agreed Ogden. "They go from the house to the barn, and then they wind over to the pond." Ogden frowned at the ragged trail, wondering why it was so irregular. He hoped that Ericson wasn't drunk. The man was mean enough sober.

"He hasn't left the farm since last night," added Portnoy. "There hasn't been enough snow since last night to cover up his tracks." The cold had brought the blood to his cheeks, and he beamed at Ogden, watching for some sign of approval. The man rewarded him with a nod, but he frowned.

"Unless Niall has learned to fly, how'd he get to Cole's home and back?"

"It must be someone else," said Portnoy. The disappointment in his voice was obvious, and Ogden knew just how he felt.

"Perhaps." Ogden had been suspicious of Cole's note from the beginning. How would a murdered man find the time to scrawl such a message? And what murderer would leave it behind, even if he couldn't read it?

"Look there," said Portnoy. Ogden's eyes followed the lad's own stare toward the farmhouse, where a fur-clad figure stomped toward them. His breath made plumes in the late morning air as the man approached.

"Well a day, Niall Ericson," greeted Ogden.

"Constable," said Niall simply. His voice was hard as winter granite. His lips were red beneath his dirty blond beard, though his skin was stone pale.

"Will we have more snow tonight, do you think?"

"What d'ye want?" said Ericson curtly. His flinty eyes invited no more small talk.

"The wizard Cole's been murdered," replied Ogden.

"And what does that have t'do with me, then?" The man's tone had turned menacing, and Portnoy began to fidget beside his uncle. Even though the boy was of a size with Ericson, Ogden knew the man must frighten him.

"Maybe nothing," said Ogden. He glanced past the man toward the house, then met his eyes again. "But the mage wrote down your name just before he died."

Ericson looked genuinely astonished. "Why would he . . . ?"

"You won't mind our looking around a bit, then?"

Ericson stared back at Ogden's face. Ragged lines creased his face, and his eyes narrowed to black slits. Ogden noticed that the clouds of Ericson's breath had halted, and he tensed for an attack. Now he wished he'd brought more than Portnoy with him.

Finally, Ericson sighed impatiently and barked, "All right, then. Make it quick!" He turned quickly and stalked back toward his house. Portnoy hesitated, looking to his uncle for a cue. Ogden nodded, and they both hurried to follow Ericson back toward his cottage.

"You follow his boot prints," said Ogden. "See where he's gone this morning. Then take a look in the barn. I'll peek inside the house."

"Aye," agreed Portnoy. He trembled with the excitement of a wolfhound pup on its first hunt, and off he went.

Ogden followed Ericson to the door of his house, but there he paused. The threshold was swept clear, but to one side a white glaze of ice covered the snow. At least he throws out the spoiled milk, thought Ogden. Ericson must be a better housekeeper than anyone expected. Ogden stepped inside the cottage.

The odor immediately changed Ogden's opinion of Ericson's domestic talents. Even through the wood smoke, the interior smelled of unwashed clothes. To Ogden's left there stood a table cluttered with dirty pots and bowls. One of them, a small shallow basin, was freshly broken. Ericson must use them all before washing any, thought Ogden.

Ogden took a step toward the table and nearly tripped on something that rolled beneath his foot. At the base of the table lay a pile of potatoes, half-tumbled by Ogden's careless step. Behind them, three full potato sacks leaned against the cottage wall.

Ogden stepped carefully away, then turned to look across the room. He saw a pile of furs and blankets covering the lone bed. Beside it, a trio of chairs lined the wall, each piled with smelly clothing. Nearby, the hearth fire snapped and hissed as Ericson stabbed it with an iron stoker.

"I haven't left my land all morning," said Ericson. His tone had softened, but he still sounded gruff and unfriendly.

"Aye, that I believe," said Ogden.

Ericson grunted in acceptance of Ogden's answer, but then he jutted his jaw defiantly. "Then what do you want here?"

"Hmm," replied Ogden, casting about a few last glances at the house. He walked outside once more. He saw Portnoy returning from the barn, frowning with frustration.

"Just sheep," reported the boy. "Sheep and feed and only what else you'd expect to find in the barn."

Ogden only nodded. He was close to reckoning some connection between Ericson's cottage and Cole's. In most ways, the two homes couldn't be more different. Something continued to niggle at Ogden's mind, however. And the man had greeted him as "constable." He knew there was trouble this morning.

"Why would a man chop ice from pond water?" Ogden asked, more of himself than Portnoy.

The boy answered anyway. "Yuck. Who'd drink pond water?" Even he knew that still water, even frozen, was likely to make the drinker sick.

"There's perfectly good snow everywhere, too."

Portnoy shrugged and looked at Ogden's face. The man's brow was creased in impatient concentration. Portnoy imitated his expression. The family resemblance was striking, but neither of the Ffolk noted it.

"He didn't want anything from the pond . . ." began Ogden tentatively.

". . . he put something into it!" finished Portnoy, grinning.

"Let's have a look," said Ogden. Both men stepped toward the frozen water.

"That's enough," boomed a voice behind them. They

turned to see Ericson, still gripping the iron stoker. Its tip glowed red. "You've had your look around."

"True enough," said Ogden. Now he knew he should have brought more men along. He knew at last how Ericson had murdered Cole, but now he'd let on what he had reckoned. By the time he could return with help, Ericson could destroy the evidence rather than just hide it. If he and Portnoy stayed, however, how would Ericson react?

"We'll be on our way, then," said Ogden. "Come along, lad." He chucked Portnoy's elbow, though his eyes remained locked on the fiery stoker in Ericson's hand. Portnoy followed dully, distracted by the problem of what Ericson had put in the cold water.

They walked toward the pond, the way they'd come. Ericson followed. When Ogden glanced back at the man, he saw that the tip of the stoker whipped up and down in agitation. Ogden instantly regretted bringing Portnoy along for this visit. The big lad's presence might be a deterrent against attack from most men, but Ericson was desperate and dangerous. Ogden increased his pace, and Portnoy did the same.

"That's far enough." Ericson's voice was calm and strong now. Ogden knew that meant he had come to a decision.

"Run, lad! Fetch help!" Ogden shoved Portnoy and turned to face the brawny Northman. He might not be able to disable the man, but at least he could give the boy a good start back to the village. Ericson growled deep and loud. Ogden whirled to face his attacker, crouching low and throwing up his left arm. He felt the blow of the stoker break his arm.

All the strength drained from his ruined left arm as the Northman raised the hot bar again. Ericson's face was a twisted mass of veins and sinew. He grimaced so hard and wide that his mouth threatened to open up over his entire face. His eyeballs rolled in their sockets.

He's going berserk, thought Ogden fleetingly. He'll tear me apart.

Ogden braced himself and stepped toward his attacker, throwing all of his weight into a low, sweeping punch. His fist caught Ericson just below the ribcage, and the northman's dirty breath blasted Ogden's face.

"Huh!" Ericson grinned even wider, white flecks dotting his beard. "Ha!" He smashed his forehead into Ogden's face. The innkeeper felt his nose go flat with a sickening crunch. Red light exploded behind his eyes. He felt his brain rolling untethered in his skull, and the earth rolled in waves beneath him. He tried to step back, but his legs betrayed him. He fell back hard, and the impact chased the wind out of his lungs. Ogden lay helpless on the snow.

Ericson loomed forward, a giant against the white sky. With both hands he raised the poker above his head. The black bar rose higher and higher, Ogden thought, high enough to pierce the roof of the world. And then he saw that Ericson himself was rising.

"No!" The hoarse cry was Portnoy's, but all Ogden could see was the great awkward figure of Ericson flying through the air. He heard a heavy thump and an inarticulate grunt. His limbs still felt stringless, but Ogden rolled toward the sound.

Not five yards away lay Ericson, stunned and blinking. A big shadow moved toward him on the snow, and Portnoy's heavy steps followed close behind, quickening in a charge.

The Northman rose to meet his new attacker, his rage broken but his desperate will intact. The poker remained in his grip.

"Portnoy, don't!" Ogden tried to yell. His voice was as weak as his battered body. The lad wouldn't have heard even the most thunderous bellow, from the way his head lowered in determination.

The lad closed as Ericson swung his bar. The weapon struck Portnoy's big round shoulder and bent, but the blow did nothing to slow him. Both giant figures crashed to the ground, and Ogden imagined he could feel the resulting tremor. He tried to stand but managed only to put his hands and knees beneath him. He looked up to see Ericson and Portnoy rising from their tumble. Portnoy now held the iron stoker.

The Northman looked at the mangled weapon in Portnoy's hand, then at the face of his foe, who seemed none the worse for the mighty blow. He turned and fled.

Portnoy started after him.

"Wait!" wheezed Ogden. His voice was returning, and with it some strength. He pushed himself up to one knee and pointed vaguely toward the fleeing Northman. "Look where he's going."

Ericson ran awkwardly, his feet sliding on the icy surface of the pond. As Portnoy and Ogden watched, the northman's feet shot out, and he hit the ice with a terrific crack. Even at this distance, Ogden could see the blue lines form under the Northman's fallen body.

He tried to stand, but first one and then his other leg thrust through the broken surface into the frigid water. Jagged teeth of ice grated and groaned, and the Northman sank deeper. He scrabbled for a hold, but found none. Ogden saw his adversary's eyes meet his one last time, and then the northman's face fell still. Without a cry, Ericson slipped into the icy pond.

* * * * *

". . . and when we searched the pond where he'd been chopping, we came up with the bag." Portnoy's voice had dropped low and frightening. He was developing a talent for storytelling. It was not easy for him, for he had always been awkward around crowds. He left out the parts where he'd been most frightened, and that helped, too.

"What was inside?" Enid whispered theatrically. She had heard the story earlier, but more villagers had gathered at the door to the Hart, waiting for Lord Donnell and Ogden to finish their private discussion of the day's events. Among them stood Lord Donnell's guardsmen, themselves commanded to wait outside with the rest. Like the other villagers, they burned with curiosity about the death of the wizard Cole. Fortunately, Portnoy was there to satisfy their curiosity at once.

"The wizard's cat!"

After an initial "oh" of understanding, the audience was suitably puzzled.

"His cat?" Mane had arrived late and was mystified by Portnoy's revelation.

"It was his familiar, you see. If a wizard's familiar dies, so does he." Portnoy hadn't known that for certain until Ogden had said so, and even Ogden had to consult Megan, who everyone was pretty sure was a witch, even though she didn't have a familiar of her own.

"Oh!" Now the listeners nodded and nudged each other.

"Uncle Ogden saw milk and a broken bowl at Niall's house. Niall was too mean to set out milk for a cat, so he must have put it out to lure the poor thing close. Then he grabbed it, popped it in a potato sack, and drowned it in the pond."

"So Niall killed Cole without ever leaving his cottage," Enid concluded for him. Mane gave her and Portnoy a suspicious glance. It made Portnoy feel uncomfortable and vaguely proud.

"Why didn't you see the cat's footprints coming up to Niall's house?" asked one of the older villagers, quite sensibly.

Portnoy nodded, expecting this question, too.

"The cat walked over across the pond, where the wind had blown away the snow before it could settle. Where it walked from the pond to the door, Niall had stamped out its tracks with his own. That's why his trail was so ragged. He had to go everywhere the cat had—"

Behind Portnoy, the front door of the inn opened. Out walked Lord Donnell, a tall, lean man who wore his dark beard neatly trimmed. His blue winter cloak was finer than those around him, but not so fine as to seem out of place. Behind him stood Ogden, his broken arm bound and splinted, and hanging in a clean linen sling. His broken nose was darkly bruised, but packed full and near to its original shape. The faces of both men were aglow, and not entirely from sitting too close to the hearth.

"Let the gossip begin!" declared Donnell. His eyes were weary from his journey and from the unfortunate news— not to mention Ogden's ale—but he seemed satisfied if not cheered by his constable's report.

"I suspect you're a bit late for that," said Ogden, looking at Portnoy. The big lad looked like a child caught stealing a neighbor's apples.

"But I thought it would be all right to—"

"Oh, it's all right, lad," interrupted Donnell. "But did you give the whole story?" He turned to address the crowd as a whole. The setting sun made his shadow huge against the wall of the inn. "Did you tell how you fought Niall Ericson single-handed, defeating an armed Northman warrior with your bare hands?"

"Well. . . ."

"You did that?" Mane's suspicious stare transformed into a look of awe. He never saw Enid's own gaze of unsurprised affection as she smiled at Portnoy.

"I knew you were leaving out your own part," said Enid.

"Well. . . ."

"Well, then," said Lord Donnell, ushering the eager crowd into the warm confines of the Hart, where they would hear the rest of the story from Ogden himself. "Let the gossip truly begin."

The Rose Window

Monte Cook

I hope against hope that no one ever reads this.

I suppose I learned the truth the day before yesterday, but it all started a few weeks before that. You see, I was there when the Abbey of Byfor was torn down. I had to go. Loremaster High Tessen had been my mentor. It was like paying my last respects to an old friend.

The late autumn day was overcast and gray, with a cold, northerly wind tearing at us with angry talons. All those attending kept their cloaks tightly wrapped around themselves like armor against the chill. I was surprised at how many had come to take part in the simony that took place.

The abbey was old, and had not actually functioned as a monastery in many years. Nevertheless, until recently, it had still served the surrounding community as a place of worship one day in ten and shelter in times of inclement weather. Now, however, the western wall had begun to collapse and the roof sagged so badly that the local masons claimed the building was no longer safe. A man named Greal had taken over the abbey after the bishop's death a few years earlier. I never was able to determine exactly what station he held in church hierarchy, if any. Greal claimed that he had no money to instigate the necessary repairs, so he began selling the stone and furnishings alike. He claimed to hope that with the money he raised he could build a new church, dedicated to Oghma, for the local folk.

I stood outside the decaying edifice and watched as young men carried pews, the lectern and even the stone-topped altar out into the barren, leaf-covered yard. I saw people come and go, purchasing all of the old accouterments that had served the abbey and its parishioners for generations. Later in the day—I had not moved—I saw the young men now brandish hammers and tools. Soon, I knew, the stones from the abbey would be taken away and used to build pasture walls and farm houses.

Something—perhaps fate, but now I'm not so sure—bid me to look up to the abbey's tall roof. There, high upon the gable, was the beautiful rose window that I remembered so well from my time as an acolyte there. The round window was fitted with light blue-green glass that formed an extremely complex rose pattern. Though it was dull in that day's gray, I knew that in any brighter sunlight it scintillated like a jewel with a brilliant cascade of light.

I left my spot and approached the man called Greal, reaching into an inner pocket in my cloak. I produced a bag of gold—all that I had. He turned toward me with a foul expression.

"Excuse me, sir," I began, "but I understand that you are selling the abbey's, ah, parts." His expression softened, and I continued. "Well, you may not know this, but I once held a position here as a seeker—an acolyte—before I was given my own parish. Loremaster High Tessen was the priest at the time—my mentor."

Greal's dark gray eyes were flat and his mouth was drawn thin. He folded his arms in front of him, but did not say a word.

"Well," I said, "that old rose window meant a lot to me." I pointed at it, and his eyes followed my gesture. "I would be willing to pay you for it, so that I could put it in my own church."

"Really," he did not ask, but stated. A light came to his eyes as he turned back toward me. His tight mouth was tense.

"Yes, it would be an excellent . . ." I searched for the right word. ". . . reminder of the Loremaster High and his steadfast faith."

Greal now smiled, and I cannot say that I liked it. It was the wide, tight-lipped grin of a predator. "Yes," he said finally. "An excellent reminder. He was an inspiration to us all."

He held out his hand, and I dropped the purse in it. Emptying the coins into his wide, soft hand, he counted slowly. The sight disturbed me, so I looked up at the window instead. Though it cost me greatly, I knew that I would enjoy the window and the remembrance of Tessen for many years to come.

Satisfied with the price, Greal told the young men to climb up and carefully remove the window for me. I had come to the abbey in my small wagon, and there was room for the window. It all seemed like fate had meant for it to be, for not long after I was driving my team back across the valley to my parish home.

* * * * *

Within a week, I had hired some men of my own to come to the church and help me install the window high above the floor of the sanctuary. There I knew it would bring brilliant light down upon the worshipers during each Binding and Covenant, our morning and evening rituals. The window would glorify Oghma as well as the faith of Loremaster High Tessen. I was gladdened. Once it was in place, I noticed that young Pheslan, my own seeker, was transfixed by the window.

"It's so wonderful," he said, "and yet so odd."

I looked up at the window myself, and then at the portly Pheslan. "Odd?"

"Forgive me, brother, I mean no disrespect. It is not odd

in an ill fashion. It's just . . . the pattern. Each time I look at it I see something new. Some different facet to the way the glass has been fitted, or some new way the light plays upon the angles. Yes, that's it. It is the angles that are so fascinating."

Looking at the window again, I had to admit that he was right. It was fascinating.

"The workmanship of those days has known no equal since," I said, knowing that such was something that elders always said to the young. I smiled at the thought, and then at the boy as we both bathed in the blessing of sunlight and looked at the beauty of the rose window.

* * * * *

As the next few weeks passed, I became concerned with other things. Oghma, the Lord of Knowledge and the Wise God, bids his servants to spread information and dispense learning as well as watch over the well-being of the worshipers as we guide them toward enlightenment. Thus, the duties of a parish priest are legion, but I suppose that this is not the time to describe them. Let it suffice to say that I was preoccupied—so much so that I paid little attention to the fact that young Pheslan was still enraptured with the rose window. One night, after Covenant, we finished our duties and sat down to our simple meal. He told me that he had seen something strange in the window. I listened only halfheartedly, for I was very tired.

"It must be within the pattern of the glass, or the facets," he explained. We sat at a small wooden table in the room that lies between our sleeping chambers at the back of the church. It was dark, the only light coming from a lamp on the table at the center of our meager feast.

"What must?" I said, my mouth full of bread.

The young acolyte was too agitated to eat. "As I said, brother," he said, "there were things that seemed to move in the window as the sun set."

"You mean the light played upon the glass," I said, swallowing.

"Yes, probably." His eyes lowered.

"What do mean, 'probably'?"

"Well, it seemed so real," he replied, looking into my eyes. "They moved."

"What moved?"

"The images in the window. It was as though something was on the other side."

"Perhaps there was something on the other side, Pheslan." I was becoming slightly irritated now. "A bird?"

"But I went outside and looked," he said. "There was nothing."

I drank the last bit from my cup and stood. "Then it was indeed the light of the setting sun playing upon the glass," I concluded. "Enough now, Pheslan. It is time for bed."

With that we retired. Pheslan was nothing if not obedient. It makes me . . .

Well, let me finish the tale first.

* * * * *

Two more days passed, and Pheslan said nothing more about the window. He was quiet, and slow to finish his duties. I knew I needed to talk to him, but I was just too busy. Later, there would be time.

The night of the second day, after retiring, I heard a strange noise. I had been reading in bed as I often did before blowing out my lamp and going to sleep. I heard the noise again. It sounded as if it was coming from outside the church. Perhaps someone was knocking at the door. I placed my marker in the book, threw the blankets back and made my way to the front of the church in my nightclothes. The sound came again, it struck me as though something was scratching on the outside wall of the building.

The stone floor was cold on my bare feet so I hurried through the dark, only my intimate knowledge of the place keeping me from bumping into anything until I entered the sanctuary. There, the light of the full moon shone through the rose window lighting my way to the narthex and the door.

Although there are dangers in the night, even in our peaceful valley, I never bolted the door. The church should always be open, I believed, always there to welcome the poor as well as those in need of knowledge, Oghma's sacred gift. I opened the door and looked out into the dark night. A bitter wind blew dead, brown leaves all around the yard in front of the church.

I could see nothing out of the ordinary.

Again, I heard the scraping. Something was outside scraping against the stone walls of the church. A tree? It had sounded big, so I had thought it best to check. Despite my lack of shoes, a cloak, or a light, I went outside. As I made my circuit of the building I saw nothing. No tree grew so close as to have its branches move against the walls. My eyes spotted no person or animal that could have done it, but my night vision is poor, and it was very dark.

Yet had there not been the light of the full moon coming through the rose window? I looked up. The clouds were thick. Besides, I knew very well—now that my wits were about me—that there was no full moon tonight.

I went back inside. Yes, both the sanctuary and nave were full of cool, blue-tinted light and it shone through the rose window. As I looked up at the window, I knew I had to check. So, steeling myself against the cold, I returned to the outside.

No light. I hurried around to the north side of the church, the side that held the rose window. No light. I looked up at the window but it looked perfectly normal, or at least as far as I could see in the dark.

Again, I returned to the sanctuary. Yes, it was still filled with light (was it dimmer now?). I looked up at the window, and then down at the lighted church. As I stood there, between the sets of wooden pews in the nave leading up to the altar, the light cast a shadow from the window all around me. To my horror, it was not the rose-shaped shadow it should have been, but that of some great inhuman beast! As I looked down at my feet, I saw that I stood directly in the gaping mouth of the creature's shadow.

I ran. Yelling for Pheslan, I rushed to the back of the church. He came out of his room, his eyes filled with alarm and sleep. Without a word, I grabbed the blank scroll that served as a symbol of Oghma's might from the night stand and led him into the nave.

All was dark.

"Get a light," I commanded with a whisper.

"What is it?"

"Get a light!"

He lit one of the many candles surrounding the altar and brought it forward. It occurs to me now that Pheslan knew the church as well as I did, for he had found the flint in the dark to strike that light. Ah, Pheslan.

In any event, the candle's light illuminated much of the room, albeit dimly. I looked around carefully, first at the floor where the shadow had been, and then up at the window.

"Please, Brother," Pheslan said, "tell me what it is."

"I thought I saw something," I said carefully—still looking around.

He replied without hesitation. "In the window?"

"Yes, I suppose. Actually, it was a shadow from a light in the window."

Pheslan looked at me. His eyes were full of questions. I had the same questions.

"I have no idea, my son." I put my hand on his shoulder and, with one last look around, led him back to our chambers.

I took the candle from him. "Oghma watches over us, Pheslan," I said. "Just because we do not understand, we can know that he does, for no secret is hidden from him. Besides, while the sights of the night are often frightening, the morning light always dispels the fear they bring. Everything will be fine. I should know better, at my age, than to be scared of shadows." He smiled and nodded.

After the boy went into his room, I paused. Still holding the candle I went to the front door and bolted it. I did not stop to look at the rose window.

* * * * *

The next day, just to be on the safe side, I performed every blessing and banishment that I've ever been taught, hoping that divine power might cleanse the rose window and the sanctuary itself. These protective rituals and prayers would surely protect us from any evil that might have been present the night before.

The rest of the afternoon I spent caring for Makkis Hiddle, who had taken ill a few miles down the road. My position as loremaster made me also the most knowledgeable healer in the tiny community. In any event, I did not return until well after dark. Like the previous night, the wind blew from the north and made my trip cold and unpleasant. I unhitched the team and put them in their stalls in the barn behind the east end of the church. They seemed uneasy and stamped and snorted until I calmed them with an apple that I had been saving for myself. As I walked to the front door, I rounded the north side of the building and looked up.

As I watched, a shadow moved across the colored panes of the rose window. It was big—big enough to be a person. My first thought was of Pheslan. Had he climbed up there somehow? I ran into the sanctuary, but all was still. I could see nothing unusual at the window.

The room was lit by a lamp on the altar. Pheslan knew that I would arrive late, and left it for me, as he always did. I knew, too, that I would find some food and wine left waiting for me on the table. I smiled at the thought, and sighed. I was making a fool of myself with all this non-sense. I ate quickly and went to bed.

That night I awoke, startled. The scraping noise was back. It sounded a little like a dog scratching at the door of his master's house, hoping to get in—a big dog. I lit my bedside lamp with a flame from the coals in the brazier that attempted in vain to keep the chill from my room. When I opened my door, I could see that the door to Phes-lan's room was already open. I looked in to find it empty. The boy had obviously risen—perhaps awakened by the noise as well?

Then I heard the scream.

I ran into the sanctuary, the flame of my lamp almost going out as it passed through the cold air. I looked frantically about.

"Pheslan?" I called out. My voice was swallowed by the dark emptiness of the room. How had I grown so afraid of my own sanctuary? "Pheslan, boy—where are you?" No answer came.

My eyes were drawn to the rose window. Dark shapes seemed to move across its surface. Was that light playing against the facets? (How long could I tell myself that?)

I longed for a closer look at the window, but there was no way for me to climb to that height without a ladder, and that would be difficult in the dark. I called out again for Pheslan.

I went outside and checked the barn. The horses and wagon were still there. I checked all around the outside of the building, still calling for my young friend.

"Pheslan!"

By the time I had searched the inside of the church again, the light of dawn was evident, and I blew out my lamp. I knew what I had to do. I returned to the barn and got the ladder. I maneuvered it into the church, despite its weight and size and set it below the rose window. I do not know exactly what I thought I would find up there, but I grabbed a heavy candlestick from the altar and held it tightly in my grip. Taking a deep breath, I began to climb.

When I reached the top, I held on to the top rung of the ladder with one hand, and gripped the candlestick in the other like a weapon. I peered through the window.

I had no idea what I was seeing. I gazed through the rose window and beheld some other place—this was not the churchyard. Instead I saw some infernal realm of shadows and slime-covered things that slithered over a blasted and dreadful landscape. Something flitted across the sky on batlike wings that seemed to leave a trail of greasy residue behind the creature. This window did not look outside. Or rather it did—but not the outside, the Outside. My eyes now saw beyond the veil of our world. My mind was besieged by the knowledge that there were places on the other side of the rose window, and they were terrible. The things in those places, I also knew, wanted to get to the inside—to our world.

Gods! I knew all at once that this window was a thing of evil. No longer (or was it ever?) a fine piece of some glazier's workmanship, no longer bits of blue-green stained glass cleverly pieced together. The rose window was a sorcerous, corrupted thing. It gave me a view no man should ever see. But what else did it give? Was it some kind of portal, or doorway?

I raised the candlestick, my eyes tearing with fear and hatred. I was going to smash the window—shatter it and its evil, to erase the loathsome view that it provided. This would be no defilement or desecration, for the window did not actually belong in a holy place, yet still I stopped. One thought came to me (from where?). If I smashed the window, would I destroy it, or would I let in those things that seethed and writhed in that infernal realm? Would shattering the window prevent them from coming through, or would it grant them passage? A burglar in the night often smashes a window to get in. Smashing it for him only makes his entrance easier.

I had to think—but not at the top of that ladder. There, I could still see into that nightmare realm, and worse, I think the things beyond could see me. I climbed down and slumped on the floor next to the altar.

I was at a loss. What could I do? Was Pheslan gone? Was that his scream I had heard, or something else? Had he somehow disappeared into the window? That seemed so impossible. What would Tessen have done in this situation?

My thoughts were always drawn back to my old mentor in times of crisis. I thought of Tessen, and the old abbey, and—

Oghma preserve us.

* * * * *

I saddled one of the horses—I cannot recall which one anymore. I am not much of a rider, but I thought that I could move faster riding just one than in the wagon. I rode through a good deal of the morning, across the valley to the old abbey.

The men had worked fast. Only some of the foundation stones were left. Everything was gone, including any clue I had hoped to find regarding the nature of the rose window. The wall where it had set for over one hundred years had been torn down. The floor where it had cast its shadows was torn apart and covered with rubble, dirt, and leaves.

I stood in the middle of all this and wept. Tessen had committed a sin against Oghma that could never be forgiven. He had kept a secret, and a terrible secret at that. Had he been a guardian over that window, or its servant? I certainly could remember no hint of the malevolence that the window now displayed.

Finally, I could weep no more and I got back on my horse. Perhaps it was just my training in Oghma's priesthood, but I needed information to confront this challenge. When I had been here last, I had learned of one more place that I could go to find the answers I sought. I beckoned my steed back onto the road, and led it into the village nearby, to where I had heard that Greal lived and had set up his temporary new church.

Once I arrived, nearly exhausted now, I slid to the ground. I knocked on the door. When there was no response, I knocked again, pounding now.

"Master Greal?" I shouted. Still nothing.

"Master Greal, it is Loremaster Jaon." I continued my pounding, stopping only to confirm that the door was locked.

"I must ask you about the rose window I purchased from you!" My pounding fist accompanied each word like a drumbeat in some southern jungle ritual.

"I need to ask you about Loremaster High Tessen!"

Completely expired, I collapsed against the door. "Tell me," I moaned. "Tell me what we were really worshiping in that abbey!"

* * * * *

As I rode back to my parish, I knew that someone had seen me. There had been eyes on me the whole time that I had spent pounding on that door. And as I had sat there, exhausted in the damp soil in front of Greal's home, the autumn leaves blowing around me like dead memories that may very well have been lies, someone watched. No one in that entire town had come when I called out. No one answered their door, but I knew that I was being watched. Even now. . . .

How many of them were there, that had taken part in the foul rites that I could only imagine must have taken place in front of that rose window? Had those rituals gone on even when I had been there? Could I have been so naïve? Could—no, I would not think of it anymore. It was too hard, and too painful, and there were still things that needed doing back in my own church.

* * * * *

Which brings me to right now.

I am writing this the day after I went to the site of the old abbey. I have not yet slept nor eaten. When I came back, I had hoped against hope that Pheslan would be here, and that somehow I would have been wrong. But I was not wrong, and he was not here. I dressed myself in the vestments of my order—white shirt and pants, and the kantlara, a black vest with gold brocade. My kantlara had been made for me by my grandmother, who had also been a loremaster. I prepared my holy symbol and brought out the staff that I kept by the door for emergencies—the staff with its ends shod in iron and made for fighting. I prepared to make my move, and take my stand against the evil that I myself had brought to my parish.

But I waited. What if I was wrong, as I had thought before? What if I let those things through? I somehow told myself that it could not be. An evil thing, like the rose window, must be destroyed. Only good could come from destroying it. Perhaps it could even free Pheslan from whatever held him. If indeed he still lived.

I spent the rest of yesterday at the bottom of the ladder, which I had never moved from its spot below the window. I looked up, but all day long, I saw only the blue-green stained glass. No movement, no shadows, nothing. Somehow, my indecision still prevented me from climbing to even the first rung.

So after so many hours of arguing with myself, pushed farther past exhaustion than I have ever been, I began writing this manuscript on the nightstand in my bedchamber.

On these few sheets of parchment, penned throughout the night, I have put my story. Now, as I finish, I prepare myself to climb that ladder. I will smash the rose window, and destroy every last shard. If I am right, and the evil is over, I will return here to this manuscript and throw these pages into the fire so that none shall ever learn of these horrible events. But if I am wrong, you are reading this now. If that is the case perhaps you—whoever you are—will know what can be done and right my wrongs.

I am ready.

The Club Rules

James Lowder

"I didn't do it," the butler said blandly.

The dozen people lining the entry hall of the Stalwart's Club remained unmoved, dauntingly so. Their hard, silent stares revealed that they had already convicted the servant, if only in their minds. Even so, the emotions displayed on those faces were oddly muted—displeasure rather than anger, annoyance instead of outrage. It was hardly what one would expect from a crowd confronting the man accused of murdering one of their own. The butler, though, was not surprised. The Stalwarts could be a bloodless lot, especially when the matter before them was anything less esoteric than the smithing techniques of long-extinct dwarf clans or the proper table wine to serve with blackened Sword Coast devilfish.

"I don't think they believe you, Uther," said the burly guardsman who had a firm grip on the butler's arm. "I don't neither."

"Either," the accused man corrected. At the guardsman's blank look, Uther explained, " 'Don't neither' is a double negative."

"That sort of talk only proves you're smart enough to

do a crime like this," the guardsman said, tightening his grip. "You already look the part."

The latter comment was as pointless as the supposed restraining hold the soldier had on the servant. A misfired spell had left Uther with a visage that could only be described as demonic. His skin had been blasted to leathery toughness and a sooty crimson hue. Small but noticeable fangs protruded over his dark lips. The pair of twisted horns atop his head were not only impressive, but as sharp as any assassin's blade. His physique was equally daunting. Had he wished it, Uther could have shaken off the guard with the merest shrug and shattered the manacles around his wrists with one flex.

"There's only one thing that'll save you now," the guardsman noted as he led Uther through the door. "A good attorney."

"A clever oxymoron," Uther said, narrowing his slitted yellow eyes. The resulting expression was an odd mixture of humor and anger. "And they say the city watch attracts only dullards."

The small knot of children always loitering before the Stalwarts Club broke into a chorus of taunts when Uther stepped outside. He regularly chased the urchins away, as they were wont to pick the pockets of any clubman drunk enough or foolish enough to give them the opportunity. For their part, the children harassed the butler whenever the chance arose, tying sticks to their heads as mock horns and feigning horror at his grim features. But the conflict had long ago become a game between the ragged children and the servant. So when they saw the manacles on Uther's wrists, they swallowed their quips and gawked in forlorn silence.

One of the boys, a puny but bold child near the back of the knot, hefted a loose piece of paving stone and mentally targeted the soldier's skull, which was unprotected by a helmet or even hair. He cocked his arm back to throw, but a gentle hand stayed the assault. The boy yelped in surprise. Few men were stealthy enough to sneak up on the streetwise group and not alert any of them.

Artus Cimber, however, had once roamed the same hopeless alleys and burrowed for safety in the same abandoned hovels those urchins now called home. His years as a world traveler had honed the survival skills he'd gained there—and tempered them with a bit of wisdom besides.

"That'll only make things worse," Artus said. He took the would-be missile from the boy's fingers and let it drop.

The clatter of stone on stone drew an angry look from the guardsman. "What's going—?" When he saw the man standing among the children, he cut his words short and shook his head. "Cimber. Still hanging about in the gutter, I see. Shouldn't you find some friends your own age?"

"I keep making them, Orsini, but you keep arresting them." As Artus started across the muddy, cobbled way, he asked facetiously, "What's he supposed to have done, let the wrong opera cape get wrinkled in the cloak room?"

"He's done the only crime that matters," was all Orsini said.

The reply made Artus stutter a step. He'd known Sergeant Orsini since his own days on the street. The man had a surprisingly flexible view of the law for a Purple Dragon as the king's most redoubtable soldiers were known. Orsini had let many a thief escape detention, so long as their need was obvious and their crime motivated by survival, not greed. But there was a single offense the soldier took seriously: murder. He pursued men and women accused of that particular crime with a passion that bordered on blind fury. It was almost as if each murder were somehow a personal attack on him.

"I stand accused of slaughtering the inestimable Count Leonska," Uther confirmed.

"It's about time someone got around to that," Artus muttered. Then, more loudly, he asked, "Why do they think you beat the count's other 'admirers' to the deed?"

Uther arched one wickedly pointed brow. "Because I am the butler, and the Stalwarts' library contains one too many Thayan murder mystery. It's happened at last—I am reduced to a cliché. They should all be very proud of themselves."

"You left out the fact that you were the first person on the scene of the murder," Orsini added. His voice was harsh, his whole body tense. "And half the club had previously heard you threaten Count Leonska's life."

The details Uther offered in reply were directed at Artus, not the guardsman. "One of the winged monkeys had escaped from the library," he said. "I was pursuing the creature through the back halls, hoping to recapture it before Lady Elynna's leopard caught its scent. During that endeavor I chanced upon the sounds of a disturbance in one of the rooms. When the door was eventually unlocked, *in front of another witness.*" The butler placed obvious emphasis on this fact, but Sergeant Orsini didn't react in the slightest "The count's body was discovered . . . in a rather unpleasant state."

Uther did not bother to explain his threat on Leonska's life. There was no need. Artus had been in the Stalwarts' game room the day the count, using methods he'd perfected in his years as a mean-spirited drunkard, provoked a very public and frighteningly angry reaction from Uther. It was rare for the servant to rise to any bait dangled before him by a clubman—so rare that the incident remained vivid in the minds of everyone who'd witnessed it.

"Well," Artus said after a moment, "we shouldn't have too much trouble clearing you."

"Am I to conclude from your use of the plural that you will help prove my innocence?"

Orsini tugged on Uther's arm, hoping to move him toward the barred carriage waiting up the alley at the main thoroughfare. The guardsman might as well have tried pulling the Stalwarts Club from its magically secured foundation. "Don't waste your time, Cimber," he said. "The city watch will do its own investigation."

Uther stared briefly and sternly down upon Orsini's bald pate. "That is precisely the reason I need someone with a feathersweight of intelligence to find the true killer." The words were snarled in such a way that the soldier was left to ponder just how deep the butler's demonic facade ran.

"I'll do my best," Artus said. "I hope my lack of standing in the club doesn't cause a problem."

"That you are not a Stalwart is all the more reason for me to desire your aid," the butler replied. He easily shrugged off Orsini's now halfhearted grip and placed his hands on Artus's shoulders. "This will not be an easy defense to build. There are the side effects of my *condition* to consider, as well as the location of the murder."

"Which was?"

"The Treaty Room."

With that, Uther started down the narrow alley. Orsini had to hurry to keep pace with him, taking three steps for each of the butler's two long strides. Artus watched them go, though only vaguely. His mind was already focused on the complexities of the task before him.

The misfired spell that had warped Uther's form left him immune to any and all further magic, including those incantations the city watch used as a truth test against a suspect's claims. Magic would wrest no clues from the crime scene, either. The Treaty Room had been rendered "magic dead" just days after Uther's misfortune, and by the same world-rattling events that had caused the innocent spell to misfire and transform him. The instability in magic caused by the crisis known as the Time of Troubles had left the Treaty Room a magical void, a place where no spell could be cast and enchanted items simply failed to function.

Artus was still considering ways in which he might get around those obstacles when he entered the Stalwarts Club.

A few members milled in the entry hall, but most had gone back to whatever had drawn them to the club that day. A mournful fellow from Armot named Grig the Younger debated the finer points of Mulhorandi entrapment spells with a pair of dwarf women, twins who had both been named Isilglowe for some reason that eluded even them. Sir Hamnet Hawklin expounded upon the hunting rituals of the Batiri goblins of Chult to Gareth Truesilver, newly commissioned as a captain for his heroics during the crusade against the Tuigan horde. In a nearby corner, an elf maid named Cyndrik tallied the money she'd gathered for the Lord Onovan Protection Fund, even though that hapless Dalesman had been quite fatally bitten in half by a gigantic lizard several months earlier.

They wrangled over topics and championed causes for which few outside the club spared even a moment's thought. It was that collective energy that drew Artus to the Stalwarts. The intellect and effort focused upon obscure matters by those famous explorers, those noted seekers of adventure, quickened his mind and reinforced his commitment to his own consuming quest—the search for the legendary Ring of Winter, the existence of which had been written off as utter fantasy decades past. At the moment, the passion for the esoteric that Uther found so chilling about his employers was, in fact, bolstering his ally's resolve to prove him innocent.

Artus threaded his way between the people in the entryway, but found himself facing a loud and impassable obstruction just a few steps down the corridor. A beautiful mountaineer named Guigenor, her temper stoked to the intensity of her long red hair, confronted one of the most influential of the Stalwarts' inner circle. Her wild gesticulations kept Artus from trying to slip past; the ceaseless, seamless character of her tirade yielded no opportunity for him to politely ask her to let him by.

"Are you feeble?" she snapped. "Are you blind? Uther had the motive and the opportunity for murder. He was standing at the Treaty Room door, alone, when I came across him. You could still hear Leonska moving around in there—drunk, but very much alive."

Without slowing for the space of a single syllable, Guigenor repeatedly battered the oak paneling with her fist. It wasn't a very good simulation of the noises she'd heard from the Treaty Room, but she was aiming for impact, not accuracy. As such, the dramatics proved a success; there were suddenly people lined up four deep on both sides of the blockage, listening to her prosecution.

"But does Uther use his strength to break down the door?" Guigenor continued. "No! He sent me for *keys,* for Torm's sake! What's Uther doing without his keys? It's obvious—he had them all along. He sent me off, used his set to unlock the door, slipped into the room, and slaughtered Leonska. Then he sauntered back out, relocked the door, and waited for me to return with the spares. Any dolt—except you, perhaps—would see that there's no other explanation!"

There was a moment of stunned silence at the tirade's end. The placid-seeming older man at whom this verbal barrage had been aimed simply shook his head. "You are overwrought at the death of your mentor, my dear," said Marrok de Landoine. "Otherwise you would not address me in such an impudent manner."

Guigenor sputtered for a moment, struggling to put together a reply. Her anger at the casual dismissal, at the murder of her friend, boiled over into tears. She roughly shoved Artus out of her way and bulled through the crowded hallway much as she had many a snowbound mountain pass.

The look on Marrok's face appeared full of fatherly concern for the young woman, but Artus had seen that smirking, fatuous expression before. Marrok reserved that empty smile for those he found distasteful, below his notice as a person of wealth and influence. Marrok was a man of remarkable resources, position, and accomplishment, even in a group as thick with decorated military heroes and titled aristocrats as the Society of Stalwart Adventurers. And, to him, Guigenor was quite unalterably an upstart.

The smile didn't alter when Marrok first noticed Artus standing there. Then it abruptly faded, transformed into a look of utter weariness. "Mystra save me from the rabble," the nobleman muttered. Artus opened his mouth to reply, but Marrok turned his back on the young man and walked away.

Grumbling through clenched teeth, Artus made his way back to the Treaty Room. He followed a route he would have found difficult to map, despite his years of practice in the field, for the Stalwarts Club was labyrinthine in design and cut loose from architectural logic by the amount of magic utilized in its construction. In some places angles did not operate as angles should. In others, straight lines were not necessarily the shortest distance between two points.

All that strangeness made the Treaty Room a haven to those few Stalwarts unimpressed by mages and spellcraft. Hidden in one of the most isolated sections of the club, the room could be generously described as four walls and a single stout door. It lacked secret passages, magical gateways, even windows. Its floor and ceiling were identical to their counterparts in most mundane homes—more carefully constructed and, at most other times, quite a lot cleaner—but essentially commonplace. The two things that most obviously set the Treaty Room apart from those average places now were the amount of blood splashed on the walls and the poorly dressed and rather overweight corpse laying atop the conference table at the room's exact center.

"Well, let's take the gorgon by the horns," said Sir Hydel Pontifax—mage, surgeon, sometime War Wizard, and full-time Stalwart. He gestured to the Purple Dragon stationed by the door, who was doing quite a good job of refusing Artus admittance. "Be a good soldier and let my scribe in. I rather need his help if I'm to complete the medical examination your sergeant requested."

Artus tore a few pages from the journal he always carried tucked into his wide leather belt; the wyvern-bound book was magical, so it wouldn't even open in the magic-dead room. Then he ducked under the guard's out-stretched arm and hurried to the table. "Thanks, Pontifax. I was hoping you'd be here."

The paunchy mage leaned over the body. "And I was rather expecting you to show up. Just the sort of messy business you can't keep your fingers clean of. They're blaming Uther, you know."

"I told him I'd help clear his name."

Pontifax glanced up. "Good for you! That puts a noble cause behind your meddling."

Artus took the statement for what it was—gentle ribbing by his most trusted friend. He didn't reply, didn't feel the usual need to fire back a cutting response. In comfortable silence, the two set about their work. Pontifax examined the corpse and occasionally murmured observations to be recorded. Artus made a very rough sketch of the body and took down notes.

"What do you make of the dagger?" Pontifax asked after they'd completed their initial examination.

Count Leonska might have died from any of the dozens of deep slashes on his body, face, and hands, but the most obvious and violent wound was caused by the knife protruding from his chest. The blade was hidden in flesh, but the golden handle burned with reflected light from the room's many candles.

"The markings are Zhentish," Artus said. "A ritual dagger of some kind?"

Pontifax muttered a vague reply. His white, cloudlike brows had drifted together over his blue eyes. The effect was something like a gathering storm. "The body should be more of a mess," he said.

Blood lightly spattered the count's hands and clothes, but most of his wounds were clean. The sole exception was his crimson-smeared mouth. Artus used the dry end of his writing stylus to pull back a swollen lip. Leonska's teeth were missing. They'd been shattered, many broken right down to the gums.

"What's this?" Artus murmured. As he leaned close, he felt a shiver of apprehension snake up his spine. It was as if the count's dead eyes were watching him. Hands trembling just a little, he picked a small, dark shred of material from between two broken teeth. "It's leather, I think. Part of a gag?"

"That would explain why Leonska didn't cry out when he was being attacked," Pontifax replied. The mage nervously paced around the room, his stubby fingers steepled. "Uther heard a ruckus, but no shouts for help. That's why he didn't break the door in."

"Guigenor thinks the count was stumbling around in here, drunk, before she ran off to get the keys. She was screeching at Marrok about her suspicions when I came in."

"That young woman is one to talk about suspicions," said Pontifax. "When the watch asked her why she happened to be roaming around back here, she said Leonska had left her a note requesting her presence in the Treaty Room. But she can't find the note now.

"As for her claim that the count was alive when she heard the noises—nonsense. This murder took a long time to commit. They heard the end of the struggle, not its beginning."

"Do you think Guigenor had a hand in this?" Artus asked, gesturing to a wall of framed treaties and trade agreements, all of which had been signed in the room. Blood had splashed across each and every one. "What kind of weapon would she have used?"

"I've heard of assassinations . . . the work of men from far eastern Kozakura who call themselves 'ninjas.' They sometimes leave behind some strange gore slinging like this," Pontifax said. "It almost looks like Leonska was stabbed and slashed, then spun quickly so the blood would cake the walls."

Neither man commented that it would take someone incredibly strong to heft the count's bulk. The thought had occurred to both—as did the notion that Uther was probably the only person in the club who could do so without the aid of sorcery.

Pontifax returned to the table and stared at the open door. "How did the blackguard get out of the room after doing this to Leonska, I wonder. Uther said the noises continued in here until just before Guigenor returned with the keys. The door remained tightly closed and locked until he opened it."

"You don't suppose the murderer is still hiding in the room."

"Already been searched three times. We've checked for sliding panels and any of that rot. Nothing. And no magic could possibly work in here."

Artus prodded a pile of threadbare clothes he'd found in one corner. The moth-eaten cloak, thick gloves, and long, dirt-smeared scarf had been folded and stacked neatly. Atop the pile rested a wide-brimmed hat dyed the black of ravens' feathers. "All these belonged to Leonska?"

Pontifax nodded. "He was seen bundled up in those rags when he entered the club this morning. It was his usual attire."

"You wouldn't think someone with such shabby clothes would bother folding them so neatly." Artus held up the corner of the rather grotesquely patterned scarf and said, "Poor fashion sense for a count."

"He had poorer social skills," Pontifax said. "As he did most mornings, Leonska made his way back here with a full wineskin and the single-minded purpose of drinking himself to the brink of unconsciousness." He idly flicked one hand toward the body. "Only today he didn't get a chance to stagger out and pick fights, like he normally did. Not a good soldier in the least—"

"For once you and I are in full agreement, Sir Hydel. No army would have ever taken Leonska on campaign, not even to haul baggage."

Artus and Pontifax turned to the door to find Marrok de Landoine standing there, surveying them with practiced disinterest. "I thought I'd find you here, Cimber. If you are done assisting Sir Hydel with his examination, I'd like a word with you."

The nobleman didn't wait for a reply. He hooked Artus's arm with his own and led him out of the Treaty Room, down the narrow hall. Stalwarts deferentially flattened against the paneling or ducked into doorways to let them by.

"I have my pass," Artus said. He reached up to his breast pocket for the thin leather card that allowed him access to certain areas of the club—the library, game room, and main bar—even though he was not a full member. The gesture was automatic; the pass was the only topic about which the nobleman had ever addressed Artus directly.

"I'm certain you do," Marrok said. "You consider Uther a friend, do you not?"

"Of course."

"He is in a considerable spot of trouble."

"I know. I ran into him outside the club," Artus noted. "He asked me—"

"Despite what some of the other members think," said Marrok, unaware or unconcerned that he was interrupting Artus, said "*I* believe him innocent."

"I agree. Uther asked—"

"Earlier you caught me in a very bad temper. We've had our differences in the past, too . . ."

Artus suppressed a smirk. Marrok had single-handedly blocked his entrance into the society three times in as many years. In the nobleman's eyes, no accomplishment as a scholar, explorer, or historian could compensate for Artus's low birth.

"Yet I have always recognized you as . . . clever." The pause made it obvious that Marrok had to cast his net far for the right word. The phrase that followed made it clear just how far. "In your own way."

The slight was unintentional, though even more annoying for its thoughtlessness. Artus slipped from the nobleman's falsely familiar grasp under the pretext of tightening a boot lace. After that they walked in silence for a time, moving toward the fabulous library at the club's heart.

Finally, Marrok spoke again. It seemed to Artus that the nobleman's superior glow dimmed just a little as he did. "Politics deserve more of your attention," he began obliquely, then checked himself. "No, let me be direct. Some of the more senior members—Hamnet Hawklin foremost among them—have declared Uther guilty. I respect them, yet I also feel they are incorrect in their conclusion. It would be unwise of me to challenge them in any open fashion, but I must also—"

"So long as you're being direct," Artus prompted, "how about skipping to the verse of this song that involves me."

"I wish you to find the killer."

Artus began, for the third time, to tell Marrok he'd already promised Uther to do just that, but decided to see what the nobleman had to say. "I suppose I could try," he offered.

Masking his feelings had never been one of Artus's strong suits. The attempt now only caused Marrok to mistake the explorer's hastily erected facade of guilelessness for actual reluctance.

"You'd do well to play along here, Cimber," the nobleman said. "At least hear me out. You have no idea how disinclined I am to ask for your help."

"Oh, I think I know. But why me?"

"Use a criminal to catch a criminal," Marrok said, and this time the insult was carefully chosen. "Don't think for an instant the club doesn't know that your father was a highwayman. You lost your position as a court scribe when you got caught breaking him out of jail. We could also discuss that murder charge outstanding against you in Tantras. There's no need for me to go on, is there?"

Anger edged Marrok's words, made them sharp as blades, but he kept his voice tactfully low. They'd reached the library's antechamber, where a small group of men and women were discussing a recent polar expedition the society had sponsored. Generally, Artus could have strolled through the club with a large spear protruding from his side and not attracted any attention at all. The moment Marrok de Landoine entered a room, he somehow became its focus.

"Here's the fellow to ask now," one of the loiterers announced. "Say, Marrok old man, when will that yeti Philyra bagged on the expedition be ready for display?"

Preparing exotic beasts for display seemed to be the one practical skill Marrok de Landoine possessed. He was loathe to discuss the craft. A fact his peers always capitalized upon in the club's near constant public banter. Marrok had never intended to reveal his odd talent to his fellows. But the supposed artists to whom the Stalwarts had entrusted their unusual, often irreplaceable trophies did such a poor job that the nobleman was forced to step forward and save the membership and the library, where such valuable objects were displayed, from further insult.

"Eh?" Marrok said distractedly. "Oh, the yeti . . . any day now."

The nobleman turned back to Artus, his own expression not all that far removed from the fearsome hunting snarl of the fabled snow beasts. "Uther is more valuable to the society than you are a detriment," Marrok growled. "Find the murderer and I'll . . . support you for full membership."

As he turned to go, Marrok worked his mouth soundlessly, as if trying to exorcise the foul taste of the offer he'd just made. The nobleman passed Pontifax on his way out of the antechamber; the mage had obviously followed them from the Treaty Room at a discreet distance. The two exchanged civil, if frigid greetings.

"Marrok canceled the pass I gave you, didn't he?" Pontifax said without preamble. "I'm sorry, my boy. He's been in a foul mood ever since his favorite hound died. Kezef, I think he called it, though why anyone would name a pet after a monster like that—"

Artus shook his head, still a bit stunned by Marrok's offer. "He's going to support me for membership. If I clear Uther's name, I'll be a Stalwart."

"It's about time," Pontifax said. "Assuming we find the killer, of course."

Artus patted the mage on the back. "We will. Look, you follow up on the leads here—the note Guigenor supposedly lost, the dagger, that sort of thing. I'm going to get some communications help."

"Communications help?" Pontifax repeated, confusion clear on his face. "Who do you need to communicate with that you can't just chat up all on your own?"

A triumphant gleam flashed in Artus's brown eyes. "Count Leonska."

* * * * *

The soul you seek is not recorded in my rolls, said the weird, disembodied head floating above the low altar. The words buzzed in Artus's mind, swarmed around his thoughts like flies. The sensation was no more peculiar than the specter's features—or lack thereof. Its smooth gray face was broken only by two bulging yellow eyes.

"How can that be, O Scribe of the Dead?" intoned the priest kneeling opposite Artus.

I do not know the reason for it, only the truth of what I tell you.

"But all dead men are your charges. Can you not tell us where the soul of Count Leonska resides?"

There was a pause. Then the two fat tallow candles on the altar began to smoke. The black, oily coils snaked upward, but rose no higher than the specter's chin. *If you insist on badgering me, minion of the Scribbler God,* said the Scribe of the Dead menacingly, *then I will give my reply in the flesh.* The smoke coalesced into a flowing cloak. The phantasmal head began to take on substance.

The priest toppled a candle with a casual stroke of one

brown hand. The conjured power lingered for a moment above the altar, black cloak billowing, then slowly faded. Its bulbous yellow eyes disappeared last. Their awful gaze seemed to pierce the small prayer room long after they, too, had vanished.

"And what have we learned from this, Master Cimber?" The priest unrolled his long white sleeves, which had been bunched above his elbows. "Not to bother the seneschal of Hell, I hope."

Artus uncrossed his legs and lay back on the prayer mat. His hopes of solving the murder quickly had not survived a few hours past leaving the Stalwarts Club. Now, days later, he had begun to wonder if he was in over his head. The ritual to summon Jergal had taken two full days in itself. Before the tenday was out, he might have to start plotting a jailbreak.

"Well, we know that Leonska isn't alive," Artus sighed. "Pontifax checked to be certain. So why hasn't his soul gone to the Realm of the Dead?"

"Perhaps a mage is concealing it," the priest noted. "Or Jergal was lying to us. I have not the power or authority to compel one such as him to tell the truth."

"There's a first," Artus said with a chuckle. "Zintermi of Oghma admits to a weakness."

"All creatures possess weaknesses," the priest replied as he dutifully collected the components for the conjuring rite. As with everything, Zintermi did this simple task methodically and gracefully. "You, for instance, lack the ability to admit defeat."

"This is a very important matter," Artus snapped.

"Any matter you take up becomes 'very important,'" Zintermi said in the same pedantic tone Artus had found so infuriating as a student in the temple school. "Have you considered the possibility that Uther is guilty?"

"I told you, Guigenor is the murderer. No one's seen her in days. She's obviously gone into hiding. And Pontifax and I have gathered enough evidence to convince me she did it."

"But not enough to convince the authorities," Zintermi reminded him. "You say that Guigenor was recently seen conversing with members of the consulate of Kozakura, but that is not proof she studied with, or hired, any of their assassins. You have uncovered rumors of a failed romance between the young lady and the count, but these rumors cannot be confirmed and do not necessarily offer motive."

Artus sat up. "Those suspicions should be enough to redirect the investigation, but Hamnet Hawklin and his allies are pressuring the watch to formally charge Uther and convene a trial. Without some sort of hard evidence against Guigenor—like finding the leather gag or the count's missing wineskin in her possession, or having Leonska's spirit identify her as the murderer—they're going to do just that."

"Perhaps you are searching for evidence that doesn't exist."

"Look," Artus said irritably, "Guigenor is hiding something. She claims to be from the Dales. She's not. Pontifax discovered she's a native of Zhentil Keep, which would explain why the writing on the dagger was Zhentish." He tapped his chest; beneath his tunic the skin was crisscrossed there with scars—the handiwork of Zhentish torturers. "And if she's connected to the Keep, she's trouble."

Zintermi finally snuffed the remaining ritual candle. The oil lamps on either side of the door kept the room from sinking into total darkness, but shadows ventured out from the corners and slipped across the priest's face. "There are things in your past you do not claim with pride," he said. "Can your suspect not be afforded the same luxury? At the very least, Master Cimber, you should be more meticulous, more evenhanded. Might I suggest you delve into Uther's history with the same eye toward inconsistency?"

"What's that supposed to mean?"

"You have often repeated Uther's quips about lawyers.

He is quite critical of anyone who pursues that profession, no? You might be surprised to learn that he was a barrister himself. In fact Uther can claim distant membership in the FitzKevrald clan, which has practiced at the bar in Waterdeep for centuries."

The content of that revelation could not have been described as ominous, but Artus found himself unsettled by it anyway. Zintermi had a way of undermining Artus's most carefully constructed theories, though he didn't seem to gain any undue sense of triumph in doing so. That was his strength as a teacher. But the reason the explorer sought his advice so often was his practice of suggesting a better, more solid foundation to replace any he shattered.

The wise words Zintermi offered that evening were predictably simple: "Gather facts before you attempt to prove a theory. Observe, then conclude."

Artus had the opportunity to put that advice into practice shortly after departing the temple. Doing so probably saved his life.

For each of the three nights since the murder, Artus had made his way to Marrok de Landoine's estate. The nobleman had instructed the young explorer—there was no hint of a request about it—to provide a regular update on his search for the killer. So after leaving Zintermi, Artus once again trekked to Suzail's most distant outskirts. There, the sprawling grounds of Marrok's ancestral home presented themselves as a last bastion of carefully gardened topiary and well-scrubbed servants before a traveler would find himself surrounded by rough rolling hills and the even rougher farmers, ranchers, and hunters who tore a living from them.

As expected, Artus found the main gate unlocked. He trudged wearily up the long gravel carriageway, the crunch of his bootfalls sending alarmed rabbits scurrying for cover. Wan moonlight cast a pall over everything. Artus assumed the ghostly look of the fruit trees, the harsh hedgerows, and the nearly dark mansion to be the product of his overtaxed and under-rested imagination. The truth of it was, even the city's most drearily practical clerk would have found the grounds strange and unsettling that night.

A dark shape stumbled from behind a tree, then disappeared into the entrance of a hedge maze. Artus saw the figure for only a moment, but it was clearly female. A poacher, he concluded. They were common enough on estates like Marrok's, where the meticulously mown lawns rendered small game easier targets. This one was clearly drunk, though, far more likely to snare herself than any dinner. Artus felt a pang of sympathy for the poor woman, who very likely had children to feed in some hillside hovel.

That sympathetic inclination was quickly tempered by Zintermi's advice, which had been lingering at the periphery of Artus's thoughts all evening. At first Artus cursed the priest for making him suspicious of a drunken unfortunate. Nevertheless, he found himself observing his surroundings with a more critical eye. Had he not done so, he might have missed a telltale rustling in the hedges right before the attack.

Artus had a foot on the lowest of the steps leading up to the house's pillared entry when she burst through the bushes like an enraged animal. She seemed oblivious to the scratches gouged into her bare arms by the branches. With both hands she clutched a large ritual knife. She drew the blade up over her head as she charged.

As he spun around to face her, Artus noticed all of these things dimly, just as he realized in a detached way that the woman was no professional assassin. The black hood concealing her face might be a favored guise of the ninja, but she was most certainly not one of their highly trained murderers. Her attack was clumsy, her movements graceless and stiff.

Artus easily ducked the blade swipe, then planted a kick in her midsection. He expected to hear her gasp, possibly even see her topple as the air exploded from her lungs. Instead she barely staggered a step before raising her blade again.

Artus drew his own dagger from the sheath in his boot. A gem in the hilt cast pale magical light in a circle just large enough to encompass both combatants. He side-stepped the woman's second clumsy charge. As she moved past, he brought the rounded end of his knife's handle down atop her skull. The blow didn't faze her at all.

It did, however, loosen a coil of hair hidden beneath the hood. The escaped tresses snaked down to her shoulders. For a moment Artus mistook the flame-bright red hair for blood, so striking was its hue. Then a look of recognition flashed across his face.

"Guigenor!" Artus exclaimed.

The shouted name accomplished what no blow could: the woman stopped her attack. With one hand Guigenor drew off the mask that hid her pale, expressionless features. The fingers of the other hand opened slowly and the knife dropped to the gravel. With its golden handle, engraved with Zhentish markings, the weapon was a twin to the one he'd seen embedded in Count Leonska's chest.

Finally the mansion's main entry flew open. A small mob of servants flooded out with cries of "What's going on there?" and "Be warned, we're armed!" Artus turned his head for just a moment as they clattered down the steps. It was time enough for Guigenor to flee back into the bushes.

Artus might have caught her, but one of Marrok's men tackled him from behind. Before he could even cry out, two others had descended upon him, pinning his arms to the ground, kneeling heavily upon his back. "It's her you want," Artus wheezed into the gravel. "She's a murderer."

"I think we've enough proof of that now," sighed Marrok de Landoine from the top step. "Well, let him up, you buffoons."

Artus accepted a helping hand from a liveried servant.

"Someone should alert the watch," he said to Marrok.

"Already done," the nobleman replied. "I will, of course, sack the dolts who assaulted you."

With an annoyed wave of his hand, Artus dismissed the offer. "Never mind that. We should be worrying about finding Guigenor before she hurts anyone else. She's obviously unbalanced."

"No fear," Marrok sniffed. "My men will track her down. In the meantime, why don't you come in. The watch will want to take your statement when they arrive."

On his previous visits, Artus had been received in the foyer. And while that grand entryway had been constructed to impress—it was as large as the two rooms Artus rented over Razor John's fletcher shop—giving his reports there left him feeling distinctly like a delivery man come to the wrong side of the house. Now Marrok led him down a long, carpeted hall, past ancestral portraits and brightly polished suits of armor, to a large book-lined study. It was all exactly as Artus would have guessed, a page out of the style handbook for old Cormyrean money.

"We should thank Tymora you escaped harm," Marrok noted from behind the generously stocked bar. He sounded a bit disappointed in saying so. "Care for a brandy?"

Artus declined politely. He started to sit on a beautifully upholstered couch, then remembered his roll on the ground and stood up. He might brush himself off, but that would only draw attention to the fact that he had walked through the nobleman's house trailing gravel and dirt. He suddenly wished himself back in the foyer. At least he knew how to act like a delivery man.

A footman arrived and spared Artus the embarrassment of trading small talk with Marrok. "Pardon me, m'lord," he said after rapping lightly on the open door. "They've found the woman."

"Do you have her securely bound?" Marrok asked, displaying no more real interest in the subject than he might have given his neighbor's dinner menu. "Where was she hiding?"

"No need to bind her, m'lord," the footman replied. "We found her . . ." he paused dramatically ". . . floating in the reflecting pool. Dead. The knife wound from Master Cimber must have killed her."

"I never used the blade on her," Artus said.

"Then it must have been a wound inflicted by one of the men in bringing her to ground," Marrok offered hastily. "Excuse me for just a moment, Cimber. I'd best be certain they do not move the body until the watch arrives."

Marrok put down his brandy snifter and crossed to the door, where he murmured a long string of commands to the cringing footman. Artus wandered across the room to the bookcases. As he might have suspected, he found little of substance, and the few scrolls or folios that were worth their ink seemed untouched, likely unread.

A low whine drew his attention to a door on his left. He paused to listen. When the sound came again, he recognized it for a dog's plaintive cry. Artus tried the knob and found it unlocked. The door swung open on well-oiled hinges.

All manner of strange creatures and even stranger apparatus filled the room beyond. Coiling tubes carried liquids of various colors to and from animal carcasses laid out on metal tables. Jars filled with hearts and brains and other organs crammed shelf after shelf. Mounted heads of assorted sizes, shapes, and species covered one entire wall, while another displayed neatly sorted saws, blades, and other tools gleaming silver in the candlelight. And in the center of it all stood a yeti, its coat the virgin white of freshly fallen polar snow, its thickly muscled arms raised over its head in perpetual menace. Marrok had preserved the trophy so perfectly that it seemed trapped between life and death.

Something leathery pressed into his palm, and Artus

jumped back a step or two. A pathetic-looking hound had nuzzled his hand with its nose. With yellow, glassy eyes, the dog stared up at the explorer. It whined once more. The cry sounded hollow, as if it came from a very long way off.

"Kezef, back!"

Marrok was suddenly beside Artus. He lifted the hound, which didn't struggle in the least, and returned it to the other side of the threshold. As he closed the door on the whimpering animal, the nobleman said, "He's getting on in years. Not much use as a watchdog, as you've witnessed." The door clicked shut. "Sentimental of me, but I couldn't bear to part with him."

Artus knew that it was the most truthful thing Marrok de Landoine had ever said to him.

The nobleman proceeded to speculate in his usual disinterested fashion on how quickly Uther might be freed from prison now that they had proven Guigenor the murderer beyond any reasonable doubt. To Marrok's way of thinking, Artus had stumbled too close to the truth, making it necessary for the woman to try to silence him. "Of course I will honor my promise," Marrok concluded, refilling his snifter for the third time. "We can hold the ceremony granting you full membership in the club tomorrow."

When Artus didn't reply, Marrok's expression turned serious.

"Is something troubling you, Cimber?"

"No, nothing," Artus replied much too quickly. Then he forced a smile. "It's always so obvious when something's bothering me, why deny it? I know it's customary for a new member to offer a gift to the society. I was worrying about what I might put together by tomorrow."

"Uther's freedom will be enough of a gift," Marrok replied. "And the soul of Count Leonska can rest easier, now that you've identified his killer."

"Of course," Artus said. "How can I come up with a

better gift than justice?" He finally sat down on the ridiculously expensive couch. "You know, I think I'm ready for that drink now."

* * * * *

The Ceremony Hall presented a welcome contrast to the rest of the Stalwarts Club. It was stark and dignified. Actual candles lit its modest confines. Craftsmen, not djinn or golems, had woven the tapestries decorating the walls. The robes worn by the clubmen there had not been liberated from some sultan's wardrobe or pilfered from the depths of Hades. They were simple garments honestly made, unadorned by jewels or excess of history. In the Ceremony Hall, that was enough.

The initiation ceremony, too, proved remarkably restrained. It was over almost before Artus realized it had begun. He had expected more ritual, more pomp. He would have felt cheated, had he not been so preoccupied with the presentation of his gift.

Until the ceremony was through, Uther kept the curious from peeking beneath the sheet draped over the long box containing Artus's offering. Once Artus was alone on the simple wooden dais at the head of the hall, ready to make his presentation, Hydel Pontifax and three other Stalwarts moved the still-concealed crate to the room's center. Uther gave a subtle tilt of his magnificent horns and took up his station by the door. The clubmen were too caught up in speculation about the gift's content to notice Sergeant Orsini of the city watch loitering impatiently on the other side of that same threshold.

"In return for the honor you've bestowed upon me," Artus began, in the words he'd been instructed to use, "I offer this noble society a gift of lasting value, a token by which you may forever gauge my worth as a member and my regard for you all."

No sooner had the final word been spoken than something rose up slowly from the box. The white sheet clung to it for a moment, cloaking a figure that was clearly human.

"I offer you justice," Artus said. "I offer you the murderer of Count Leonska."

The sheet slipped away to reveal Guigenor standing within the pine crate. Startled gasps and cries of outrage echoed through the hall. "Necromancy!" bellowed Sir Hamnet Hawklin. "This is how you demonstrate your worth to us, you—you—*weasel.*" There was no more damning word in Hawklin's vocabulary.

"Guigenor did not kill the count!" Artus shouted over the throng. "She was a victim to the same assassin, for the same reason!"

The dead woman stepped from the box. Her unblinking eyes scanned the crowd, searching for her murderer. When she found him, she stiffly raised one arm and pointed him out.

Marrok de Landoine did not attempt to escape. Neither did he utter a single word of protest. He simply stripped off his robe, revealing a finely tailored doublet, expensive custom-made breeches, and dragon-leather boots. As Sergeant Orsini approached, he presented his dagger, handle first, to the nearest Stalwart. "Please see that this is returned to the armory on my estate," he droned.

"Evidence," was all Orsini said as he snatched up the dagger and slipped it into his belt. With vindictive glee, the Purple Dragon ordered an immediate and humiliating search of Marrok's person for hidden weapons or, more dangerous still, any bits of arcane matter he might use for a spell.

A crowd of clubmen had surrounded Artus, demanding the true story behind the murders. He explained it all as best he could.

"Count Leonska sealed his doom when he used his influence, and a significant part of the club's liquor reserve, to gain his protégé entrance into the Stalwarts," Artus began. "Marrok had been away on business at the time, unable to block Guigenor's ascendance to the rank of full member. Upon his return, he set about to ensure the count would foist no more upstarts upon the membership."

How Marrok had murdered Leonska remained a mystery to Artus, though no one had to stretch his imagination too far to picture the count drunkenly stumbling onto a blade or downing a snifter of poison. What happened next the explorer could explain with more certainty.

"Marrok raised the count from the dead and put him to the task of incriminating Guigenor," Artus continued. "The count was sent back to the club, his wineskin filled with his own blood. He made his way to the Treaty Room, already dead, and set about laying clues—stabbing himself with the Zhentish dagger, splashing gore on the walls in the fashion of a Kozakuran assassination. . . . Marrok had already made certain those things tied the crime to Guigenor. He'd even arranged for her to meet her 'victim' at the crime scene."

"There really was a note," Pontifax said with a nod.

"And Guigenor really did manage to lose it," Artus offered. "It'll turn up somewhere in the club one of these days."

"So what happened to the wineskin?" someone asked from the crowd.

Artus shuddered. "Marrok must have ordered Leonska to get rid of that bit of evidence—so he ate it. His teeth were all shattered from trying to chew up the stopper before swallowing it."

Pontifax cleared his throat sententiously. "It was a fiendishly clever plan," he announced. "You see, the undead are not magical, *per se,* so the Treaty Room had no effect upon the poor creature's actions. There was also the added benefit of having Leonska's soul trapped in his corpse, which meant the watch could not raise it for questioning."

Artus stepped down from the dais. "Marrok really only needed me to uncover all the evidence he'd laid out. He killed Guigenor, too, and had her attack me to sew up the case—and maybe just murder me in the process." He plucked at his ceremonial robe. "Oghma knows he didn't really want to let me join his club. I probably would have turned up dead eventually if I hadn't figured this out."

Pontifax continued to expound upon the minutiae of their investigation, anchoring the crowd in place as Artus drifted away. He passed the small group of priests who had already begun the task of freeing Guigenor's soul from her animate corpse. Artus only wished the priests had been able to do the same for Count Leonska, whose body had been burned the previous night. The man had surely been conscious of his fate to the end, staring at the flames of his pyre with the same lifeless expression with which he'd regarded Artus that day in the Treaty Room.

"There's a dog on Marrok's estate you'll want to have exorcised, too," Artus called to Sergeant Orsini. The soldier was finally leading Marrok away. "The thing's called Kezef. You'll find it in the workshop off the study."

"You'll do no such thing," Marrok snapped. He swept the Dragons with an imperious stare. "That hound will be waiting for me when I return home in a day or two, or I'll see the lot of you scrubbing gull droppings from the king's yacht."

The stunned expression on Artus's face drew a sneer from Marrok de Landoine. "I have influence rabble like you can never counter. Even if the charges are true—note, please, that I said 'if'—I'll certainly never hang for them. Just look around if you doubt me."

Artus did just that as Sergeant Orsini hustled Marrok from the room.

For each person who looked upon the newest Stalwart with admiration and approval, there was another who glowered at him. More telling still, the most senior and influential members were the ones who offered Artus their undisguised animosity. A disdain for upstarts had not been a trait of Marrok's alone.

"You appear glum when you should be celebrating, Master Cimber," Uther said.

Artus shrugged. "I'm not all that certain I want to belong to this club anymore."

"Nonsense." The butler regarded the frowning, sulking Stalwarts with his slitted yellow eyes, then turned back to Artus. "They may not welcome you with open arms, but they will most assuredly offer you respect. You've brought down one of their own—whether he swings for his crimes or no."

"They hate me for it."

"Perhaps," Uther said. "But they fear you for it, too. Fear is a useful thing when dealing with powerful men and women. To be honest, it's the reason I am just a bit pleased they think me capable of murder."

"And you're not?" Artus asked. He hesitated before he spoke again, but when he did, he said something to Uther few would have dared. "I thought lawyers—especially FitzKevrald clan barristers—were capable of anything."

The look that comment engendered on Uther's horrible features was truly unsettling. A smile spread across his black lips. Then quietly, deeply, the butler began to laugh.

Thieves' Justice

Mary H. Herbert

Spring was coming to Rashemen—eventually. That
night, early in the month of Ches, spring's presence had
not yet been detected in the frost-bound capital city of
Immilmar. The snow in the streets and on the buildings
had been there for months, layer after layer of hard-
packed ice, dirt, soot, and frozen debris. The air was still
bitterly cold, and icicles hung like prison bars from the
eaves of many buildings.

Teza wiped her face and hurriedly pulled her wolf-fur
collar up closer to her nose and mouth. Muttering to herself, she left the Guardian Witch Inn behind and marched
up the street, paying no attention to her direction or the
people around her. The streets were quiet, for most people
had already sought the warmth and light of well-lit
hearths. The many inns were doing a rollicking business,
but most of the shop fronts and the city markets were
closed.

The young woman gritted her teeth and stamped into
the gathering darkness. Mask take that wizardess, she
fumed. It was not fair that the one person in all the East
that she considered her best friend had to be so stubbornly
honest. Why couldn't Kanlara look past Teza's profession
to what lay within the horse thief's heart and mind?

Resentment flared anew in Teza's thoughts. What right did Kanlara have to tell her what she should not do? Who made her the guardian of Teza's integrity? Kanlara's rigidity and her lack of faith in her friend had pricked the horse thief's hide one time too many.

Teza frowned at the night sky. Last autumn, tolerance had been easy for both of them. At the risk of her own life, Teza had freed Kanlara from a wizard's spell that had trapped her in the shape of a book for over thirty years. Kanlara, overjoyed at her freedom, had been grateful and ready to embrace the world. Teza took Kanlara to her home and into her life. To the delight of them both, a fast friendship had formed. But in the ensuing months, winter had locked them into constant close proximity and forced them to delay their plans to travel beyond Rashemen's borders. Little differences blew up into heated arguments, and the subject of Teza's profession threatened to cause an irreparable rift.

As if on cue Teza's palms began to itch, a sure sign she had not stolen a good horse in days. Belatedly, she slowed and took her bearings. She was in an area of large workshops and houses just to the east of the center of the city. The grim fortress of the Huhrong's citadel lay behind her, its iron and steel walls pockmarked with pools of torchlight. Ahead and to the north lay the houses of the wealthier merchants and many of the city's nobles.

It wasn't the houses that drew Teza, however. She had tried her hand at burglary and did not like it. She preferred the subtlety of picking pockets or the excitement of horse theft. Even in winter there were places to find crowds with full purses and stables with interesting horses. One of her favorite spots was an inn and livery on the eastern road to Mulptan. It was often frequented by merchants, travelers, and traders, and their many beasts of burden, and it was not always well guarded.

Teza picked up her pace and continued east. The snow crunched under her boots and the biting wind drove in from Lake Ashane, the icy Lake of Tears. She hunched her shoulders against the cold and plowed on, not hearing a faint voice that called behind her.

She passed over a low stone bridge that spanned a small but swift river that still resisted the grip of the freezing wind. Several minutes later she saw the bulk of the Red Stallion Inn hunched back into a thick stand of evergreens. The timbered walls were lit with lanterns and lamplight blazed from every window. Smoke rolled from the inn's several chimneys and the smell of cooking food wafted into the dark. Teza noted all the activity with satisfaction. The inn was busy this night, which meant there were probably good pickings in the stable.

Niall One Hand ran a fine establishment that included the convenience of large corrals for livestock and beasts of burden and warm stables for the finer mounts of his guests. Teza, not wishing to abuse a good source, only visited Niall's place rarely to remove a few of the finer steeds from customers who could well afford it. Fortunately, Niall had no idea who raided his stable, so Teza was able to return the favor sometimes by bringing him stock to sell or passing a good deal his way. She liked Niall's easy wit and his flexible sense of honesty.

She turned away from the light and warmth and worked her way through the trees toward the stables. As quiet as a snowcat she slipped through the night to the back of the large barn. The building was timber, built on a stone and earth foundation, and it could house twenty horses or thirty ponies in a double row of stalls. A set of double doors opened onto the inn's courtyard, but there was also a smaller groom's door that opened from the back into the alley between the stalls. This door was usually kept locked—a fact that rarely bothered Teza—but this night it was also guarded.

Teza hesitated. The presence of the guard was unusual, but the fact that he wore the emblem of the clan family, Vrul, seemed strange. Most of the Vrul lived in Mulptan. Not that it really mattered. The Vrul were well known in Rashemen for their fine taste in horses.

It took the horse thief just a moment to slip back her hood, loosen her long dark braid, and find the small bag she always wore. Within, among the other tools of her trade, were the circles of fabric permeated with a quick-acting sedative. Very useful for unsuspecting guards.

She stumbled out of the trees close to the inn and ambled, in her best drunken fashion, toward the guard by the door. He watched her approach with some amusement.

"Sir, I was looking for the outhouse," she slurred, stumbling closer. "Do you know where it is?"

He lifted his hand to point, his head turning naturally in that direction, and in that instant Teza leaped forward and pressed the fabric to his nose. He took one gasp and fell like a stricken rothé.

Teza solicitously dragged him into the barn where he would not freeze. As she hoped, the grooms were in the inn and the stable was empty of humans. One by one she began a rapid inspection of the stalls' inhabitants.

"Teza!" a whispered voice called to her from the door.

Teza and the horse she was patting leaped sideways as one and crashed into the wooden partition. "Kanlara!" Teza snarled. "What are you doing here?"

The wizardess, cloaked and booted, strode forward, her face pinched with cold and annoyance. "I followed you," she said. "I wanted to apologize, but I couldn't catch up with you. I had a feeling you were going to do something like this."

"Of course I am!" Teza stormed out of the stall and into the next where a creamy white mare rolled her eyes nervously. "I told you from the beginning I was a horse thief. It's what I am."

"But it's not what you can be!" Kanlara insisted. "You are intelligent, strong, and beautiful. You could be anything you set your mind to."

Teza made a rude noise of disbelief. Those words, coming from a woman with exquisitely beautiful features, long red hair, jewel-green eyes, and the advantage of being wizard-trained, did not carry a great deal of weight with an untalented street rat. There were some realities of life Kanlara had never had to face—like starvation and loneliness and poverty.

Teza had learned to be a thief to survive and now it was all she knew. She threw her hands up. "You want me to change. You want us to leave Immilmar. You want a new wizard's staff and spell components. Well, all of that takes money. How do you propose we get it? You are forbidden to practice magic while you are in the jurisdiction of the Rashemi witches and the only jobs the Rashemaar will give an outlander are menial . . . they barely pay for our room. So that leaves me."

She realized her voice was rising with every word, and she quickly lowered it so as not to draw outside interest. "I can't sew. I hate serving in taverns. I have no learning or talent. I cannot be a witch, and I won't be a berserker. There is little left for someone like me in Immilmar. How can I make you understand?" She ended her tirade and leaned against the mare, breathing heavily.

"I am trying to understand," Kanlara replied sadly. "But please stop before something happens to you. I couldn't bear to lose you. You are the only family I have."

Something in Kanlara's tone rang true to Teza. Nonplused, she left the mare's stall and walked into the next without looking.

To Kanlara, the stall looked empty. But Teza found more than she bargained for. Her foot caught on something solid and heavy on the stall floor, and she stumbled forward into the manger. "By Mask! What is that?" she gasped. She squatted down and pushed the straw off a dark form.

Kanlara hurried in and the two women knelt together in the straw. They carefully rolled the form over onto its back. The strong smell of fresh blood filled their nostrils. Their hands slipped in the warm, dark fluid that covered the man's neck and chest.

"Oh, gods, he's been stabbed," Kanlara cried. "We must

get some help. Run to the inn and have someone summon the guards."

"What?" Teza yanked her hands away and frantically wiped them on cleaner straw. "The guards," she hissed, appalled at the very suggestion. "Don't be a fool. We have to get out of here, now!"

Kanlara stiffened. "There's been a crime committed," she said firmly. "We have to report it."

"Like the Abyss we do. One look at us, sneaking around where we don't belong, blood all over our hands, and they'll arrest us without a blink." She grabbed her friend's arm to pull her to her feet. "Come on!"

Kanlara yanked free. "Don't be ridiculous, Teza. There is nothing here to tie us to this. We simply found the body."

"You are so naïve. I have lived in the thieves' world all my life. I know how this will look to the Elders. We must go . . . now!"

A sudden call outside the door brought Teza to her feet like a panicked horse. "Kanlara," she begged, "please! He's a *fyrra,* a lord. Look at his clothes. We are riffraff to him, and the guards are not well known for their far-reaching intelligence. They will convict us on the spot."

Footsteps crunched on the snow outside.

"Kanlara, come on!" Teza cried one last time.

The wizardess stood still, staring down at the dead man, then she lifted her eyes to Teza's. Before either could react, someone pushed open the wide front door. Lanternlight spilled into the stable.

Teza's will broke. Like a fox bolting for cover she whipped around the stall door and fled silently into the shadows and out the back door. She did not hesitate a step until she was well back into the trees. Belatedly, she slowed. She turned, against all her instincts, and angled toward the road and the front of the inn. Through the trees she could hear the uproar of voices and the blare of a horn as a guard signaled to his captain.

The sounds of authority approaching and the noise of

the angry crowd were more than Teza wanted to face. Let Kanlara handle it. She could explain far better than Teza. The guard would question her and let her go. Teza decided to go home and wait. Kanlara would surely be along soon.

But she wasn't.

By midmorning the next day, Kanlara still had not returned and Teza had paced and worried to the point of nausea. As angry as Kanlara probably was, if she was able, she would have come back by that time.

Just before noon Teza tied her hair into a tight braid, piled it up on her head, and pulled a loose fur hat over the whole thing. She dressed in a pair of men's pants and boots and strapped a dagger to her side. Her smooth cheeks were dusted with a shadow of charcoal dust and, to finish off her disguise, she added a false mustache carefully crafted from horse hair. It was a disguise she had used successfully before and one few in Immilmar had seen. With luck it would get her safely where she wanted to go.

Teza hurried outdoors and strode just a few short blocks to the communal longhouse. The morning was overcast; the air cold and biting. Quite a few citizens were out on their daily business, and quite a few more were heading in the same direction as Teza, for the daily *kohrtar*, or charging of criminals, at the longhouse.

The squat longhouse sat on a short hill overlooking one of the main roads leading to the busy docks on the Lake of Tears. It was a large, if rather plain building used by the citizens of Immilmar for all the meetings of the Elders who ran the city, as well as gatherings of various guilds and parties. Every day at noon, or when needed, the Elders held the kohrtar to charge suspects of crimes and to hold trials for those already charged.

Teza knew if Kanlara had been arrested for the murder that she would be brought before the judges this noon. Keeping quiet, Teza mingled with the crowd moving through the open doors. Obviously, word of the murder had already spread through the city, and curious onlookers were coming to have a look. The young woman squeezed into an open space by the back wall and waited, her heart in her throat.

In just a few minutes a Fang guardsman slammed his sword on his shield to signal the arrival of the Elders. The noisy room fell silent. At the far end of the long room, three Elders practiced in the rudiments of Rashemi law (and law in Rashemen was rather rudimentary), entered and took their seats at a table placed on a dais. A fyrra, wearing the emblem of the Vrul clan stood to one side, his hawk glance fastened intently on the proceedings.

A second Fang guard read the day's charges from a roll of parchment. Several minor infractions were quickly dealt with by imposing fines or several days in the Iron Lord's dungeon.

At last the guard announced, "For the murder of the Lord Gireth StoneHammer of the Vrul Clan we hold the outlander, Kanlara. She was found beside the body with blood on her hands. Although she claims innocence and, as yet, no weapon has been found, the court feels there is enough evidence to try her."

A shock of guilt and fear jolted through Teza. "This can't be," she groaned. But she had predicted it herself.

At the sound of the sword clashing on the iron embossed shield, Kanlara was led in between two more armed guards. Her bright red hair stood out like a lick of flame among the black-haired Rashemaar.

Teza stared at her friend's face and she felt her hands begin to shake. Kanlara's beautiful features were slack; her bright gaze dulled. She walked with the stiff, uncaring motions of a lich between her two guards, going where they pushed her, stopping when they pulled her to a halt.

"The sewer scum," Teza spat. "They've put a feeble-mind spell on her."

"Of course," said the woman beside her. "She's an outland wizardess. It's a wonder she's been allowed to stay here at all. Usually the Witches send other magic-wielders running for the border."

"Yes, and look what happened—one of our own murdered. There's good reason for keeping strange wizardesses out of Rashemen," observed a second bystander.

Teza bit her lip hard to keep back a retort. She did not dare draw any more attention to herself. Instead she left the wall and pushed a little closer to the front where she could see Kanlara better. The wizardess's face was pale and her dress was torn and stained with blood. Bruises discolored her wrists where guards had tied her hands with too much enthusiasm.

The horse thief thrust her hands into her pockets and clenched her fingers into tight fists. Not once in her ill-begotten life had someone she loved suffered the consequences of her actions. Now, the thought that she might lose her friend because of her own cowardice hurt more than she ever believed possible. If she had only stayed with Kanlara to talk to the guards . . .

"The charges have been read and entered in the city's rolls," intoned an Elder. "Are there any who wish to stand for her at trial?"

Teza's eyes widened. She had not thought the judges would offer that boon to a foreigner. Usually the right of defense only went to citizens of Rashemen. The crowd around her murmured in surprise. They hadn't expected that either.

"Oh, by all the gods," Teza breathed. "What do I do?" Although few people remembered, there was still a long-standing price on her head. If she stood forward to defend Kanlara, she could expose herself and risk imprisonment in the Iron Lord's dungeon, or worse. The penalty for thievery in Immilmar was often the loss of a hand to the axe. Yet, if she didn't try to help Kanlara, it was a foregone conclusion that the wizardess would be found guilty and executed for a crime she would never commit.

Teza shivered. Never had she been so torn in two, but

never had she had a friend quite like the strong, obstinate, honorable Kanlara.

"I ask one last time," boomed the judge. "Is there anyone—"

"I will," Teza cried abruptly. She cringed at the high note her voice hit. She dropped her tone immediately and tried again. "I will stand for the accused."

A babble of voices broke as people turned to stare.

"And you are?" the judge demanded.

"Tezan, citizen of Immilmar. The accused is my friend."

"So let it be written. The wizardess will be held for trial in three days' time. You have until then, young man, to make her defense."

The sword clashed again and Kanlara was led away. The crowd slowly dispersed and Teza turned on her heel, pushing her way out of the longhouse. There was only one thing she could think to do at this moment. She walked to the nearest tavern, ordered a mug of *jhuild,* Rashemen's famous firewine, and downed it all in one long, fiery pull until her throat burned and her eyes watered. The other customers cheered her, astonished at her prodigious feat.

Thus fortified, she set out do the only other thing she could think to do—face the witches in their den. The witches of Rashemen were a powerful and secretive sisterhood that ruled and protected the country. Although the majority made their home in Urling, a contingent kept a longhouse in Immilmar to support the trio of Hathran who in turn supported and advised the Iron Lord. Teza deeply respected and feared the powerful witches. After her encounter with a witch two years before, she usually went out of her way to avoid them. Now, though, she marched to the front entrance of the Witches' Hall and boldly knocked on the carved wooden door.

The door immediately swung open of its own volition. Teza peered into the dim interior. When she saw nothing, she swallowed hard and walked inside.

A tall, black-robed woman stepped out of the shadows to meet her in the foyer of a long hallway. The witch's face was covered with a gray mask and her hands were tucked in her long sleeves. She said nothing, but waited for Teza to speak.

The horse thief bowed low and tried to keep her voice smooth and even. "I am sorry to disturb your peace, but there is one here who knows my friend, Kanlara the wizardess. May I speak with her?"

"I am she, Teza," replied the witch.

Teza's hand flew to her false mustache. The witch knew her and since she was waiting, she must know what was happening to Kanlara. Without thinking, Teza burst out, "You know Kanlara didn't do it. She was following me and the man was already dead when we found him. Please, is there anything you can do to help her?"

"There is little we can do. She is an outland spellcaster accused of murder by the city authorities. She must continue through the trial."

"The trial," Teza repeated bitterly. "That is a joke. She is already condemned."

The black figure did not stir. "Unless you prove her innocent."

"The only way I can do that to the Elders' satisfaction is to find the real killer."

"Precisely." The woman raised an elegant hand and beckoned to Teza to follow. "We do believe Kanlara is innocent. We have been keeping a close watch on Lord Gireth for some time, and his enemies are as numerous as the tears in Lake Ashane."

While she talked, the witch led Teza down a long, empty corridor lined with doors. The hall around them seemed empty and silent, yet Teza knew without a doubt they were being watched by numerous pairs of eyes. She stifled a shudder and tried to pay close attention to her guide.

"While we cannot help Kanlara directly, we can help you solve her problem." So saying, she pushed open a door and escorted Teza into a dim, windowless room. The only light radiated from a single small fire that burned in a high-legged brazier sitting alone in the room. Just above the flames hovered a nebulous shape that wavered and swayed with the smoke.

"Lord Gireth!" the witch commanded.

Teza gasped. The indistinct form quickly coalesced into the head and sharp features of the dead Rashemen fyrra, and his ghostly face turned toward them.

"We summoned his spirit back to talk to you. He did not see his killer, but perhaps he can give you some clues."

The young woman looked from the spectral head to the witch and back again, then said, "Lord Gireth, why were you in the barn that night?"

The ghost frowned at the memory. "I was to meet someone. A spy of mine who had information for me."

"What sort of information?"

"I don't know. I received a message to meet him outside in the barn. He knew I was staying at that inn."

"Why did you come to Immilmar?"

The spirit suddenly grinned wickedly. "To betray my brother-in-law. He abused his privileges one time too many."

"Did he know you were coming?"

"No. No one knew but my spy."

Teza paused, thinking hard. "Did you see anything before you were . . . killed?"

"No. I was alone, waiting for Alfric. He is a serving man for my brother-in-law. I did smell something, though." The ghost gave a hideous chortle. "Even over the horse manure I thought I caught a whiff of the lake."

Teza nodded once. The witch raised her hands, spoke a strange word, and snuffed out the fire. Lord Gireth's spirit form vanished from sight.

"Now," said Teza's black-robed companion. "There is the matter of your vulnerability. You cannot concentrate on this quest if you are constantly dodging into taverns and racing home to change disguises."

Teza tore her eyes away from the now dark brazier and frowned. Her eyes narrowed suspiciously. "That is my problem," she said.

"True. But we can temporarily relieve you of that difficulty. You only have three days to find the killer."

"Teza crossed her arms. "How?"

"A disguise no one will penetrate."

Teza thought she heard a hint of laughter in the witch's words. Her mental alarms began to clang. "That's kind, but . . ." She got no further.

The witch lifted her palms up and blew a pale, glimmering powder into Teza's face. Even as the woman chanted her incantation, Teza felt an alien feeling crawl over her. Her skin tingled; her nose lengthened. Her legs and arms shortened so quickly she fell on her side on the cold stone floor. Her clothes sagged on her body. Worst of all, she was assailed by an explosion of sensory stimulation: hundreds of smells she had never experienced, new sounds that filled her sensitive ears. Her vision sharpened in the dark room and lost most of its color. Terrified she closed her eyes and shouted, "Stop!" She heard a dog bark so close it could have been beneath her.

Oh, no, she thought.

"Teza," a gentle voice said above her. "It's over now. Stand up."

Slowly, carefully, Teza opened her eyes and climbed to her feet. All four of them. Too astounded for anger, her rump sagged to the floor and she sat.

"Excellent. This spell will last only three days, so don't worry. Think of the advantages and put them to use. You will retain your own intelligence, but you will also be able to communicate with other animals and with those creatures, human and otherwise, who are a part of magic. Do you understand?"

Teza growled, "Yes." She had a hundred other well chosen questions and opinions she wanted to add, but she was too bemused. Besides, her human memory reminded her, to disobey a witch was to ask for immediate death. If this witch thought Teza would be more effective as a dog, then that's how it would be.

Grumbling to herself, she padded after the witch back to the front entrance. The door stood open.

"Chauntea go with you," said the witch softly, and she shut the door behind Teza.

For a long while, Teza the dog stood immobile by the hall, her head lowered and her tail tucked between her legs. Of all the stupid, manipulating things to do to someone. At least the witch could have turned her into a horse.

This was all so bewildering. There were too many smells and too many sounds. Her vision was different and her body was aligned in a strange new way. Her perspective had changed, too. As a human she could look many people in the eyes, now all she could see were legs. Thankfully, the witch had made her a large dog, one people would not try to kick or eat or catch.

Just then the breeze wafted a scent toward her that even her dog sense recognized. She lifted her eyes to see a man walking along the road toward her—a young man in a shaggy coat and a jaunty knit hat and a smile that had melted her human heart on many occasions.

"Jereth!" she called as he passed.

The young man heard a woof. He glanced around at her, flashed his grin, and ruffled her shaggy ears. "Good day to you, too, big dog. Out watching the people? Well, maybe you'd better find another door to sit by before those witches turn you into a doorstop." He patted her again and sauntered away, his boots crunching on the snow.

Teza watched him go, her ears cocked thoughtfully. Perhaps the witch's spell had merit. If Jereth, a man who knew Teza very well indeed, did not suspect she was anything more than a dog, then no one else would either. Teza's confusion melted away in the warmth of a growing curiosity. She had always been good at disguises, but this was the best one she'd ever had. This might prove rather interesting.

Hesitantly at first, Teza set out toward the Red Stallion Inn. As the witch pointed out, there were only three days to help Kanlara. So, dog or no dog, Teza decided she had better get busy. To her surprise and pleasure, her mind quickly adapted to the strange new ways of her canine body. Before long she was swinging along at a jaunty trot with her long tail high and her ears flapping. The distance to the inn vanished quickly under her long-legged pace.

The inn lay quietly in its shelter of trees with only a wisp of smoke from the kitchen chimney to show a sign of life. Teza trotted around the back and into the stable through the groom's door. There were many more empty stalls this afternoon. A few ponies nibbled hay in a pen at one end and one horse dozed in a stall.

Teza inhaled deeply, astonished at the intensity and variety of the smells she could identify. The stall where Lord Gireth had died was all too easy to find by the intense, metallic scent of old blood. The bloodied straw had been removed, but nothing could disguise the smells that had soaked into the earth floor. Teza began a slow and careful search of the stall's interior.

"New around here?" a husky voice asked. "I hope you're not planning to stay."

Startled, Teza looked up to see a large yellow tomcat perched on the wooden wall. "No, no," she hastened to reassure. How she knew how to communicate with him so easily she never knew, but her speech was a richly varied combination of vocal sounds, body language, and an instinctive enhancement of mental images. It was remarkable, and it just seemed to come with the disguise. "The people think my friend killed this man. I want to find out who really did." She continued to sniff around under the close scrutiny of the yellow cat.

There were any number of human scents in this stall, including her own and Kanlara's. She also identified

Lord Gireth's smell on the floor and on the door of the stall and two others that were quite fresh. "How many people have been in the stable today?" she asked the cat politely.

The tom ignored her as he settled down in the hay of the feed rack.

"Don't pay attention to that lazy floor rug," another voice squeaked. A small black rat poked her nose out of a hole under the hay rack. "He is older than this inn and just as set in his ways. If you want to know, ask me. There were three people who came in here last night to remove the body and one more who cleaned it out this morning. That was some excitement. We haven't seen such goings on since the last midwinter festival."

Teza lifted her lips in a dogish smile at the rat's cheerful chatter. "Did you see anyone else before the man died?"

"Oh, certainly. There was the man, the selkie that met him, a guard, a woman who—"

"What?" Teza barked. "A selkie. Are you certain?"

The rat stuck out her whiskers and lifted her nose. "As certain as the darkness. Smell it yourself. She leaned against that wall."

Teza sniffed and there it was, just as Lord Gireth had said, a whiff of the lake.

In the flick of an eye, the rat disappeared and like an iron fist a hand grabbed Teza's ruff and hauled her out of the stall. "Here, you cur. Get out!" A man, tall and well dressed, planted a boot viciously into Teza's side. Pain lanced through her ribs. She yelped. He pulled back his foot to kick her again, but this time her dog instincts took over.

Fast as a weasel she slipped around in her loose skin and sank her teeth in his arm. His scent and the smell of his blood filled her nostrils. A cry of furious pain escaped his lips. Teza wrenched herself free from his grasp. She caught one glimpse of his face before she whirled away and galloped out of the barn to the safety of the trees.

She went just far enough to get out of sight, then she stopped and sat thoughtfully staring at the road through the evergreens. That man had looked familiar. Somewhere she had seen him very recently. Then she had it. He was the lord in the communal longhouse who had watched the kohrtar with such interest. So what was he doing in the stable where Lord Gireth was murdered?

Without realizing what she was doing, Teza's tongue lolled out and she started panting while her mind ranged over a hundred questions. Particularly, why was a selkie, a freshwater creature of the gentlest nature, in a stable with a murder victim? Why hadn't Lord Gireth's shade mentioned her?

Keeping one eye on the inn for the lord with the heavy boot, she searched the road and the paths leading to the inn for some tell-tale hint of the seal woman. The ground was frozen and the snow had been tramped by dozens of humans and animals, but finally, Teza's keen nose found another trace of that odd watery smell. It lay along a frozen path seldom used that wound through the trees and made its way at an oblique angle to the river and the city.

Others had left their trails behind but here and there, clinging to the frozen ground lay that elusive scent. With the utmost care Teza snuffled down the path until it intersected the road at the low bridge. She trailed onto the bridge, her tail wagging, and came to a stop in the middle. The selkie apparently paused there, for her scent covered a spot on the low stone wall and two delicate feet had scuffed the snow along the edge.

Teza lifted her front paws to the stone wall and peered down at the swiftly flowing river below. What had the Selkie done here? Had she resumed her seal form and fled back into the water? Had she dropped something?

Thoughtfully, Teza went back to her search of the road, and there, beyond the bridge, the selkie's trail continued. Teza followed it toward Immilmar and the section of the city where the large houses of the wealthy merchants and the lords crowded against the banks of the river. She was nearly among those houses when the road joined a larger thoroughfare and she lost the scent in a bewildering mob of smells from people, ponies, wagons, and other dogs.

She flopped down under a tree to rest and think. Her paws hurt from ice balls that had collected between the pads of her toes, so she gnawed them out while she pondered everything she had learned so far, which, she had to give the witch credit, she would not have discovered as a human. Being a dog had some interesting advantages. In fact, learning this new identity and trying something so different was positively exhilarating.

Twilight crept into the city by the time Teza decided what to do. There was one creature, a resident of Lake Ashane, who just might—for old time's sake—help her. Her mind made up, she ran easily out of the city and down to the shores of the Lake of Tears to look for the aughisky. Several times she had slipped down to the lake just to see how he fared. She knew his habits and favorite haunts, and she hoped to find him quickly.

Just as she suspected, he was in the second cove she tried. Blacker than night and exquisitely formed, the aughisky was a carnivorous water horse who preyed on human flesh. Teza had once bound him to her with the attraction magic of a hippomane, but early that winter she had freed him. She hoped fervently he would remember her and stay on shore long enough to hear her plea.

The horse stiffened when he saw a tall, shaggy dog trot toward him, then he dropped his glorious head and touched noses. "Oh, it's you," he snorted in amusement.

Teza stared up in surprise. "You can talk?"

"To animals. I do not eat them. I smell magic on you. A spell?"

She woofed a yes. "The witches did this to help me. I have to find someone."

"The witches. Interesting." He eyed the water's edge and made a move as if to leave.

"Don't go," Teza barked hastily. "Please, I have a favor to ask. For Kanlara."

The aughisky turned his attention back to her. "Why?"

"She is in trouble. I must find a selkie who is living on land now. Probably close by."

The aughisky lowered his head. His fiery green eyes peered at her through his long mane. "There is only one I know of. She was taken by a man and lives with him in the city."

"Do you know who?"

He snorted contempt. "They are all the same to me."

"I think she may have dropped something off the bridge."

"And you want me to look for it."

Teza nodded once. He would either do it or refuse, and all the begging in the world would not sway him.

The aughisky nickered a sound that reminded Teza of laughter. "Wait here," he said, then plunged into the dark water and was gone.

* * * * *

The cloud cover broke during the night and sunlight streamed over the lake at dawn. Teza crawled from her nest of dead leaves under a tree and stretched deliciously in the clear light. The cold did not seem so biting that morning, and the wind had died to a mere breath. She was about to look for some breakfast when something large and heavy plunged out of the lake. She whirled around, hoping it was not a water troll, and saw the aughisky prance out of the water carrying something in his mouth. He dropped his trophy at her feet.

Teza took a long look and a longer sniff and barked her gratitude. The soggy, cold things lying in the snow still reeked of Gireth's blood despite their immersion in the river. One was a dagger shoved askew into a beautifully tooled leather sheath; the other was a lady's coin bag that had been badly stained and thrown away. Embroidered in the fine fabric was the emblem of the Vrul clan. Teza grinned wolfishly.

"Now I know where to look," she told the aughisky. "Thank you."

The water horse bobbed his head. "You can thank me by helping the selkie if you can. She did not ask to be taken from her family."

Teza nodded and watched the black horse return to his watery home. Full of excitement, she headed back to Immilmar where she carefully hid the dagger and the bag in a place she often used for her stolen goods. Everything was falling into place. Perhaps, with a little luck, she would find the selkie, learn the truth, and have Kanlara out of that prison by nightfall.

Ears high and tail waving, she ran along the road to the houses by the river and soon came to a stop before a wall of stone that surrounded a large house. Above the gate hung the same emblem she had seen on the lady's bag.

A voice suddenly shouted in the courtyard. Its harsh tones sent a chill of fear through the dog. It was the same man who had driven her out of the stable the day before. On swift feet she bolted around the wall to the back of the house.

Luck was with her twice that day, for as she came around to the rear of the residence, she saw an open postern gate in the wall. She was about to turn into it when she noticed a path that led down a grassy slope to the banks of the river. Teza slowed her gait to check the path for people. The path was empty, but there was one person sitting on a dock that extended into the river.

Teza ducked behind a shrub to study the silent form. It seemed to be a slender woman, and a crazy woman at that, for she was sitting on the edge dangling her feet in the frigid water. Teza's ears came up. There was only one creature that slim and lovely who could do something like that with impunity.

Keeping an ear perked toward the house, she walked

quietly down to the dock and sat beside the woman. All of her doubt disappeared. The scent was the same and the appearance was correct for a selkie down to the pale green hair and the enchanting green eyes. The woman slanted a startled glance at the strange dog who just sat down with her, then she threw her arms around Teza's neck and burst into tears. Teza did not move.

"I hate him," the selkie sobbed. "I hate him! Why won't he just let me go?"

"Because he covets you?" Teza guessed.

The selkie let go as if stung. "You're not a real dog," she said. "I see now . . . you're ensorceled. Who are you?"

"I am a friend of the woman who was charged for the murder of Lord Gireth."

"I'm sorry," the selkie said bitterly. "That was not planned. But Lord Rath found her capture very convenient."

"She didn't do it."

"I know." Tears streamed down her lovely face and she leaned into Teza's warm, furry sides. "Lord Rath ordered his death because Lord Gireth was going to expose him to your *huhrong*. His own kin! Rath is a brute!"

"Can't you leave him?"

"He holds my seal skin." The selkie let her breath out in a sigh of total misery. "I even know where it is now, but I can't get to it."

Teza remained silent. She understood the selkie's fear—she had felt a small part of Rath's brutality herself. But just sitting out on a cold, damp dock was not going to free Kanlara. She had to find convincing proof of Kanlara's innocence—without convicting herself, if possible. At this point, only the selkie seemed to have the truth Teza needed.

"How about a trade?" the dog suggested. "I will get your skin for you, if you will come to my friend's trial and tell the Elders what you know."

The selkie's expression was transformed by a radiant hope. "Agreed. Let's go now. Rath was leaving to meet the *huhrong.* He should be gone by now, and most of his men with him." She drew her feet out of the water and slipped them into her shoes.

Teza observed with interest that the selkie's feet were delicately shaped and webbed between each toe. When she rose to her full height, the selkie was not as tall as Teza used to be, but her form was as slender as a lake reed and fully proportioned in breast and hip. It was little wonder human males desired the voluptuous seal maidens.

Silently, the two walked up the slope to the postern in the surrounding wall. The selkie slipped through, gestured to Teza, then led her to the house. Teza stared wide-eyed at the edifice.

It was huge, by Rashemi standards: a two-story stone and timber building set over a deep undercroft. A narrow wooden stair led up to the single back door. The windows, set in the thick walls, were mere arrow-slits. The house gave Teza the impression of being both a fortress and a prison. Little wonder the selkie hated it.

The two entered into a long, shadowed hall that extended the width of the house. The selkie led Teza to a staircase and paused at the first step. "He keeps my skin in a chest in his room on the second floor," she whispered. "Go right. Second door."

"Are there any locks or guards or spells on it?"

The selkie nodded reluctantly. "There is one thing he uses to guard the skin. Salt."

"Salt?" repeated Teza skeptically. "What kind of a deterrent is that?"

"I am a freshwater selkie," the seal-woman explained. "Salt burns us like acid."

"Why couldn't one of the house servants get it for you?"

"They are terrified of him."

Teza waited no longer but flew up the stairs on silent paws. Following directions, she found the room and drew open the bar on the door with her teeth. The chest was easy to find, being the only one in a large and very sparse room. It sat against the wall near a bed. Teza trotted over, her toenails clicking softly on the bare wood floor. Opening the big rectangular box proved difficult because there was a latch that defied canine teeth and claws. Finally, though, she worked it open, and rising to her hind legs, she thrust her head into the chest and began to pull out clothes and personal items right and left. She made no effort to be careful or circumspect. There wasn't time, and she felt an ever-increasing sense of urgency. At last, near the bottom, she scented the strong odor of salt. A package wrapped in salted leather lay at the very bottom of chest.

Teza snatched the bundle and ran. She scooted out into the hall just in time to hear the selkie cry a warning. "He's coming! Hurry!" Out in the courtyard sounded the shouted voice of Lord Rath. Booted feet pounded on the stairs outside. Teza scrabbled to the top of the stairs, tore open the salty leather, and heaved the velvety soft skin of the selkie over the banister.

It fell directly into the selkie's arms.

At that instant the front door slammed open and Lord Rath strode in. His haughty glance caught sight of the selkie clasping the seal skin in her arms, and he roared with rage. Faster than a bird, the selkie whirled on her toes and raced for the back door and the path leading to the river.

"After her, you scum!" he bellowed to his men. He and all his guards charged after the fleeing seal-woman. Teza watched them go from the cover of the second floor balcony. As soon as it seemed clear, she bolted down the stairs and ran for the front door. It was then that her luck ran out.

An armed guard stepped into the doorway just as she reached it. "Hey, you mutt," he shouted at her. "What are you doing in the house?" He adroitly grabbed the scruff of her neck and brought her to a scrabbling halt by his leg. She growled and snapped at his hand, but this man had experience with dogs. He cuffed her hard, then dragged her down the stairs to the courtyard. She struggled to get away from him. A second ringing blow to her head nearly knocked her off her feet, and in that moment of weakness, the guard hauled her to the kennels, threw her unceremoniously inside, and slammed shut the gate. Teza collapsed on the straw, her mind reeling.

Three other dogs in the kennel with her withdrew to their own places and left her in peace. Teza was glad. Her ribs ached, her head pounded, and her hopes were crushed. She was trapped in a pen as stout as a prison and her one witness was beyond her reach. She had hoped to escort the selkie out of Lord Rath's reach and bring her to the longhouse for the trial. Now the selkie was gone. If she escaped to the river, she would never dare return to the city for fear of Lord Rath. And if Rath caught her now, he would surely imprison her in the house for her attempted escape.

Teza whined. Tomorrow was Kanlara's trial. Tomorrow she needed to present evidence to the Elders to prove Kanlara's innocence. Yet nothing she had was tangible, and who would take the word of a wanted horse thief in the shape of a dog?

She lifted her muzzle to the sky. "By all the gods," she howled, "if Kanlara is freed, I swear I will try to find honest work. Something new. Something she and I both can accept. If I can be a dog, by Mask, I can be anything to keep my friend."

"Shut up, you stupid dog!" bellowed one of the grooms.

Teza climbed slowly to her feet and sat by the gate. A few minutes later Lord Rath returned, roaring like an enraged bull. Teza snorted to herself. The selkie had obviously escaped. At least she had the satisfaction of that. Thankfully, Rath was too busy taking his fury out on his men to notice a strange dog in his kennel. She turned her back on the uproar in the courtyard, curled up in the straw, and went to sleep.

She was more exhausted than she thought, for not even the arrival of the dogs' dinner that evening roused her from her deep sleep. When she finally awakened, it was dawn. Early dawn, thankfully. She opened her eyes and discovered that the witch's spell had worn off. She was human again, miserably cold and without a scrap of clothing to cover her. The dogs lay in their corner and eyed her askance.

"Good dogs," she whispered. As quietly as she could, she slipped the latch on the kennel and eased out. The main gate was closed and there were guards standing nearby, but in the early morning gloom, no one saw the young woman slip into several outbuildings by the wall. Soon, a shuffling figure in an old skirt and heavy coat came out and made her way around the back of the house. She found the postern gate, picked the lock, and vanished into the awakening city.

* * * * *

A short time later, a young woman walked to the front gate of Lord Rath's house and presented a letter for the fyrra to the guards there.

Teza smiled at them winningly, and they in turn were quite willing to oblige. She handed them her carefully penned missive, winked at them both, and walked away, swinging her hips like a tavern girl. Kanlara had spent the winter teaching her to read and write, and this letter she had written to Lord Rath made every difficult hour she had spent struggling to learn her letters worthwhile. If Rath fell for her threat of blackmail and came to the place she suggested to meet, the selkie would not have to worry about him again.

Just to ensure that the trap would be waiting, she hurried down to the lake to find the aughisky. He was still by the shore, still hoping for a meal. Winter was a difficult time for the waterhorse, and Teza hoped his hunger would make him linger.

Although she could no longer understand him, he still seemed to know what she was saying. When she explained her plan, his eyes lit with a greedy, green glow.

Satisfied, Teza fetched the dagger and the purse out of their hiding place and went back to the room in the Guardian Witch. There was only a short time left until the trial and she needed every minute of it to resume her identity as a young man and to try to plan what she would say to the judges. There was nothing left but her own truth.

The communal longhouse was crowded when she reached it, and Teza had to push her way to the front where she could wait for the judges to appear. They soon came, accompanied by the Fang guards and Kanlara. The feeblemind spell had been removed so Kanlara could hear the evidence against her and tell her own side, but her hands were firmly tied and a witch stood guard beside her to prevent any sorcery.

The Elders quickly silenced the crowd and the trial commenced. In Immilmar tradition, the evidence against the accused was presented first, and even Teza had to admit it sounded damning. The Elders called for Tezan to stand forth in Kanlara's behalf.

The wizardess stared at her friend, her eyes pleading, begging Teza not to say anything that would condemn the horse thief to imprisonment and amputation.

Teza would not look at her. She stood before the three men and drew a deep breath. "Most revered sirs," she began. "I have known from the beginning that Kanlara was innocent of this charge of murder because I—"

"Because I did it," a voice called from the back.

The onlookers erupted in an uproar of excitement and curiosity. A path opened through the crowd and a Rashemi witch and a figure in a voluminous cloak walked forward to meet the judges. People bowed in respect to the witch and stared in open curiosity at the slender woman accompanying her. The two walked to Teza's side and stopped before the judges.

The figure in the cloak threw back her hood to reveal the green hair and lovely face of the selkie. She gave Teza a beaming smile of gratitude. "Lord Rath is dead," she whispered. "He fell for your bait. The aughisky came for me as soon as he finished with the man." Her eyes sparkled like gems. "I went to your friend the witch as quickly as I could. She has promised me protection for my information."

"Your friend, the witch." Teza liked those words. She lifted her gaze to the enigmatic mask of the black-robed witch and nodded her thanks.

"Young woman," boomed a judged. "Are you the one who just confessed to killing Lord Gireth?"

The selkie turned to the men at the table. "Yes. My captor, Lord Rath, forced me to kill Gireth in the stable at the Red Stallion Inn. Lord Gireth had learned through his servant that his brother-in-law was about to betray him to the huhrong over a small matter of smuggling and bribery. He despised Gireth, but not enough to dirty his own hands with the crime, so he threatened to destroy my skin and beat me to death if I did not do his bidding. Even then I might have wavered, so he drugged me with a poison that weakened my will to fight him. He gave me the dagger, hid me in the stable and lured Gireth out with a false message."

Teza silently produced the dagger and laid it and the bloodstained purse before the Elders. The witch watched impassively. Kanlara's face brightened with rising hope.

The judges asked many questions of the selkie and Kanlara and they carefully examined the dagger and the purse. To everyone's surprise, the witch with the selkie filled in a number of details about Lord Rath's activities in Immilmar and other cities in Rashemen. The judges decided a full investigation of his crimes needed to be held immediately and they recommended that word be sent to the huhrong to have Lord Rath arrested.

Teza glanced at the selkie and dropped her eyelid in a slow wink. She didn't think there was a need to rush.

"In the face of such clear evidence, we free Kanlara from the charges of murder and release her," announced the judges.

Teza whooped with joy. She sprang around the Fang guard and untied Kanlara's hands herself. The wizardess fell into her arms and returned her overjoyed hug.

"Thank you, my sister," she whispered to Teza. "Thank you for everything."

The horse thief grinned. "Wait till you hear the rest of the story."

Ekhar Lorrent:
Gnome Detective

Steven "Stan!" Brown

Have you traveled along the Way of the Dragon, southeast from Espar to Waymoot? Curving across the empty plains and through the quietest parts of the King's Forest, it is a lonely stretch of road. You may feel there is not another living creature within a griffon's flight.

Would it shock you to know there is a village not five miles from where the Way plunges into the tree line? Nestled in a fragrant dale, where the dusty foothills of the Storm Horns almost touch the fragile leaves of the forest rests a little town with little houses where little folk live languorous lives. The hearth smoke that climbs to the clouds is usually mistaken for campfires by travelers who, on their journeys, happen to glance away to the south. The place cannot be found on a map; in fact, it is too small to have a name of its own. The halflings and gnomes who live there simply call it Home. Not a building in sight stands taller than ten feet at chimney top, and each one has a garden filled with the fruits, flowers, or herbs its owner fancies. Visitors often mistake fields of corn, standing tall beside the tiny houses, for orchards filled with saplings of some strange, leafy willow tree.

Gardening is the passion of these folk, and so it should surprise no one that on a sunny spring morning, Ekhar Lorrent was up to his gnomish elbows in mud and muck. The rains of the last few days threatened to drown his beloved snapdragon tomatoes—a stock he'd gotten as an import from Maztica and crossbred himself—ruining his dreams of lazy summer evenings contentedly chewing on the fruit, pickled in vinegar and sugar. As the planting bed drained, he gently held the fragile roots, speaking softly to them.

"Not to worry, my sweets, you will make it through. Summer wouldn't be summer if it were not for you. Your spicy juice helps cool a long humid night. And your flowers keep filling me with the delight of the thought of pies cooked in a tomato crust. No, you must all survive. Yes, you all simply . . . must . . ."

Ekhar's voice trailed off as though he could no longer remember the thought he had begun. For a full minute he sat there, hands buried in the ground cradling the tomato roots, with an odd look on his face. Some folk have this look when they try to remember long ago times and places, others when they are listening for a sound that only dogs and elves can hear. Ekhar had the look for another reason, a far too familiar one. So he was not at all surprised when his great gnomish ears began to wiggle, then flap as though blown by a terrible gale. He was not at all worried, as he stood up and wiped the dirt from his hands, that the sound of his lobes slapping against the side of his head could be heard clearly ten yards away. It bothered him not a bit, as he went inside to wash up and change, that his ears were now a brighter red than a salamander's scales. And he didn't even notice his fallen snapdragon tomatoes wilting in the mud as he put on his cloak, grabbed his sturdiest walking stick, and left his house and Home.

Ekhar's neighbors rolled their wide halfling eyes, chuckled to one another, then went back to tending their own gardens. This was hardly the first time the daft old gnome had mysteriously dropped everything and walked off into the world, oblivious of everything and everyone around him. They knew he would return in a day, or a week, with tales of intrigue and violent death. For, though gardening was Ekhar Lorrent's passion, murder was the gnome's one true love.

* * * * *

"What I want to know is what you're going to do about the damage that . . . that . . . thing did to my inn!"

The dull ache Jäg Dubblspeir felt at the base of his skull grew suddenly to a constant pounding above his left eye. The danger was past, the town was safe, but if one of his men didn't escort Kethril Fentloque, owner of the recently demolished Dancing Roc Inn, back behind the barricade, there would be one more name added to the list of today's casualties.

Luckily, the problem was averted as a throng of villagers rushed up to the barman, slapping him on the back, perhaps a bit too enthusiastically. They lifted Kethril over their heads and carried his kicking, screaming, spindly frame to the center of town. Along the way, cries of "that's some boy you have there!" and "you sure must be proud!" nearly drowned out the undertone of "better your inn than mine" and "somehow, this is just too fitting!" Jäg was left alone with his deputies to contemplate what their next step should be.

"Dang thing sure is big!"

"Not much point in calling it a giant otherwise." Jäg, who was widely considered to be the most patient man in Minroe, had no time for the naïveté of his men. They all came from this small town or its outlying farming communities, and signed on as deputies only to save themselves from ending up working behind a plow from sunup to sundown every day of their tiresome lives. Besides, the local maids were crazy for anyone dressed in a tight-fitting, dull-gray deputy's uniform. On most days, the unprofessional attitudes of his men were nothing more than a minor annoyance. Today, however, they factored heavily into Jäg's headache, which now throbbed above both eyes.

Unlike his deputies, Jäg lived in Minroe by choice. You might not guess it to look at him, with his unkempt hair, scruffy beard, and stained and wrinkled uniform, but Jäg Dubblspeir was perhaps the finest officer ever to grace the Waymoot garrison of the Purple Dragons. He worked his way up through the ranks, earning every promotion he got with blood, sweat, and more blood. By the time he was made a commander, Jäg could no longer count the number of close friends he saw killed in the line of duty, nor how many times he came within an arrow's breadth (or dragon's breath, or sword arm's length) from joining them, but every single one of those memories haunted him. When he finally realized that he had to retreat from this life if he wanted to have any life left at all, Jäg chose to come here because, according to every map he knew, nowhere was farther off the beaten track than the tiny village of Minroe.

When he first arrived, Jäg was surprised at how big the town looked. The buildings, while weather-worn and of an architectural style that went out of fashion three generations ago, were tall and strong and well kept up. In the last century, Minroe was a bustling mining town, the caverns in the surrounding hills yielding rubies, emeralds, and other gems by the bucketful. When the lodes ran dry, though, the town nearly did as well. The people who stayed were hardy folk who made their livings farming the rocky, uncooperative soil, or collecting pixie cap mushrooms and selling them to Suzailan merchants. They took a great pride in their little town and did everything in their power to maintain it. Of a summer afternoon, it was not unusual to see several neighbors working together to repair the shingles, fix the garden wall, and add a new coat of paint to a building that no one had lived in for twenty years. That's just how the people of Minroe were, and it suited Jäg just fine.

From time to time, friends who yet served with the Purple Dragons visited Jäg, though they often seemed most interested in inspecting his deputies for someone worth recruiting. So far, he'd lost a half-dozen fine officers—not to mention the only true friends he had in town—to the Dragons. After all, who would remain in a dying town like Minroe when the Purple Dragons offered to show you the world? Who indeed, except for Jäg. Before they'd leave, though, old comrade and departing deputy alike invariably would comment that Minroe was no place for Jäg to be. "You're like an eagle roosting in a henhouse," they'd say. "A man like you should go out and meet the world head on."

In his years with the Purple Dragons, Jäg met, fought, and killed practically every creature native to the Heartlands, and a few from other regions, continents, and even planes. Truthfully, he'd had quite enough of it. He figured that moving to a backwater town like Minroe meant that the most dangerous creature he was likely to face was a drunken dwarf or love-sick half-ogre. That illusion was shattered within weeks of his arrival. Minroe's trouble with medusas is well-chronicled, and talk of it is partly what has kept the town from regaining any of its lost status or population, all this despite the fact that Jäg, who suddenly found himself saddled with the position of Chief Constable, successfully brought the medusas under control in less than a month and with only three deputies (all of whom the Purple Dragons soon recruited). Being this far off the beaten track, he came to realize, meant only that he was the sole mechanism keeping the chaos of the wilderness at bay. Today, that chaos expressed itself in the form of a twenty-two foot tall cyclops rampaging through the heart of Minroe.

Jäg spat on the ground.

It was no surprise that giants lived in the hills surrounding his sleepy little town. It was an unusual week that passed without one farmer or another running into his office, blue in the face over the fact that he'd seen a hill or mountain giant casting a hungry eye at his livestock . . . or his daughter. Nothing ever came of these incidents. The giants wanted no trouble. They lived their tremendous lives in the hills and, occasionally, the smaller ones even visited Minroe to buy large quantities of supplies. They were generally good, if unruly, neighbors.

"Ow!" he was startled back to the here and now by a rap against his ribs, the kind you might get from a mischievous friend's elbow. Unfortunately, Jäg didn't have any mischievous friends. The headache beat savagely across his brow.

The constable turned, ready to take all his frustrations out on the person attached to that unwanted elbow, but only stared in bewilderment at the empty air beside him. No one was there. Then he felt another dull rap, this time against his knee.

"If you look nose-to-nose there is nothing to see, but mind your feet, Constable Dubblspeir, or you'll trip over me!"

Jäg's teeth clacked as his chin snapped against his chest, and the pain behind his eyes soared like a Waterdhavian opera. This might have been from changing his gaze so dramatically, but more likely it was the sight of the gray-haired gnome puffing on a long-stemmed clay pipe and gently tapping a walking stick against the constable's leg.

"Ekhar Lorrent! Gods above, that's all I need!!"

"You've trouble, friend Jäg, that much I know. Murder most foul, my wagging ears tell me so. Ekhar is here, set your mind at ease. Together we'll solve this case, quick as you please!"

Jäg covered his eyes and counted to ten under his breath, then looked down at the gnome and said, "Look, Ekhar, I don't want you to take this the wrong way, but would you get the hells out of my way? There haven't been any murders in Minroe since that time Jenna the seamstress found out Taña Fellbrook was having an affair with her husband, and sewed the pair of them into a suit and evening gown."

" 'The Case of the Tailor-Made Corpse,' I remember it well. But come now, Jäg, have you nothing to tell?" His steel-gray eyes glanced at the debris that surrounded them. The gnome winked and said, "Quite a large corpse I see lying prone over there. Something untoward happened, the scent's in the air."

Ekhar Lorrent could be counted on to show up every time things got out of control and blood was shed. He seemed to have a sixth sense about murder. The Fellbrook case was only one of a dozen or so that Ekhar had gotten involved in over the years. The gnome had a head for investigative work, Jäg had to give him that much credit. But his knack for being in the right place at the right time and tripping over clues was more than outweighed by the fact that he was so damned annoying.

"I'm only going to say this one time, Ekhar. We've had a little giant trouble today. A bit of property damage, a few broken bones, but no one's been murdered—so go home!"

"No murder, you say? Can it really be true? You don't mind if I just look about town, do you?"

The constable let out a long sigh of relief.

"No, no. Go ahead. Look around all you like, Ekhar. Just stay out from under my feet."

"You've much work to do, that much I can see. What happened to bring this giant trouble on thee?"

Jäg groaned. His headache now encircled his skull like a crown of pain. He wasn't sure whether Ekhar's rhyming patter was an affectation or a curse placed upon the gnome by some witch, but the lengths to which the diminutive detective would go for a rhyme was maddening.

"I don't know Ekhar, and that's most of the problem. It's been a quiet few weeks, which is fine with me. There haven't even been any bar fights for my men to break up. Then, out of nowhere, this cyclops was seen circling the town." Jäg pointed absentmindedly at the dead giant. "It showed up for a few hours each day, crawling around in the scrub brush, watching the comings and goings around town. I think it was trying to be surreptitious. Who knows. Those giants are dumb enough to think that just because their heads are buried in bushes, no one will notice their enormous butts sticking in the air."

"It spied on the town for a few days you, say?" Ekhar had his face scrunched up in a look that Jäg knew only too well. "Please, finish your tale, and I'll be out of your way."

"There isn't much to tell," Jäg continued. "It stopped showing up about three days ago. I figured that it'd grown bored with whatever game it was playing and gone back into the hills. Then, this morning, it comes screaming down the main road. I mean, we could hear it coming a good ten minutes before it got here. It was waving its hands in the air and shouting about how mean we all were and how it was going to wreck the town.

"You can see all the damage the damned thing did. It kicked in the front of the schoolhouse, tore the roof off M'Greely's general store, and was absolutely wrecking the Dancing Roc Inn when we finally brought it down. I figure the confounded thing was mad, or maybe it ate some brainfever berries."

Ekhar, who had been gazing at the buildings that had been ruined, or perhaps at the half dozen or so intervening ones that had not been touched, was struck by this last comment.

"Bainfevered, you think? Or under a spell? What makes you say this giant was unwell?"

Running his hand through his short-cropped gray hair, Jäg accepted the fact that the gnome, like his headache, was not going to just go away. "You mean besides the fact that we peppered it with at least six dozen arrows before it fell? Man, I've never seen anything take that much punishment without even batting an eyelash. But, my first big clue was that it started foaming at the mouth just before it fell over."

Ekhar tapped the stem of his pipe against his thin lips and raised one eyebrow. Tyr save me, Jäg thought, he's got a theory.

"The mad giant's rampage was a tragedy nearly, but no murder's been done, you've shown me quite clearly. You've much work to do, Jäg, and I've no wish to delay. May I look at the giant, before I'm away?"

The constable nodded mutely. The gnome had listened to reason. He was going to leave. Jäg's prayers had been answered.

Ekhar bowed deeply, clamped his clay pipe in his teeth, and walked purposefully toward the lifeless cyclops. He stood there for a while, hands clasped behind his back, and stared at the dozens of arrows sticking out of the body. He paid particular attention to those around the giant's face and neck, especially the one poking directly out of its sightless eye.

All of this would have been interesting, possibly even amusing to Jäg Dubblspeir, except that he still had so much to do. He called four of his men aside and they huddled around him as he squatted in the muddy street.

"Three of you go around to every barn, stable, and manger in town" he pointed to the three newest recruits. He knew it was best to send them on an assignment together. It just about guaranteed that they'd stay focused on the job at hand. "Gather up every plow horse, oxen, and mule in Minroe and bring them to the hitching post in front of the Dancing Roc. While you're at it, grab every coil of rope you come across. Make sure they're strong and at least twenty feet long, though. We're going to drag that cyclops out of town before it has a chance to start stinking up the place."

The three young men stood up, saluted, mumbled "yes sir" at least five times each, saluted again, and headed off toward the Happy Horse Livery repeatedly tripping over one another the whole way.

"You, stand guard over the body" he said to the remaining deputy. His name was Riktus, and he was a few years older than the other three. While not a born soldier, Riktus had learned a lot in the three years since Jäg took him on. "People are already gathering around and poking at it. If the cursed thing really was brainsick, I don't want anyone cutting slices off it to take home as souvenirs."

The lad snapped off a crisp salute and trotted over to his post. He could handle responsibility, Jäg reflected, which meant that the Purple Dragons were sure to snatch him up when next they passed through on a visit. This job was never going to get any easier if he couldn't find some way to get the qualified soldiers to stay. Still, knowing that the things were beginning to come under control eased the throbbing in Jäg's head. The worst of the day was surely over. Now all the constable had to worry about was that no one got too rowdy in the celebratory atmosphere that pervaded the unaffected quarters of Minroe.

As if on cue, a crowd of cheering people rounded the corner and marched toward the wreckage of the Dancing Roc. Kethril Fentloque and his son Abril led the way. Jäg met them at the barricade.

"Where do you think you're going?" he asked. He made sure to keep his posture civil, but spoke in the voice he mastered as a Purple Dragon commander, the one that made raw recruits wet their tabards. Kethril flinched.

"W-we're going to remove the head of that giant. The Dancing Roc may have been destroyed, but I'm going to rebuild the inn and name it 'One Shot In The Eye.' We'll get the head stuffed and mounted to hang over the bar." The frail man pulled his even frailer son close against him. "My boy killed that giant. We have the right to a souvenir!"

Jäg knew it would come to this.

"I'm sorry, Kethril, but we've reason to believe the giant may have some disease. You wouldn't want to hang a trophy that would poison all your guests now, would you?"

The sour old man looked unconvinced.

"If it's so dangerous, why is that gnome touching it?"

As the constable turned, the pain in his head surged again. There stood Riktus, obviously at his wits' end, helplessly trying to convince Ekhar to stand away from the corpse. The gnome, for his part, tut-tutted and pooh-poohed the guard, continuing to merrily poke and prod at the cyclops.

Jäg's eyes narrowed. "He won't be for long!" the constable muttered half to himself as he stalked over to the site.

"Sir!" Riktus almost whined. "I tried to stop him, but—"

"Don't worry, son" Jäg said. "Ekhar! What the hells do you think you're doing? I already told you we think the thing was brainsick. How am I supposed to keep the citizens away from it when here you are sticking your damned hands in its mouth? By the gods, that's disgusting!"

"Oh, my friend, that you're here I am glad. I'm quite certain now, this giant was not mad." He held a finger aloft and it was covered with some of the frothy yellow foam that still clung to the giant's lips. "A brainfevered or sick thing might spew a white lather, but only a poison makes this foam I gather. It may seem I do this just to be bold and defiant, but the truth is I know someone murdered this giant!"

"Blessed Torm, give me strength—of course it was murdered! I shot it half a dozen times myself!!" The constable turned to the crowd. "How many of you shot the giant?"

Several dozen hands shot into the air along with a resounding "Huzzah!"

"See the arrow that sticks from the poor creature's eye? It felled this great beast—who let that one fly?"

The crowd shouted, "Abril! Abril! Abril!" and the frail boy flushed with pride.

"That fragile youth killed such a monstrous attacker? Not a well-seasoned knight, not a slasher and hacker? Come now you Minroeans, you're all genteel folk. Such an end to this battle seems like a poor joke."

Jäg looked at Ekhar in bewilderment. "'Slasher and hacker?' What the hell is a 'slasher and hacker?'"

"It's true!" came a shrill voice from the crowd. Kethril Fentloque broke the barricade and walked straight up to Ekhar Lorrent. Jäg marveled at the fact that next to an elderly gnome, even the spindly Kethril looked hail and hardy. "My boy did it! Everyone else was shooting the blasted thing in the arms and chest and back. But only my Abril was smart enough and brave enough to wait until it turned to look at him, then shoot it square in the eye."

"A wise move it's true, and not easily done. The boy stood and fired when most others would run. It's an action to be considered uncommonly brave, since the boy's family and home were in danger so grave."

"Is that so hard to believe?" Kethril fumed. "That my boy has a backbone?" The innkeeper turned to face the crowd. "You all teased him so. Every day he would come home from school battered and bloodied, but he kept going back. All you did was toughen his spirit!"

Several of the young men who had earlier carried Abril on their shoulders looked abashed and scuffed their shoes in the mud, unwilling to meet the elder Fentloque's gaze.

"Though brave he may be, and remarkably quick, neither of these two skills today did the trick. The giant died not from a piercing of marrow, instead he was poisoned by the tip of the arrow."

Jäg, who had been mouthing the words 'slasher and hacker' over and over to himself, suddenly regained his focus. "By all that's right and just, Ekhar, who cares? The giant attacked the town. Do you think it matters to anyone that the lad used poison instead of muscle to kill it?"

"Yes! Yes!" cried Kethril. "I think he showed uncommon sense. I've always said he was a bright one, my Abril. Not like you, Alon M'Greely, who gave him a job and snatched it away all in the same week. So he sometimes gave back the wrong change—bah! That was no reason to fire him, let alone embarrass him the way you did!"

Ekhar Lorrent nodded to himself. Of all those gathered only Jäg noticed, but then he was also the only who knew the gnome well enough to guess at the gesture's significance. He was sure now that the pounding in his head would never stop.

"But you, innkeeper Kethril, you believe in your boy. Have you filled his whole life with nothing but joy?"

Someone from the back of the crowd yelled, "What about when the lad wanted to go to Waterdeep to study at the bardic academy? I thought you were going to flay the skin off him right there in the main room of the Dancing Roc!" And everyone gathered murmured their agreement.

"Bah! It was for his own good!" Kethril snorted. "Bardic academy indeed! We Fentloques run inns, we don't perform in them!"

"The murder is solved, I'm happy to say. I know who it was killed the giant today!" Ekhar bounced about like a squirrel with its tail caught in a bear trap.

"Oh, Ekhar!" Jäg groaned. "Abril killed the giant. I've been telling you that since the minute you arrived!"

"The boy killed the giant, that much is true, but how and why he did it just might surprise you!"

The gnome had every eye in the crowd on him. As much as Jäg wanted to tell him to close his fool mouth, he knew that at this point the citizens would demand to hear Ekhar's wild theory. Best just to let him go, the constable thought.

"Wary was I of the giant's foamy lip. The odd yellow froth gave me my first tip. You don't care that the boy used poison to fell the cyclops, but the next thing I tell you may make your eyes pop. The poison he used is called yellow-root-brew. Inn cooks use but a drop to spice their stew. But if a man were to drink a cup full of this mix, he'd be dead as that giant lying still on your bricks. In order to kill such a tremendous beast, the boy would need use a gallon, at least."

The crowd stood mesmerized by the gnome. His explanation was the best theater Minroe had seen all year. Between his excited hopping about and his rhyming cant, it seemed to be a mixture of ballet and opera. Only Jäg shook his head ruefully. He prayed Ekhar wasn't going to say something they would all regret.

"He couldn't possibly fit that much poison on an arrow," shouted a man from the crowd.

"Yes!" yelled a woman closer to the front. "How did he do it?"

"I'll tell you," the gnome continued, "but first I must pray, that you listen quite closely to all that I say. Look, if you will, at the monster's still feet. The mud you see there will quite closely meet, upon closer inspection if you only stare, the same exact type found on Abril's shoes there."

Even Ekhar was taken aback by the volume of the gasp that escaped the crowd. It was true. The mud on the cyclops's boots was a rich brown hue since it came from the dark soil of the creature's mountain cave, very different from the tan-colored dirt found in town. And, when they looked, the same dark mud could be clearly seen on Abril's shoes and pant cuffs.

"The boy has been spending his time in the hills, befriending the monster, bending it to his wills. He'd bring it food from his father's own inn, to make it believe it could trust only him. But on the gift food he would liberally sprinkle, the yellow-root brew mixed with raw periwinkle. This covered the scent so the giant could smell just the food not the poison, he never could tell."

It seemed to Jäg that the crowd was closing in on Ekhar, leaning in closer and closer so that they didn't miss a word of this explanation.

"Something I must tell you about yellow-root-brew, it remains long in your blood whatever you do. Though each time the giant ate but a wee tiny drop, he was slowly being poisoned and the boy did not stop. He fed the beast more until he was certain, just one sprinkle more would bring death's black curtain."

"Why?" someone shouted, though he needn't have. Everyone was pressed so closely together that a whisper would have probably been heard by most of the crowd. "Why would Abril do this? I mean, no one here would mourn the killing of a cyclops, but why do it in such a round about way?"

"Yes," cried Kethril, who was growing quite nervous at this sordid tale the gnome wove about his son. Actually, the tale didn't bother him as much as the thought that it might be true. Could Abril be so cunning?

"Why, you ask? It's quite easy to tell. To strike back at those people who made his life hell! When he fed the dumb giant he also did show, the bruises he got from his life in Minroe. Abril shared with the giant his pain and his sorrow, in hopes that the creature would beg steal or borrow, to help his new friend take revenge on his foes. Just a pawn in his plans, but that's how it goes.

"And what buildings suffered in the giant's attack? Why those the boy hated, if you'll only think back. The school where he learned to suffer daily torment, had its door torn in half and it's portico rent. Then the store where he worked till his boss kicked him out, had its roof torn right off then littered about. And his father, innkeeper of the Dancing Roc, abused the poor boy, beat him merely to shock him from going away to pursue a career as a singer of songs that fall light on the ear. For his father he saved the most horrible loss, to see his dear inn turned to rubble and dross.

"The creature crushed everything Abril did ask, and what reward did he get for this terrible task? Once the damage was done, the revenge carried through, his friend shot him dead where he lies before you. And the final insult to both giant and town, is that Abril's the 'hero' who brought the beast down.

"So there you have it, my story's complete. Abril has blood on his hands and damning mud on his feet. I know not what punishment you'll likely mete out, but let justice be served—the truth's been let out!"

All was silence.

Jäg stared at Ekhar, then at Abril, and finally at the crowd who still stood transfixed. It was as if they were mentally chewing on the tale the gnome told. And slowly, one by one, they swallowed it—and they began to laugh.

"That's the most ridiculous thing I've ever heard!" cried Alon M'Greely. "I can see Abril getting in a lucky shot with his bow, but weaving such an intricate plot over imagined slights? The boy's so scatter-brained he's lucky he remembers to put his pants on in the morning!"

The laughter rose and rose. Jäg imagined he even saw the buildings of the town shaking with mirth. Although most of the town had a higher opinion of the lad's intellect than M'Greely did, no one believed that Abril was capable of hatching such a heinous plot. No one, that is, except Ekhar Lorrent—and Abril himself.

It was only after five full minutes of raucous laughter that anyone noticed the boy sitting in the mud. His head buried in his hands, Abril wept. And when every eye was on him, he looked up red eyed and said simply, "It's true."

The entire crowd took a single step backward, and Jäg felt like his head would explode.

"It's true! It happened just the way the gnome said. Everything, everyone in this town holds nothing for me other than painful memories. I'd gone up into the hills to run away when I came across the cyclops. He was my first true friend. But his friendship was nothing compared to my need to be revenged."

Now the lad stood, radiating more menace than his slight frame should have been capable of holding.

"So I figured a plan to get my revenge, and make myself the hero of Minroe at the same time! It would have worked too, if not for that meddling gnome!"

The crowd, who had been standing stock still, suddenly came to angry life. They screamed for Abril's head on a pike—none louder than his own father—and surged toward the lad, bent on getting it themselves.

"Riktus! Help me push these people back!" Jäg yelled

as he grabbed a fallen beam that used to support the roof of the Dancing Roc Inn. The young deputy was already at work, though, pulling Abril away from the clasping mob, then coming back to help Jäg press them back. It was a fight they were destined to lose.

Luckily, the three other deputies chose that moment to come around the bend leading seven horses, twelve mules, four oxen, and a camel toward the fallen giant. The commotion of the crowd spooked the animals such that they all reared up, knocking the hapless deputies off their feet, then sprinting out of town.

"My plow horse! You stole my plow horse!" one member of the mob yelled.

"What are you doing with Sand Treader?" another one cried.

As quickly as it had begun, the riot ended as the citizens all ran off either to rein in their frightened mounts, or to get home as quickly as possible to ensure that they too had not been the victims of looters. Within minutes, the only people left on the streets were Jäg Dubblspeir, his four deputies, Abril Fentloque, and Ekhar Lorrent.

"Take him to the stockade." Jäg said, grabbing Abril's arm and handing it to Riktus. "Quickly . . . before they decide to come back."

The young man hurried off with his prisoner.

"Well, Ekhar, I hope you're satisfied. You took a town in the midst of a celebration and turned it in against itself. The hero of the day is now likely to spend the next year or more of his life in prison, if his friends and family don't decide to hang him instead."

"I know, I know. I've no need for thanks. Just knowing the boy and his deadly pranks will receive justice most swift is all that I need. Now my job here is done, I'll go home with all speed. And tell often the story of what I've seen here today. The lessons I've learned will not soon fade away. 'The Case of the Really Big Corpse' is my true masterpiece. This pride that I feel may never surcease.

"So I bid you farewell, Jäg, my one truest friend. The mystery is solved, this is finally the end."

With that, Ekhar Lorrent dusted off his lapel and headed toward Home, never once looking back to see Jäg Dubblspeir, sword in his hand and murder in his eye, barely being restrained by his three deputies. The only clue available to the gnome, had he cared to observe it, was a slight twitching in his left earlobe.

The Devil and Tertius Wands

Jeff Grubb

There's a common saying that I have recently taken to heart. It's normally the type of phrase you hear among adventurers, freebooters, tax collectors, and other individuals of low moral character. The phrase, if you pardon my language, is "a special place in the Hells."

Normally such a comment would be heard in adventuring dives, usually uttered when a particularly large barbarian, laden heavily with scars, tattoos, and other body modifications, heads for the door. One of the other adventuring types would give a head-nod toward the barbarian's slouched, fur-covered back and say something like, "There's a special place in the Hells for that one." Sometimes they might just say "hell," or something more exact "the Nine Hells," or "the Myriad Pits," or, if they are among the intelligentsia, they would call it "Baator," home of the baatezu. In any event, said adventurer-type would invoke that lower dimension of lava pits, imps, devils (another name for baatezu) and brimstone. His companion would probably grunt in agreement. Or start a tavern-clearing brawl. Such is the way things are done among professional adventurers, as I understand it.

Never would I imagine that my own name, Tertius Wands, would be connected with that dark domain, nor that I would potentially have my own named parcel of abyssal real estate. But such might have been the case, if not for my ever-present and ever-wise companion, the genie Ampratines.

Let me start at the beginning, which in this case is not in the However-Many Hells but in the city of Iriaebor, crown gem of the upper reaches of the River Chionthar. Iriaebor consists of two cities, an upper city built along a narrow ridge overlooking the river, and a lower city bunched up along the sides of that selfsame ridge. The upper city is a tight jumble of important buildings, all stacked next to each other like children's blocks. Space is at a premium in the upper city, and none of the various merchant lords wants to move from their lofty (if crowded) perch into the Lower City.

And for good reason. While the Upper City basks in the relatively warm sun of those climes, the Lower City is usually draped in a miasma of morning fog, noonday drear, and afternoon industrial smoke. Down below are the tin foundries and the ironmongers, the steelworks and the lime bakers, the tanners, hide-men, hat-makers, coach-works, stables, and working offices of the various trading costers, with their attendant collection of stables, wagons, warehouses, hostels, festhalls, and all manner of entertainments for the laborers, teamsters, stevedores, and other haulers. The Lower City, in short, operates under a continual cloud, both figuratively and literally, as far as those of the Upper City are concerned.

At the time I was lodging at the Wandering Wyvern, highly-touted in the guide books for its view. Unfortunately the view is mostly of the aforementioned L.C., as it was situated directly above the tanneries. As a result, I kept to the Wyvern's drawing room for the most part of my stay, and broadened my horizons primarily by reading.

At that time of my life, I was moving eastward, slowly but unyieldingly, seeking to put as much of Faerûn as possible between myself and my home city of Waterdeep.

The wondrous City of Splendors has a special place in my heart, and I would choose to reside there, if not for the presence of my assorted relatives in the Wands family. The fact is that the vast bulk of said relatives are mages. Powerful mages. The most powerful of them is my great-uncle Maskar, who is cause enough to make any young man showing no more interest in spellcraft than he does in killing dragons for a living, head eastward. I had earlier thought that Scornubel was far enough, but recent encounters there convinced me that relocating further inland from the Sword Coast would be a wise decision. At the time when all hell (or hells) was about to break loose, I was comfortably ensconced in the drawing room of the Wandering Wyvern, with my nose in a book.

At this point, I can hear the reader saying to him- or herself, "Aha! some fell tome of magic, wrested from some elder crypt." Actually the book I was reading had been penned the previous spring by an aspiring young author, Allison Rodigar-Glenn, published by Tyme-Waterdeep, and sold by the august offices of Aurora's mail-order catalog. It was a historical mystery book, or "mystoricals" as they were called, and I must confess I could not get enough of them.

"I say, this Miss Rodigar-Glenn pens an excellent tome," I commented to Ampratines, my djinni and personal manservant.

"If you say so, sir," responded the djinni, replacing my expired drink with a fresh one. "I wouldn't know."

For a creature as large as Ampratines was he moved with a silence and a grace that were almost as valuable as his drink serving abilities. He was, of course, the tallest being in the room, tipping the yardstick at ten feet and change. However, he was dressed not in the flowing desert robes so common to his kind, but rather a respectable and immaculate servant's jacket and trousers, with an unfrilled shirt beneath. The most remarkable thing about him—other than being a powerful native of the plane of elemental air, which is remarkable enough—is his head. I swear its larger than most others of his breed, if for no other reason than to contain the masterful brains within. There are greater treasures beneath his broad forehead than beneath all the domes in Calimshan, and his visage is more sage than any vizier's.

However, while Ampratines remains one of the most puissant of the air elementals I have ever met, he has an unfortunate tendency to under appreciate much of the culture of this plane of existence. This marked disdain for the more interesting things in life often creates rifts in our otherwise illustrious relationship.

"No, I'm not jesting," I said, perhaps a little too loudly, for a few heads in the drawing room turned our way. "These mystoricals are filled with derring-do and secrets revealed and all manner of goodly material. The stuff of adventures and heroes, with a fine eye to the details. This current mystorical centers around 'Who Put the Galoshes in Madame Milani's Stew?' "

"Riveting," said Ampratines, who set the remains of my early-afternoon cocktail down on the tray, "I can understand why they are so popular, with such deep subject material."

"Joke not," said I, "This is classic stuff. Miss Rodigar-Glenn is a master at her craft."

"It is my understanding," said Ampi, "that Miss Rodigar-Glenn is really an entire family of halflings living in the basement of the Tyme-Waterdeep building, churning these books out at a clip of one a week."

"Churning? Churning?" I said indignantly. "These books are obviously not churned. They are lovingly crafted and carefully scribed. They speak to the heart of the matter, as it were."

"If you say so, sir," responded Ampi, with that resigned sigh that never fails to infuriate me. It bothers me greatly that such a big-brained djinni as Ampratines would be so small-minded at times. "These books do have one advantage, sir," he said.

"And that is?"

"Why you are reading about them," said the djinni, "You have less of a tendency to go out and do anything dangerous."

I scowled up at the djinni, looking for some sign of humor. As usual, that response was missing from Ampi's stony features. Instead I said, again a trifle too loudly, "I believe another shipment of books is coming in today at Aurora's. You will check this out and retrieve them. Else I might just go out and do something. And don't think I'm not capable of something adventurous."

If it were possible for a djinni to deflate in defeat, Ampi would be leaking air at that moment, "As you wish, sir." And with that he wafted out, as silent as a church patriarch leaving a festhall past midnight.

I don't remember muttering aloud to myself about Ampi's lack of good taste, good sense, and a goodly amount of other attributes, but I probably did so. I tried to fling myself back into the book, but was interrupted by another voice, this one soft and sweet and gentle. A sudden ray of light in the darkened drawing room of the Wyvern.

"Did you mean that?" said the voice, in a tone that was halfway between a crystal bell and a silver dinner chime.

I looked up from Madame Milani's Stew and into wide, open eyes of the purest sky blue. It took a few seconds to recognize that the eyes were set into a heart-shaped face, marked by a button nose hovering above a trembling set of bee-stung lips. The entire assemblage of facial features was framed by curled locks of honey blond hair.

I must have gurgled something along the lines of "excuse me?" though I could not be sure. She repeated, "Did you mean what you said about being a capable adventurer?"

The components of my brain, shattered by her beauty, quickly scrambled to re-combine into a generally operating form. Fortunately, Waterdhavian manners do not require an operating brain, and I was already on my feet, taking the young lady's offered hand and bowing deeply while I re-gathered my wits. My brain was just catching up with my mouth as I said, "Tertius Wands of Waterdeep, capable adventurer and world traveler, at your service."

Actually my brain wanted to say "I said I was capable and adventurous, but not necessarily a capable adventurer." But brains are like that, coming up with the right thing to say right after you've said something completely different.

"Drusilla. Drusilla Vermeer," she said simply, replying with a perfunctory curtsey and almost stumbling in the process. At once I leaned forward to steady her, and caught the scent of honeysuckle in bloom. She seemed faint and I walked her to the chair facing mine. The ultimate gentleman, I offered her my untouched drink. She sniffed at the mixture (one of Ampi's specialties), then waved it aside with a delicate hand.

"Sorry, so sorry," she said, even the wrinkle of concern that lined her eyes making her all the more beautiful. "I shouldn't bother you, really, but I need a capable adventurer for a matter of some delicacy."

I returned to my seat and nodded, then half-turned to order Ampi for some hot tea or some other suitable nostrum. But of course the djinni had already left for my new shipment of books, so I turned back to the young and beautiful Drusilla.

"I fear I've done a terrible, terrible thing," she said, "And I need someone to help me."

"There, there," said I, unsure of what the terrible thing was, but confident that it would be no more than a lost pet or a misplaced locket.

"My family is one of the investing households that provides capital for the various traders. I was entrusted with a family keepsake, an amber box containing an heirloom belonging to my great, great grandmother." She pulled out a lace handkerchief at this point and held it to her lips. I wondered if she was going to go to pieces entirely. In a small voice she said, "Its about three inches on a side, like a cube. I'm afraid I've lost it."

I nodded, and realized I was nodding altogether too much, "How did you lose—"

"I was such a fool!" she sobbed, "I was careless. I shouldn't have trusted . . ." She snuffled again, and even her snuffling was musical and sweet. "The fact remains that I lost it, and it is my responsibility to get the box back. It is very important!" She buried her lovely face in the handkerchief.

"So," I said, reprising the situation so far. "You've lost the family thingummy, an amber box. You need to find the box, and need a capable adventurer to retrieve it." This was the sort of thing the heroes of Miss Rodigar-Glenn would say. Repeating exactly what someone has just told you in hopes of gaining more information.

"Then you'll help?" she said, blinking back the tears at me. Not quite the response I had anticipated.

Despite myself, I fell back on an earlier mannerism and merely nodded. Her face blossomed in a flower of relief and she warbled sweetly, "I knew I had chosen the right man."

She made to rise, and I fought to regain control of the conversation. "This box, I have to say . . . if you lost it, we'll have to spend a long time looking for it."

"Oh, I know where it is," she said brightly, canting her head to one side as if to reassure me. "It's in the hands of a terrible person. I'll need you to retrieve it from him."

And then she smiled and gave me his name.

* * * * *

" 'Big Ugly,' " said Ampratines later as I recounted the story to him. "Not the most reassuring of appellations."

"He's a crime lord, apparently, in the Lower City," I countered, trying to determine which set of trousers was appropriate for a meeting with the aforementioned Mr. Ugly. "Crime lords are not supposed to have reassuring names. The truly evil ones put a lot of X's and Z's in them.

Sort of like a verbal 'beware of dragon,' sign, or 'no peddlers.'"

"Indeed," said the djinni, holding out a dependable set of leather riding pants. I shook my head and chose instead my red satin trousers. I would send my own message to the crime lord, I thought, that we Wands are both stylish and not to be trifled with.

I hopped into the trousers while continuing, "Said B.U. operates a tavern as a front for his various nefarious operations, a place called the Burrows. That's where I'm going to meet him."

"And this Master Ugly stole the amber box?" said the genie.

"Unclear but likely," I said, thinking back about what Drusilla had said specifically. "She said that she had lost it and this Ugly fellow had glommed onto it, and she wants it back. Money is no object, but this Ugly has refused to budge. I'm supposed to place the offer on the table and, as they say in the parlance, 'put the lean' on him."

"And a lean fellow you are," said Ampi without the merest of smiles. "And I suppose you'll want me to attend you in this madcap mystorical escapade?"

I blinked at the genie and fastened the clasp of my cape (the dark one with the red satin lining that matched the pants). I had not thought about it one way or another, but had merely assumed that Ampratines would be tagging along. Still, there was something in the genie's tone that bothered me, as if this were some adventure he'd rather watch from a safe but discrete distance.

"If you're not too busy," I said simply, the frost in my voice wilting the nearby potted ferns.

Ampratines merely nodded and we set out. Hiring a carriage outside the inn, we started the long descent into the Lower City. Ampi was silent for most of the trip, apparently brooding in thought. Only when we were deposited at the Burrows, a small tavern built into the hillside itself, did he speak up.

"I'm afraid I cannot accompany you," he said, in a matter-of-fact manner.

"I say," I responded, "If this is about your not liking my choice of reading materials, I . . ."

But the genie was already shaking his head, and motioned toward the door of the Burrows. There was an ornate squiggle of pounded brass over the door, surrounded by arcane markings. The markings covered the entire frame of the doorway, and, I noted in the flickering street-lamps, extended along the entire building. It looked like unruly scribes had targeted the tavern's outer walls as an impromptu scriptorium.

"Mystic wards," he said simply, "Magical symbols that keep creatures from other dimensions at bay. Master Ugly must be very worried about such beings, from the looks of things. With these wards in place, the tavern is proof against all manner of demons, devils, devae, archons, undead, elementals, efreet . . ."

". . . and djinn," I finished.

The tall genie gave a small shrug which he turned into a bow of admission. "I cannot enter. Indeed, I must confess that this many wards in one place give me a rather intense headache."

"Very well," I said, trying to imagine Ampi with a ripper of a hangover, "You'll just have to keep an eye out on the street then. That happens in the books all the time, anyway. One of the investigators goes in, while the other one stays outside 'riding crossbow,' as it were. Do you have a crossbow on you?"

"I neglected to pack one," said the djinni, "But I could scare one up if you thought it necessary."

I waved off the suggestion, "It matters little. Stay out here and keep your orbs glued to the building. If anyone suddenly leaves I want you to be ready."

"As you wish," said Ampi, again with a small bow. He took two steps backward and disappeared among the shadows of the buildings directly across from the tavern.

I straightened my cape and climbed the six low stairs

leading to the door in two large strides. I took a deep breath and plunged into the bar.

Now I had been in taverns from Waterdeep to Iriaebor, oftimes wearing something similar to my red satin cape and trousers. Usually, upon entering, there is a brief lull in the conversation as some of the resident bar flies check out the newcomer, and, once ascertaining that the new individual meant no immediate threat, turn back to their ales.

Not this time. The noise level dropped to an imperceptible level. One moment it was a typical tavern noise, the next it was dead silence. The last time I had witnessed something like this was when cousin Halian did his impression of grand-uncle Maskar while the old goat had suddenly appeared, unseen, behind him.

In this case, however, it was my own arrival that had squelched the conversations. I took the opportunity to look around. If the outer walls were decked with mystical wards, the inner walls were positively festooned with arcane designs. No wonder Ampi was getting headaches, I thought. The crisscrossing lines and whirls were enough to give anyone without sufficient alcohol in their system a splitting migraine, and was probably an inducement for those within to keep drinking.

But it was the patrons that were the clue to the sudden silence. There were about thirty of them altogether—a trio of halflings on high stools alongside the bar, a gaggle of gnomes plotting in a booth, a morose-looking dark elf (male) at the end of the bar, and a clutch of dwarves playing cards in the far corner. A pair of large, scaly ogres who apparently did the heavy lifting, and who were converging on my location at flank speed.

I put my finger on the problem at once. There were no humans present. Or to be more correct, there were no humans other than myself.

"You're in the wrong place," said the slightly taller of the two ogres, his words lisping around his oversized lower fangs.

I looked the ogres up and down (more up than down), and thought what the mystorical heroes would do in such a situation. I decided to grab the conversational bull by the horns and responded, "This is the Burrows, is it not?"

The ogre blinked, apparently unused to such a direct approach. He nodded.

"And there is someone named Big Ugly in charge around here?" I continued, arching an eyebrow most archly.

Another nod.

"Then I am in the right place," I said, stepping down toward the bar. "Please inform Mr. Ugly that Master Tertius Wands, of the Wands of Waterdeep, is present and wishes to converse with him."

All thirty sets of nonhuman eyes followed me as I strode to the bar (at the far end from the drow), pulled out a stool, and sat down. Or at least tried to sit down.

The stool disappeared beneath me, snatched by one of the ogres. The other one, the slightly taller one, simultaneously grabbed me by the collar and breathed hotly in my ear, "this way." He propelled me toward a door in the back of the tavern, keeping me slightly above the ground so I could only graze the floorboards with my flailing toes.

Beyond the door lay darkness. Most nonhumans have some form of ultra-, infra-, or arcano-vision that allows them to see in the dark. Unfortunately that gift was not extended to the human race, so I merely strained my eyes against the ebon blackness. I was set down and found a chair in the darkness.

There was movement about me in the dark, followed by a sharp clicking noise. Then there was light, all of it funneled in my direction. I held up a hand against the brightness, and was vaguely aware that the two ogres were now flanking me.

"Who are you?" said a voice behind the light. I could not see anything other that a blaze of whiteness, but the voice came from above the light source.

"Ter—" I said, my voice breaking, "Tertius Wands of

Waterdeep. I'm looking for the one called Big Ugly."

"Why do you seek him?" said the voice.

I shifted in my seat. I was the one supposed to be asking the tough questions. "Ugly, er, Mister Ugly has something in his possession that I am interested in." I shut up at this point. In the mystoricals, the hero would always give away as much as he had to, but no more.

I was rewarded with another sound I had not heard before, a sound of soft whispers behind the light. Big Ugly had advisors, it seemed. The voice said aloud, "What is the item in question?"

"A box. Amber. About so big by so big," I motioned with my hands and immediately the ogres on either side of me tensed. "Belongs to a woman. She wants it back. She'll pay a finder's fee for it. Very generous one, indeed."

I pulled out a slip of paper, on which I had written Drusilla's offer. It seemed high to me for even an heirloom, but people are funny that way about family possessions. One of the ogres snatched the paper out of my grasp and took it to behind the light.

More silence and whispering. Then the voice said, "Come again in two nights time. Now go."

"Now wait just a moment," I said, trying to rise as I spoke. Two large ogrish paws clamped down, one per shoulder, and I was lifted again from my perch. The light was doused again and I was suddenly moving quickly through the main room of the tavern as fast as ogres could run.

A gnome at the front door flung it open as our party approached it. The ogres stopped but I did not. They released their grips and I was flung out into the night air.

Or rather, flung through the night air and into the arms of Ampratines, who manifested himself while I was mere inches from the cobblestones.

"Unsuccessful?" he said simply, helping me to my feet.

"A small setback," I responded, readjusting my tunic where the ogres had left small claw tears. "They as good as admitted they had it, and that I should come back in two days time. The lovely Drusilla should be pleased when I give her that news. At least its a start."

* * * * *

"This is horrible," said the lovely Drusilla when I gave her the news. She had been waiting for us at the Wyvern. She seemed a little nervous around Ampi, which was odd because the djinni normally had the ability to remain unobtrusive. "Two days is far too late."

"I don't see why," I said simply, "It will probably take a few days for them to pull it out of whatever file drawer they've parked it away in."

"Or to appraise the item and solicit competing bids," said Ampi softly. Drusilla started at the sound of his voice. Then she nodded and put the kerchief to her soft lips again.

I looked up at the genie, "How do you figure that?"

"While I was outside watching the tavern, I noticed that a number of individuals entered by the front door. Elves, dwarves, and gnomes, with an occasional orc or two."

"No humans," I said, agreeing, "The Burrows does not cater to that clientele."

"No halflings, either," said the genie, "even though there were apparently halflings within the bar. I noticed that they used another entrance."

"So they used a shorter door," I said, then stopped. "No, then dwarves and gnomes would use that other door as well. Let's say that this 'other door' was the employees entrance, correct?"

Drusilla looked from one of us to the other, totally out of the loop.

"I'm sorry, I don't understand," she squeaked. It was a very sweet squeak.

"Halflings run the Burrows, which makes sense," I said. "Big Ugly is a shadowy figure whose face is unseen. Indeed, there was a lot of whispering going on while I talked to him. Therefore, Big Ugly is probably a halfling. Or a group of halflings."

"Much like Miss Rodigar-Glenn of Waterdeep," said Ampi. I generously ignored the dig.

"But if this Big Ugly is a halfling," she said. "Why is that a problem?"

"Consider," said the genie, "A halfling has something you want. You tell them you want it. What do they do?"

I thought for a moment, then leaned forward and put my head in my hands, "They'll try to get as much as possible for it."

"They know its valuable?" said Drusilla, her voice rising a half-octave as she said it.

"They know it is valuable to you," said Ampi levelly, "That is all they need to know. The next day will be occupied with them sending out the word and soliciting other bids. Only if they do not get a better offer will they sell it to you in two days time."

"Oh." hiccuped Drusilla, "Oh, its going to be horrible. Daddy will find out I lost the box and that will be the end of everything."

"Perhaps if you could tell us what is in the box. . . ." began Ampratines, but just the thought of Daddy's disappointment set the lovely Drusilla on a longer crying jag. I shot the genie a fell look and he merely nodded and retreated to the hallway. After about five minutes of assuring the girl that everything would be all right and promising to help her recover the box, I sent her out as well. The genie reappeared as she vanished down the hallway.

"If I might suggest—" he began.

"You may not," I snapped, "I think you've worried that poor girl enough."

"Sir, that poor girl is not being entirely honest with you," said the djinni.

"Anything in particular?" I asked. Drusilla had left her kerchief on the drawing table. I picked it up and it smelled of salt and honeysuckle.

"She has a nasty tendency to break down in tears whenever asked a direct question," said the genie. "The smartest move in this particular situation would be to retire from the field in good order and leave her and her family to recover the amber box on their own. Perhaps we might suggest they hire a halfling or gnome to place a bid on her behalf."

I waved the genie's suggestions down. "Objections duly noted and ignored," I said. "No mystorical hero would abandon a woman in need."

Ampi sighed, one of those great genie sighs that threatened to suck all the air out of the room. "As you wish," he said at last, "What will you be doing next?"

"I'm thinking about keeping a watch on the place," I said. "See who goes in and out. Then we'll know who we're bidding against. Yes, that's it."

We returned once more to the Burrows, after I had changed clothes. This time I chose sturdy leather trousers and a dark shirt. I abandoned the cape for a dark cloak and an oversized black hat with a huge brim to mask my features.

We found a bench across the street from the Burrows, and set up shop there. Ampi took first watch while I retreated under my oversized hat to catch a few winks.

The few winks turned into a full night's sleep, during which nothing much happened. When I awoke the morning sun was making its best attempt to pierce the smoky haze of the Lower City, and Ampi was still standing beside the bench.

"Anything?" I said.

"A lot of non-humans," said Ampi briefly, as if I had picked up a conversational thread abandoned only a few moments before. "Mostly drinkers and revelers. A lot of halflings through the side door. Three wizards, all of whom were elves. A half-orc barbarian. A couple human merchants, who were turned away at the door. A priest of Gond with three gnomes. Only the gnomes were admitted, then left a few minutes later. A dwarf dressed up as a pasha of Calimshan. A dark elf that might have been a priestess of Loviatar. I could not be sure. All stayed a few moments, then left."

"Interesting," I said, "Conclusions?"

"They are the rival bidders solicited by Big Ugly," said the genie. "The word is being spread and these are early buyers. They are being shown the merchandise, then they leave. Some will undoubtedly be back."

"No humans," I noted.

"No humans," agreed Ampi.

"Right then," I said. "We keep an eye on the place at least until noon. Then we meet the fair Drusilla for lunch and figure out what she wants to bid for her heirloom."

Ampratines was silent at the suggestion, so I prompted, "Yes?"

"With your permission," said the genie, "I would like to investigate in another direction. I know a marid, another genie, in contact with a local sage named Prespos, and I would like to seek that sage's advice as to this situation. Discretely, of course."

I thought about the request for a moment, then nodded. Ampi faded from view immediately, and I sat down again on the bench, waiting for the world to unfold before me.

Morning in the Lower City is a clamorous affair, and the first of the coster caravans were already clattering through the streets. The last of the night wagons were long gone at this hour, replaced by cargo haulers and teamsters, sprinkled with carts of the hand-, dog-, and pony- varieties. And of course all manner of luggers, toters, handlers, and haulers and various day laborers. I thought from my perch I would be able to observe without being observed.

I was wrong. After about half an hour a shadow moved alongside my left. I did not turn my head toward it, but instead dipped my head forward, trying to keep as much of the broad-brimmed hat between me and the new arrival as possible. For all I knew it could be one of the city guard, seeking to roust a malingerer from the main thoroughfares. Or worse yet, a particularly strong ogre. The Burrows was closed at this hour, and there was no sign of life either from the front door or the halfling door to the side. Perhaps, I thought at the time, it would be best to move back to the Wyvern for an early start at lunch.

The shadow's owner, in a wheezing, nasal voice, said, "So, you've seen anything interesting?"

Despite myself, I raised my head slightly, and was rewarded with a nasal laugh that sounded like migrating geese. My cheeks reddening with embarrassment, I looked at the individual addressing me.

He wasn't much to look at. A neat set of leggings and a nondescript tunic, topped with a vest of moderately valuable brocade. A trim, balding head. His eyes, however, were overlarge, made almost monstrous when viewed through his thick spectacles. The latter were like sheets of block crystal and continually slid down his nose. When he talked they would slide further down, necessitating he push them back with a finger. He seemed human, but at best would reach up to my shoulder.

"I said," repeated the little man with the thick lenses. "See anything interesting?"

"Sorry," I tried. "Not from around here."

"Indeed you aren't," said the short man. "Otherwise you'd know that while that outfit was suitable for nighttime surveillance, you stick out like a sore thumb with the light of day."

I scowled at him. In the mystoricals this would have the effect of melting him where he stood, and forcing him to leave me alone. Instead the short human smiled.

"You were watching the Burrows," he said. "I was watching you. Oh, and your tall companion as well, but he's gone. Word has already gone out that the place will be closed for tonight. Private business with Big Ugly. And I think we both know what that means."

I tried scowling again, but the short human remained

unmeltable. "Who are you?" I said at last.

"Ah," he said, as if rewarded with my attention, "a response. The first step to a conversation, and from that a lasting relationship. Its always so horrible when no one wants to talk to you."

"Who . . . ?" I began again, but the man waved me silent.

"I heard you the first time," he said with a smile. "I was just enjoying the moment. Call me a collector. A hunter of rare and unique items. Let's say that it has reached my ears that there is a certain item, such as an amber box, that is currently in the possession of the owner of that establishment. And let's say that the owner does not like to deal with individuals such as I."

He meant human. Ampi had mentioned that several humans had been turned away. They were not welcome. I waved for him to continue.

"As a collector," he said, "I would be more than eager to lay my hands on that box and its contents. And I thought that you might be willing to help me."

"I'm not . . ." I started, but then paused. "I don't know what you're talking about."

"Hmmmm, yes," said the little collector, "I don't think you do, at that. I assumed that you were working for some accumulator of curios or an enterprising hedge mage. But I think you're involved deeper. You want the amber box as well, for what it is."

"Only to return it to its true owner," I said hotly.

"Ah!" the small man spread his hands wide. "And here I am before you, the true owner."

"No, you're not," I exclaimed, feeling my face burn from more than embarrassment. "The true owner never mentioned you. I don't think she ever would."

The collector put a finger to his lips and hummed. "A 'she,' is it? Well, I can think of one 'she' in particular, and your answer is, while she was an owner, she is not the true owner. The rightful owner. The legal owner. She traded it away, long ago. You understand that?"

I said nothing, and the small man continued, "Its good to know she's in the hunt, at least. Do me a favor, young man. You look like a reasonable individual. And when this is all over and done with you might find an offer I have to be very appealing. But for the moment . . ."

He fished around inside his tunic for a moment, then pulled out a thin black wand. "I suspect you'll want to get in for the bidding tonight, without being noticed, and without the price being driven up for your human appearance. This will let you get past the bouncers. Here, take it. I offer it free and without strings."

Despite myself, I reached out and took the wand. It had an oily touch to it, and almost seemed to want to squirm out of my grasp.

The collector smiled, "There, that wasn't so bad, was it?" and touched his forehead by way of salutation, turned smartly on his heels, and headed off. I watched him until he disappeared from sight. Then, regarding the cold, empty building of the Burrows, I walked two blocks over, hailed a carriage, and returned to the Wyvern.

Drusilla did not show up for lunch as promised, which added to my consternation. I wanted to ask her who the little man was and exactly what the box was all about. As it was, the luncheon hour arrived and passed without so much as a note from her. After spending most of the previous evening on a cold bench, I was in no mood to wait any longer than I had to. I was halfway through the shell-fish course—Prawns du Chionthar—when there was the slightest waft of air over my left shoulder. Long experience told me who had arrived and I did not even look up from my crustacean.

"She has not shown up," I said simply.

"I did not think she would," said Ampi calmly. "The idea that a simple acquisition would turn into an auction has probably upset her. She is probably making other plans to acquire the box even as we speak."

I frowned at my prawn. I didn't want to believe that Drusilla would abandon me so easily. "Perhaps she is in trouble herself. Waylaid by bandits or short collectors or something."

Ampi drifted slowly into my line of sight. His face was drawn with concern. Say whatever else you want about genies, when they are concerned you know they are concerned. Still, he would not voice them until I asked. "How was your research?"

The djinni nodded slightly and said, "Productive, but I fear expensive. The sage Prespos could teach the dao something about hard negotiations. What I discovered was of interest, however."

"And that is?"

"The Vermeers were an Iriaebor household," said the djinni. "But their forte was more magic than money. They were a household of spellcasters."

I nearly choked on my shellfish. "Like the Wands?" I managed, suddenly having visions of the patriarch of the Vermeer clan showing up in my bedroom late in the evening.

"Similar, but not exact," said the genie. "The biggest difference being that the last of the line died out almost a hundred years ago. If the girl Drusilla is a member of that clan. . . ."

" 'Daddy' must be very ancient indeed."

"You do not seem surprised."

"Hardly," said I. "If one thing these mystoricals prepare you for it's that the heroine rarely tells the truth the first time out. Indeed, most of the heroes ignore whatever the heroine says until after the third attempt on his life. Most likely some far flung fragment of the family trying to regain its insignia and ancestral lands. Or perhaps Vermeer was a name she pulled out of an old book, as a cover."

My logic was irrefutable, for Ampratines remained silent, if only for a moment, before resuming the argument "If you say so, sir. However, in the light of this, I would recommend we reconsider the situation and our employment with the mysterious lady."

I shook my head and motioned with a prawn claw, "No. In the stories, whenever a hero gives his word, he lives by it. It doesn't matter if the heroine is not what she says she is. Often, she's better."

"I cannot dissuade you?" said the djinni.

"Not a whit." I pulled out the black wand, "What do you make of this?"

The genie took the thin black rod from my hand. He had a look on his face akin to revulsion. "Unpleasant material. Not from around here, as you would say." He held it up to a light, then handed it back. "It is a spell rod. Arcane device, sometimes used in the south. You break it to release the spell within. The runes say that the spell can alter your appearance. The illusion would last until you were struck or choose to drop the charade. Where did you get it?"

"Someone with a mutual interest," I replied, "Someone who thinks I should get into the auction tonight. And yes, there will be an auction tonight."

The genie's face creased with concern again. "Someone?"

"A collector, who argues a separate claim on the box," I said, holding up the claw again. "I know, I should not trust him either, but I think the first order of business is to get a hold of the box. Then we can sort everything out."

A deep sigh, again. "As you wish, sir."

* * * * *

That evening, after breaking open the wand, I turned to Ampi and said, "How do I look?"

The genie frowned, canted his head to one side, and asked, "Something's wrong."

"Wrong? How can anything be wrong?" I turned back to the mirror. Looking out was a rather dapper-looking dark elf in my clothes. My hair was ghost white, and my skin the color of night, a purple verging on ultraviolet. I smiled and primped for a moment.

"I think its the smile," said the genie at last.

"Too flashy?" I asked.

"Too present," replied Ampratines. "I can't think of any drow smiling, unless the situation dealt with accidental dismemberment. Try to frown."

I attempted a scowl.

"Better, but not quite," said Ampi. "You don't look angry, only petulant. Try to look more tragic. More angst-ridden."

I scowled harder.

Ampi let out a sigh, "I suppose that's the best we can do. Here, take these." He handed me several long strips of white cloth.

I gave the genie a quizzical look and he explained, "The drow often communicate by a language of signs. Should you be challenged on the matter, you can complain you have been wounded and unable to respond."

I looked at the bandages, and took them from him. At least he had stopped trying to convince me to abandon Drusilla and was trying to be constructive. As I wound the bandages around my wrists and palms, he continued. "I'll summon a carriage. I would keep the hood of my cloak up while in the Wyvern, though. I don't think the Upper City gets much in the way of underground conqueror races and might not appreciate your continence, and I will not be there to aid you."

I blinked at the genie. "You aren't coming? I was looking for someone to ride crossbow on this adventure. Just in case things go wrong."

"I will be along presently," said the genie. "I asked the sage Prespos for a particular item, and will be along myself as soon as I retrieve it."

And with that I was off for the L.C. again, bundled in the back of the carriage, my face hidden beneath a voluminous cloak. The illusion had provided the cloak, along with a pair of ridiculously curved long swords. The latter were extremely dashing, but made sitting properly impossible. I ended up sprawling across the back of carriage, wondering if this inability to sit was what made dark elves so surly.

Night had fallen in the Lower City, which meant the gray of the day had surrendered at last to the smoky blackness of the evening. There was a halfling guard posted outside the Burrows this time, vetting the various individuals. Traditional revelers and regulars were being turned away at the door, along with a few angry humans. I waited my turn in the queue, practicing my scowling. Being made to wait helped my acting immeasurably.

Finally the party ahead of me was turned aside, a group of dwarf laborers bitterly disappointed that their evening game of "toss-the-darts-at-the-elves" had been interrupted. The halfling at the door scowled at me and said, "Private party tonight."

"I know," I said, trying to out scowl him. "There is an item up for sale. I wish to be included in that bidding."

"Name?"

My mind went, for a tragic moment, blank.

"Ziixxxita" I snarled at last, trying to string as many Z's and X's together as possible.

"How do you spell that?" he asked.

"You spell it how it sounds," I said, spreading my cloak and resting my hands on the hilts of the blades.

The halfling looked at the curved blades, then at my face again. Then he nodded toward the door. I gave the small humanoid a sullen snarl and passed within.

I was a late arrival. The half-orc barbarian was there, along with the fancy-dressed southern dwarf and a drow woman dressed in a low-cut gown that denied gravity, morality, and several local zoning ordinances. There were no less than seven mages of various nonhuman types in the room, and a few creatures that were wrapped in thick cloaks, species unknown.

Most of the tables had been cleared to the sides of the room and the chairs organized in a rough line facing the bar. A buffet table had been thoughtfully set up at the opposite end. As I entered one of the halflings was standing on the bar, thundering a large stave against the top and calling for order.

As I scanned the room my eyes locked on those of the drow woman. She looked as imperious as drow women were reported to be, but was not fully a drow matriarch. A drow debutante, then, but still one that could expose my masquerade.

She raised a hand, and her fingers drew intricate patterns in the air. I froze for a moment, suspecting a spell, but realized immediately that she was greeting me in her unknown language. I raised my bandaged flippers and gave the best dourful look I could manage. She in turn gave me a frosty glare, but nodded.

I exhaled slowly, mentally thanking both the gods and Ampi, and took a seat on the far side of the room from the drow woman. I did not trust my disguise against a true native of the Underdark, and did not wish to press my luck. I ended up next to the half-orc.

"Whaddya bid onnit?" said the half-orc, without preamble or greeting.

I thought for a moment. Actually, if the bidding brushed the crystal sphere, I was planning on just noting who had bought the box and approaching them later. Would be better than dealing with halflings. Still, a reply was called for. "Whatever it takes," I said, and scowled deeper.

The half-orc gave a deep chuckle. "Yagreed. Whativer i'takes," He pulled a barbed dagger. "Just don' git'n m'way, eh?"

"Take your seats," said the halfling. As our motley mob took our places, he thumped his staff thrice more and the show got on the road.

The back door swung open and a procession emerged: one of the ogres, a pair of halfling guards with spears, a well-dressed halfling with a serving dish, two more halfling guards, and the last ogre. Any of the halflings could be Big Ugly. Or all of them.

The well-dressed halfling climbed up behind the bar and set the serving dish on it. The two ogres took up positions on either side, also behind the bar. The halflings guarded the doors. The halfling with the staff said, "We are the representatives of the owner of this establishment, known to the humans as Big Ugly. We thank you for coming on short notice. A foolish fop of a human has approached us in regards to an item that we have in our possession. While we wish to be rid of it, we want to give our non-human brethren"—and with this he waved a small paw at the assemblage—"the opportunity to bid on it first. Many of you have had the chance to examine the item in question, though not all. Therefore, there will be a brief examination session before we begin to accept bids."

The halfling with the serving dish lifted the lid and the assembled group milled forward in roughly two adjacent lines down the center of the room. I could not see the box itself from the back of the pack, but the group was generally orderly, like mourners at a funeral. Each paid their respects and then returned to their seats.

I let the half-orc pass ahead of me, but ended up alongside the drow woman. "Where are you from?" she said with a cold smile. She was looking ahead, but her question was obviously for me.

I mumbled something indistinct, then said, "Waterdeep," at last.

"Skullport, you mean, the city beneath the city?" she nodded, "I've heard of it but I've never been. Who are you?"

"I'll tell if you will," It was almost our turn up to the box.

The drow looked at me, and it was a curious look. Apparently drow males were not so forward, but she said "Fair enough. I am Marinanta, loyal follower of the Demiurge of Despair, faithful to the Maiden of Pain. And you?"

"Ziixxxita," I muttered, keeping to my original story. Then the mage and the half-orc in front of us parted and I got my first look at the box.

It made me think of Drusilla immediately. It had that same sort of purity, a radiance that seemed to embody the young woman. It was a cube of translucent yellow gold, only about three inches on a side. The faces were incised with numerous carvings and mystic wards, similar to the walls of the Burrows themselves. I daresay that this little number would give Ampi a nasty head-pain as well. There was no obvious latch or hinges. Within the translucent box, something indeterminate seemed to glow of its own power.

In a moment I knew why Drusilla wanted the box, or at least thought I knew. It was one of the most splendid things I had seen in my life. I also knew in a moment that I could not afford what the others would bid on this.

I looked up at the drow in the low-cut gown next to me, expecting to see in her eyes the same look of wonder and appreciation. Instead, I saw a set of narrowed eyes that pierced me to the core.

"Ziixxxita is a woman's name," she hissed, "Who are you, really?"

Had I been thinking about my mystoricals I could have toughed it out, have thought of some glib explanation, but in truth I had been wowsered by the beauty of the box. I did the one thing a drow never should do. I smiled.

Her eyes flew open in recognition immediately. "You're not a drow," she snarled. Louder, she shouted, "We have an impostor among us!"

I spun on my heel immediately, looking at the shocked faces of the others. "We have an impostor!" I agreed loudly, "And that's him!" I pointed at the back of the half-orc barbarian, who was at the moment ensconced at the buffet table.

I had chosen a perfect target, if only because the barbarian had at the moment a mouth full of roast beef and could not defend himself verbally. Instead he dropped his plate and reached for his blades, which was as good as an admission of guilt. Both ogres vaulted the bar, while around the room there was the sudden, deadly whisper of blades, wands, and spellcasting materials being pulled from sheaths, holders, and pockets.

The drow woman shouted, "No, not him, the other drow!" But by that time I made my move. As everyone was turning toward the half-orc, I lunged forward and grabbed the amber box. The artifact felt warm to the touch, and that warmth comforted me to the core. I felt a need to protect it, to take it back to Drusilla.

There was an explosion from the side of the buffet table as one of the mages decided that the half-orc was guilty of something, if not of being an impostor. That half of the room was bathed in a shining radiance, followed by the smell of singed orc-flesh and the cries of temporarily blinded non-human mages. By the time the drow woman had shouted her correction, I was already halfway to the door. I intended to vault the two halfling guards and make my escape into the night.

That was the intention. Instead I found an overturned chair and got tangled in its legs. With a shout I pitched forward and downward, still clutching the box in my bandaged hands.

The fall probably saved my life. Over my head there were a scattering of lightning shards, fire bolts, and other magical missiles. The ward-covered walls glowed as they were infused by the energies, then began to smoke as the mystic wards themselves were overloaded by the assault.

I picked myself up as everyone was reloading and charged for the door. The two now slightly-singed ogres had reversed direction and were bearing down on me, hammerlike fists raised in assault.

The first time I fell was by accident. Now I did it on purpose, tossing myself behind an overturned table. The ogre fists slammed into the wall behind me. Then I was up again, making for the door as ogre curses berated my back.

The haft-end of a spear swung upward from out of nowhere and caught me in the face. My brain would have recognized it as belonging to one of the halfling guards, and would have realized that was why halflings would carry spears. The better to swat tall thieves with. Instead my brain was concentrating on getting back off the floor. If it had any spare room from that task, said brain would note that I had regained my true Tertius form.

My spinning sight came to rest to reveal an ugly tableaux. Five angry halflings. Two ogres with broken hands. An enraged female dark elf. A badly burned but still standing half-orc. And all manner of non-human mages. None of whom seemed particularly happy with me at the moment.

I was dimly aware of the fact that I still held the box, and stumbled to my feet. I held the box high, intending to threaten to smash it unless they let me leave.

I intended to make the threat, really, but that was when the wall collapsed.

The wall had been spell-smashed and ogre-bashed, and now was crumbling of its own accord. Long cracks crawled up the remains of the masonry, and the plaster began to give way under the damage it had suffered. There was a moment of silence, then the entire west half of the building collapsed with a roar, and the night wind blew the dust into the Burrows.

Something else came in with the dust. Something tall and proud and very, very dangerous. At first I thought I recognized the form, but convinced myself I was just confused by the sudden disappearance of the wall. Then I cleared the dust from my eyes and saw that it was indeed Drusilla who glided into the room.

Indeed it was Drusilla, if Drusilla had grown another foot, had her back stiffened, and lived through several bad wars. Her clear eyes were now filled with fire, and her button nose and bee-stung lips were twisted in a snarl. Her golden locks of hair extended in all directions, as if she had just shaken hands with a lightning bolt.

Her voice was no longer quiet, but still in perfect pitch as she said, "I have come for my property. Your wards no longer protect you. Give me what is mine!"

One of the elven mages choked out the first two words of a spell. Drusilla barked out a few unhuman words and the entire assemblage was treated to the sight of an elven skeleton, standing for a moment after the flesh had been blasted off. I thought of Ampi's warning about the Vermeers being magicians and inwardly groaned. Drusilla might be of that family after all. I noted that she was not taller, but rather floated a foot above the debris.

The disintegration of the elven mage was enough to convince most of the other guests, and the halflings as well, to abandon the entire business. They fled through both doors and the new aperture in the wall. Drusilla was more than willing to let them go. Instead she turned to me and snarled, "Fool!"

Not the best of greetings, I must admit. I said, "We missed you for lunch. We were worried. Well, I was, anyway."

Sparks seemed to glow from Drusilla's eyes, and flames danced from her fingertips. "If you had not bumbled so badly, I would have regained the amber box quietly. Now I must take it. Give it to me."

I nodded and was about to hold it out. "Don't do it!" said a nasal voice from the doorway. "You are protected from her as long as you hold it. Give it up and she will kill you."

The small human, the collector from earlier in the day, stepped through the gap in the wall as well. Drusilla gasped and stepped backward, toward the remains of the buffet table, "Go away!" She snarled. "This isn't for you."

"I'm afraid it is," said the short, balding human. "And we both know it."

"Hold on," I said, fed up with the smoke, noise, and danger. I held the box out. "What's in here that's so important?" I reached to try to pry the box open.

Drusilla screamed and flung herself at me. I had the good sense not to drop the box, but instead clutched it to my breast like a precious talisman and stood my ground. Drusilla hovered before me, her face slightly above mine. "You promised to recover it," she said, "to give it to me. What about your promise?"

"A promise made under false pretenses is not binding," said the small human calmly, as if he conducted all his business dealings in a ruined bar with a floating, frightening looking woman. "Don't hide behind that."

"You're the one hiding, Collector," snapped Drusilla, floating a few paces back and turning toward to the short human. "Why not show your true self?"

The small man stared at the floating woman for a moment, then gave a thin smile and nodded. "As you wish," he said, and as he spoke the words he began to grow.

The Collector's skin turned reddish and erupted with ridges of black. His hands and arms elongated, ending in yellowish talons. The nondescript face grew fangs, and horns sprouted from his forehead. There was a tearing noise as ebon bat wings sprouted from his back. Ridiculously, the thin glasses remained perched on his broad nose, making his eyes look like great yellowish platters.

"Look at him!" cried Drusilla, "Look at what wants the box!"

"A Baatezu!" I shouted, aware that my voice cracked as I spoke, and for the moment not caring.

"A Devil, if you please," said the creature in the same nasal tone as before, "I don't stand on ceremony, and its a much clearer, simpler, and concise word. And speaking of hiding, you haven't told your minion here what was in the box, have you, Drusilla?"

The floating woman hissed and retreated a few paces. The devil pulled up the wreckage of a chair and sat down. "You see, young mortal, 'Collector' is not a hobby, or even much of a name. Its more of a job description. It is my task to collect on old debts, regardless of age. This one has been outstanding for over a hundred years."

I clutched the box to my chest and could only nod, A hundred years? Then Drusilla was more than the descendant of magicians. She was probably one of the original Vermeers herself.

"Feel the warmth of the box, mortal?" said the Collector. "That is Drusilla Vermeer's soul. She traded it away years and years ago, but hid it before we could collect. She studied necromancy in order to keep herself alive until such a time she thought we would forget. But we,"—he pushed his glasses back up on his nose—"never forget."

Drusilla said "He's lying. He's a devil. They're evil creatures. They'll do anything to get what they want. You know that. You know me." As she spoke she drifted slowly to the ground. Her face, contorted with anger moments before, now smoothed itself back into pouting lips and wide, angelic eyes. "You know he's lying. If it were not mine, why would I ask for your help? I didn't want to get you in so much trouble. You know he's not telling the truth."

The fact was I did not know. I scanned my memory for every one of Miss Rodigar-Glenn's mystoricals and nowhere did I find a situation anything like the one I now faced. Miss Rodigar-Glenn was woefully mute about the subject of devils and necromancers.

Yet it was Drusilla who made the request, and she did ask me first, regardless of her true appearance. I had promised, even if the devil was correct about the promise not being binding. Slowly, I took the amber box from my chest and held it out to her. With a shy smile she reached out for it.

"Master Tertius, no!" shouted Ampi, appearing suddenly at the hole in the wall. Despite myself, I jerked the box back away from Drusilla's fingertips. The sound of Ampi's voice was ingrained in my bones, and a sharp command was enough to change my mind.

Drusilla spun on her heels toward the genie and the snarl returned to her face. "What do you want, servant of the ring?"

"I want a resolution," said Ampi calmly, and produced a small scroll. "A just resolution. Do you know what this is, Drusilla Vermeer?"

Drusilla's face turned ash white. It seemed to me to be the natural color for her. Her hair, once golden, was bleached out as well, the ringlets looking like smoke instead. "No," she said simply. "No."

"May I?" said the Collector, and Ampi turned the scroll over to the devil. The infernal creature scanned the scroll quickly. "Yes, its what I thought it was. The original agreement between you, Drusilla Vermeer, and the Infernal Court. Power in exchange for your immortal soul. Power enough to destroy the rest of your family, if I remember right. And you've almost gotten your soul back. Not bad work, for a ghost."

A ghost, I thought. Yes, that was what Drusilla was looking like at the moment. She had turned almost immaterial, fading almost entirely from view as the devil spoke. Her face had become bone white and skeletal. With one last cry she launched herself against the devil and genie. The pair ducked, but they were not the targets of her attack. She floated over the top of both and out into the town, bellowing like a banshee as she fled into the night.

"Hmmm," said the Collector. "I believe that takes care of that. Now for the last matter. The box, if you please."

I looked at the box, then at Ampi.

"It is his legally," said the genie with a resigned tone. "The right thing is to return him his property."

"There is another way, of course," said the devil. "I could see fit to let Drusilla's soul go, if one was able to find a replacement." The devil took a step forward, continuing, "Another soul, noble and innocent this time, in return for hers. Perhaps if you would care to offer your own immortal spirit. . . .?" The devil reached out to me and Ampi's hand closed tightly on the devil's arm.

"You have your deal," said the djinni sharply. "Ask for no more, or you will have to deal with me."

The devil hesitated for a moment, and I saw a feral gleam in its bespectacled eyes. Then it retreated and Ampi let go of its arm. The devil rubbed the arm and said, "Well put. No need to get greedy here."

I looked at the box, then at the Collector, then I held

the box out "Take it, then," I told the devil. "But know that this truly sticks in my craw. I don't like dealing with devils, even if they are in the right."

The devil smiled and took the amber box, "I know," he said, "That's what makes it so wonderful doing business with you."

And with that the infernal creature laughed and disappeared in a puff of pungent smoke. In the distance there were the signs that our battle had roused the city, and there was already in the distance a hue and cry of the town guard.

I looked around. We were the only ones left in the Burrows, and it seemed like a bad idea to be present when the guards finally arrived. "I think its time to leave," I noted.

"Agreed, sir," replied Ampi. "I took the liberty to have a horse stocked and provisioned at a stables not more than two blocks from here."

"Always thinking, aren't you?" said I. "Well, one thing you should not pack is those dratted mystoricals. Completely unrealistic, as it turns out, and a danger as well to follow them. We'll toss them down the first well we reach."

"Already taken care of," said the genie with a straight face.

I looked at Ampratines with an amazed look.

"I told you Prespos charged dear for his aid," said the genie, "It turns out he is a fan of those mystoricals as well, and was extremely interested in finding out who put the galoshes in Madame Milani's stew. He is now the proud owner of your entire collection."

H

Richard Lee Byers

The stars shone brightly through the thin, cold mountain air. Basking in their beauty, lulled by the crackling of the campfire and the drone of his comrades' snoring, Halladon Moonglade reflected that this adventuring life was passing tolerable, even when a fellow pulled watch duty in the middle of the night.

Behind him, something thumped and rustled.

Halladon turned. Osher of Torm, the company's priest, lay feebly flailing and writhing, while all around him, the other five members of the band slumbered on, oblivious.

It looked as if Osher was having a nightmare. Rising nimbly, Halladon moved to wake him. After two paces, the young, slender, platinum-haired half-elf saw the wetness darkly gleaming on the cleric's chest, and caught the coppery smell of it. He flung himself down at Osher's side.

Even as Halladon applied pressure to his friend's wounds, he was horribly certain that the effort was in vain. Something had torn Osher's throat to shreds. Only the bald, beak-nosed priest's own healing magic might have served to preserve his life, and his injuries manifestly rendered him incapable of reciting a spell.

Osher fumbled at Halladon's wrists. "Don't!" said the

half-elf. "I'm trying to help you!" But the cleric wouldn't relent. Somehow finding a strength that should have been beyond the capacity of any man so gravely wounded, he caught hold of Halladon's forearms and forced his hands away.

Halladon would have continued striving to minister to him, but Osher gave him an imploring stare. A look full of desperation, yet entirely lucid. Overawed by the maimed man's resolution, the half-elf hovered helplessly beside him and allowed him to do as he would.

Osher dabbed his fingertip in the terrible inkwell of his own blood, and, his hand shaking violently, began to write on the ground. He managed only an H before his eyes rolled up in his head and he gave a long, mournful sigh and was still.

"What's wrong?" rumbled Kovost of Mithral Hall. Halladon looked around. Bushy black beard, upturned mustache, and eyebrows bristling, the dwarf stood with his battle-axe clasped in his callused hands. Stray tufts of hair protruded from beneath his hastily donned steel-and-leather helmet like the petals of a withered flower. Behind him, the other members of the company were hastily but belatedly stirring themselves.

"Something killed Osher," Halladon said. He strode back to the place where he'd been sitting, picked up his longbow, nocked an arrow, and peered about.

"Make more light," said Perys, a lanky, soft-spoken ranger and former scout for the Elders of Everlund, taking up his broadsword and shield.

Halladon opened his small pouch of spell components, fingered a wisp of phosphorescent moss, and murmured an incantation. A silvery glow flowered from the top of his bow. Everyone gazed tensely into the darkness, weapons at the ready.

"I think it's gone," the half-elf said at last.

"What was it?" demanded Moanda the Spike, a javelin in one hand and a buckler with a wickedly pointed boss—the source of her epithet—in the other.

"I don't know," Halladon said, feeling, whether it was warranted or not, a pang of shame.

The pale-eyed barbarian, who'd grown to womanhood in the trackless reaches of the frozen north, glared at him. "You were on watch. How could something sneak into camp, kill someone, and slip away without you ever seeing it?"

"Unless you fell asleep," said Silbastis, a stocky, tattooed former sailor from the Sword Coast. His cutlass and golden hoop earring glimmered in the magical glow.

Halladon bit back an angry retort, knowing that, in their place, he might well have suspected the same. "I swear I didn't. I just . . . didn't see it."

Stooping, studying the ground, Perys walked slowly back to Osher's body. "Whatever it was, it didn't leave any sign. Which is curious. The soil isn't that hard."

"Osher tried to tell us what it was," Halladon said. "Since he couldn't speak, he was going to write it. But he only managed the first rune—H—before his heart stopped."

"Hobgoblin!" cried Gybik, the company's thief. An apple-cheeked, snub-nosed little man who, though middle-aged, looked as if he were still a stripling. He possessed a positive genius for picking locks and finding hidden booty which was offset by a certain obtuseness in other matters.

Kovost rolled his eyes. "A hobgoblin couldn't slip in and out of camp without being seen, Lightfingers. It likely couldn't avoid leaving tracks, either."

"Mielikki only knows what Osher meant to write," Perys said, returning his sword to its scabbard. The blade went in with a soft metallic hiss. "I'm afraid there are simply too many possibilities for us to puzzle it out. What we can do is set double watches for the remainder of the night."

Moanda nodded grimly, a motion which set her grizzled braids bobbing on her breast. "Wise idea. Somebody help me carry Osher to the edge of camp."

"I will," Halladon said. "But first, everyone . . ." His comrades gazed at him. "If this is my fault, if I wasn't vigilant enough, I'm sorry."

For a moment, no one replied, and he wondered if henceforth they all were going to despise him. Then Kovost said, "Don't blame yourself, lad. We're deep in the Nether Mountains. Things happen here. Shift the body, then try to get some sleep."

* * * * *

Dawn revealed the wilderness in all its splendor. Mountains rose in every direction as far as the eye could see. Their pristine caps of perpetual snow reflected the ruddy sunlight, while gloom still veiled the gorges and valleys below. Nowhere could one discern so much as a hut, a road, a thread of smoke rising against the vast blue sky, or any other hint of civilization. On many a morning, the desolate beauty of such vistas had lifted Halladon's heart. But not today. Not when he and his fellow adventurers faced the melancholy task of sorting through the belongings of a dead friend.

They kept the valuable items—the rubies, fire opals, and sapphires that had been Osher's share of the treasure—and those that were personal, like the leather headband his sister had braided for him, the slide whistle he'd played at idle moments, and the steel amulet, cast in the form of a gauntlet, which was the emblem of his faith. These they would deliver to his temple. The rest, including his heavy steel breastplate emblazoned with the gauntlet of Torm, they buried with him.

After a cheerless breakfast, they set out on their way, trekking westward. Perhaps in tribute to Osher's memory, Halladon found himself recalling all that had happened since the company formed.

They'd met by chance, in a dilapidated fieldstone inn in Jalanthar. At the end of a night of carousing, Kovost had grandly proposed that they all go treasure-hunting in the craggy wasteland to the east. Everyone knew the ancient wizards of Netheril had left sacks of gold and diamonds stashed in every cave and hollow tree, and they were just the clever fellows to retrieve them.

Less drunk than most of his companions, Halladon had accepted the proposition with equal enthusiasm. Why else had he roused his Moon elf father's ire and his human mother's worry by refusing to live the safe, sensible life of a wood carver like everyone else in the family? Or trained with his master of arms and, a shade less diligently, with his magic teacher, until crotchety old Hlint had declared him a crude, bumptious warrior at heart and terminated his lessons? Why else but to join a fellowship of adventurers and sally forth on bold expeditions like this?

Although, had he known what lay in store, he might have thought twice, for it soon became apparent just what an ill-matched and contentious lot they actually were. Sober, Kovost remembered the usual dwarf prejudice against elf and half-elf alike. Moanda, like any rightthinking barbarian, distrusted mages and was inclined to scorn all her companions as prime exemplars of everything that ailed effete, decadent civilization. Silbastis vexed the others by shirking his share of the chores, Gybik by pilfering, and Perys by his phlegmatic imperturbability.

The way they bickered, it was a marvel they lasted a week in the Nethers, and in fact, one of them didn't. While they were still in the foothills, an ogre had slain Bax, the company's only genuine wizard, with a well thrown rock. But the rest survived by learning to work together, and eventually, they even started to like one another. Prejudices faded, or at least ceased to apply to the fellow tramping along at one's side, while reprehensible character flaws and odious personal habits softened into endearing foibles.

Finally, weeks after the chilly autumn winds began to whine out of the north, the company found a ruined keep and the crypts beneath. Much to their frustration, they'd nearly run out of time to explore the place. They had to set out for Sundabar before the first blizzards sealed the passes. But on the last afternoon before the morning on which they'd agreed to depart, Gybik discovered a fortune in gems concealed behind a stag-headed bas-relief of some long-forgotten beast.

The adventurers could have lived comfortably on such a prize for the rest of their lives, but as they swaggered, jesting and crowing along the ridges and through the vales, not a one of them had any patience for a tame, timid notion like that. They'd spend the winter roistering like lords, then return for more treasure in the spring. Nobody doubted it was there for the taking, just as no one felt daunted by the prospect of a second expedition.

In the wake of Osher's death their cockiness had flown. They trudged along silently, dull-eyed or peering nervously into the pines clinging to the steep, rocky slope above the trail. Around midmorning, when the sun finally rose above the lofty peaks at their backs, Perys pushed back his green woolen hood to uncover his tousled chestnut curls and turned to regard his comrades.

"Enough of this moping," he said. "We'll miss Osher, but he served Torm well. The god has surely given him a high place at his table. We should be happy for him."

Striving to cast off their melancholy, the others nodded, smiled wanly, or murmured their agreement. "And whatever killed him," Kovost said, "it's far behind us now, and won't trouble us again."

* * * * *

Halladon woke to a hard nudging in his ribs. From prior experience, he knew it was the steel toe of Kovost's boot. "Get up, sluggard," boomed the dwarf.

"It's good that a season of living rough hasn't spoiled those exquisite manners of yours," Halladon replied. When he pushed his covers aside, the cold pierced him like a blade. He hastily clambered to his feet and wrapped himself in his bearskin mantle, which he'd been employing as an extra blanket. "Evidently we came through the night all right."

"Of course," Kovost said. "Didn't I tell you—"

Someone gasped.

The half-elf turned. His face ashen, Gybik was squatting beside Silbastis. Gybik had no doubt attempted to rouse him, but Silbastis wasn't moving.

The other adventurers hurriedly gathered around the corpse. This time, the throat wasn't shredded. There was only a single neat, round puncture.

"Whatever killed Osher," Gybik said shakily, "it followed us."

"And this time it apparently slew its victim in his sleep," said Halladon, queasy with grief and dismay. "Stealthy as it is, I wouldn't be surprised if that's how it usually kills. It was likely only a fluke that Osher awoke."

"Poor man," said Moanda, gazing down at the body. "I enjoyed his tales of the sea. Even if I was sure he lied with every other word."

"Poor him and poor us!" said Gybik. "If the killer came twice, it'll come again."

"I'm afraid you may well be correct," Perys said, crouching. "Hmmm. Once again, the creature didn't leave any tracks."

"There isn't much blood on the ground, either," Halladon said. "That's odd, too, don't you think?"

"Everything about this is 'odd!' " Gybik snapped. "Blessed Tymora, what terrible thing is stalking us?"

"Perhaps we roused something in the catacombs," Perys said somberly. "Some sort of guardian the mages of Netheril left behind to ward their treasure."

Halladon shrugged. "We didn't notice any signs of such a thing while we were there, but you could be right."

"Whatever it is," Perys mused, "how can it come, kill, and depart at will? Unseen . . . without leaving a trace?

In my experience, even invisible creatures generally give some sign of their presence. Why did it only slay one of us, when others lay sleeping and thus at its mercy as well? And most importantly, how do we protect ourselves from such a thing?"

"It attacks in the dark," Kovost said. "We could travel by night and sleep by day."

The long-legged scout shook his head. "Not in this country. I understand that you and Halladon see better at night than we humans, but there's still an excellent chance we'd take the wrong path or blunder over the edge of a precipice."

"Now that we know the killer's tracking us," Moanda said, "let's lie in wait for it."

"That's worth a try," Perys said. "If it doesn't work, we'll simply have to try to shake the creature off our trail, set up camps that are more difficult to sneak into, and maintain the double watches with especial wariness."— he looked at Halladon—"Unless you can do something more with your sorcery."

Feeling useless, the half-elf shook his head. "As I've told you, I've only mastered a few spells, and I don't see how any of them could help."

Moanda made a spitting sound.

"H," muttered Kovost, his brow furrowed. "Damn it, what was Osher trying to tell us?"

"I'm afraid that what Perys said still holds," Halladon said sympathetically. "I don't see how you can possibly guess it."

"The Soulforger smite you!" snarled the dwarf. "At least I'm trying to help!" Shocked by his comrade's outburst, Halladon stepped backward.

* * * * *

"No!" Kovost bellowed.

After burying Silbastis, the adventurers had marched about two leagues, then wasted precious hours lying in ambush for a foe that never came. Afterward, they pushed themselves hard to cover as much ground as possible. Despite the weariness their pace engendered, Halladon had at first been too apprehensive to sleep well. But the next two nights had passed without incident, inspiring the brittle hope that the company had outdistanced its nemesis, and this evening exhaustion had finally dragged him down into a profound slumber.

Still, when Kovost's shout jolted him awake, he comprehended instantly that someone else was dead. Groggily, he disentangled himself from his covers and stumbled over to where the dwarf and Moanda were standing. Gybik joined them a moment later.

The companions regarded the inert form at their feet. To all appearances, Perys, like Silbastis, had perished without ever waking. Once again, there was little blood on the ground.

His boyish face contorted with anger, Gybik rounded on Kovost and Moanda. "What's the matter with you? You knew this fiend was skulking about. You were supposed to check on us!"

"We did," Moanda said. "Again and again. I . . . I don't know how it got to him without us spotting it."

" 'H,' " said Kovost, gazing at his feet. His fist clenched on the haft of his axe as though he thought he could pound the solution into his skull.

Shivering, wishing he'd had the presence of mind to pick up his mantle, Halladon crouched beside the body. As he'd expected, he didn't find any tracks.

"None of us will reach Sundabar," said Gybik in a fey voice. "We're all going to die in these awful mountains. Unless . . ." He dashed to his pack, tore it open, scooped out a handful of gems, and brandished them at the night. "Take them back! We don't want them anymore!"

The darkness didn't answer. "Be a man," said Moanda in disgust.

" 'H!' " roared Kovost suddenly, no longer perplexed but inspired. " 'H,' by all the gods!"

Halladon felt a thrill of hope. "Do you actually know what Osher meant?"

The dwarf gave him a savage grin. "Oh, I believe so, Elf-get. I should have figured it out before, but I was overlooking the obvious. No one ever saw the killer sneaking into or out of camp because he was here all the time, using magic to murder his comrades silently from a distance. He made sure to butcher Osher first lest the priest divine the evil in his heart, then did his level best to persuade the rest of us to ignore the clue our poor friend left us. 'H' stands for Halladon!"

The half-elf gaped at him. "That's insane! You've seen my magic, paltry thing that it is. You know I can't cast a spell that could kill someone without the sentries noticing."

"We've only seen what you've chosen to show us," Moanda said. "Who knows what other filthy sorceries you command?" Her broadsword with its eagle-head pommel whispered out of its scabbard.

"But why would I kill Perys and the others?"

"That's an easy one," Kovost said. "You want all the gems for yourself." Behind him, Gybik was approaching. He looked less angry, less certain of Halladon's guilt than the others, but he had his short sword in one hand and a throwing knife in the other.

Loath as he would be to strike at his friends, their demeanor was so menacing that Halladon could only wish he'd buckled on his own sword. But like his bow, quiver, and pack, it still lay next to his cloak and blankets. All he had were the dirk and pouch which never left his belt. "You're wrong," he said. "Think about it. I reached Osher's body ahead of everyone else. Were I the killer, I would have wiped the 'H' away."

"Maybe you didn't notice it in time," Moanda said. "At any rate, we see the truth at last, and your serpent's tongue won't convince us otherwise. Take him!" She and Kovost surged at him, with Gybik bringing up the rear. Scrambling backward, the half-elf rattled off a spell.

A quartet of Halladons, identical to the original in every respect, flickered into existence around him. Wheeling, he broke for the trees, his illusory twins aping his motions as swiftly and precisely as reflections in a mirror.

His comrades gave chase. Gybik's knife whizzed through one of phantasms, bursting it like a soap bubble. A slash of Moanda's sword dispersed a second illusion, and she snarled in frustration.

Halladon plunged into the pines. Kovost's axe spun past him and for an instant, the half-elf grinned. The weapon wasn't balanced for throwing, and the short-legged dwarf wouldn't have hurled it if he hadn't fallen behind.

Moanda and Gybik began to collide with the branches and trip over the gnarled roots which Halladon, with his superior night vision, was avoiding. By the time the remaining illusions winked out of existence, he'd lost himself in the night.

* * * * *

The wind howled and snow flurried down from the sky. A rampart of towering storm clouds, like a second tier of mountains stacked atop the first, veiled the midday sun. As he trudged along shaking, hugging himself for warmth, Halladon strained to listen. He didn't think his erstwhile companions would attempt another ambush, but then, he hadn't thought they'd mistake him for a murdering traitor either, and in any case, it wouldn't do to catch up with them before dark.

After his escape, he'd felt a bitter rage at the way his friends had turned on him, but the emotion hadn't lasted. He knew that Moanda, Kovost, and Gybik hadn't wanted to believe him a murderer. With the company dying one by one, it was imperative that they figure out how it was happening, and the dwarf's accusation had had a superficial air of plausibility. It should have come as no surprise that Halladon had failed to persuade the others of his innocence, especially since he had no alternative explanation of his own to offer, just as it was only natural that they'd taken up arms against the supposed author of their misfortunes with such dispatch. He understood why they'd behaved as they had, and he forgave them.

Which was just as well, because it was vital that he reunite himself with them. No doubt with malice aforethought, they'd taken his gear with them when they moved on, and, inadequately clad and armed, bereft of his grimoire, rations, and water bottle, he had virtually no chance of making it out of the Nether Mountains. Even if properly equipped he likely couldn't survive the trek alone. The rugged, predator-infested country was simply too dangerous.

Obviously, he could only regain his comrades' trust by revealing the true killer, and it occurred to him that he might now be in a better position to do precisely that. The foe was adept at concealing itself from whatever guards the adventurers posted. But perhaps a hidden observer, lurking just outside the camp, someone of whose presence it was unaware, would be able to spot it.

It seemed a promising plan. To try it, all he had to do was make it through the day.

His extremities grew numb, and his breath crackled in his nose. Occasionally he trudged past a hollow in the ground or in the escarpment beside the trail. He'd feel sorely tempted to huddle there to escape the freezing wind, but he didn't dare let his friends get too far ahead. Instead, he imagined dancing hearth fires, steamy saunas, drafts of mulled red wine searing his throat and kindling a glow in his belly, and a feather bed heaped with eiderdowns with a warming pan tucked underneath.

It didn't seem to help much. He promised himself that if by some miracle he survived this nightmare, he'd flee to sunny Chessenta where winter was a myth, and never wander north again.

By mid afternoon, the cold had reduced him to a miserable, shambling somnolence, his consciousness wavering in and out of focus. Once he roused to find himself plodding down the wrong side of the path, a mere inch from a prodigious drop. The danger jolted him back to full awareness, and that was when he heard the guttural orcish voices whispering from somewhere back up the trail. Thank Corellon he had sharp ears, and that sound carried well in the mountains.

It would be suicide to confront the creatures here, where there was no room to maneuver. Halladon ran, and though he tried to do so quietly, he heard the orcs immediately break into a run as well. They were hunting him.

After a switchback turn the way widened out into a promontory supporting a stand of stunted spruces. Panting, his heart pounding, Halladon hid behind one of the trees and prepared to cast one of the two spells left in his memory.

Three orcs trotted into view. They wore ragged garments crudely dyed with ugly, clashing colors—muddy mauves, garish oranges, and mustard yellows. Deep cowls shadowed their swinish faces, protecting their bloodshot eyes against the hated daylight; had the sun been shining, they likely wouldn't have ventured from their lair at all. Even from across the bluff, Halladon caught the sour stink of their blemished olive flesh. Grateful that he hadn't attracted the notice of a full-sized war party, he let them trot as close as he dared, then took hold of his piece of moss and whispered the incantation.

On the far side of the orcs, white light flowered amid the branches of an evergreen. On a brighter day, they might not even have noticed, but on this gray, overcast afternoon the shimmer caught their eyes. Exclaiming in surprise, they pivoted toward the glow.

Halladon rattled off his final spell. Two slivers of azure radiance streaked from his fingertips and buried themselves in the closest orc's back. The creature collapsed. Halladon sprang to his feet and charged. The remaining orcs began to blunder back around. The nearer one, a pot-bellied specimen with a necklace of mummified ears, caught sight of the half-elf rushing at it and its piggy eyes widened. It tried to swing its spear point into line, but was an instant too slow. Halladon thrust his dirk into the creature's chest.

Knowing he had no chance of taking the last orc by surprise, the adventurer yanked his weapon free and whirled to face it. The creature, a hulking brute with delicately wrought bands of gold—perhaps plunder from some massacred caravan—gleaming on its corded, simian arms, threw its spear. Halladon dodged it by a hair. The orc whipped out a scimitar and rushed him.

The half-elf had to overcome the advantage of his foe's longer, heavier blade, and he knew he'd only get one chance to do it. He retreated several steps while the scimitar, whizzing through the air, missed him by inches. When he'd taken the measure of the orc's attacks—the creature favored a high, horizontal, potentially behead-ing cut—he faked another step backward, crouched sud-denly below the arc of his adversary's stroke, and drove his dirk into its belly.

With a grunt, the orc doubled over. Halladon stabbed it again, this time in the heart. The brute dropped.

Halladon could scarcely believe he'd single-handedly bested all three of his attackers. Corellon grant that no other creature wanted to pick a fight.

In any case, there was no time to stand and savor his victory, not when Moanda, Kovost, and Gybik were get-ting farther away by the second. Halladon bent over the third orc, then hesitated. In normal circumstances, he would have deemed it a shabby, churlish deed to rob the dead, but it would be even more dishonorable to allow himself to freeze to death when his friends needed his help to escape a killer. Hoping it wasn't verminous, he appropriated the orc's malodorous but warm-looking fleece-lined leather cloak, and then the creature's curved, brass-hilted scimitar.

* * * * *

Shivering, envying his friends their little fire, Halladon surveyed the camp from behind a granite boulder. Gybik and Moanda lay shrouded in their blankets, with only Kovost—who'd wrapped himself in Halladon's bearskin mantle—standing guard. Perhaps the adventurers believed that now that they'd chased their companion away, they were no longer in any extraordinary danger. Or perhaps they'd decided that with only three of them remaining, double watches simply weren't feasible anymore.

The sun had set several hours ago, and by now Halladon had begun to suspect that the killer intended to stay away tonight. The half-elf's stomach was already hollow and achy with hunger, and he wondered grimly how he'd feel after another day without food. Perhaps he should have searched the orc corpses for provender, although the notion of eating the kind of rations such creatures typically carried was almost enough to quell his appetite for the nonce.

Gybik shifted beneath his covers, and the motion drew Halladon's eye. No shadowy ghost or assassin was crouching over the thief, and the half-elf was already looking away again, into the darkness beyond the wavering yellow firelight, when it struck him that there was something subtly wrong about the way Gybik had moved. When he peered at the thief more closely, he realized what it was. The small man hadn't just rolled over, changing position in his sleep. He'd raised his head ever so slightly, as if looking about.

It almost certainly meant nothing. Why shouldn't Gybik wake for a moment, glance around to make sure nothing was amiss, and then drift off again? But the motion had seemed sly, stealthy, as if the thief was peeking at his companions, making sure that Moanda was unconscious and Kovost's back was turned. And thus Halladon continued to watch him.

Even so, in the darkness, he almost missed what happened next. A shape crawled from under Gybik's blankets. At first the half-elf thought it was a rat, and then, from the length and number of its limbs, some sort of enormous insect. Only when it scuttled away across the ground did he discern that it was a human hand. Gybik's hand, apparently, detached from his wrist.

I finally understand you, Osher, thought Halladon in amazement.

As the hand scurried noiselessly along, it changed. The skin darkened, and the fingers lengthened until they resembled a spider's legs. Kovost glanced casually around, and the hand instantly flattened itself against the ground. When the dwarf turned away again, it scuttled on to Moanda and crouched by her neck. Its nails lengthened into claws. The one on the index finger was particularly long and narrow, like a knitting needle, or a mosquito's proboscis.

Halladon had been watching the hand in horrified fascination. Now he abruptly realized that unless he intervened, the barbarian had only seconds to live. He grabbed his scimitar, sprang up from behind the stone, and raced forward. "Kovost!" he shouted. "Help Moanda!"

At once the disembodied hand crouched down, concealing itself among the folds of Moanda's blanket a split second before Kovost reflexively jerked around to peer at her. Obviously seeing nothing amiss, the dwarf surged to his feet, Halladon's cloak falling away from his brawny shoulders. Teeth bared in a snarl, battle-axe at the ready, he darted to intercept the half-elf.

Halladon halted. It was either that or give his friend a chance to strike at him. "Look again!" he pleaded. "The creature, the true killer, is right there beside her!" But when he looked again himself, he saw that it wasn't, not any longer.

"You were mad to think you could fool us a second time," Kovost said, still advancing. At his back, Moanda and Gybik, who possessed two normal-looking hands again, threw off their covers and scrambled up from the ground.

"Listen to me," Halladon said. Moanda and Gybik stalked up to stand beside Kovost, swords leveled. "I've been spying on the camp since just after dusk. I reasoned that the killer might not be as able to hide itself from someone whose presence it didn't suspect, and I was correct. I saw it, and it has been among us all along. You, Kovost, were right about that much. Gybik—or rather, some shapeshifting creature that caught our friend alone, slaughtered him, and assumed his identity—is the murderer. I imagine we attracted its attention while we were exploring the fortress."

The false Gybik goggled at him in perfect imitation of the original. "I . . . what are you talking about? I'm me!" He looked wildly about at Moanda and Kovost. "I promise I am!"

"We know that," the barbarian said soothingly, or as close to soothingly as her acerbic nature would permit.

"Of course we do," said Kovost. "You couldn't move around the camp killing people without the sentries seeing you. Nor does Gybik begin with an 'H.'"

"No, but 'hand' does," Halladon said. "Our impostor is a kind of glorified leech. It insinuated itself into our company because it craves human blood, and it has a clever way of getting it without being detected. It can detach its hand to skitter about like a little animal. The hand slips a hollow needle of a talon into somebody's neck, killing him so deftly the victim never wakes. The hand siphons its victim's blood and carries it back to nourish its body. Our guards never saw the thing scuttling around because it's too quick and small, and can darken itself to blend into the shadows. Perys never found tracks because it's too light to leave any. The wounds didn't shed as much blood as we would have expected because the shapeshifter took it. It only killed one of us at a time because that was all the sustenance it needed. And Osher didn't try to write Gybik because he never saw Gybik attacking him, just a disembodied, inhuman hand. Don't you see—"

"We see that it's all preposterous," Kovost said.

"Yes," Moanda said, an unaccustomed hint of pity in her voice. "Halladon, you must be mad in truth, to imagine you could cozen us with such a tale. Perhaps it was your dark studies that deranged you. I'll be sorry to slay you, but the shades of Osher, Silbastis, and Perys cry out for vengeance."

"Besides," said Kovost, raising his axe, "you're too dangerous to live."

"Wait!" said Halladon. "Let me prove he isn't Gybik. Let me demonstrate that he doesn't know things the genuine Gybik should know"—he looked the shapeshifter in the eye—"Where did we first meet?"

"The Crowing Cockatrice," the creature said.

The half-elf felt a pang of dismay. "With what drink did we toast the founding of our company?"

"The cider. Jalanthar amber, it was called."

"What did we fight in our first battle together?"

"Three ogres."

Halladon realized he wouldn't be able to trip the creature up. Either it had somehow assimilated the real Gybik's memories when it had taken on his form, or else it had gleaned all it needed to know from conversations along the trail.

"That was your final ploy," said Moanda, slinking forward. "We'll give you a proper burial, in memory of the comrade you once were."

Halladon knew he couldn't defeat all three of them, but by Corellon, if he had to perish, he meant to take the shapeshifter with him. He shifted his weight as if preparing to retreat, then dived forward in an all out attack, swinging the orcish blade at the false Gybik's skull.

The creature recoiled, and the scimitar merely gashed its shoulder. Moanda sprang at Halladon from the right, and Kovost, from the left. Off-balance, the half-elf struggled to flounder back on guard, knowing that he wouldn't make it in time.

"Wait!" Kovost barked. "Look!" Moanda somehow halted her stroke an inch short of cleaving Halladon's spine.

Surmising what Kovost must have seen, the half-elf turned back toward the shapeshifter. Sure enough, the pain of its wound had evidently disrupted its ability to maintain its borrowed form. Its flesh expanded and flowed, erasing all resemblance to Gybik, or to anything human. In a heartbeat, it grew half as tall as Halladon. Its body was dead black, its limbs coiled with the boneless fluidity of an octopus's tentacles, and its surface bulged and hollowed as if new muscles and organs were constantly forming and dissolving inside it. Is head was hairless, and without ears, nose, or mouth, but from the center of a triangle of bulging white oval eyes extended a tapered prehensile proboscis as long and pointed as a spear.

"Kill it!" Moanda cried. She edged toward the creature, and it struck at her with Gybik's short sword. She blocked the blow with her buckler, jabbing the spiked boss into the shapeshifter's arm in the process. Pivoting, she swung her broadsword down and hacked the limb in two.

Had her opponent been human, such a maiming blow would almost certainly have ended the combat. But the raw stump of the shapeshifter's arm instantly sprouted a tangle of chitinous pincers resembling lobster claws, and it struck at her again. Caught by surprise, she couldn't quite bring the buckler up in time to deflect the blow completely. She reeled backward with a long gash in her temple.

Bellowing a war cry, Kovost darted forward, intent, like any dwarf facing such a huge creature, on getting inside its reach. The shapeshifter, which didn't seem to be experiencing any particular difficulty keeping track of more than one opponent at a time, slashed at him with one of Gybik's knives. Kovost ducked the stroke, then chopped at the monster's knee, half severing its leg. The shapeshifter stumbled and, grinning, the dwarf ripped his weapon free for another attack. But then six new appendages, each terminating in a pointed shaft of bone like a scorpion's stinger, erupted from the beast's abdomen to stab at him. Driven backward, he dodged and parried frantically.

Meanwhile, Halladon circled behind the shapeshifter and drove the scimitar deep into its back. For a moment the creature froze, affording Moanda and Kovost a precious respite from its onslaught, and the half-elf dared to hope he'd hurt it badly. Then another blank, round eye opened in the nape of its neck, and a huge hand shot from the center of its back to snatch at Halladon's head.

Halladon sidestepped and hacked at the thin, snaky arm to which the hand was attached. The shapeshifter's flesh parted with surprising ease, and the severed member tumbled to the ground. Turning, Halladon lifted his blade to cut at the creature's back.

Something struck the half-elf's leg, hurting him and thrusting him off-balance. He fell heavily onto his side. A headless thing resembling an enormous black starfish, each of its arms tipped with a jagged talon and a fanged, slavering maw gnashing in the center of its body, scuttled up the length of Halladon's body toward his head, jabbing at him as it came. He realized it was the severed hand, acting independently of the shapeshifter's body.

He slashed at it awkwardly. The starfish pounced over his blade and onto his shoulder, plunging two of its claws into his flesh to anchor itself. The other three arms poised to stab at his head.

Dropping his saber, which was useless at such close quarters, he grabbed his attacker and pulled. In a flash of pain, the starfish tore free of his flesh. He tried to fling it away from him, but it instantly attached itself to his hand and started to bite him.

Halladon frantically drew his knife, then stabbed and sawed at the creature. After a few seconds, it stopped moving, and with a final flailing of his arm, he freed himself from its excruciating embrace.

The half-elf seized his scimitar, scrambled up, and surveyed the battle. His friends were hard-pressed. The left side of her face red with blood, warding herself with her buckler and boot knife, Moanda tried vainly to work her way back to the broadsword she'd lost, until one of the shapeshifter's hands snatched it up to use against her. Gasping, Kovost lurched desperately back and forth, striking at the ropy limbs that lashed at him from every side.

But all the shapeshifter's arms were currently deployed in front of its body, away from Halladon. Praying it would ignore him just long enough for one more sword stroke, the half-elf charged it.

Since his cut to the torso hadn't slain it, he decided to attack the monster's head. Scimitar raised, he leaped into the air, and at that instant the shapeshifter's proboscis whipped all the way around its skull to hurtle at his face.

He was certain he was a dead man, but his sword hand knew better. It beat the proboscis to the side, then buried the scimitar in the creature's skull.

The shapeshifter stiffened, let out a ghastly buzzing sound, then dropped. Within moments, it began to melt into a foul-smelling slime.

Dead as it looked, Moanda and Kovost approached it warily.

"Are you all right?" the dwarf asked Halladon.

At first, too winded to speak, Halladon merely nodded. "It stuck me a few times," he wheezed at last, "but not too deeply. What about you two?"

"The same," said the barbarian, hand pressed to the cut on her brow.

Kovost peered down at the rapidly dissolving carcass. "What in the name of the Keeper's beard was this thing?"

Moanda snorted, her usual response to anything she considered a foolish question. "It was unpleasant, and now it's dead. What more do you need to know?" She turned to Halladon, inclined her head, and grumbled a phrase in her native language three times over. Then, when he peered at her in puzzlement, she gave him an exasperated scowl. "That's how my people apologize. Don't you cityfolk know anything?"

"I'm sorry, too, lad," Kovost said. "We should never have doubted you. I'll carry the shame of it to my dying day. Tell me how to make it up to you."

Halladon grinned. "Depend on it, it will be a long, arduous process. But after we tend to one another's wounds, you can make a start by building up the fire and cooking me a gigantic supper."

Strange Bedfellows

Keith Francis Strohm

"Fair travel, Captain Aidan, 'tis a chill wind blowin' this eve," called the young guardsman, his purple cloak drawn tight against the cold.

Aidan turned to face the officer standing within the guard post of the Upper City Gate and grunted. In the dancing light of the torches, he could make out the lad's beardless face. No matter how hard he tried, Aidan couldn't shake the feeling that the Purple Dragons recruited younger every year.

"Luck yerself," his gravelly voice carried across the deserted stretch of the Gateguard Road, "sunrise is still a fair bit away."

With a gruff laugh, he turned and continued somewhat unsteadily up the road into Tilverton proper. In truth, the Dragonet was right—the night air carried a chill bite. Aidan could feel his old bones throb under the wind's lash. Still, winter's bluster couldn't touch the warmth that flooded from his recollection of the past.

Tonight had marked his last official day as a captain in the Purple Dragons. He was mustering out, and the memories of his former companions—many of whom had spent the evening toasting his health in the taproom of the Windlord's Rest—covered him like a comfortable quilt.

He'd come a long way since leaving Skull Crag and wandering the West Reaches of Cormyr—certainly further than he had ever dreamed after signing with the Dragons in Greatgaunt. For the past twenty seasons, he had made Tilverton his home, working hard to keep peace and uphold law. He loved the city and felt that, in his own small way, he had helped make at least this part of Faerûn a better place. It was tough to put that behind him.

Aidan sighed and turned off the main road, wending his way through back alleys toward his home. In the distance a cur barked, and the captain's hand strayed reflexively to the dagger at his belt. The weapon was new, given to him this very evening by Commander Haldan Rimmersbane, and its weight pulled unfamiliarly at his side.

A slight scuffling sound brought him to a stop. He peered into the shadows, the dagger drawn almost without thought, and waited.

Nothing.

Cursing himself for a beardless cadet, Aidan relaxed. It took a few moments for him to realize that he still held his weapon. The dagger felt natural in his hand, almost like an extension of his fingers, and he marveled once again at its gem-inlayed hilt and razor-sharp edge. Truly it was a noble's blade, a gift he had received this very evening from Commander Haldan. It was a token, Haldan had said to him later, of Lady Alaslyn Rowanmantle's appreciation for his "unswerving dedication to Cormyrean justice."

He chuckled out loud at this memory. Haldan always did have a flair for the melodramatic. Even when they were cadets struggling through training, Aidan had thought his younger friend had missed his true calling.

Still, the dagger was a great gift, and he would carry it with pride as a reminder of his service to Cormyr.

Ahhh . . . you're still drunk, he thought.

Aidan sheathed the blade, hawked, and spit before

resuming his weaving journey. The taste of Thungor's bitters lay heavily in his mouth, and he still had a fair distance to go.

The tight alleyway eventually turned, opening into a slightly wider street. Aidan walked in the center of the road, careful to avoid the refuse and offal piled on either side. Rats were common enough in Tilverton, but the captain had seen enough savaged corpses to know that other creatures sometimes lived on the castoffs of civilization.

The shadows in the lane suddenly shifted. Several cloaked shapes melted out of the darkness, quickly forming a wide circle around him. His attackers moved forward slowly, tightening the circle. Aidan once again drew his dagger, grateful for such a practical gift.

"What is it that you want," he asked, pitching the question like a command.

The menacing figures stopped their advance, and for a brief moment he thought he had a chance to control this situation. A voice spoke from deeper within the alley's shadows, and he knew that these were not common footpads, frightened by the first display of resistance.

"I believe you have something we require," the voice said.

Aidan shook his head and started to protest, until he remembered the dagger. Even in the pale moonlight, its gems burned incandescently, like a beacon to every greedy eye.

"Ahh," the voice said again. "I see we understand each other . . . captain."

Aidan's mind whirled. This was no chance robbery; the thieves had come for the knife. He could hand it over to them, in which case they'd probably cut his throat and be done with it, or he could make them think twice about ever tangling with another Purple Dragon. Either way, he didn't expect a fair fight—only a quick death.

With a silent curse, Aidan made his decision. "The only way you'll get this dagger," he shouted at the shadows, "is by pulling it out of your own chest!" Crouching low, he centered his balance and tossed the dagger from hand to hand.

Silence greeted Aidan's declaration, punctuated only by the rapid beating of his own heart. After what seemed like an eternity, the voice spoke again.

"You have made an unfortunate choice, captain."

The twang of a fired crossbow propelled his body into action. Aidan dove to the side, feeling his heart race as it pumped the blessed fire that sustained him through a lifetime of battle. He rolled to his feet and met the first of his cloaked attackers with a thrust to the gut. His dagger cut through the figure's leathers and bit deeply. He turned the knife and withdrew it quickly, ignoring the thief's dying gurgle. Several more attackers rushed in, and he soon found himself parrying a flurry of kicks, punches, and sword thrusts. Grizzled muscle and old bones no longer moved as quickly as they used to, but Aidan's years on the battlefield kept him alive—at least for the moment.

Gods, I can't keep this up for too much longer, he thought desperately. His breath came laboringly now, like a desert steed's on its last length. Another sword swept close to his head. He ducked under the swing and lunged forward, scoring one of his opponents across the leg, but the move left his flank exposed. Aidan turned quickly, trying to shield the vulnerable area—and wasn't fast enough.

He cried out as a blade pierced his side, shattering the bones of his ribs. Another sword raked across his thigh and he fell to the ground, dropping his dagger. Aidan lay on the floor, struggling to breathe, to move, to grab his weapon, but to no avail. His limbs were cold and sluggish; he was no longer their master. With great effort, he looked up at the cloaked figures approaching him with their swords drawn. They moved slowly, unhurried, almost calm. That's when he heard it, a roaring in his ears like the raging of an ocean of blood. It grew louder, drowning out the creek of leather, the cries of the wounded, and even his own heartbeat. This is it, he thought, this is death.

Somehow, he had always believed there would be more to it.

Aidan watched as one of the thieves raised a sword above his head. Silently mouthing a prayer to Tyr, Tymora, and any other god who would listen to an old, dying soldier's last words, he waited for the final blow.

It never came. Instead, the alleyway burst into light. Aidan could see another cloaked figure step from the shadows, green fire arcing from its hand to his executioners. In the sick emerald light he caught a glimpse of the newcomer's face, small-nosed and boyish, beneath a thick cowl. Again and again, his mysterious ally called down eldritch flames upon the thieves, who fell back, screaming.

He struggled to stand and fight, wanting to help the cowled man, but the pain of his wounds called him back. He collapsed and watched his own blood pool out into the road, reflecting green tongues of flame, until the darkness claimed him.

* * * * *

Aidan awoke in a simple, run-down room. A small fire burned in an old mantle, casting flickering shadows against the walls. He lay still for a moment, wondering how he had survived. The straw mattress upon which he had slept was lumpy, pressing uncomfortably against his lower back. But, he thought wryly, it's better than bleeding to death on a cold dirt floor.

Aidan sat up slowly, expecting a great deal of pain. He gasped, partly in wonder and partly in disbelief, as his movements offered him only slight soreness. What's more, his wounds looked as if they had been healing for weeks. He ran his fingers along the length of two angry looking scars, their puckered redness the only thing distinguishing them from the countless marks upon his warrior's frame.

"I see you have decided to join the ranks of the living."

The captain bolted up from the bed and whirled toward the sound of the voice, ignoring the protests from tight muscles. A thinly built man in purple robes stood in the open doorway. The shadows from the fire caressed the stranger's face as he entered the room. His lips were full, almost pouty, and Aidan recognized his thoughtful, brooding look as one that often captivated young women.

The man handed Aidan some clean clothes and moved toward the fire, idly poking at the burning wood. "Whom do I have to thank for my life?" asked the captain as he changed into the simple pair of leather breeches and wool cambric.

"My name is Morgrim," he said simply, not turning from the mantle. His voice was smooth and somewhat breathy. It sent a chill down Aidan's spine.

The captain finished changing. "You have my thanks, Morgrim," he said, extending his hand.

Morgrim stopped tending the fire, faced Aidan, and bowed. "Do not thank me. I am a simple priest, it's my duty."

Aidan smiled and awkwardly returned the bow. He'd been around long enough to know that there was nothing simple about priests—especially in Cormyr. "Which god do you serve, Morgrim?" he asked.

"Cyric," the priest replied softly.

Aidan fell back as if struck by a crossbow bolt. He stared at the young priest in disbelief. A joke, he thought, though why anyone would make light of such a thing was beyond him.

Morgrim moved toward Aidan slowly, arms held out in front of him. In the flickering light of the fire, the captain could see the glint of silver bracers, the symbol of Morgrim's enslavement to his dark god, on the priest's arms.

"Why?" Aidan asked, searching the room for some weapon he could use against the foul priest. "Why did you save my life?" If he could just edge toward the door, he would have a chance to bolt out of the room before Morgrim called down Cyric's power upon him.

"Relax," the priest said. "I mean you no harm."

Aidan stopped, instinct warring with the earnestness he heard in the young man's voice. "Why should I trust you?" he asked, firing the question like an arrow at the approaching priest. "When have the servants of Cyric ever told the truth?" Aidan was angry and confused. He knew about the priesthood of Cyric, its dark rites and shadowy assassins; it festered like a tumor upon the land. But why did this priest pretend kindness? It didn't make any sense, and he wasn't about to let down his guard until he found out.

Morgrim hissed sharply at the question. Aidan watched the priest's handsome face transform into a mask of bitterness, his sensual lips curling like asps. "Truth!" he shouted. "You want me to tell you the truth?"

Aidan felt the priest's power gather in the room, a predatory silence that filled every corner of the chamber. It swelled, a hungering beast threatening to blot out even the fragile beating of Aidan's heart. He closed his eyes against the funereal force, struggling to breathe. It was as if he had fallen into an abyss, a dark womb from which nothing ever emerged. Then, as suddenly as it appeared, the silence fled. With a gasp, Aidan opened his eyes.

"The truth is," Morgrim continued softly, as if regretting his loss of composure, "if the Prince of Lies had called you, your soul would be serving him even as we speak."

The priest moved even closer to Aidan, brushing his fingers across the captain's chest as he finished speaking. Aidan stood transfixed, his heart pounding wildly, whether from Morgrim's words or his featherlight touch he wasn't sure. He only knew that at this moment, he stood closer to death than ever before.

Nervously, Aidan cleared his throat, looking away from the promise in Morgrim's steady gaze. "Why," he repeated his question, "did you save my life? Tell me, priest."

Morgrim walked toward the old, scratched table and poured himself a glass of wine. "I have need of you."

Aidan sat down on the bed. "You have need of me," he repeated, his voice quavering between disbelief and incredulity, "For what? I will not participate in your murderous rites—even if you send me to Cyric as a slave."

The priest shot Aidan a glance, bright eagerness alight in his eyes. "And what of yourself? Do you not kill? Does your sword not taste the blood of the living?" Morgrim took a quick sip of wine and thunked his goblet down on the table.

"I am a Purple Dragon," Aidan protested. "I fight against injustice for the honor of Cormyr—"

"You are a soldier! You fight where you're told to," interrupted Morgrim. "When the Cormyrean king unleashes his Dragons upon Sembia or the Zhentarim, what do you think the Sembian farmers say to comfort their families? They say, 'Do not worry, I go to fight for the honor of our people and our land.' And when those farmers die, pierced by the teeth of your swords and your spears, who is it do you think greets them on the other side of death?"

Aidan tried to reply, to say that he was different. He knew in his heart that he was no murderer, but the words died on his lips. Finally, he said, "I cannot find the words to debate you, priest. But I know what I am."

"Peace, Aidan," the young man said. "It is not your words that I require." Morgrim's voice was gentle, sliding once again into velvety tones. The sound soothed the old warrior, calming him so much that he barely heard the priest call him by name.

He looked up, surprised. "How did—"

Morgrim held up a thin, graceful hand. He took another sip of wine and said, "The thieves weren't the only ones waiting for you in that alley. Someone stole an object of great importance from my order, an object that I have spent many months searching for."

"The dagger," Aidan cut in.

The young priest nodded. "Yes. The dagger, as you so elegantly call it, is the Lirithane—a high priestess's ceremonial blade and the symbol of her authority."

Aidan drew his hand across his grizzled gray beard, trying to make sense of the priest's words. "I don't understand. The blade was well crafted, something far beyond what an old soldier like myself would carry, but—"

"It didn't resemble an unholy blade consecrated to the Lord of Three Crowns?" Morgrim finished. "Believe me, the Lirithane does not look like any weapon you would want to carry. Whoever ordered the theft wove powerful illusions about the blade, making it difficult to track."

Aidan sat for a few minutes, weighing what the priest had said. He didn't believe Morgrim—at least not fully. Oh, the young man sounded earnest, that was certain, and his eyes, dancing with the reflected light of the fire, looked as guileless and trusting as a doe's. Unbidden, Aidan found himself thinking of Morgrim's feather-light touch. . . .

The fire hissed and popped as he brought himself back to the present. "All right, let's assume for a moment that I did carry the blade of the high priestess of Cyric last night. How did I come to possess it, and who were the cutthroats who attacked me?" he asked. Despite the warmth of the fire, Aidan felt a queer chill in the pit of his stomach, as the events of the last day swirled around in his mind. He wasn't sure he really wanted an answer to his question.

Morgrim hesitated before speaking, as if sensing his thoughts. "I do not know how you received the Lirithane—though the identity of your attackers is easy enough to impart; they were members of the Fire Knives."

Aidan shook his head. "Impossible. The Purple Dragons and our allies destroyed the Fire Knives." He had been a young lieutenant then, and the memories of that fierce struggle still pulled him screaming from his sleep.

"In Tilverton, perhaps" Morgrim replied, "but remnants of the cult survived your attack. They were lost without their little god, and it was a simple thing to take them in and bend them to our purpose. They were our dark hounds, and we sent them out to hunt across the face of Faerûn."

Aidan's blood froze. "Then why did they attack me?"

The priest sighed and said, "The hounds have gone feral. They used their familiarity with our temple to steal the high priest's blade. They aren't smart enough to carry this off by themselves; someone put them up to it. I tracked them across Cormyr until they ended up here, where they delivered the blade to their unknown master. Apparently, this person felt the blade was too dangerous to keep in their possession and used you to 'deliver' it back to the Knives."

Morgrim paused and Aidan sat still as the priest finished, "I need your help in finding their leader."

Nothing made sense! Aidan had spent a lifetime battling the forces of chaos and darkness, struggling to carve out a safe haven in the world, and now, on the eve of his retirement, an agent of darkness called upon him for help. His choice should have been clear.

Then why, by Tymora's Thrice-Damned Tresses, isn't it? he thought.

"Look, if you won't help me out of the goodness of your heart, do it for yourself." Morgrim whispered as he crept closer to Aidan's silent form. "Someone set you up—someone who didn't care whether you lived or died. Don't you want to find out who that was?"

Aidan held his breath. Gods it was hard to think with the strange young man so close. Still, the priest had a point: Someone in Tilverton was trafficking with dangerous forces. Retired or not, he had a duty to find out the identity of that person. With a silent prayer, he made his decision.

"What do I have to do?" he asked.

* * * * *

The midmorning sun shone brightly as Aidan walked down the Street of the Sorceress, heading toward the marketplace. Tilverton's streets were crowded at this time of day, and the city seemed to take on a life of its own. Horse-drawn wagons and carriages pushed valiantly against the steady press of people, carrying loads of flour, wool, and other items for the marketplace. The people, in turn, parted reluctantly for the transport, immersed in their own private conversations. Musicians dotted the street corners, playing wildly for small groups of onlookers, their music a rhythmic counterpoint to the constant hum of conversation.

Aidan felt comforted by the sights and sounds of the city. He had spent most of the last tenday since his attack peering and poking throughout Tilverton for any information regarding the mastermind behind the Lirithane's disappearance. So far, the results were frustrating. Whereas before his rank in the Purple Dragons opened the tightest lips, he now found himself facing a wall of silence. He was just another citizen. There was little he could do to force information from the unwilling. Even so, he managed to get a few nibbles. Unfortunately, each one had led to a dead end.

To make matters worse, he had finally returned to his own house after spending the last six nights in the mausoleum that Morgrim called a room only to find a letter from Commander Haldan requesting his presence this very afternoon. It was easy to guess what the commander wanted. Even when they were both lieutenants, Haldan had resented any civilian interference in official Dragon business. Not only had Aidan not informed his friend about the fateful attack in the alleyway, but he had also begun an investigation without official sanction. By now, the commander had most likely discovered both those facts. Aidan didn't look forward to this interview.

A rough bump jolted Aidan from his ruminations. He looked up to find a burly fur-clad man shaking his fists; a stream of guttural language poured out from the man's mouth. All around the angry giant, a number of animal skins lay dashed in the mud. A small crowd gathered behind the incensed man as Aidan realized with a shock that he had just stumbled into a trader's stall. He hastily mumbled an apology and gave the irate merchant a gold coin for his troubles. Shaken, he entered the marketplace proper.

If the press of people were the lifeblood of Tilverton, the marketplace was its heart. Every road flowed into it, from the Street of the Sorceress to the Great Moonsea Ride, all paths met here at the city's center. He ignored the tantalizing smells of the marketplace—the heady aroma of spiced meats and the thick, gooey sweetcakes designed to entice a man's coin from his pocket. Instead, he made straight for the Council Tower, a white stone bastion rising up from the marketplace like the finger of Torm.

The sounds of merchants hawking their wares seemed to fade away as he approached the tower. It was always like this. Standing in the shadow of the tower, his concentration intensified and his strength seemed to increase. It was the strength of assurance—that whatever befell the city, this tower, and the Purple Dragon garrison within it, would strive to set it right.

He approached the guards at the tower gate, sighing inwardly as they struggled to decide whether or not to salute. It's all different, now, he thought. No matter how recent his retirement, he was an outsider. The memories of his service in the Purple Dragons were just that—memories—and the camaraderie he shared with his shieldmates, while no less real, would eventually fade. He felt an aching loss inside, like a wound to the gut.

Quickly he jostled past the guards, sparing them any further discomfort, and entered the building. As always, the tower's first level literally hummed with ordered chaos, as uniformed soldiers and messengers scuttled about making reports and planning the watch. The captain entered the building with measured practice and walked up to a young soldier filing papers behind a desk. He knew the officer, a steady-nerved man named Joran.

"Excuse me, Sergeant," he said in measured tones, "but may I see the commander?"

Aidan watched as Joran looked up, the officer's face transforming from steadied boredom to carefully concealed joy.

"Captain Aidan, 'tis good to see you again, sir." Joran stood up quickly, scattering papers to the floor.

"At ease, son. It's simply Aidan, now." It hurt less if he said it quickly. "I'm supposed to see the commander. Is he in?"

Joran nodded. "Yes, Ca . . . sir. He asked not to be disturbed, but he's expecting you."

Aidan smiled gratefully and followed Joran up the stairs to Commander Haldan's private office. The chamber was simply appointed, almost spartan, and very much like the commander himself. A sturdy desk took up one corner of the room, and a small fire burned in the mantle. Military accouterments hung on the walls, a testament to a lifetime of soldiering.

Haldan looked up as Aidan and the sergeant entered, breaking off a quiet conversation with a white-robed man. The captain saw his friend's eyes widen in surprise, only to crease immediately in a familiar, wolfish grin. A quick word sent the white-robed man from the room, but not before Aidan caught a hostile glance from the stranger as he shouldered roughly past.

Aidan waited for Joran to shut the door before speaking. "Sorry to barge in Commander, but you wanted to see me. I hope I didn't come at a bad time."

Haldan rose from his seat, rubbing a salt and pepper beard. "Nonsense," he said with a smile. "I always have time for one of my best captains—and friends."

Aidan returned the smile, relief flooding through his body as he looked upon Haldan once more. The commander was solid and well built, an imposing officer whose martial training did not waver in the face of age and promotions. The man's career was dotted with acts of bravery and selflessness, and his soldiers followed him as much out of love as duty. The two had met while recruits, both learning to hold a sword for the first time. Haldan had risen through the ranks quickly, leading with boldness and distinction. Thinking back on his friend's career, Aidan knew that the commander deserved every accolade and promotion. He is the best of us, Aidan thought.

Standing in Haldan's office once more, Aidan felt pride at their friendship. No matter the outcome of his present situation, he knew that he could always rely upon Haldan.

"So, Aidan," the commander spoke, his resonant baritone easily filling the office, "I don't suppose you know why I've asked you here?"

The question hung in the air like pipeweed smoke. Aidan began to answer his former commander's lightly phrased question and then stopped. For just a second, he thought he saw an expectant gleam in Haldan's eye. Then it was gone, replaced by the officer's ever-present mask.

Haldan cleared his throat, and Aidan realized that he'd been staring silently at the commander. He breathed deeply and said, "Yes. It's about the attack in the alleyway."

Haldan rubbed his beard before speaking. "Go on."

Slowly, Aidan recounted the events that had occurred on the night of the attack. Strangely enough, he found himself reluctant to speak about Morgrim and the dark priest's purpose. It all seemed like an empty dream, a substanceless fear that vanished in the light of Haldan's solid presence.

When Aidan finished the tale, the commander leaned forward. "How did you survive against such odds?" he asked.

Aidan heard the keen interest in his old friend's voice. He wanted to tell Haldan the truth, to confess his involvement with Cyric's priest. Instead he laughed and said, "It'll take a lot more than a few cutpurses to kill this old soldier."

Haldan's answering smile hit him like a spear. There it was. He had lied to his friend and former commanding officer. Why? Aidan tried to think, but his shame and guilt snapped at his thoughts like hounds upon the hunt.

Haldan rose and walked toward a bright shield on the wall. "Well, that explains what happened, but why didn't you report this to me instead of going off on your own?"

Aidan turned toward the commander, inwardly cursing the night he had met Morgrim. "At first, I was too shaken. Then, I decided that I could make more progress using unofficial methods. Believe me Haldan, I was going to report to you as soon as I uncovered anything solid."

How easy the half-truths came now that he had lied once.

Haldan nodded as Aidan finished and said, "Perhaps you can tell me what you've already uncovered." He turned from the shield and looked at Aidan.

The commander's dispassionate tone confused Aidan. He wasn't quite sure how he had expected Haldan to react, but it wasn't like this. Unsure of his footing, he answered the question as truthfully as he dared. "I don't believe the attack was an accident. The thieves seemed intent upon stealing the dagger I received as a gift from Lady Rowanmantle."

"Are you sure of this, Aidan?" Haldan asked.

"Yes," he replied. "Whoever attacked me knew exactly where to find me." Once again, he hated not telling Haldan everything, but Morgrim had planted a dark seed of doubt and it had sprouted.

"I agree with your assessment," Haldan said after a moment's pause. "Rest assured that we will send out our best investigators to get to the bottom of this."

"With all due permission, sir. I would like to assist in the investigation."

Haldan sat back behind the desk and steepled his fingers together. "I'm afraid that's not possible, Aidan. You are no longer a member of the Purple Dragons, and I can't risk putting a Cormyrean citizen in harm's way."

"But—" Aidan started to protest, but Haldan interrupted.

"I'm sorry Aidan, I really am. You'll always have an honored place among the Dragons as long as I'm in command, but I can't involve you in official inquiries."

Aidan stood up, trying hard to control his growing anger, his hands clenched into fists. "Haldan," he said, trying to appeal to his friendship with the commander, "I have the best chance of identifying whoever attacked me and finding out exactly who planned it. I'm the most logical candidate to—"

Haldan's fist smashed down on his desk, "Aidan, for the last time . . . you are not to pursue this investigation at all! Do you understand me?" he thundered, not waiting for Aidan's nod. "If I find that you went against my orders, I'll jail you for interfering in official business. Is that clear?"

Aidan, stunned at his friend's outburst, didn't reply at first. In all the years he had known Haldan, the man had never shouted at him. Anger and hurt gave voice to his reply. "Abundantly clear," Aidan said in a clipped tone.

Haldan let out a deep breath and leaned forward. "Look, Aidan, I didn't mean to yell like that," he said. "Overseeing the safety and security of this city is a tiring job, and Lady Rowanmantle isn't making it any easier. What I meant to say is that you should relax and enjoy your retirement. You've served Cormyr faithfully for many years and now its time for someone else to do it. Spend your time in peaceful pursuits; gods know you've earned it."

Aidan looked closely at his old friend. The worry lines had increased around his eyes, and his face looked tired, almost haggard. Clearly, something was bothering Haldan. Damn you, Morgrim, he thought. He wanted to reassure his friend, but the face of the dark priest kept drawing him forward.

He stood up to leave and said, "Don't worry, Haldan. You have my word."

"Thank you, my friend" the commander said.

Aidan left the tower feeling lost and adrift, like a

storm-damaged galley on the Trackless Sea. He had promised his obedience, gave his oath to a friend—an oath he never intended to keep.

How, he asked himself, have I changed so much in such a short time?

Such were his thoughts as he numbly exited the tower.

* * * * *

The Sow's Ear had more connections to the underworld of Tilverton than Grimwald's Revenge. Aidan looked around nervously as he approached the warped wooden door of the establishment. He had spent most of his career pursuing the very elements that made up the tavern's clientele, and here he was walking into the dragon's lair without a single weapon. Morgrim's choice of meeting places left much to be desired.

He grimaced as he pushed open the door, walking into the establishment. Although it was midday, the inside of the Sow's Ear was dark and shadowy. Aidan could see several figures lying scattered around the common room in various states of drunkenness. Those who could still sit up squinted against the tavern's smoke-filled haze, playing traitor's heads or swords and shields. The walls, floors, and tables of the place were chipped and rotting, and the place smelled of stale beer and urine.

As he approached the bar, a fat, gap-toothed man in a greasy apron flashed him a scowl and asked for his order. Not wishing to draw attention to himself, Aidan bought an ale and found an empty table in a deserted corner. He sipped the drink slowly, grimacing at the flat taste.

Where was Morgrim? The damned priest said he would meet him here at midday. He scanned the common room again, a queer feeling rising in his stomach. Despite the confusion he brought on, the captain found himself anxiously awaiting the priest.

The door suddenly crashed open, and he nearly dove to

the ground as three men staggered drunkenly into the common area.

Torm's Teeth, he thought, you're as skittish as a cadet on review.

Aidan sniffed distastefully as he watched the three men swagger to the bar and bellow for some ale. He knew by the look of them that they were trouble. He sipped his own ale quietly and kept his eyes studiously away from the three braggarts, hoping they would ignore him.

He was wrong.

One of the oafs swayed toward his table and began to laugh. "What have we here," he slurred. His companions must have heard the grizzly sound, for they turned their attention away from a full-figured barmaid and onto the object of their friend's interest.

"I don't see nuthin', Durm," replied the blondest, and fattest, of the toughs. "Nuthin' but a graybeard taking up our fav'rit spot."

Aidan rolled his eyes. Why did they always use that tired old excuse for a fight? Lack of imagination, he supposed.

As the rest of Durm's friends approached, he stared intently into his beer. All he had wanted to do was wait quietly for the priest. Now it looked like there would be trouble. The three men surrounded him, blocking off any chance of escape.

"What's wrong, old man," taunted Durm. "Don't ya remember how to talk?" He laughed again, a vulgar sound somewhat between a belch and a snort.

Aidan sighed. He knew how this would most likely end. If only Morgrim would arrive, he could walk away without a fight.

"I guess he can't remember, Durm," replied the fat one. "Maybe we should refresh his mem'ry."

They all laughed self-importantly. Suddenly, the last of the men, a giant, red-haired fellow with the build of a field ox, slammed his meaty hand on the table. Durm leaned forward.

"My friend here would like you to move so we could have our table."

Aidan looked up at the three men. Smiling invitingly, he said, "There's no need to get upset. Why don't you and your friends sit down here and join me for a drink?"

As he finished the sentence, he threw the remainder of his drink at Durm, then slammed the cheap metal goblet on the red-haired giant's hand. Both of the men recoiled from the surprise attack. He took advantage of that opportunity and got to his feet.

As soon as Aidan stood up, the fat man charged in. Aidan quickly sidestepped the attack and grabbed the man's arm. Raising it over his head, he pivoted his hips and watched with satisfaction as his attacker flipped in the air and landed with a whumpf on his back.

By this time, Durm and his companion were ready for another go-around. Aidan sized up his two opponents with a practiced eye. He could handle Durm easily enough, the man was all bluster and soft muscle. It was his companion, the ox, whom he worried about.

They moved forward and he braced for the attack. Before he could raise his arms, however, he felt a sharp blow to the back of his head. Someone had thrown a bottle. Aidan's head spun and before he knew it, the giant had both of his hands locked behind his back. Durm strutted forward, producing a thin dagger from his belt.

"Not so fast now, are you old man," Durm said. "I think I'll gut you right here for what you did to me and my friends."

Aidan shook his head, trying to recover from the thrown bottle. If he could just shift his weight a little, he'd be able to kick the gloating man in the face.

Before he could do this, however, a soft voice floated from the bar. "I think he's had enough, don't you."

Durm spun to face the voice. Aidan looked over to see Morgrim, dressed in a simple brown robe. Even without his vestments, the man had a malignant air. Durm must have sensed this, for he chuckled nervously and said

"Yeah, sure. We was just havin' a bit of fun, weren't we boys." He nodded to the giant. "Let the man go, and let's be on our way."

The mighty grip relaxed, and Aidan made his way toward Morgrim, rubbing his wrists to restore the circulation. The three men looked at Morgrim once and then quickly left the bar.

"What took you so long?" Aidan asked.

Morgrim flashed him a grin. "I was busy doing some research," he replied. "Besides, you looked like you had everything under control. I especially liked the way you blocked the flying bottle with your head."

"Demons take you, man!" Aidan nearly shouted. "Do you think this is some gods-blasted prank?" He was too angry and confused to deal with the priest's newfound levity.

Morgrim's smile vanished. "I see your meeting didn't go so well. Come, let's talk business if it's a dark mood you're having." The priest pulled Aidan into a corner and whispered. "I found out a couple of things that might interest you. First, Alaslyn Rowanmantle did commission a blade for you from Khulgar's weapon shop. You should lay a few inquiries up that tree and see if it yields fruit."

Aidan nodded. "What's the second thing?"

Morgrim looked about the room before continuing, "Apparently, there are rumors of some sort of transaction, purportedly over a dagger, that will take place tomorrow in the sewers. If we can witness that transaction it would be most beneficial.

At last, something constructive to do, Aidan thought.

* * * * *

It was early evening by the time Aidan found himself in front of Khulgar's shop. Briefly, he stared at the evening sky, splashed pink with the last rays of the setting sun, and paused at the door. The air was still, poised as if the slightest breeze would shatter the twilight scene. He breathed deeply, gathering the stillness into himself. His life had changed so much in the last tenday that it took something as unfailingly regular as the coming of night to remind him of who he was. With a sigh, he entered the shop.

Blades of various shapes and sizes, from short-hilted daggers to elaborately crafted two-handed weapons, hung promisingly on display, and a number of finer ones lay behind rune-inscribed glass. The heat from the back forge poured over him in waves. He shuddered once, trying to expel the cold that had settled into his bones. Winter was never kind in Tilverton, and every year his old body found it more difficult to fight the chill. He waited patiently for a clerk, gratefully soaking in the heat, until a lad finally came out to assist him.

He quietly handed the boy a few silvers and spoke Khulgar's name. The young apprentice dashed off, only to return a few minutes later with the dwarven smith in tow. Khulgar was short, like all of his people, but he possessed thickly corded muscles and a mighty barrel of a chest. His skin was ruddy and heat-baked; a thin sheen of sweat covered his naked torso. Aidan noted with interest the smith's tightly braided beard, now tucked neatly into his heavy pants. This, he thought, was a dwarf of whom Moradin himself would be proud.

"Here now," barked Khulgar, folding his callused arms across his chest. "What's this you been doing to my boy, that he drags me away from the forge so early?"

Despite the dwarf's gruffness, Aidan suppressed a smile. He doubted that Khulgar spent much time away from the forge. Not wishing to waste any more of the smith's time than necessary, he got right to the point. "I'm wondering if you remember working on a dagger commissioned by Lady Rowanmantle herself."

If the invocation of the regent's name impressed Khulgar at all, the dwarf didn't show it. He stood there for a minute, a scowl sculpted upon his craggy face, before answering, "Hmmph . . . I receive a lot of commissions from the Lady."

"Yes, I quite understand," Aidan put in hastily, "but this would have been a gift intended for a retiring Purple Dragon officer."

Khulgar's stony face cracked into a smile. "Yes, I remember that one . . . carved the Purple Dragon's symbol into the hilt myself." The smith paused. "Unusual, that's for sure."

"Unusual in what way?" Aidan asked excitedly. Here, at last, was his first real lead!

"Well, I usually deliver the regent's commissions myself—I don't much trust anyone else to handle them—but when the commander came in and said that he wanted the dagger, I let him have it. Who am I to argue with—"

"Excuse me," Aidan interrupted, not sure if he heard the smith correctly, "did you say the 'commander'?"

Khulgar nodded. "Aye," he said. "Commander Haldan. I wouldn't have just given it to him, but he said that Lady Rowanmantle charged him with its safety. He was supposed to deliver it to its intended recipient personally," the dwarf replied. "Look . . . why do you want to know this, anyhow?"

Aidan didn't hear the question. Sweat broke out on his face and his knees trembled. The heat from the forge seemed to treble in intensity, as the interior of the shop, so comforting just moments ago, closed in upon him like the jaws of an ancient red dragon.

Ignoring the smith's startled exclamations—for Aidan's skin must have looked as sallow and gray as the roaming dead—he threw open the door of the shop and ran out into the night. He stumbled hurriedly through the streets and alleyways of Tilverton for hours, not knowing, not caring about his destination. His thoughts, if one could call them such, were a chaotic jumble.

Impossible!

Let them pry the dagger from my heart!

He was the best of us!

Moradin would be proud!

Morgrim, my friend?

How could he?

Finally, Aidan tripped and fell on the uneven stones of a darkened alleyway. He struggled to rise, but couldn't, his mad strength spent. Defeated, he panted hard into the night air. Winter wind whipped through his sweat-soaked body, sending a chill down his spine. The sensation hurt, but the pain cleared his mind; it was like awakening from some ensorceled dream.

Aidan lay in the alleyway for a few more minutes, marshaling his strength. When he finally arose, his steps were unhurried and steady. Although the night grew ever colder, he didn't feel it. He was numb, empty, like the husk of a soldier after his spirit has fled—except that he wasn't dead.

He trudged on and reached the door of his simple house. Once inside, Aidan slumped on his bed and waited in vain for sleep's blessed relief. When it didn't arrive, he sat in the darkness of his room, searching for some other way to resolve the situation—but nothing came. Haldan had used him, broken every oath of friendship and honor known to a warrior. For that, he had to pay. As the hours passed and dawn threatened the night sky, Aidan's resolve hardened. Emptiness gave way to a hungering need for vengeance. When Morgrim appeared at his door in the pre-dawn light, adorned in a thick purple robe and bearing a skull tipped obsidian staff, Aidan didn't even acknowledge the young priest's greeting. Instead, he threw an old black cloak over his own leather armor, buckled on a sword. and uttered a silent prayer to Cyric as they marched out into the fog-shrouded morning.

He was off to kill his oldest friend.

* * * * *

Aidan walked through the old sewer tunnel and grimaced at the ankle-deep sludge through which he and Morgrim were trudging. The priest's staff spat feeble illumination into the darkened tunnel, revealing slime-coated stone walls and horridly wilted roots. The air was dank and warm, heady with the stink of decay, and everywhere Aidan could hear the echoing squeal of sewer rats.

He and Morgrim had spent much of the early morning wandering through this endless array of crumbling sewer tunnels in a frustrating search for the correct series of passages. At first, his memories of this place had threatened to overwhelm him. He had lost a lot of men within these tunnels during the final battle against the Fire Knives, and their dying screams seemed to carry throughout the sewers. But these memories had also spurred his thoughts toward Haldan—with whom he shared command that awful night—and he used the surge of anger brought on by the thoughts of his former commander to tame his tortured remembrances. Now, every step brought him closer to the truth—a truth he knew would be difficult to face.

At last, the two neared the center of the Fire Knives' old headquarters. Aidan stopped and turned to Morgrim, pointing down a tunnel that angled to the east.

"This is it," he whispered. "Straight down this tunnel lies an old storage room used when the sewers were still active. That's where we'll find the Lirithane."

Aidan's hands were shaking now. He placed both of them on his sword hilt while Morgrim stepped off to the side.

The priest nodded and said, "We'll need to be careful; there are bound to be sentries." With that, he held his staff

aloft and spoke a single word. The light from the staff went
out, plunging the tunnel into darkness.

"I have something that will help us deal with our enemies," Morgrim said softly. "Hold on to me and don't let go."

Aidan reached out toward the direction of Morgrim's
voice, grasping for the priest's hand. When he found it,
the captain almost shouted. The young man's hands were
as cold as ice.

Morgrim chanted softly in the darkness of the tunnel,
a harsh grating sound that cut through the air like a
knife. Aidan winced at the sound and tried to cover one
ear with his free hand. The sound swelled for a few seconds, then stopped abruptly.

Silence. Aidan began to panic until he felt Morgrim
squeeze his hand. The panic receded, and he continued
down the tunnel, guiding both himself and the priest by
holding on to the wall. They followed the angling tunnel
for a few hundred feet until Aidan saw a dim light in the
distance. The two figures kept close to the walls and crept
toward the light. As they approached, Aidan saw two
cloaked figures guarding an old stone door. He squeezed
Morgrim's hand and pointed at the sentries.

The priest's answering smile chilled Aidan to the bone.

Morgrim released Aidan's hand, pulled out two daggers, and flung them at the sentries. The weapons kissed
both thieves in the throat, and they fell to the floor.

Aidan and Morgrim moved quickly, dragging the now
still bodies into the shadows. When they were done, Morgrim threw a small coin back down the tunnel. The
silence seemed to follow it, and soon Aidan could make
out voices from the room beyond the door. He pressed his
ear closer.

". . . the note of credit, Paidraig, and my associates will
present the knife."

Aidan's heart lurched. It was the voice of Haldan Rimmersbane! He had hoped, even at the last, that the evidence was wrong. Now, with the knowledge that Haldan
truly was involved in the theft of the dagger, the final fab-

ric that held his former life together tore. The pain of that tearing was worse than any sword wound, and Aidan nearly toppled to the floor with the strength of it. Instead, he banked the smoldering fire of his anger and drew his sword in a white-knuckled grip. With a shout of fury, he pushed open the door and ran into the room, not caring whether Morgrim followed.

Haldan and a familiar white-robed figure turned at the sound.

"Traitor!" Aidan shouted.

He did not have a chance to hear Haldan's response as four figures detached themselves from the shadows and attacked. This time, Aidan was prepared. He swung his sword in a wide arc, denying the thieves an opening. Although he was once again outnumbered, Aidan fought with a mind unsullied by ale. This battle would cost his attackers dearly.

The room flickered in a shower of sparks and blazing lights as Aidan ducked under a hasty attack. Dimly, he was aware of Morgrim locked in a deadly mystical duel with the white-robed man. Again and again the two opponents called upon magical forces beyond his ken, and the room nearly trembled with their power. With a shake of his head, Aidan blocked out the thundering display of pyrotechnics and turned his attention back to his opponents.

Fortunately, the arcane battle seemed to unnerve the cloaked figures, and he quickly took advantage of their distraction, dispatching two of them with a well-timed reverse stroke. The two remaining thieves were noticeably less enthusiastic and soon fell beneath the furious onslaught of his attack. He stood above the two corpses for a moment and carefully wiped the blood from his blade. It was then that he realized the room lay silent.

Desperately he cast about the chamber for any sign of Morgrim. He found the priest in the corner, struggling to rise to his feet. The body of his opponent lay scorched in the center of the room. Aidan shot off a prayer of thanks and started toward his companion. As he neared the corner, he saw Haldan step out of the shadows and raise a sword above Morgrim's head. The priest tried feebly to defend himself, but it was obvious to Aidan that he was too hurt to do any good.

"No!" shouted Aidan, running toward the two. "You've lost, Haldan. Let him be."

Haldan spun. Even in the dim light of the storage chamber, Aidan could see the runes engraved upon his former friend's sword.

"Lost?" Haldan said. "I haven't lost. I'm still alive."

Aidan shook his head and tried to speak. He wanted to give voice to the anger and hurt that festered inside him, to condemn this man for destroying his faith in the world, but the words were stuck in his throat as surely as if he were bespelled. All he could do was blurt out a single word.

"Why?"

Haldan looked at him and chuckled. "Why?" he taunted. "For the money, of course. With the gold from this sale, I'll buy a seat on the Council, and from there my associates and I will slowly pry Tilverton out from under the thumb of Cormyrean rule." Haldan raised his voice and began to shout. "The regent has done nothing but drain the life from this city. She is unfit to lead us. It's time for a new rule, a new ruler, in Tilverton!"

A light shone in the commander's eyes as he spoke. At first, Aidan thought it madness, but soon realized it was something far worse . . . fanaticism.

"I suppose that you will lead Tilverton in this new era?" he asked, hoping to divert Haldan for a few more moments. He knew that there was no hope of convincing his former friend to surrender.

"Of course," the commander replied. "Who else is more suited to handle the responsibility? And I will start right now by ridding Tilverton of this scum!" Without warning, his sword whistled down to Morgrim's bleeding form . . . and rebounded as it met Aidan's own blade.

The look of betrayal that passed across Haldan's face only angered Aidan more. Ignoring the numbness in his wrist, he slid his blade out from under the commander's and aimed a high strike at Haldan's head. Engaged in battle, Haldan's sword began to glow with bright blue intensity. Faster than any weapon had a right to move, it deflected Aidan's blade.

Haldan grinned fiercely and sent his own sword snaking after Aidan's blood. "It seems that you have made a choice, Alassalynn Aidan," he hissed through clenched teeth. "So be it. Even if you kill me, there are others who won't rest until Alassalynn and her Cormyrean lapdogs are nothing but a memory."

Aidan said nothing, conserving his strength for the battle ahead. Although he was still quicker than the commander, Haldan possessed greater strength and a magical blade. Even now, he could feel his muscles weakening; every parry brought the rune-encrusted sword closer to his flesh. He crouched low, hoping to find an opening in Haldan's guard. The commander attacked high and to the right. There was his chance! Springing forward, he thrust his sword at Haldan's exposed midsection. Too late, Aidan realized his mistake. The commander completed his feint and angled his blade at the captain's neck. Desperately, Aidan raised his sword, hoping to deflect at least part of the blow.

With a sickening twist, his sword flew from his hands.

He watched helplessly as Haldan moved closer. The commander could end this at any time, and they both knew it. He braced himself for the final blow, but Haldan just stood there with a surprised look upon his face. When he pitched forward, blood frothing from his mouth, Aidan automatically moved forward to help. Forcefully, he stopped himself. Behind the fallen commander stood Morgrim, holding two bloodied knives. The priest panted heavily in the silence of the chambers and smiled at Aidan before collapsing to the ground.

Slowly, Aidan retrieved his sword and knelt beside Haldan's body. The commander was dead, his face frozen in a permanent rictus of surprise. Gently, and with more care than he thought possible, Aidan closed the corpse's eyes.

"Rest well, my friend," he whispered. Whatever had passed between them, he would always honor the man he knew as a young Dragon.

He sighed and moved to Morgrim's crumpled form. The priest lived—barely. Aidan watched the shallow rise and fall of his chest and marveled at the priest's vulnerability. Morgrim's life was an ember smoldering beneath Aidan's boot; a simple step would grind it into ash.

And yet, he knew that he would not take that step.

Though the priest served the whims of a dark god, he had more than proven himself worthy of respect. Aidan didn't believe he possessed a heart of gold—that kind of naïveté shattered in a dark alley late one night—but Morgrim's actions spoke of friendship more eloquently than words.

Aidan watched the wounded priest for a few more moments, then turned away to search for the Lirithane. He didn't want to stay in the sewers any longer. A few minutes later, he found the familiar blade clutched in the cold hands of Morgrim's spell-wielding opponent. Prying it loose, he discovered a disc shaped symbol—the sign of Lathander—attached to a chain around the corpse's neck. With a curse, he tore the symbol from the chain and tossed it back down the sewer tunnel. Haldan had spoken the truth; his allies would never rest until they fulfilled their plan.

Carefully, Aidan bent down and lifted Morgrim up from the dank floor. As he retraced their furtive passage through the tunnels, he thought about the events of the past tenday and smiled. He would speak to Lady Rowanmantle this very afternoon and pledge his help in rooting out the conspiracy.

Perhaps there was a place for an old, tired soldier after all.

Whence the Song of Steel

J. Robert King

In my line of work a fellow gets used to lots of things—
ear-splitting screams, daggers in the shadows, leering
masks, wicked smiles, wailing widows, back alleys, bodies, and blood . . . lots of blood. I'd just never had to
endure all of them in one night.

Opera's what the Sembites called it. The word means
"works." Still, out of a cast of thousands, I was the only
one working. Everybody else primped and bickered,
pranced in parti-colored silks and grease paint, and gestured to a couple fat men who bellowed. Meanwhile, I
stood there in the dark lee of a stage curtain and watched
and listened.

That was work. Real, hard work. It's tough for a man of
action to stand around and watch something happen that
isn't even happening. Still, something real was about to
happen. Death was in the air that night—real death and
real blood—I could smell it. Murder was only moments
away. I edged closer to the stage. The two fat men there
were my responsibility. Usually a person doesn't become
my responsibility until he's lying facedown in an alley
puddle. But these two stuffed sausages were still very
much alive, and it was my job to keep them that way.

I'm Bolton Quaid, watch captain-for-hire and, lately,

bodyguard. I'd landed this particular job back in Water-deep—my stomping grounds—when the opera had toured there. No sooner had it opened than death threats had started rolling in. Understandable. If I'd paid a handful of gold to hear this, I'd've been in a mood for murder, too. Still, the head of the company hadn't wanted to take chances. He'd sought out the best bodyguard in the city and ended up with me. Five cities and ten months later, I was still along for the ride . . . and the death threats still rolled in.

From the beginning I knew most of the threats were sent by one tenor to the other. Singers are like that, I'm told. But a few came from somebody else, somebody who could've been sitting in the audience even now. I looked out past the bobbing heads of the chorus, toward the dour, jewel-decked crowd. They sat in the Grand House as still as statues. The best of the best. Everything about them shone—diamond necklaces, gold earrings, silver hair, bald pates, and glassy eyes. Mostly their eyes. Boredom, resignation, sleepiness. Not the usual motives for murder. Most of the crowd couldn't even muster up interest, let alone malice.

Still, death was in the air. I could smell it. Somebody was planning murder.

It could have been one of the singers. While the crowd had no passion, the singers had too much—roaring, stomping, wailing, collapsing, trembling, swaggering, staggering, leaping, sobbing, fighting, swooning, and, of course, bellowing, bellowing, bellowing. . . . They were mad with passion, lunatics capering and drooling and howling at the moon.

Tonias, the younger tenor, led the bedlam. He was a stout lad with golden hair and beard standing straight out in a ring around his head. The sheen of his hair was accentuated by the crown he wore, which designated him King Orpheus, conquering lord of Distalia. He wore a fat white ruff, a tunic of bright yellow silk, a stiff brown waistcoat, an ermine-lined cloak, and a yellow stocking that showed every line of his legs. On high notes, Tonias would loft his gleaming sword, giving everyone in the front row an intimate view of the effect of his tremolo. He seemed more a puff pastry than a killer.

The older tenor, on the other hand, seemed perfectly capable of murder. In this opera he played the villain Garragius, one-time king of Distalia. Displaced and outlawed, Garragius posed as a leprous beggar in order to sneak up to Orpheus and kill him. The animosity was not all acting, though. It was jealousy, pure and simple. While Tonias got to strut center stage, V'Torres had to lurk near stage front. The old tenor wore no finery, only black rags charred from encounters with the foot candles. His lines were full of growls, barks, and guttural threats. On low notes, he sounded like a rutting bull, on high notes like a cat in heat.

That hadn't always been the case. He'd once been a young tenor sensation, the toast of Sembia. Then, he'd had the voice of a hero—high, pure, and crystalline. Bold but tender. Powerful but tragic. Especially tragic. His career had ended at its height, turning on itself like a snake swallowing its own tail. To escape ever-present fans, V'Torres had begun to drink himself unconscious. The problem was he would invariably wake up beside one of those fans. Eventually, drink rotted his liver, and pox rotted his brain. By the time he got dry on both ends he was empty in the middle, and had no voice left. V'Torres, now, was next to nothing, and jealousy consumed him.

Perhaps murderous jealousy.

Tonias was worthy of it. Occasionally, he would stop bellowing and actually sing something soaring and sweet. Then, even I could tell he was good. In those moments his voice held all of hope and fear, desire and devotion. The sound struck me in the breastbone and moved in waves through my ribs, into my spine, and up to buzz in the base of my brain. It was like my ears heard only the smallest part of that sound, most of it resounding directly in my bones. Even now he sang such a passage. Among a rapt and adoring throng of choristers, King Orpheus stood, belly thrust outward, head thrown back, and battle sword lifted high:

"I rise. I rise upon the dawning hope of Distalia,
Like pollen in the teaming air of Spring.
I rise. I rise as all life rises, green and soft
Through iron-hard ground to daylight gleam.
I rise. I rise from roots that turn your dark decay
To golden finery, turn grave soil to wind-borne seed.
I rise, as all of life, I rise!"

While King Orpheus sang, Garragius growled out a counterpoint. Tattered black rags swayed around his twisted frame. Within the cloth, a wickedly curved dagger glinted with little flame teeth from the foot candles. Clutching the blade, Garragius made his way toward the king.

"Death also rises,
Or didn't you know?
In every blossom, every fruit,
The worm will also grow.
The worm that eats away the home.
The worm that winnows flesh from bone.
The worm, implacable, alone
Eternal, worm. Eternal worm!"

Garragius groveled his way to the foot of the singing king and lifted the dagger in tremulous hands. King Orpheus sang on, oblivious, as his foe rose from the shadows to slay him. Giving a final shriek of animal fury, Garragius rammed the curved dagger into the King's bulging gut. A gout of blood sprayed forth.

I was impressed with this bit of stage magic, more realistic than in the fifty-some last performances. The blood even steamed in the cool air.

Tonias's song turned into a shriek of agony and he stared in horror and shock at the knife jutting from his stomach. "He's killed me!" Tonias cried out unmusically. The pit orchestra ground to a halt. The lead rebec player—a thin, pale woman—rose to stare, aghast.

Tonias lifted a crimson hand from his belly. "V'Torres has killed me!"

V'Torres? I flung back the curtain and rushed onstage.

Too late. Tonias's whole body shuddered. His sword arm went limp and dropped, blade still in hand. The steel flashed in an orange arc and struck V'Torres in the neck, bringing an instant spray of gore.

V'Torres's scream was taken up by many members of the crowd. The audience recoiled from the stage, clambering over seats and bustles and miles of satin to get away from the blood. I was drawn to it. I reached the scene in time to catch Tonias, slumping unconscious to the floor. The dead weight of the man bore me down in a heap beneath him. Next moment, V'Torres added his body to the pile, hand falling from his spurting neck.

That's when I began bellowing. Hot blood soaked my clothes, and three hundred pounds of tenor crushed me. But mainly I bellowed because the men I'd been hired to protect had, in front of thousands of elite witnesses, killed each other dead.

* * * * *

Well, not exactly dead, thanks to the priests of Lathander in the front row. I commandeered the healers, who accompanied body-bearing guardsmen to separate dressing rooms where ministrations began. After issuing orders for crowd control, I got the blood cleaned off me and headed for Tonias's dressing room.

I knocked on the door. The lead rebec player answered. She blinked big moon eyes at me. Her hair bristled in a brown, unkempt mat and her mannish tunic and trousers were stained in blood. "What?"

"I'm Bolton Quaid, the bodyguard."

"A little late, aren't you?" she asked caustically. She stepped back and let me in.

The room was as sumptuous as it was crowded—wool rugs, glazed windows, silvered mirrors, embroidered chairs. . . . Tonias lay, huge and sweating, on a too-small fainting couch, midsection covered by a rumpled yellow shirt. At his head stood one gray-garbed guardsman. Another stood at his foot. The rebec player drifted quickly in to kneel beside the couch on a lush Shou Lung carpet. Her knees settled just beside the bloody sword that had almost killed V'Torres. I made my way past red-and yellow-robed priests and stood over the tenor.

Tonias groaned to see me. "There's the man. There's the man whom I was told would ensure my safety, my very life. There he is, Waterdhavian sewer rat, keeping track of his pay but not his responsibilities. . . ."

"That's why I'm here, actually," I said, dragging a notebook and a fat-nibbed hunk of lead from my pocket, "my responsibility. It's not just guarding you. It's also convicting anybody that attacks you—or V'Torres."

Tonias's face grew a fiery red beneath his crown of gold hair. "Why aren't you questioning him?"

"Hard to question an unconscious man." I shoved a couple music scores off a chair, drew it up beside the bed, and straddled it. "Besides, he's looks guilty enough. Everybody saw him stab you. That was no accident. That was attempted murder. The real question is, what happened with this sword of yours? Was that an accident, or. . . ."

The flush of Tonias's face waned the moment I'd pronounced V'Torres's guilt, but his eyes still blazed as he said, "I wish to the gods I'd killed him. I wish to the gods the sword had cut his head clear off. I assure you, if I'd done it on purpose, it would have killed him. I hate the man. But the blow of my sword was completely accidental."

I made a line of nonsense scribbles on my pad of paper. I never write real notes, but scribbling keeps people off balance. "That's a funny kind of argument. You're saying you had motive, means, and opportunity, and yet you didn't try to kill him? That'll be hard to prove."

He glanced down. His jowls rippled as he chewed over

a decision. At last, he said, "It's easy to prove. It's the easiest thing in the world to prove, only I won't do it with all these people here."

I glanced up. The priests of Lathander returned my questioning gaze, most of them young, clean-shaven, and naïve.

I gestured toward the man's belly. "What's the prognosis? He well enough for you folks to step outside?"

The chief healer nodded and smiled—even his eyes smiled. "The Morninglord has been generous, indeed. The wound closed with the first prayers uttered, and the patient is resting comfortably—"

"That'll be the day," sniped Tonias.

"—so I suppose we could step outside and see how V'Torres is doing."

"Fine," I said, dismissing them.

The priests filtered out, robes rustling in the stale air, and I closed the door behind them. Tonias glanced meaningfully at the guards at the head and foot of his bed.

"Not a chance," I said. "They're working with me."

Grimacing reluctantly, Tonias said, "I had the motive and opportunity, but not the means. I would have loved to kill V'Torres, but I never would have tried to kill him with that sword." He nodded down to the blood-crusted blade beside the couch.

I reached down and lifted the thing, amazed at its heft. This was no mere stage sword. The blade was broad and balanced, its hilt expertly wound.

"Look at it, Quaid. This is the real murder victim tonight," said Tonias cryptically. The blade certainly was bloody enough to be a murder victim. V'Torres's gore was drying all across its fine etching. "Do you have any idea what . . . whom you hold in your hand?"

"Whom?"

"That is . . . was Ranjir, an ancient elven singing sword. An intelligent weapon," said Tonias sadly. "It was forged before the time of Myth Drannor. It fought in thousands of battles, many for the elven homelands they still hold today. It has changed the course of Faerûn. And now, it is dead."

"Dead?" I glanced up and down the blade. "How can you tell?"

"Look at the ruby in its hilt. It once shone with an inner light. Now look at it," he urged. "Look at it!"

I turned the sword over, gazing into an eye-sized gemstone set in the silver filigree of the basket handle. The stone was cracked, shot through with sooty blackness. I tried to keep the humor from my voice as I asked, "How did it die?"

"Blood," Tonias responded, miserable. He folded his arms over his chest. "The sword was forged so that if ever in battle it was touched with blood, it would be slain."

I was still studying the blown-out stone. "How did the sword fight in thousands of battles and change the face of Faerûn if it never drew blood?"

"By singing, it could create mass hallucinations, make a small force seem like an army, make enemies think they were wounded, make them faint, unconscious, believing themselves slain. It won its wars by singing, not by slaying . . . not by blood."

"A singing sword," I said, admiring the weapon. "Perhaps even an operatic sword? This would be quite an item for a person such as you to have. A wonderful prop that could turn a fine actor into a magnificent tenor."

"He is a magnificent tenor," the rebec player protested. "He has a beautiful voice. Sing for him, Tonias. Sing for him!"

Tonias patted her hand, defensiveness melting as he comforted her. "It's no use. He'll know soon enough." He lifted his eyes to me, and the fire and irritation were gone, leaving only the red, wounded look of a lost child. "I am a good tenor, yes, but not a great tenor. Not the great tenor Tonias of Selgaunt. That was all an act. It was the sword singing, not me. So, you can see, Ranjir was my career, my life. I'd never have drawn blood with it."

I nodded, sliding my notebook away. He was telling the

truth, I was sure. Otherwise, he was throwing his career away for nothing. "So, you're finished then, yes?"

Tonias snorted. "I'll say the belly wound stole my breath. I'll say I can't sing four bars straight through. I'll say something and retire from opera forever."

I got up to go, still carrying the sword, but turned with one final question. "You said Ranjir was a murder victim. If you didn't murder the sword, who did?"

The heat returned to his eyes. "V'Torres. He must have found out about the sword, that it sang for me. He must have found out how to kill it, and stabbed me to provoke me into using it on him. He may have attempted to murder me, Quaid, but he succeeded in murdering Ranjir."

"Why?" I asked. "Why kill the sword?"

"Jealousy, pure and simple. He wanted to destroy my career just like he destroyed his own."

It all seemed to be falling into place. I headed toward the door. "I'm confiscating the sword till this thing gets cleared up."

Tonias waved the blade away. "It's worthless to me, now. Do whatever you want with it."

"I'd like to show it to V'Torres and see what he has to say." I motioned to the two city guardsmen. "And I'm going to ask these fellows to stick with you until we've got this whole mess sorted out."

"I understand," Tonias said snidely, patting his girlfriend's hand. "After all, somebody's got to guard me."

The other tenor's dressing room was down in the bowels of the opera house—no windows, no silver mirrors, no fainting couch, no Shou Lung carpets. It was a cramped space of drippy brick. Flanked by guards, V'Torres lay on a moldy pallet on the floor. He wore black rags and clutched a metal flask in his hand. His face was grimy with stage makeup, his black hair a tangled mass above dissipated eyes.

The yet-smiling priest met me at the door. "We've been doubly blessed today. The Morninglord saw fit to heal this man, as well. He's lost much blood, but is no longer in danger."

I raked the bloody sword out toward V'Torres. "We'll see how long that remains the case. Thanks for your help," I said by way of dismissal. The priest made a shallow bow and ducked from the mildewy place.

I considered the wounded man, real-life equivalent of the leprous, murderous Garragius. "So, what do you have to say for yourself, stabbing your rival onstage, before thousands of witnesses?"

"I didn't do it," he rasped out miserably, and took another bitter swallow.

I nodded. Every man in the dungeons was innocent. "So, your dagger just slipped. Maybe you'd been drinking and started to lose your balance. Maybe the blade couldn't help hitting the biggest thing around."

"Not even that," the man said darkly, coughing as the rot-gut brought tears to his eyes. "I stuck the dagger in the space under his left arm, just as I always do."

"When you're seeing double, it's hard to know which left arm—"

"I'd had nothing to drink before the performance. It was only after . . . everything that I. . . ."

"Then where did all the blood come from? And how did ten priests get a look at Tonias's bowel? And why am I here having to talk to you?"

"I didn't stab him."

I towered over the supine man. "Tonias thinks you did. Tonias, and me, and the rest of Selgaunt. Not only do I think that, but also that you killed his sword, too . . . this sword." I held out the bloody blade.

V'Torres blinked at the gory steel, then screwed his eyes closed in torment. "Ranjir was mine, Quaid. Why would I murder my own sword?"

I was incredulous. I crouched down atop my heels and held the blade on my knees. "Your sword? Then why was it in your rival's hand?"

"Why, indeed?" V'Torres nodded, eyes still closed. "Back in my heyday, it had been mine. I'd used it just like Tonias did. It was the voice behind my career. But then it got stolen. I was ruined. I refused to perform. Drank heavily. Woke up in a lot of odd places. People came to their own conclusions. But the real end of my career was losing Ranjir." He took a shuddering breath. "May I see the blade?"

I handed him the blood-stained sword, and V'Torres positioned it on his body, point down like a weapon laid on a corpse. V'Torres's nostrils flared as he drew in the scent of the metal. Eyes closing tight once again, he smiled in pain. "In my hands again, at last."

Tonias's blade? V'Torres's blade? It made sense. Two great tenors, one great voice. "If it's yours, why didn't you try to hunt it down?"

"What do you think I've been doing for the last five years? I suspected Tonias at his debut, but couldn't get close enough to find out. I'd been banned from concert halls, you know. Offstage he kept the sword in a triple-locked iron trunk. I knew for certain it was Ranjir only when we began rehearsals for *Terra Incognita*. Since then, I've been trying to take it back. I even went to the Guild of Thespians, Bards, and Choristers—"

"Why would they help you? You're a fraud. Tonias is a fraud."

"Ranjir was just an instrument, like a cittern—that's what I told them. They turned me down flat. Guild or no guild, I was determined get the sword back. As long as I was alive I wouldn't give it up. Tonias knew that. He just didn't know what my blood would do to the sword."

"He's the one that told me how the blade died."

"He'd tried it once before . . . took a swipe at me. I'd warned him then, but he scoffed. Now he knows the truth."

Tonias might have known the truth, but I didn't. The stories of both men were plausible enough, but still stories, still lies.

"You'd stop at nothing to get the sword back," I said. "I'm sending you off with the city watch, suggesting you be charged with attempted murder." I took the sword from the tenor and glanced up at the guardsmen. "Shackle him and take him to the dungeons. I'll be by shortly to explain."

Even as the men set to work, rolling V'Torres on his side, the tenor said, "And what about Tonias?"

"He'll be charged with attempted murder, too."

"And what about Ranjir? Who killed Ranjir?"

I turned the crimson blade slowly in my hand. "That, I still don't know."

* * * * *

I delivered the bad news to Tonias and his girlfriend and endured a whole new opera of bluster and threats. That was enough. I'd had a bellyful of singers and silk, hubris and hoi polloi. I wanted dark streets and smoking chimneys, stray dogs and the smell of old fish. I wanted some good honest dirt, dirt that called itself dirt and looked dirty. In the end, even gold and diamonds were just dressed-up dirt.

I took Ranjir with me and headed out alone to the city garrison. On the way, I stopped to get a breath, to get my bearings.

I stood in a small circular courtyard, a cobbled alley surrounded by fieldstone townhouses. The crescent moon was a bright scar on the belly of the night. Thin clouds wrapped the sky in torn gauze. The roof line of the city rankled below. Black tiles, seeping shakes, and shaggy humps of thatch. Widow's walks bristled like vulgar crowns. Water whispered in gutters and glinted in the distant cup of the sea.

Selgaunt. A quarter the size of Waterdeep, but still embroiled in nastiness. Fakery. Mendacity. Rich fat prima donnas attacking rich fat prima donnas. All that I could've stood—I was used to it—but caught in the center of this fight was something fine, something noble and beautiful.

I hefted the sanguine blade before me. Ranjir, ancient singing sword of elven kings, forged for battle, hero of a hundred wars, shaper of continents . . . and forevermore dead. Killed as an evening's entertainment. That wasn't even the worst of it. Before all that, the sword had been enslaved to two stupid, petty men. They'd made it sing for applause, perform like a trick monkey, and spend the rest of its time in triple-locked darkness. It might as well have been used to slice watermelons and pry open stuck doors.

Standing there under gauze clouds and frightened little stars, I knew with a sudden certainty that Tonias and V'Torres hadn't been the sword's first taskmasters. How many of the other great tenors of Semmite opera had used this blade? For how many hundreds of years had the singing sword of elven kings been enslaved by puffed up blowfish like Tonias and V'Torres?

Suddenly, there it was again. The smell of death. . . .

I was no longer alone in the cobbled courtyard. From beneath crumbling arched alleyways they came. They emerged from behind ragged wooden tool sheds, abandoned flower boxes, a pile of rotten barrels. Lean, black-suited fighters with eyes like candle flames. They were all around me, blocking all exits.

I crouched, holding out the sword before me, and noticed that not a single one wore any armor over their body stockings.

An eloquent and dramatic voice came from one of my attackers, "It would seem, Agent Quaid, that you are at our mercy, and mercy is perhaps the rarest coin in our realm." Not assassins. Thespians. "Surrender the sword to us, Quaid, for we have taken your mettle, and our taste is for a much finer alloy." Bad thespians. There was a bit of whispered protest after that line, and a small slap fight to determine who would get to address me in the future.

"This sword is at the center of this investigation," I said flatly. "You can't have it. Besides, it's dead. What would the Guild of Thespians, Bards, and Choristers want with a dead sword?"

That brought more nervous whispers. Someone argued they should make a run for it. In the end, a new voice won out. "Believe what you will about who surrounds you, Quaid. We will believe what we will about the sword. Now, hand it over or taste our own tongues of steel." That speech was the most popular so far. Heads nodded in the darkness.

Thespians or no, there were twenty of them. They could kill me with prop swords. Still, Ranjir had been through too much already. I wasn't about to surrender it to another batch of simpering fops. "Come, take it."

"We will!" someone improvised, though the group seemed anything but keen on charging me.

The circle slowly tightened. I shifted my feet, turning to keep them all in view. Quick footsteps came behind me. I whirled. Ranjir whistled into the space. Steel struck steel and sparks flashed before a black goatee. With another swipe, I drove the attacker back.

And whirled. Two more swords darted toward my back. Ranjir cracked against them, one, two. . . . I charged after the swordsmen, needing more room. They staggered back, fashionable berets outlined against the starry night, and foundered on a pile of barrels. Staves popped and rusty hoops groaned as they tumbled.

I'd gotten room enough to breathe but wanted to keep it. I swung Ranjir in a wide arc to my right and let the weight of the blade spin me around. With an audible gasp, the black body-suits fell back.

I assumed a fighting stance and growled out, "The damned blade is dead. Give it up, or you may be as well."

They seemed impressed by this speech—literarily, not literally. One shouted back, "Give it up, or you may be as well." That pleased the crowd even more, and hardened my resolve. Dead or alive, Ranjir would not end up in the hands of more theatrical taskmasters.

I took the battle to them, rushing a pair of men outlined by an alleyway. If I could bash past them. . . .

Swords rang angrily on each other. The attackers' blades sounded tinny mixed with the bell-tones of Ranjir. Even dead, it was a beautifully turned blade. I lunged. The tip of Ranjir catching in the basket hilt of a foe's sword. As I struggled to wrench the blade away, something lashed my sword arm. My shoulder felt suddenly hot and achy. I won free and backed up, carving space around me.

Blood was creeping down my arm, dousing the sleeve of my shirt. One of the leotard crew had gotten in a lucky strike. The blow was superficial. It stung, but I could still wag Ranjir well enough. Then one of the actors was counting to three in an ominous stage whisper, and they all rushed me. I shouted in surprise, but there was no time for threats or words or even breath.

A thicket of blades surrounded me, jabbing in, nicking my side, my back, my neck. Ranjir danced with a will all its own, seeming to drag my wounded arm behind. All the while my blood crept down from shoulder to elbow to forearm to wrist. I was losing, and I knew it.

Ranjir knew it, too.

Light suddenly flashed through the courtyard. Thirty-some lanterns were unhooded at once, surrounding us in glare. Lances of light sliced through the circle of thespians. They shrank back, muttering about watchmen and dungeons and the fact that the world never recognizes true genius. Then they bolted, scrambling away through the shadows like so many rats. I expected to hear sounds of struggle and eloquent protests as the watchmen collared them.

But there were no watchmen, no lanterns. The light, in fact, radiated from the ancient elven sword I bore. The ruby blazed with light and life. The sword sang sadly:

> "Lift me, if you please.
> The blood on your hand
> Could kill me."

I complied, raising the blade overhead and watching the trickle of blood on my hand reverse, flowing back down my wrist. And there I stood, sword lifted high, a shabby, common version of King Orpheus. And, as in the play, the sword sang:

"I rise. I rise upon the dawning hope of Distalia,
Like pollen in the teaming air of Spring.
I rise. I rise as all life rises, green and soft
Through iron-hard ground to daylight gleam.
I rise. I rise from roots that turn your dark decay
To golden finery, turn grave soil to wind-borne seed.
I rise, as all of life, I rise"

"So," I interrupted wryly, "it was you all along. You used your mass hallucination powers to fake your own death?"

"How else could I get shut
Of simpering, bellowing fools?
They wouldn't let me go
Except in death.
Death also rises,
Or didn't you know?"

"And you faked the stab wounds, too. No wonder they healed so easily. I was surprised even the Morninglord was so solicitous. I wouldn't be surprised, though, if you somehow sent some of those death threats, too."

"Yes, I've been waiting these centuries
To find a hand such as yours,
The hand of a real warrior.
I've been pining for real battles again,
No more snake-oil stage shows."

"Oh, no," I said, fetching up the edge of my shirt and wiping the blood from my hand. "I work alone. I can't be seen singing whenever I get in a fight." Once the blood was well stanched, I lowered Ranjir and looked it square in the ruby. "Still, I wouldn't mind some company on the way back to Waterdeep. And I know a certain weaponsmith who supplies fine swords to real warriors. I imagine I could enlist his aid to find you a fist headed for battle."

The sword seemed almost to laugh as it sang out again:
"I rise. I rise upon the dawning hope of Waterdeep,
Like buds and flowers from wintry sleep.
I rise!"

An Unusual Suspect

Brian M. Thomsen

There were three corpses laid out on the dock before me; two of them were burnt beyond recognition, the pungent smell of charred flesh wafting up from the ashy remains.

The third corpse had miraculously avoided incineration . . . and it was Kitten's.

Others knew her as Nymara Scheiron, just another tousled-haired dockyard coquette of dubious alignment (if you know what I mean), but for me she has always been Kitten. She was my oldest friend despite the fact that I've only known her for three months. That being the exact period of time I can claim to know anything or anyone; before that point others might know, just not me.

Don't get me wrong or mistake me for some lunatic, liar, or lover. I'm not some bardic romantic whose life metaphorically began when he first set eyes on his lady love. Kitten and I are, I mean, were friends, not lovers, at least not as far as I can recall. Three months ago I woke up in a Waterdeep dockyard alley with my mind wiped of all knowledge concerning my past. A walking *tabula rasa*, you might say, perfect prey to everyone and anyone, a wandering stranger unto himself with naught to confirm his existence except a splitting headache and the scent that comes with being unwashed for longer than polite company wish to be aware. I don't remember exactly what happened (something I say a bit too often for even my own comfort), but somehow Kitten came upon me and nursed me back to health. Not just satisfied with mending my body, she even found me a useful place in the society at hand and lined up work (of a sort) for me, to keep my belly fed and the rest of me adequately warm and comfortable until my memory returned (which it hasn't yet).

She got me back on my feet when no one else seemed to give a damn.

Kitten was the oldest memory still in my head, and now her lifeless body was laying before me and I knew I would have to avenge her death.

* * * * *

I had been sleeping off a celebratory bender on a recent job's successful completion when I was aroused from the golden slumbers of the inebriated by a dockyard lad of the streets who had been sent to fetch me. (This was the usual way I was drafted by the mysterious group who I had to look upon as being potential clients.) Throwing just enough cold water on my face to enable me to see clearly (and not enough to cause frost in my close-cropped whiskers in the pre-morning chill), I followed the boy as I knew that my potential clients usually didn't like to be kept waiting.

As was the routine, I was led down a number of back alleys and through a few abandoned buildings (throwing off any potential tails) before the lad handed me off to a cloaked figure who tipped the boy a coin and beckoned me to follow. The cloaked figure walked briskly, his boots tapping a staccato beat against the stone streets as he raced against the ever encroaching dawn whose early light was just beginning to cast out the shadows from the dark side of Waterdeep.

The sun was just about to clear the horizon when he motioned me into a nearby warehouse and quickly closed the door behind us, sealing us into the dark while the rest of Waterdeep began to enjoy the first light of a new day.

As my guide fumbled with a torch, I mused to myself gratefully. Well, at least my first fear has been dismissed; a vampire racing against the dawn would never pause to light a torch. We must always be thankful for small blessings.

A few seconds later his efforts were rewarded and the torch ignited with a temporarily blinding blaze that quickly settled down to a reassuring illumination that provided me with my first good look at the guide who had led me here.

There wasn't much to see.

He was about my height and build with rather expensive taste in clothes. His cloak was heavy and cowled, the hood of which he carefully rearranged so as to remove it from his head with minimal muss and bother.

The hood fell back from my guide's head to reveal a closer, more form-fitting mask that completely obscured his face, hair, and features, leaving me with little more of a clue to his identity than I had upon the first moment of our meeting.

This wasn't unusual really, as many of my clients seemed to prefer to keep their identities well under wraps, even from me, their humble and obedient mind-wiped servant. It almost seemed to go with the territory in the line of work to which I had become accustomed.

The masked man lead me down a set of cellar steps to a subterranean passage. I was immediately struck by a cool, moist breeze that seemed to be coming from the direction in which we were headed. The sing-songy lapping of waves grew louder as we approached a larger, well lit chamber.

A highly functional dock, receiving, and storage area (not to mention two burly stevedores, arms emblazoned with tattoos of numerous savory and unsavory ports of call from the Sword Coast to the Moonsea) lead me to believe that we had arrived at one of Waterdeep's numerous clandestine ports of call. I began to wonder if perhaps I was being taken to a meeting by means of some underground nautical transport (to fabled Skullport perhaps) until my guide lead me to the three waterlogged forms that appeared to have been recently dragged from the sea and set out on the docks like recently unloaded refuse.

Whatever had befallen the three sorry corpses must have happened very recently. The sodden state of their garments had not yet washed away the smoky residue of partial human incineration that must have occurred within the last two hours.

My eyes were immediately drawn to the only body that seemed to have escaped the flames, whereupon I recognized its identity. I held my breath and controlled my rage at what fate had befallen my benefactor, silently swearing an oath of vengeance.

"Your thoughts?" inquired the stentorian voice of the masked man. The voice seemed vaguely familiar. (But then again all of the other masked voices I've dealt with in my short past sounded familiar, too.)

Obviously I had not been brought here to identify the bodies. The patrons who hired me had numerous necromancers, scryers, and other magic men specializing in the recently deceased who were easily more suited to such a task.

"Life's cheap, unfair, and brutal, as luck would have it," I said, "but whatever happened here, didn't happen by chance."

"How so?"

"Two of the bodies were burnt beyond recognition, and whoever did it was no second rate firebug. They were flamed by some blast of intense heat, probably some sort of spell—"

"Spellfire," the masked man volunteered, interrupting my impromptu dissertation and dissection of the matters at hand.

"Whatever," I said quickly, dismissing the interruption as irrelevant to my thought processes. If there were two mortals on all of Toril possessed of spellfire that was a lot. Any garden variety fireball would have sufficed. "All I know was that it was powerful enough so that a good dunking in the sea failed to dampen the heat left from the blast . . . as evidenced by the fact that the bodies and what remained of their clothing are still smoldering." I pointed at the lifeless husk that had been my friend. "Except for this one."

"Kitten's," the masked man volunteered in an emotionless tone.

"Right," I said quickly, trying not to dwell on the consuming wave of grief and rage that was beginning to tangle in my gut (emotions that did not seem evident in the monotone of my client's voice). "She hasn't been burnt at all. The other two were probably incinerated to forestall identification. Maybe they wanted someone, us, to know that Kitten has been killed."

"Not likely," the masked man volunteered.

"Then perhaps the fellows with the hot hands were interrupted before they could finish their flaming handiwork," I offered, and quickly inquired, "But why isn't my initial scenario likely?"

"Because at this moment, in the pub known as the Bloody Fist, a woman going by the name of Nymara Scheiron—also known as Kitten—is drinking on the tab of a recently acquired friend."

"An impostor?"

"A doppleganger," the masked man answered.

"Go on," I demanded, impatient to be brought up to speed. I felt no necessity to confess my ignorance of such matters to the patron. Personal experience of the past few weeks had already clued me in that these hooded guys always knew a lot more about me than I knew of them. (That was why, after all, I agreed to work for them.)

"Dopplegangers," the masked man elaborated in a tone

more than colored by a tint of condescension, "are creatures that have the ability to shapeshift and take on the appearance of any other creature. Their exceptional mental powers allow them the ability to read the mind of anyone in their close proximity, thus providing them with the details and data to effectively masquerade as anyone, even when they are in the presence of that individual's loved ones. Needless to say, once an individual has been removed from sight, kidnapped, enchanted or killed, there is nothing to prevent this unholy creature from taking their place in society. Over the past few years we have been troubled by a crime ring known as the Unseen under the leadership of one of those devils, a criminal genius who goes by the name Hlavin who aspires to replace key figures of our community with his unholy minions and thus bring all Waterdeep secretly under his thumb."

"And as goes Waterdeep," I said, "all Faerûn does follow."

"A few years ago he operated out of a local festhall called the Inn of the Hanging Lantern hoping to get its surprisingly upper class clientele under his spell, but his operational cover was blown by some journalist by the name of Volothamp Geddarm."

"The name's familiar," I volunteered, remembering his connection to a certain Waterdhavian publishing concern.

"He's not important," the masked man stated. "Somehow Hlavin has implemented some new, fiendish plan. He's already replaced this sorry threesome, and we need to know his next move."

"Who are the other two?" I asked, gesturing at the two soggy victims.

"That's the problem. All three bodies are ensorcelled, and the best wizards in Waterdeep can't crack the spell."

"So no deathbed interrogation or revelation."

"Exactly," he concurred. "Which has forced us to utilize much more mundane methods in our search for the truth."

"Namely me."

"Your charge," he ordered with the authority of some pompous magistrate, "is to follow the doppleganger that is passing as Kitten and uncover the identities of her two associates who have taken the place of these poor bastards."

"I accept," I answered quickly, eager to get to work, and avenge the death of my friend.

"Not so fast," his lordship ordered. "Remember, dopplegangers are telepathic. They can read minds. This Kitten can't see you or she will know what you're doing."

"Don't call that thing Kitten," I said defiantly, adding, "and once I've found the other two, I assume I can deal with them with the extreme prejudice that all three deserve."

"No," he ordered, "you will report back your findings, and accept your payment. You are solely to gather information, and no direct contact is to be instigated. After your . . . shall we say research . . . is complete, the matter will then be turned over to the proper authorities."

"I want to be there when their heads are removed from their shoulders."

"That is not for you to concern yourself with."

I was taken aback for a moment.

"They will be executed, won't they?" I demanded. "Last I heard, cold-blooded murder was still a capital offense here in Waterdeep."

"Again," the patron said without hiding his tone of condescension, "that is not your concern. I assure you, cool and competent minds will handle the matter."

I nodded to concede the patron's point so that I could expedite the matters at hand and get on with the case, all along knowing that I would not rest until I had personally laid Kitten's killer to rest, no matter who I angered while doing it.

The masked man snapped his fingers and one of the burly boys escorted me back to the surface. Messages and updates were to be left in the usual clandestine places, and I was to go about fulfilling my assignment as I saw fit. The instructions on leaving the resolution of the matter to others was considered to be more than enough of a warning not to proceed with any plans for vengeance, but I was out for blood.

Kitten deserved no less.

* * * * *

My assignment wasn't by any means an easy one. The creature that had killed and was now posing as Kitten would obviously pick up my thoughts once we made contact. The only one deceived by the thoughts of a mind is it's own possessor.

Tailing her undetected wasn't a problem. The Dock Ward was filled with urchins willing to do anything for a gold piece or two. In the short time of my memory I had recruited a sturdy stable of cast-off minions whose effectiveness at following orders was only surpassed by their greed and fear of my displeasure.

Gross and Waters would be perfect for the job. Both were used to doing my background dirty work and neither knew Kitten personally. The two would spell each other and report back to me twice daily at dusk and dawn. Though neither could read or write worth a damn, they nevertheless always turned in comprehensive reports on their day's (or night's, as the case may be) observations.

I knew Kitten's usual routine like the back of my hand and hoped that I might observe some discrepancy in my two lads' reports that might lead me to the identities of that hellion's accomplices. Newfound friends, secrets, rendezvous, and such would no doubt provide me with an avenue worth pursuing.

Minions dispatched, I decided to spend the rest of the day avoiding the target of their tails, and do a little research on the dastardly dopplegangers myself.

My patron had mentioned a certain Geddarm who broke up the ring that operated out of the Hanging Lantern. I seemed to recall a loutish would-be actor

(Pisspot, or some such name) who was always bragging about his great comrade Volo with whom he had shared many an adventure. As I recall, the thespian hung out at an after-hours place frequented by actresses and their patrons. The hostess was a bosomy wench named Blondel who owed me a favor or two for services rendered. As luck would have it, the actor in question was engaged in a discussion with the lady of the house as I entered the establishment.

"But Blondie," the rotund fellow persisted, "I assure you it would be wonderful."

"For who?" Blondel replied with a tolerant grin. She patted his hand firmly before moving on to another patron.

I scanned the rest of the crowd, a scant lot not unusual for the daylight hours, and turned back to take a seat at the bar. A glass of my midday usual was already in place before me. I reached in my purse for a silver piece, but my hostess wouldn't hear of it.

"I'm still working off my tab from last week," Blondel replied with a coy wink. "At this rate I'll be paying it off all year. I wish you'd consider some of my more expensive services."

"I'm in no hurry," I answered slyly. "I like to take my time."

"I bet you do."

Lowering my voice I asked, "What's the price on information these days?"

"Reasonable."

"What can you tell me about the crowd that used to hang out at the Hanging Lantern?"

Blondel furrowed her brow for a moment. "Not much," she answered. "They did a brisk trade catering to the crowd's wishes. More than a few of their clientele really hated it when they closed down even if it was rumored to be a den of demonic dopplegangers."

"Any word of the survivors regrouping and re-establishing themselves elsewhere in the trade?"

"Not that I've heard. Things have been awfully quiet lately. Word in the alleyways is that the Unseen has left town in favor of greener pastures, and speaking of greener pastures have you considered—"

Blondel's proposition was rudely interrupted by the boisterous boom of the thespian lout Pisspot.

"You want to know about dopplegangers, my good fellow," the bag of wind announced to the world (or at least those who were within earshot in the room around us). "Well, allow me to be of service. A drink for me, wench, and put it on his tab."

Blondel looked at me in gentle amusement. I nodded and she went about serving the fellow who had situated himself beside me, giving me a quick and hearty hale-and-well-met pat on the back.

The drink arrived, he drained it, and beckoned for me to draw closer as he intended to speak in a hushed tone. Secrecy is always best maintained by whispering, I thought, especially when you have already announced the subject matter to everyone in the room.

"I am an expert on dopplegangers," he whispered pompously.

I nodded, and said, "So I've heard. You're an associate of that Volo fellow. Pisspot's your name."

"That's Passepout," he corrected, "son of Idle and Catinflas, circumtraveler of Toril, and scourge of all dopplegangers. What would you like to know? Do you want to hear about how I uncovered a plot to replace Khelben or how I saved the heir of one of the leading families of Cormyr or how I single-handedly secured the balance of power in the Moonsea region? It's all very hush hush you see."

"What can you tell me about dopplegangers in Waterdeep . . . lately?" I inquired.

"Another drink?" he requested.

I nodded to Blondel who quickly accommodated him. The rotund fellow raised the tankard to his lips and replied, "Nothing, I'm afraid, but thanks for the refreshment. You are a gentlemen and a scholar."

As he drained the tankard, Blondel quickly placed another in front of him, which he quaffed in similar fashion and immediately passed out.

"That settles that," she announced, and then, pointing at the stout fellow who had just begun to snore, asked the crowd, "Know anyone looking to shanghai a crew member or two? He'll be out for at least a day and a half, more than enough time to get persuasively out to sea."

"I'll send word if I hear of anyone," I replied. "And you do the same if you hear anything new about the matters we discussed. You know how to get hold of me."

I was swiftly back on the street and in search of information, the sound of two bouncers placing a rotund thespian in a holding sack quickly diminishing in the distance.

Word would be out in no time that I was on a doppleganger hunt. The loudmouthed Pisspot had seen to that. If I didn't find them they would find me.

Either way I'd soon be facing Kitten's killers.

* * * * *

Things didn't move as swiftly as I had assumed.

Three days and six reports from my minions later and I was no closer to achieving my objective, and the hunger for vengeance began to consume my belly like day-old Baldur's Gate rotgut.

Gross and Waters had both reported that the thing that was passing for Kitten seemed overly wary in her one-on-one encounters, as if she were always on her guard, but other than that nothing suspicious. (Gross postulated that it could be a "woman thing" and that she was just self-conscious.) As always I didn't comment, just listened.

My patron sent a missive indicating that he and his associates were growing impatient, and that the fate of Faerûn was probably hanging in the balance. What else was new? I had heard that all before and really didn't care. They would get their information soon enough (and a few corpses as well, if I had my way) even if I had to beat it out of someone who looked like my best friend.

* * * * *

On the fourth day of my quest I almost ran into Kitten but quickly managed to remove myself from her presence before she had a chance to sense me. I'm not really sure how these doppleganger telepathic powers work, but I'm pretty sure I made it away clean. Waters included his observation of my near-miss in his daily report, but as per usual didn't make any query about it.

A good minion doesn't ask questions unless they are told to.

On the fifth day I received a missive from Blondel. Someone wanted to see me. Concealing various bladed instruments on my person, I quickly set off for the rendezvous that had been arranged for me.

The meeting was set for an after-hours place a block over from the waterfront. Blondel's missive had indicated that a well dressed fellow from the North had asked her about the Hanging Lantern and dopplegangers a night ago. A follower of synchronicity over coincidence, her feminine sixth sense told her that she should put him in touch with me.

The dockyard was my home turf and she knew I could take care of myself. I arrived at the meeting an hour early so as to have the advantage. I was about half an hour too late.

I realized this only when I felt the initial blow of a firm cudgel on the crest of my cranium. My adversaries had already laid claim to the advantage by arriving even earlier.

* * * * *

I came to a while later, lying on some cold and damp

cellar floor, my wrists and ankles bound, Blondel and a nondescript gentleman standing over me.

"He's coming around," the unknown figure announced.

"It's about time," the creature that had become Blondel answered. "Though I guess we really couldn't have asked for a more cooperative opponent, walking right into our clutches and all. I probably would have let you go on living if you hadn't posed a threat to our other associate."

"The one posing as Nymara Scheiron," I replied.

"Exactly. Your queries were getting in the way of her fulfilling her part of our mission, and our master was growing quite impatient. We never really feared that you would uncover the full extent of our plot since you had obviously chosen to settle the matters at hand before carrying out your patron's wishes. Such arrogance and rage can only get in the way, and for what? A slim chance to avenge the death of a friend? A person of your abilities should have known better. But then again, if memory serves, experiences are the best teachers, and you seem to have forgotten most of yours. At this point I would like to add that it was quite refreshing to read such an uncluttered mind as yours."

"I'm glad I could accommodate you," I replied cockily. "Little did I realize that I would have to avenge the deaths of two dear friends."

"Blondel's crime was being in the wrong place at the wrong time," the thing that was passing for Blondel explained. "Your Kitten on the other hand was very necessary for our plot. The new Kitten should be on her way here now. Too bad you won't be around to meet her."

"Why didn't you just kill me and get it over with?" I asked. "It would have saved you the trouble of tying me up and all."

"True," it replied, "but unfortunately my nondescript colleague whose appearance was dictated by an equally unlucky nobody applied his cudgel to your skull a little too quickly. I hadn't yet had the chance to leaf through the pages of your mind to make sure that you hadn't informed your unknown patron of our little meeting, and unfortunately such reading of thoughts is more difficult when the subject is out cold."

The thing that had become Blondel looked in my eyes. I sensed hunger in her thoughts.

"You have so many questions inside of your head," it said with a sigh. "I'm afraid I can't answer any of them for you. It's a shame, going to your death without ever knowing your own identity, your past, or even your own name."

"You could at least tell me the reason Kitten and Blondel had to die."

"Beyond the simple reason that we had to take their places?" it replied, and shrugged. "Too bad you can't read minds. Oh well, I can't see the harm in it, and besides, Kitten should be here soon. We probably should wait for her."

The thing leaned in close to me, and purred in the manner Blondel used to when she wanted to get me hot and bothered. The knowledge that this wasn't the member of the gentler sex with whom I had shared a few passing evenings did little to quell my response to her seductive tones.

"Our master has engineered a new plan to reassert his influence in the fair city of Waterdeep. He has recognized the necessity of controlling the, how should I say . . . 'word about town' in order to carry out his plan. The Inn of the Hanging Lantern was brought down quite inadvertently by a busybody hack writer and a know-nothing publisher. Our job was to replace the publisher with one of our own so that such a turn of events wouldn't happen again."

I laughed sardonically at the black humor of it all.

"All of this for one lousy publisher who would probably have been open to a bribe anyway," I said in ironic resignation.

"Indeed," it replied, "but the master didn't want to take that chance. Bribes don't usually instill loyalty, and most publishers seem to relish the idea of renegotiation even after a deal and price have been set provided that the matters at hand seem to be in their favor. It was to be the first cautious step in his great new plan . . . but I am afraid that we can't wait any longer. Kitten or no Kitten."

It withdrew a poisoned black blade dagger from it's bodice and began to place it beneath my chin, ready to insinuate its deadly edge into the fleshy part of my neck.

"Good-bye, man without a past. Give my best to your Blondel. She should be happy to see you, if I recall correctly," it purred.

The poisoned tip of the deadly dagger had furthered its insinuation into my flesh and was about to penetrate and seal my fate when the sound of the whistle of flying steel breezed through the cellar.

The thing that had become Blondel slumped to the side, quite dead, the poisoned blade barely missing my throat with nary a nick, as her associate also crumpled to the floor.

A familiar face stepped out of the shadows pausing momentarily to retrieve her blades from their well aimed destinations deep in the dopplegangers' backs before turning her attention to me.

"Now that wasn't too hard," the familiar voice of Kitten exclaimed. "There's a whining tub of lard in the other room. He's in a large sack labeled 'bad actor for shanghai', but I don't think he'll mind if I tend to you first."

My oldest friend explained the matters at hand as she undid my bonds.

"Sorry that you had to be kept in the dark about all of this," she said, "but it was the will of the Lords. When the doppleganger tried to remove me and take my place, it woefully underestimated me."

"A common mistake . . ." I interjected.

Out of the corner of my eye I discerned a movement from the direction of the supposedly dead doppleganger accomplice of Blondel, and with my recently freed hand extracted a throwing knife from one of my secret harnesses and let it fly in the direction of the noise, hitting home in the forehead of the now really dead doppleganger. It seems Kitten's dagger had lost most of its killing power when its mortal flight had been interrupted by some well placed chainmail.

". . . and common mistakes do have a way of continuing to crop up," I added.

"Point well taken," Kitten conceded.

"I immediately sent word to Khelben Arunsun, who alerted the Lords. It was they who concocted this plot to uncover this latest conspiracy of the Unseen. We needed to know who the others were and what they were doing. Given their exceptional mental powers, the Lords knew I would never be able to pass myself off as one of them. We therefore needed a reason that I would cease interacting with the others in the plot, namely that I was being followed by one of the Lord's men."

"Me," I offered, mentally making a note that my current patron was one of the Lords, confirming a suspicion that I had been harboring of all of my so-called benefactors, "the perfect blank slate."

"Exactly," she replied. "Your well intentioned quest for vengeance—yes, the Lords knew what you intended to do—made you the perfect judas goat to draw them out while providing me with the perfect cover."

"I was the bait, and you were the trap."

"Exactly."

With her help I stood up and rubbed the circulation back into my wrists and hands. "Blondel is still dead."

"I'm afraid so," Kitten replied, a supportive hand placed on my shoulder, "but her killers are now dead also."

"All to protect a stupid publisher whom the Lords have had numerous problems with."

"Indeed, Justin Tyme is no friend of the Lords," Kitten answered apologetically, "but we didn't know that he was their target at the time. And we could rule out the usual suspects like Khelben, Danilo Thann, Myrt the Money-lender, and others. If we had known, maybe things would have been different. Maybe we would have taken a different tact."

I secretly made a second note of her use of the word "we."

"Blondel would still be dead. Some things don't change."

Kitten looked down at the toes of her boots as if to avert my stare.

"It's a small consolation, but the Lords' plan worked as well as it needed to. A new Unseen plan nipped in the bud." Kitten raised her head, and looked me in the eye. "Let's get out of here. It's time for you to claim your payment for services rendered. But first we should free the hapless actor . . . unless of course you think we could fetch a good price for him on the seagoing market."

"Not likely," I replied, still distracted by the new revelations at hand. I quickly regained my wits and, not wishing to alert my feminine benefactor to my realization, I added, "It wouldn't be worth the effort."

It took bare minutes to free the terrified Pisspot from the very large sack that imprisoned him and an interminable few minutes more to get him to stop groveling.

We quickly gained the streets of Waterdeep at which point the rotund thespian sped off in search of a bar where he would no doubt soon be bragging about his latest adventure. Kitten and I set off to claim a new piece of the puzzle that was my past, the taste of unnecessary death still fresh in my mind as well as new suspicions about whom I could really trust.

Darkly
Through A Glass of Ale

Peter Archer

The sun sank into a golden haze of clouds and darkness rolled gently from the east over the port of Tharkar on the borders of Ulgarth and the Free Cities of Parsanic. At the gates that breached a thick wall dividing the two states, guards yawned sleepily in the evening heat. Steam rose from the softly waving fronds that bordered the Free Cities, northernmost kingdom of the Utter East. On the Ulgarthan side, a horse-drawn cart kicked up a thick cloud of dust that obscured both driver and passenger. The guards bestirred themselves and raised hands.

"Who seeks entry into the Free City of Tharkar?" inquired one in a bored tone, as he grounded his halberd by his side.

The driver of the cart coughed and shook his head, clearing the dust from his eyes and throat. "I am Necht of the Free City of Whitevale. This," he said, gesturing to his companion, "is Avarilous, a merchant of Ulgarth, with goods to sell."

"What nature of goods?" The guard yawned.

"Fifty kegs of ale for the Tavern of the Tall Tankard," said the driver.

The guard, coming more awake than he had been all day, stepped back a pace and whistled loudly. From the long evening shadows of the gate behind him emerged the chief guard, a rotund fellow barely contained in his stretching chainmail. The chief glanced at his fellows and chuckled, turning his attention to the passenger.

"Well, Avarilous of Ulgarth, as you're doubtless aware, none pass into Tharkar without paying tax."

"Tax?" The merchant stared angrily at the guard. The driver put a hand on his companion's shoulder and whispered urgently, but Avarilous shrugged him off. "There's no entry tax. I paid for an import permit and for a scroll of sales submission. They cost me enough."

The fat guard stepped a pace nearer. Sweat streamed down his face, dripping onto the rolls of flesh that surrounded his neck. From the corner of his mouth came a tiny dribble of dark juice; he had been chewing kalava leaves, a mild narcotic that, while technically illegal, were nonetheless widely available in the Free Cities. He rested a hand casually on his sword.

"This is a new tax," he grunted. "A special tax on Ulgarthan slime-dogs. It comes to exactly two kegs of ale. And since you're so anxious to pay it"—he glanced back at the other guards and grinned—"you can get down from there and unload the kegs yourself."

Avarilous stared at the dirty faces of the gate watch and snorted contemptuously. The driver descended into the roadway and smiled ingratiatingly at the guard. "You'll forgive my employer, sir," he said. "He's new to the Five Kingdoms, and our ways."

Without moving his eyes from Avarilous, the guard brought his fist around in a smashing blow that knocked the driver on his back five feet away. Blood spilled from his lips and ran down his chin. The guard smiled at Avarilous, showing all his teeth. "Well, slime-dog?"

The merchant hesitated and glanced at the driver, who

sat up in the white dust of the road, wiping his mouth. A subtle signal seemed to pass between the two men. Avarilous climbed from his seat and, going around the wagon, unhitched the back flap. He quickly rolled out two of the barrels, setting them upright on the ground, and refastened the wooden flap. He began to walk back to the front of the wagon, but the guard hadn't finished his game.

"Just a minute," he growled. "Let's see if you're paying this tax in good coin. Leethron, get a spout to tap this keg."

One of the other watchmen disappeared into a narrow recess in the wall, then reemerged a moment later with a tap and mallet. Swiftly, with the air of one well accustomed to such duty, he tapped the keg and, taking a dirty tin cup from one of the other guardsmen, filled it full of the frothy ale and passed it to his chief.

The head of the watch took a long draught, then looked at the merchant and smiled soapily.

"Pig's piss. That's what this is. But what do you expect from the hogs of Ulgarth? They've nothing to do all day but brew foul-smelling rot-gut like this." He chuckled. "Here, merchant, you try some of this swill."

He held the glass toward Avarilous, but as the latter reached for it, the captain suddenly upended it and poured the ale onto the ground while his other hand, holding a blade, came up to Avarilous's throat. "Well, merchant, go on. Drink up."

Avarilous gave him a disbelieving look and stared at the muddy spot on the ground. The driver, who had regained his feet, started forward with a cry, choked off as one of the other guards clamped a hand round his throat. Another, coming up behind the merchant, gave the back of his knees a violent kick, knocking him to all fours. The captain thrust his foot on the smaller man's neck, pushing his head down. "Drink, Ulgarthan pig!"

There was a roar of laughter from the rest of the watch. Avarilous twisted away and came to his feet, mud splashed around his mouth, streaking his cheeks. With as much dignity as he could muster he remounted his wagon and sat still, waiting for his driver. The man from Whitevale hastily climbed into his place and shook the reins. They drove down the winding street and out of sight. The guards laughed scornfully, then the captain thrust his glass at his lieutenant. "Here, lad. I'm off for the evening. Where did that fool say he was going?"

"The Tall Tankard?"

"Aye. Well, maybe I'll seek him out there and make him pay another tax."

* * * * *

Avarilous and his companion proceeded through the streets of Tharkar in silence for some moments. Silent groups of heavily armed men glared suspiciously at the wagon from arched doorways. Avarilous took no notice of them; he was well aware of the tense stalemate that existed between the Five Kingdoms, whose rulers jealously guarded their most powerful magical items. The bloodforges allowed them to conjure armies to defend against attacks from fiends and from each other. In the Utter East, temporary, armed truce was the status quo.

The oncoming evening was hot, and steam rose from the horses' flanks. After passing a few streets, the merchant cleared his throat. "How is your mouth, Necht?"

The driver shrugged and touched the blood crusted on his lip. "Could be worse." He turned to Avarilous. "But you really must be more careful, sir. This isn't Ulgarth, and our ways aren't yours. The gate watch almost always steals from goods wagons, especially those from Ulgarth."

The merchant nodded humbly. "I see. I'll try to do better in future."

He sank into a thoughtful silence, broken by Necht asking him, "Just what are you selling, sir?" Avarilous glanced at him, surprised. Necht, looking resolutely ahead, continued, "Mind, it's really none of my business, but if you're planning to get me into any more fights, I think I should know what's going on." He turned from the road and looked his employer full in the face. "So what's really in the barrels?"

Avarilous gave him a look of astonishing blandness. "Why, ale, of course. Just what we told those louts at the gate."

Necht shrugged and shook the reins again. "Whatever you say, sir. Ale's as good a story as anything else."

There was a moment of silence between the two men. Avarilous glanced sideways at his companion, then cleared his throat. "Just in case something does happen, though, I'd much appreciate a pair of eyes at my back." He stared hard at Necht, who grinned back cheerfully.

Necht swung his wagon into the courtyard of the Tavern of the Tall Tankard and leaped easily from his seat. The merchant descended more slowly, as befitted his greater age and weight. In the dark beneath the stars, his eyes glittered. From the open door of the tavern came light, music, and a blast of beery air. A figure emerged, observed the wagon, and approached Avarilous.

"Ahoy, good sir. Have you goods for my master?"

"Aye, boy, fetch him and some stout fellows to unload these casks."

In a few moments, the landlord came out of the door, a fat, oily man with the air of being constructed of badly pressed butter. Behind him were four helpers who, without a word, set to removing the barrels from the wagon and carrying them through a small side door into the tavern while the landlord directed their work. When they were done and his helpers had gathered behind him, he turned to Avarilous.

"Now, sir, how much for the kegs, then?"

Avarilous and Necht had watched the proceedings without saying a word or moving a muscle. Now the merchant spoke in a soft voice. "As you well know, Daltrice, the amount we agreed upon was five crowns per barrel. Forty-eight barrels makes two hundred and forty crowns."

Daltrice shook his head, smiling and rubbing his

greasy hands. "Now, sir, you are mistaken!" the landlord exclaimed. "Why, I was right here all the time, and I'll swear by Umberlee I counted only thirty-eight barrels carried into my establishment. I believe that brings your total to, let me see, one hundred and ninety crowns."

Avarilous shuffled his feet impatiently. "Come, Master Daltrice, stop this fooling. Two hundred and forty crowns is the sum owed, and two hundred and forty crowns I'll take."

Necht tugged nervously at Avarilous's sleeve. "Remember," the driver hissed. "Discretion in all things. We don't want trouble."

Avarilous snorted. "There won't be trouble if Daltrice pays what he owes."

Daltrice laughed, a giggle of pure delight. "Oh, my dear Avarilous," he said, "such a foolish man. But perhaps they don't educate you Ulgarthans in the complex ways of commerce, as do we of Parsanic. Very well. One hundred and fifty it is, then." He motioned to the largest of his helpers. "Sirc'al, pay the merchant."

The big man stepped forward and tossed a small sack on the pavement. Avarilous, hesitating a moment, picked it up and counted the money it contained. He looked sourly at Daltrice.

"There's one hundred here."

"That's right. Payment in full." Daltrice laughed again. "Come now, my good fellow. Come into the tavern and have a drink on the house." Turning his back on the merchant, he squeezed through the doorway.

Avarilous glared after him, then at the landlord's employees, who eyed him stolidly. He shrugged his shoulders and snorted under his breath. "Thank you very much," he muttered to no one in particular.

Passing through the door of the inn, Avarilous and Necht emerged in an arched passageway with doors penetrating the walls on either side and torches flickering in iron sconces. At the far end of the tunnel was a pair of wooden doors, paneled and intricately carved. These swung open as Avarilous and Necht approached them, and they passed into the main area of the Tall Tankard.

Of all the ports along the Utter East, Tharkar was the most popular with traders, travelers, and pirates. Ships put into its docks carrying goods to Doegan, slaves to Konigheim, and mead and battle-axes to the far-off halls of the northmen. Because of its position, the city was also the first port of call for the infrequent ships from Ulgarth, Chult, and even more faraway places in Faerûn. The taverns of the city were famous throughout the Five Kingdoms for their food, ale, dancing girls, and other, less explicitly defined forms of entertainment. Among these houses, the Tavern of the Tall Tankard was the most well-known.

Smoke from a hundred pipes rose to the night sky, sparkling with stars, above the open courtyard that was typical of Parsanic inns. Palms waved, and hrashaka—tiny lizardlike creatures—ran to and fro beneath the feet of the patrons snatching scraps of food from the unwary and disappearing down holes and into cracks. A chorus of raucous voices continuously called for ale, wine, brandy, and tareetha-girls, whose services could be purchased for a few coins. Serving wenches moved about bearing platters of steaming elephant and zebra meat and tall tankards of ale with which to wash it down. Snatches of broken song resounded from the room's corners and escaped through the open windows.

Avarilous cast a swift eye over the courtyard. He gestured to a raucous group of drinkers in one corner, away from the light of the torches. "Who are those people?"

Necht narrowed his eyes, squinting at the group. "Those are the inquisitors from Whitevale, sir. The ones I told you about."

"Ah, yes. Looking for adherents of the Fallen Temple." Avarilous apparently lost interest in them and glanced at the other side of the courtyard, where a collection of tough-looking bearded men were swiftly and silently downing tankard after tankard of ale. "And those?"

"Northmen. Daltrice had better watch them closely, or they'll drink up his entire cellar in one night." Necht sniggered at his own wit.

Avarilous gave a perfunctory chuckle. "And that group?" He gestured at a long table near the fountain at the center of the courtyard. A fine spray came from somewhere in its center, and rivulets of silver ran down the figure of a coiling python in its midst.

Necht smoothed out the lines in his face and looked properly serious. "Those are the trade delegates from Konigheim and Doegan. They've been here almost six months, negotiating a pact."

The merchant stared thoughtfully at the crowd. His eyes traveled slowly across the courtyard, pausing once at the sight of a stout back and dark hair hanging greasily over a rumpled collar. Necht followed his gaze, started, and began to speak, but the merchant's hand on his arm stilled him. "All right," Avarilous murmured to Necht, "Be careful . . . and remember what I asked of you."

White teeth flashed in Necht's dark face. "Yes, sir. Don't worry." And he was gone.

Avarilous cautiously edged his way closer to the bar, behind which stood the fat landlord contentedly surveying the anarchic scene before him. At the merchant's sharp rap on the counter, he glanced around, smiled unctuously, and slid across a tankard drawn from a barrel of the ale Avarilous himself had brought to the inn.

A balcony ran around the four sides of the courtyard. Vines hung down from its banisters. Avarilous, admiring the lush greenery, was startled to see within the foliage the undulating forms of serpents sliding smoothly over the soft leaves. He shuddered involuntarily, then remembered the special regard in which the people of the Free Cities of Parsanic held snakes. It was even rumored that somewhere in the kingdom, in a cold underground room kept secret from all but a chosen few were evil men with hooded eyes and shaven scalps. These priests of Talona sat amid wriggling mounds of serpents and, as the snakes wove beneath their ragged robes, spoke prophecies in hissing voices that were not their own. Avarilous glanced at the python statue in the sparkling fountain and shivered once more.

Beneath the balcony, he spotted a seat at a table set in the shadows, away from the torchlight that illumined the courtyard. The table was already inhabited by two men who looked up in irritation as Avarilous joined them.

"This table's occupied, friend," snapped one, a tall, grim-looking man with a scar disfiguring his cheek.

Avarilous smiled ingratiatingly. "Surely you'll not begrudge me a place to sit in peace? I've been traveling the whole day, and I long for an entertaining evening away from the dusty road."

The men looked at each other for a moment; then the blond one shrugged. A colorful scarf slanted over his forehead, concealing one eye and giving him a rakish, careless appearance. "Suit yourself," he growled ungraciously, turning back to his drink.

Avarilous pulled up a chair and slowly lowered his aching body into it. Before his bottom touched the well-worn seat, though, there was a crash. The chair spun away and the merchant fell sprawling on the floor. The scarred man who had kicked away the chair at the last minute gave a shout of laughter. "Next time, Ulgarthan scum, don't presume to sit at the same table with Tharkarmen." He gestured toward a dark nook nearby. "Get over in the corner and slurp your swill there, out of my sight."

Avarilous's shoulders tensed for a moment; then he shrugged, rose, and with as much dignity as he could muster, made his way to the place indicated. Tharkar natives sitting nearby, who had witnessed the incident with amusement, turned back to their drinks.

The merchant relaxed, leaning his chair against the wall, and observed the scene. After a time he drew a small pipe from within the recesses of his cloak and lit it.

The two men who had humiliated him drank steadily. Every now and then, one would rise and go to the bar for a fresh round of ales. They spoke little, but Avarilous overheard enough to learn that the tall, scar-faced man was named Kreelan, while his companion, shorter and blond, was Spielt.

From where he sat, Avarilous had plenty of leisure for observation. The crowd appeared at first to be a typical gathering of sailors, soldiers, and rogues from the Utter East. As he watched, though, he became increasingly aware of a subtly different dynamic in the courtyard, a tension that seemed to grow quietly among the various groups.

Avarilous's attention was gradually drawn to the boisterous group of well-dressed men gathered at the table near the fountain. It was a large party, and their penetrating voices rose above the clamor.

"Slaver scum! Traders in human flesh. The men of Konigheim! Who knows from what port they'll draw slaves next. Citizens of Tharkar, look to your children!"

"Fool of a Doeganer! We of the Mighty Kingdom of Konigheim, Beacon of the Utter East, Favored of the Five Kingdoms, take slaves only from the kingdoms we conquer. And yours will be next, unless I miss my guess. The fish-people at last caught in a net." The speaker chuckled heavily and belched. "We've all seen the neck gills you Doeganers sport. What's next for you? Will you grow fins? A kingdom of codfish? We'll serve you up in a lemon sauce. Or perhaps you'd prefer to be fried in batter!" He roared with laughter at his own poor wit, as his companions sycophantically echoed him. Avarilous noted with interest the patch of wrinkled skin in the middle of his forehead, a patch surrounded by a multitude of complicated designs executed in dark ink.

Near the center of the table a man rose, evidently with some authority. As he spoke, the men at the table fell grudgingly silent.

"Now then, citizens! Peace among us all! Put aside

those differences that divide us, and together, united as one powerful force, we can confront the fiendish enemy, while improving our mutual wealth and power!" The speaker lifted his glass. "A toast! A toast to our success in these negotiations. Neither shall be the loser in the pact we conclude."

There was an embarrassed scraping of chairs, and both sides in the dispute halfheartedly lifted their glasses in assent. Once again, talk at the table sank into the general babble of inn voices.

Avarilous listened with apparent indifference to this dispute and its conclusion. The men at his table seemed at first equally unaware of it. But as he observed them closely, the merchant saw that this was not so.

As Kreelan went to the bar he spoke a word in passing to one of the Doeganers. As Spielt, a colorful scarf slanting over his forehead so that it concealed one eye, passed near the delegation he seemed to stumble and murmur something to the Konigheimers. The men at the large table drew together in a tighter circle, their voices hushed, suspicious looks passing between them like summer lightning.

Avarilous watched this with growing interest, waiting for the spark that would set off open conflict. It was not long in coming.

Kreelan leaned his chair back and stretched. As he did so, Avarilous saw him, with a flick of his wrist, toss a small rock, so accurately that it upset a full tankard of ale on the Konigheimers' side of the table. A hulking, dark-haired Konigheimer with the white skin and tall build of the Ffolk, instantly leaped to his feet with a curse. He turned angrily to one of the Doeganers sitting across from him.

"Clumsy fool! Watch what you're about!"

"Slaver dog!"—the Doeganer was on his feet now—"The curse of the mage-king upon you!"

Rather than reply, the slaver picked up his chair and bashed it across his opponent's head. Other denizens of the tavern sprang up, and the brawl was on.

Avarilous slid further into his nook, avoiding flying furniture and bits of broken glass. To his right he could see his table companions watching the battle with evident satisfaction. The conflict was conducted with broken chairs and tables. Fists flew. Bottles crashed. The smell of spilled ale was overwhelming. Then, as one fighter staggered back into the dark nook in which Avarilous was standing, the merchant was plucked forth and swept into the midst of the battle.

He found himself parrying a myriad of blows, slashes, and flying cups. Out of the corner of his eye he saw Spielt and Kreelan had entered the fray. He worked his way into the middle of the courtyard, now jammed with thrashing bodies, most of them held upright by the press of people. Then, just as the fighting was heaviest, the crowd drew apart to reveal a man's body sprawled face-down, floating in the waters of the fountain. Crimson ripples spread in a ghastly halo around his head.

"Murder!" The cry came from a hundred throats. The crowd poured into the street, and in five minutes the only ones left in the tavern besides the owner were the two men from Avarilous's table, the merchant, and the dead man. A second later, the landlord and his band of helpers emerged from behind the bar and ranged themselves before the door. Avarilous sank back into his nook, watching the scene with glittering, attentive eyes.

The two drinkers would have followed the rest of the crowd, but their way was barred by the landlord, who came at them in a furious rush.

"You fools! What have you been doing? This fight will bring the watch down on this house for sure!" The landlord's voice ended in a shriek as Spielt seized him by the throat and pinned him against the wall with one hand, while his other drew a wickedly curved sword from beneath his robes. His friend stared grimly at the landlord's henchmen as they started forward.

"Call off your dogs," he growled, "unless you'd care to end the evening as a corpse,"

The landlord gestured frantically with one hand, and the large guard, Sirc'al, stepped back a pace. His hand was on his own sword, and his eyes looked death at the scarred man.

The ruffian nodded to his companion, who loosened his hold on the landlord. The fat innkeeper choked and gasped for a moment, then sank into a chair. Kreelan gave his friend a ghastly smile and the two stepped confidently toward the door.

Light flashed suddenly from a blade, as one of the innkeeper's men drew a broadsword and pressed it against Spielt's throat. "Halt! Or your friend dies!"

Kreelan stopped, his mouth slipping sideways in anger. He glanced down, making a visible effort to regain his temper. Then he looked up again. "Go ahead! He's less than nothing to me. I can pick up a better helper than him in any dockside brothel." He took another step.

Spielt's face had turned ashy, but his voice, when he spoke, was surprisingly calm. "Death's waiting that way, Kreelan. Another step and you'll be food for the Fallen Temple." He flicked his eyes upward, toward a shadowed balcony that ran around the second story of the room. "Right now there's a crossbow aimed straight at your head. Raeglaran was keeping an alternate escape route open for us. Well, that's what he's doing for me, all right."

Kreelan began to look upward, then thought better of it. "You're bluffing, Spielt."

Spielt's laughter had a touch of hysteria about it. "Am I? Then walk ahead. You'll find out soon enough."

Sirc'al's stance appeared to relax slightly. He laughed deep in his throat and brushed a hand over his balding head, the skin mottled and scaly. "So you've betrayed each other. What more could I expect from such slime? Well, I'll have you first, Kreelan."

Kreelan grinned tightly. "Not quite." Slowly he brought up the hand that until now had stayed clenched in a fist by his side. It held a small glass sphere that the others could see was divided in half by a thin partition. One half held a black powder; the other contained a clear liquid. "Know what this is?"

The smile froze on Sirc'al's face. "What?"

"Smoke powder," Kreelan crowed. "And next to it, oil of phosphorus. You know what happens if the sphere breaks, don't you? The oil will ignite, and the smoke powder will explode."

Sirc'al laughed. "Go ahead, fool! There's barely enough powder there to blow yourself up."

Kreelan said calmly, "Ah, but there you're mistaken, my friend. This is just one sphere. In my pack, I have two more. True, there will be only one small explosion from this one, but it will be followed by a somewhat larger explosion. I shouldn't care to be standing next to me."

Sirc'al snorted. "You're bluffing."

"Am I? If your friend over there kills Spielt, Raeglaran will shoot me. I'll fall. And with me will fall this little sphere. This little glass sphere." He smiled nastily. "Spielt, if Raeglaran kills me, and the sphere breaks, I and our friend here will be dead. But his other friends will have no reason not to attack you. Five against two? Not good odds. And that assumes you won't be taken down when I fall."

Kreelan shifted his eyes upward. "Raeglaran," he called. "In case you're getting some bright ideas, shooting me now will only get your boss killed. And do you think you'd make it out of the tavern with these fellows, not to mention the watch, on your trail?"

Sirc'al grunted contemptuously. "You needn't worry about the watch."

"Why not?"

"Because we're already here."

Kreelan started, and the hand holding the sphere wavered visibly. The guard tensed.

The scarred man's voice was brittle as fine crystal. "How did you come here tonight?"

"Ask your friend." Sirc'al made a minute nod toward Spielt, who smirked at his former comrade.

Kreelan's voice rose to an outraged shriek. "You? You bastard! You planned to betray me all along."

"No more than you were planning for me," Spielt snarled. "You'd sell your mother for a handful of copper pieces if the opportunity came along. But now the tables have turned, thank Umberlee."

Spielt's mercenary companion had recovered his aplomb and managed to give the impression of shrugging his shoulders without actually doing so. "Well, well. Perhaps I would have. I've always admired initiative, Spielt. Possibly you have a bit more than I was willing to give you credit for, though any would be more than that. And now you're caught in your own trap, tightly as a Tharkaran lobster."

"Ah, but what about you?" Spielt's voice was poisoned with hatred. "How are you going to get out of here, pray tell?"

Kreelan rolled his eyes. "I don't know. At present the situation's a bit of a standoff."

"And a remarkably entertaining one, I might add," observed Avarilous, stepping out of the shadows.

Kreelan's hand jerked, and the sphere nearly slipped from his fingers, bringing forth an anguished cry from Sirc'al. The other watchman's fingers whitened on his sword hilt.

Kreelan was the first of the group to recover fully. "By all the foul beings of the Abyss, who are you, and what are you doing here?"

For the merest instant, Spielt's eyes flicked toward Avarilous. "I know him. I thought there was something odd about him from the moment he sat down at our table." His hysterical giggle pierced the damp air. "I knew we should have taken care of him earlier."

Avarilous smiled agreeably, taking care to keep his hands in plain sight and make no sudden movements. "Gentlemen, a word from an impartial observer seems as if it would not come amiss just now." He picked up his ale from the window ledge where he had set it.

Kreelan spoke before the others. "Perhaps it would, but I don't know exactly what game you're playing. Are you an agent of one of the other cities?"

Avarilous permitted himself a small shrug. "My concerns in this affair are my own. For all you know, I could be an innocent bystander. But I know enough of what's occurring in the Five Kingdoms these days to understand something about who you're all working for."

Spielt sneered openly, the veins in his neck turning purple. The watchman's sword rested closely against the largest of these, and Avarilous could see the tip of the blade denting the dirty skin. "If you know so much about it, Whoeveryouare, tell us about it." The blond mercenary glared at Kreelan. "I'd love to know who this tanar'ri-spawned bastard is working for."

Avarilous cleared his throat perfunctorily and, righting a chair, sat down. "Well, then. To begin, the political situation between the Five Kingdoms is, as usual, at a stalemate. But some people would like to change that, and here's where things get interesting. Who gains if the trade pact is signed between Konigheim and Doegan?"

There was a minute stir, as if both Kreelan and Spielt had shifted positions slightly. Spielt's hands, held stiffly up to his chest, caught a thread from his robe and began to twist it back and forth. Sirc'al shrugged. "They both gain. That's why they want to sign it."

"Correction." Avarilous picked up an unbroken plate from the table nearest him and, placing the center on his forefinger, spun it. "The two kingdoms want to negotiate about it. Neither wants to sign anything."

Spielt wet his lips. "That's ridiculous."

Avarilous's eyes followed the spinning plate. "The Konigheim slave lords see negotiations over the pact as a chance to gain breathing space for their accumulation of naval resources, preparatory to an invasion of Doegan. The mage-king, on the other hand, sees an opportunity for a small step toward his eventual goal of unifying the Five Kingdoms under his rule. I suspect he planned to use the period of negotiation about the pact to infiltrate more spies and agents into Konigheim to undermine the council's power."

Abruptly he tossed the plate from his finger and caught it skillfully. "Edenvale, the Northmen, and the Free Cities of Parsanic opposed the pact to different degrees. From their point of view, it's essential to maintain the balance."

Sirc'al spoke. "I see. So these two were working as agents of one of the other three kingdoms to sabotage negotiations and prevent the pact."

Avarilous smiled tolerantly. "Not quite. It's a bit more involved." His eyes moved slowly from Kreelan to Spielt to the watch commander. "I've developed something of a nose for sniffing out treachery. And there's a good deal of it here tonight."

The Watch commander gave a short bark of laughter. "Yes, by Tempus, I should say so. These two soldiers of fortune were willing to cut each others' throats simply in order to earn their pay."

Avarilous shook his head. "Not quite. It's true they were prepared to trade each others' lives, but the motive was stronger than mere money. In fact, neither intended the other should leave the tavern alive."

"Explain!" Sirc'al's voice was sharp.

"Well, our friend Kreelan here, judging by his clothing, has passed himself off as a native of Tharkar. But if you look just where his neck meets his robe, you'll see something else.

The Watch commander craned his head and stared in the flickering lamplight. "Gods be damned! Gills!"

"Yes, gills. The man's from Doegan. On the other hand, looking at Spielt, we find something else a bit curious."

With both hands raised, he stepped closer to the blond man. Then, with extreme delicacy, he plucked the scarf from the mercenary's head. Light gleamed on a complex array of tattooed lines and swirls, surrounding a perfectly formed, lidless, golden eye set in the middle of the man's forehead. It stared angrily at the rest of the room.

There was an audible gasp from the others. Sirc'al was the first to recover and gave vent to a burst of foul oaths invoking Umberlee and the blackest inhabitants of the deep. "A Konigheimer, by all the fiends!"

Avarilous smiled and mopped the sweat from his brow, using the scarf he had wrenched away from the disguised slaver.

The watch commander's eyebrows were wrinkled in thought. "But wait a minute! Why in the name of the gods would Konigheim and Doegan want to break up the pact. They were the ones signing it."

"Not signing it," patiently corrected Avarilous. "Negotiating about signing it." He sighed. "As long as discussions dragged on, both the Konigheim Council and the mage-king benefited. Meanwhile both secretly planned to sabotage negotiations at the last minute. Each planned a murder of a member of its own delegation in a public place on neutral ground, so the other could be accused not only of murdering an innocent delegate, but so that the Free Cities could be drawn into the conflict on the side of whichever party's delegate was killed.

"For that reason I'm quite sure Kreelan, as an agent of the mage-king, had orders to murder a Doegan delegate. Spielt, working for the Konigheim Council, was supposed to kill one of their representatives." He sighed again. "It seems a bit ironic, really."

He paused and the stillness seemed to grow thicker in the heavy night air. The landlord, long forgotten where he lay against the wall, stirred and bumped against a metal cup, knocking it over. The dull metal thump sounded loud.

Sirc'al, looking thoroughly confused, broke the silence. "So who was murdered? A Doeganer, or a Konigheimer?"

Avarilous turned and regarded the corpse with a touch of regret. "Well, now, that's the odd thing. Neither."

"Neither?" The overwrought commander was practically screaming. "How can you possibly say that? Both these scum provoked the fight in order to gain cover for their planned assassinations—I can work that out, thank you very much! One of them was successful before the other, both prepared to flee. Now you say neither completed his mission?"

Avarilous walked over to the fountain. Setting down his tankard, he reached in and, with an expression of distaste, grasped the corpse by the scruff of its jerkin. With a sudden heave he brought it out, dripping, onto the flagstones. He cautiously turned it over with his foot so they could all see the face. Water ran from the fat seams, from the mouth and nose, and merged with the smeared blood on his cut throat. From the inside of his sodden clothing a small scarlet viper emerged, hissed angrily at the merchant, and wriggled quickly into the bushes.

One of the watch behind Sirc'al started and cried out, "Sir, that's Sergeant Vilyous. Him that's on the north gate. I spoke to him there yesterday."

The commander's eyes widened. "Vilyous! Whoever helped him out of this world did us all a favor. He'll not be missed." He chuckled and spoke to Spielt and Kreelan. "A fine pair of assassins you turned out to be! Couldn't even kill one of the men you were aiming for."

Spielt giggled. "Yes, Kreelan. I imagine if you get out of this, you'll have a pretty time trying to explain things to the squid-master of Eldrinparr. He'll turn you into fish bait."

Kreelan scowled. "Come off it, Spielt! You bungled this completely. I wonder to what slave pit they send assassins who kill the wrong man."

There was a moment of painful silence. The watchman holding the blade to Spielt's throat gave a slight murmur of one whose arm muscles are beginning to ache intolerably. The sword in his hand shook, drawing a thin line of blood on Spielt's neck muscles.

Sirc'al broke the pause. "Do you two mean to tell me," he said ominously, "that neither of you killed this lout?"

Spielt said cautiously, "I mean to tell you that I didn't."

"Liar," snarled Kreelan. "I never touched the fellow. I saw him fall while you were near him. Since I thought you were working for Doegan as well, I assumed you'd completed the mission and we should get out."

"Wait a minute," sputtered Spielt. "I thought you were employed by Konigheim."

There was another silence while everyone digested the import of these words. It was broken by Avarilous casually moving toward the wooden doors that led outside, still holding a nearly full tankard of ale. Spielt's eyes followed him. "There!" he shrieked. "There, commander! There's the murderer!"

Slowly Sirc'al's eyes swung toward Avarilous. "Who in the nine hells are you?

The merchant looked at him apologetically. "The Ulgarthan government rather prefers to see the political situation in the Five Kingdoms remain the same," he observed. "I came here to make sure the balance was preserved. And the man was extremely rude to me when I entered the city."

He turned to go.

"Hoy!" cried a half-dozen voices simultaneously.

Avarilous turned back toward the yard. At the same instant, his left foot kicked back against one of the doors, slamming it as hard as he could.

The terrific crash precipitated a flurry of action within the courtyard. The watchman's sword arm jerked violently, and his blade slid into Spielt's neck. The blond man fell to the ground, writhing in his death throes. Almost at the same instant there was a dull twang, and a crossbow quarrel suddenly protruded from the back of Kreelan's head. He staggered forward against the commander. Two of the watchmen whipped crossbows from beneath their dark robes and fired at the balcony where Raeglaran was standing. There was a cry and a crash of rending wood as Raeglaran's lifeless body plummeted to the floor of the inn.

Kreelan's nerveless fingers jerked in a dying reflex,

flipping the glass ball upward. The commander snatched it out of the air. "Thank the—" he started to say, then watched in horror as the ball slipped from his sweaty grasp.

Sirc'al screamed in frustration and anguish. Then he felt a sudden blow to the back of his knees and unexpectedly sat down in the chair thrust beneath him. The glass ball landed on his lap, unbroken, and his hands clasped round it. He could feel his heart thudding against his ribs.

There was a quiet cough behind him, and he looked around to see who had saved him.

Necht, Avarilous's driver, stared at him with his hands still outthrust. Avarilous himself stood before the door watching calmly the havoc he had wrought. In the silence that followed, the merchant stepped carefully back into the courtyard and strolled over to the still recumbent landlord.

"Daltrice," he observed calmly, "I do have time for one short drink. And I think you owe me something." He picked up a tankard and drained it. At the same time, he bent and effortlessly jerked a heavy purse from the landlord's belt. He scattered its coins on the polished bar top and, swiftly flicking his forefinger, counted out one hundred and forty pieces. No one moved as he scooped them up and dropped them in his own pocket. Jingling slightly, he put down his drink and moved toward the door.

"I forgot to tell you," he said to the landlord. "I won't be back again. Urgent business elsewhere. New accounts to service. You know how it is." He grinned, beckoned to Necht, and was gone.

Lynaelle

Thomas M. Reid

Lynaelle awoke suddenly to find herself face to face with a cocked crossbow. Hurlonn Davenwiss was at the other end, aiming it at her with a snarl on his face. Hurlonn was a generally sour fellow who had lost his wife two winters ago in an orc raid. "Get up, you ungrateful wench!" he yelled at her, even as she noticed others looming over her bed. The girl blinked, trying to clear the cobwebs of sleep, even as the sheets were yanked back and she was dragged to her feet. Teress Turlgoode's husband Shastin was there, and behind him Gorlin the hunter stood, a long dagger in his belt, a lantern in one hand, and a coil of rope in the other.

"What's the matter?" Lynaelle asked, shivering from the cold in only her thin shift.

"Shut up!" Hurlonn spat, keeping the crossbow trained on the girl. "Tie her, Gorlin. Don't let her use any of her infernal magic on us. Ungrateful little whelp."

Shastin spun Lynaelle around and pushed her against the bed, then grabbed her arms, jerking them cruelly behind her back. "Ow!" she cried out, not understanding. "Please! What's wrong?" She could feel rope being threaded around her wrists, burning her skin as the slack was drawn up. "Please, Gorlin, someone, tell me what's going on!" Lynaelle sobbed, desperately wishing Ambriel would arrive and call off this mob. She did not struggle as Gorlin finished tying her hands and began to bind her fingers, immobilizing them completely.

"I say we kill her now and be done with it," Hurlonn raged. "No sense in waiting."

"No," Gorlin said quietly but firmly as he helped Lynaelle to her feet. "The Lady's law says she gets a trial. There will be no killing."

"Fah!" spat Hurlonn. "A trial is a waste of time." Outside her small one-room cottage, Lynaelle could see that dawn was breaking, but the sun was still behind the mountains.

"Nonetheless," Gorlin pronounced firmly, "the Lady's law is clear. There will be a trial. Let's go, girl." He gently pushed Lynaelle forward, toward the door, steering her by his grip.

"Please!" Lynaelle said, moving forward woodenly, shivering, her feet aching from the cold floor. "I didn't do anything! Somebody please talk to me." She felt numb, as if none of this were real. Where is Ambriel? she wondered. Or Daleon?

"Don't pretend you didn't kill him!" Hurlonn fumed. "Don't pretend you didn't go up there last night and blast him with the very magic he taught you to use!"

Lynaelle stumbled then, her head spinning. Ambriel! No! She sank to her knees, unable to breathe. Someone had taken Ambriel from her. I didn't do it! her mind screamed. No, it can't be real. She began to shake uncontrollably. "P-please," she sobbed quietly. "I didn't do that. I would never—" Never kill the only person who ever really cared about me, she finished in her head, remembering the previous day, the last time she had seen him.

* * * * *

"No, no, Lynnie, twist it. Like this," Ambriel chided as he tore another strip of parchment from the sheet in his lap. His gnarled fingers, steady despite their age, pulled the strip taut and then deftly looped it back on itself, giving it a half twist. "There, like that," he said, pinching the ends together between his thumb and forefinger and holding it for the girl to see.

Lynaelle chewed her lower lip as she studied the twisted shape in the older man's hand, wanting to make certain she understood what he had done. She nodded finally, confident she could duplicate it. She took her own strip and pulled it taut by the ends, as he had done, then mimicked his movements to form the endless loop.

"Good, very good," Ambriel smiled, absently stroking his whiskered chin with one hand as he peered at the object in Lynaelle's grasp. She smiled briefly to herself as she looked at him, crouched as he was upon the granite outcropping where they were studying, a coil of rope before him on the stone. He kept his cloak, the same sky-blue color as his eyes, wrapped about himself, for the air held a chill this late in the summer, even at the peak of a sunny afternoon.

To most, Ambriel still seemed impossibly spry for his age, but Lynaelle had begun to notice little changes that hinted otherwise. Their walks through the woods never seemed to last as long as they once did, and his lessons on magic with her came less frequently. Mostly, she had begun to notice where the lines in his face had deepened and multiplied. He's getting old, the back of her mind whispered, but she ignored it and concentrated on the lesson.

"Now, the rest." His voice was deep and rich against the hushed roar of the tumbling water at their feet. "Say the words slowly and clearly."

Lynaelle nodded again and rose to her feet, positioning herself so that the coil of rope was directly in front of her. She focused inwardly for a moment, concentrating, as she held the looped parchment before her. Then she began to speak, firmly citing words in an arcane tongue. As she formed the final syllables, she held her other hand up, palm to the sky, and blew a bit of cornstarch she had been grasping so that it passed through the twisted loop and settled on the coil of rope. She shivered, that now-familiar tingle engulfing her, as the incantation opened magical connections both within and around her body. She watched expectantly as the rope began to uncoil, one end climbing magically upward toward a dark, shimmering opening that appeared for an instant in the sun-dappled air.

A deluge of water suddenly cascaded from the sky, crashing directly into Lynaelle and knocking her off-balance. She stumbled backward from the rock and fell into the icy stream, toppling onto her back and submerging. The torrent of water continued to slam into her, pinning her under the surface, and Lynaelle flailed about in a panic, unable to breathe. She inadvertently swallowed several mouthfuls of both icy fresh water and warmer salt water before she managed to roll to one side and escape the deluge. Just as quickly as the torrent of water had appeared, it vanished, leaving Lynaelle on her hands and knees in the stream, thoroughly drenched and shivering from cold.

Lynaelle crawled from the stream onto shore, wiping water from her face and trying to catch her breath. She barely noticed Ambriel standing safely upon the bank of the stream, still clutching his spellbook. He gaped incredulously into the open air where the magical doorway had been spewing water only seconds before. All evidence of the rope, the parchment, and the cornstarch had been washed away from the outcropping of rock.

When Lynaelle saw that her teacher was unhurt, she fell back upon a bed of dried fir needles, her eyes closed, breathing deeply and trying to calm her pounding heart.

"Obviously, That wasn't supposed to happen," Lynaelle growled in frustration.

Ambriel shook his head slowly, still stunned at the unexpected display of raw nature. "Amazing," he answered absently, stroking his whiskers. "I don't know exactly what you did. . . . Some sort of wild surge, I'd warrant. I think you accidentally opened a planar portal, instead."

"That's it," the girl grumbled, her amethyst eyes flashing as she scowled upward at the sky. "That's the third time this week, and this time I nearly drowned both of us. I quit." She sat up, impatiently dragging her long, delicate fingers through her wet, bedraggled hair, sweeping a few straw-colored strands behind her noticeably sylvan ear with a trembling hand.

"Gods," she continued. "I'm a menace to both of us. Forget studying at the university in Silverymoon. I can imagine everyone's faces when I accidentally drown the headmaster while auditioning for enrollment." She huddled miserably, shivering and wet.

Ambriel laughed. "I suppose we should be glad you opened a portal to water, rather than something more dangerous," he quipped, "such as magma."

Lynaelle groaned. "Oh, that would be even better. 'I'm really sorry, Your Ladyship, I didn't mean to melt your university.' " She sighed and tucked a small, simple stone amulet back into her blouse, pausing to run her fingers over its smooth surface. Ambriel had given it to her some years before, when she had first begun to study magic with him. She always wore it on a leather thong around her neck. Ambriel made a few subtle gestures and Lynaelle was instantly dry again. She was grateful for the cantrip.

"I told you it would take more effort to learn this new magic, child," the old man said. "If it were easy, everyone would be a great wizard casting spells all over the damned place, and I wouldn't be sitting out here freezing my old bones, trying to keep from getting killed while I teach them to you." Lynaelle sighed again, nodding glumly, still feeling the chill of being wet, even though she was completely dry. Ambriel laughed at her dour expression. "Oh, stop it. You learn faster than anyone I ever knew, including me. Your logic is sharp and sometimes you even apply yourself. Patience, Lynnie! You'll get it. The Bright Lady herself would be jealous of your ability."

Ambriel got a distant look on his face, then. "I remember when I was first studying with my old teacher in Silverymoon. I was as impetuous as you, eager to learn, thinking I could master it all in an afternoon." The elder man stared off into nowhere then, and he said nothing for a time.

Lynaelle watched him, wishing he would share this vision of his past with her. She loved it when he told her stories about his younger days, about when he had studied magic at the university at Silverymoon, and then later, when he had actually served for a time as a member of the Spellguard. She often imagined what it would be like to be a member of that elite enclave of wizards charged with protecting the Gem of the North. She often vowed to herself to make it a reality.

Seeing Ambriel's craggy face now, and the gnarled hands that absently stroked his snowy beard, it was harder than ever to imagine him young. Yes, he's definitely growing old, Lynaelle's mind whispered. The elven half of her heritage made his aging pass so quickly before her eyes, and in turn, to him, she had hardly changed at all in the twelve summers he had known her. Lynaelle knew Ambriel would be long dead before she fully matured into adulthood, and the age now showing in his face filled her with sudden sadness. She hated envisioning a life without her mentor to protect and guide her, and yet she knew that day would soon be upon her. His days with you may be few in number, Lynaelle Shalandriana, but you are a fool to waste them grieving before he's gone! she scolded herself.

As if sensing her troubled thoughts, Ambriel shook his own head, returning to the present. "You must keep working on focusing the energy you feel into the loop. Only then will the magic hold." The girl nodded, her sadness dispelled. She briefly considered trying again, but remembered that all of their components had washed away. The next lesson would have to wait for another time.

Ambriel drew the girl's attention to the horizon with a nod of his head. Lynaelle turned and spied the darkening sky near the top of Emrund's Peak at the head of the valley. The late afternoon showers were coming.

"All right," Lynaelle acknowledged, sighing. She rose to her feet and turned to follow Ambriel. With careful, measured steps he strolled along the path, his buckskin boots making little noise. Lynaelle hiked along beside him, absently toying with the amulet around her neck as she soundlessly picked her way along the trail. The path meandered through a copse of large, arrow-straight firs, their great trunks rising like huge columns to an arched canopy of thick boughs overhead. It was cool and dim here, and with the late afternoon sun already settling behind the far ridge of mountains and the clouds gathering overhead, it was growing into twilight. Lynaelle inhaled deeply, delighting in the scents of the forest. She also detected the faint smell of a cookfire and roasting meat in the chill air, and her stomach reminded her it was almost dinner time.

The pair crested a small ridge along the path to behold Galen's Ford. The little hamlet before them had grown up near a shallow ford in the stream. Here, the forest floor was open and spacious, uncluttered by smaller undergrowth. The cottages, many nestled against the huge trunks of these great trees, were simple earth-and-timber affairs with thatched roofs. In what might pass for the center of town, a large, open-sided pavilion constructed of rough-hewn logs dominated the other structures. Beneath its sheltering roof there were several simple wooden tables with plank benches.

It was near this central structure that most of the folk of Galen's Ford now gathered, preparing for a communal evening meal. A half dozen or so men and women, plates and bowls in hand, huddled around the large cookfire that burned in a pit in the middle, where a hole in the roof allowed the smoke to escape. Others had already found seats at the tables. All told, some three dozen people dwelt here.

Lynaelle could distinctly smell the roasting venison even before she spied it on a large spit over the fire. She also detected the odors of steamed potatoes and carrots, fresh pan bread, and baking sourberry pie. At the table, she knew there would be hard cheese and pitchers of cold milk, both brought up from Quaervarr farther down in the valley.

Ambriel sniffed the air deeply. "Mmm," he sighed. "Sourberry pie always gets my mouth watering. I love this time of the year." The old man headed directly to the cookfire to inspect a pie cooling on the hearth. As he reached out to sample a bit of the crust, however, Teress Turlgoode, a plump, rosy-cheeked woman, swatted his hand away.

"Keep your paws off my pie, old man. There will be plenty for you after dinner." Teress was trying to sound stern, but Lynaelle could see the twinkle in the woman's eye as she scolded him. Ambriel yanked his hand back and tried to look wounded but couldn't resist chuckling.

Lynaelle smiled, sharing in the joke, then turned to follow Ambriel to a table, nearly running headlong into a thin, bony woman carrying an armload of dishes. The girl pulled up short at the last moment and the woman, Mavin Holcott, snarled at her. "Watch where you're going, you stupid half-breed." The hatred in the woman's voice was plain.

"Sorry," Lynaelle mumbled as she ducked her head and scurried out of Mavin's way. Lynaelle's cheeks burned with anger as she caught up with Ambriel and she could almost feel the other woman's eyes on her. That woman—! She's just not happy unless she's scowling at me, she seethed to herself.

Ambriel looked at Lynaelle intently for a moment. "What's troubling you, child?"

Lynaelle shook her head. "Nothing," she said dismissively. "I'll get us some food." She started to rise again, but his hand shot across the table and fastened on her wrist with a surprisingly strong grip.

"You know better than to think I'll buy that. What happened?"

Lynaelle sighed and sank back down onto the plank bench. "Oh, Mavin Holcott is staring daggers at me again. It's nothing."

Ambriel frowned, his watery blue eyes flashing. "I'll speak to her about it later. Her sour insults have gone on long enough."

"No, please don't. That'll only make things worse. I'll just stay out of her way, like I always do."

Ambriel smiled and patted Lynaelle's arm gently. "You're a good person, Lynnie. You deserve better than what that unhappy old woman dishes out. But I'll stay out of it, if that's what you wish."

Lynaelle smiled back at the elderly man, gladdened by the kindness showing in his face. "She doesn't matter, Ambriel, as long as I know I have your undying love," she teased, her voice smooth as honey.

Ambriel nearly choked. "Hush, child!" he hissed under his breath. "I'm old enough to be your father, and I look old enough to be your grandfather! Don't give these nosy people any ideas. If they got the notion I was making untoward advances, however insane that idea actually is. . . ."

Lynaelle giggled, imagining Mavin Holcott's face at such a thought. She'd turn purple and choke on her own waggling tongue. She giggled again, delighted at such an image.

Ambriel was peering around, obviously nervous at the thought someone had overheard the girl's joke. When he had assured himself that no one had, he relaxed once again and glared at Lynaelle. "You really like making me old before my time, don't you?" he muttered, but Lynaelle could see the twinkle in his eye.

She smiled at him and stood up. "I'll get us some food.

Just stay here and rest your weary bones, grandfather."
Ambriel sputtered unintelligently at her insolent comment and took a half-hearted swat at her, but she easily dodged it and traipsed toward the cook fire.

As Lynaelle stood in line, hands suddenly covered her eyes and a male voice behind her said, "Guess who?"

It was Daleon, one of the woodcutters. Lynaelle ducked and twisted out of his grasp and turned to face him. Daleon was handsome enough, Lynaelle often thought, but something about him made her uneasy. Despite the fact that he was quite friendly, she often sensed that he was up to something. Nonetheless, he was handsome, and his interest in her seemed genuine.

"I knew it was you. It's hardly a surprise when you are the only one who ever does that," the girl said, smiling and poking him playfully in the chest.

Daleon snorted. "That's because you spend all your time with the old man. If you weren't so set on becoming a great sorcerer"—he said this last bit with mock awe—"more people might pay some attention."

"Hey!" Lynaelle said indignantly, punching Daleon on the arm. "I like studying magic with Ambriel. Besides," she continued, frowning when she noticed Mavin Holcott scowling at the two of them, "I can do without some of their attention. Mavin Holcott would just as soon put a bolt through me as look at me. She doesn't think too highly of you talking to me, you know."

Daleon shrugged, seemingly indifferent to the woman's disapproval. "Hey," he said, changing the subject, "do you want to go for a walk after dinner tonight?"

Lynaelle had reached the front of the line and turned away from Daleon. Gorlin, a retired tracker who now did the hunting for Galen's Ford, handed her two bowls of steaming food. He was a quiet man who treated Lynaelle with indifference, but then, he treated everyone in the hamlet with indifference, so she had taken that as a good sign.

"Maybe," the girl replied to Daleon's question. "It

might rain. Ambriel and I noticed a storm moving in before."

"Then maybe I could come over for a while. We could talk. I'll bring some firewood; I noticed you're getting low. I'll even build you a fire tonight."

Lynaelle arched one eyebrow at this suggestion, looking askance at Daleon. Well, it's pretty obvious what mischief he wants to get into tonight, she thought. Mavin Holcott would choke on her own wagging tongue for certain. "I imagine you would even stay long enough to make sure I was warm, wouldn't you?" Daleon merely grinned, and Lynaelle suddenly got that uneasy feeling again. "We'll see," she replied. "I have to take Ambriel his dinner." She then turned and walked briskly away before the young man could press her on the issue.

Once back at the table with Ambriel, Lynaelle attacked her meal with relish. The afternoon's mishap by the river had left her famished. As they ate, a light and friendly banter sprang up around them, people enjoying a good meal among extended family.

"Ambriel, how harsh will the winter be this year?" asked Hurlonn Davenwiss, a carpenter and blacksmith of sorts. Ambriel paused to finish a bite, then patted his mouth with a napkin.

"I performed an augury only yesterday, Hurlonn," Ambriel answered, "and the winter won't be too cold, but there'll be a lot of snow this year."

There was a general murmur among the gathering at this news. Heavy snows made it difficult to harvest timber, for the wagons frequently got stuck in the high drifts. It also meant that Gorlin would need to step up his hunting so that the community would have plenty of smoked meats to see them through until next spring. There would be a lot of work to get done this fall.

Ambriel cleared his throat as he pushed his now-empty bowl away. The folk grew quiet, for this generally meant the elderly man had more to say. "Of course, the deep snows are going to be good for growing harperroot and basilisk's tongue, and the heavy melt-off next spring means there should be lots of hammerfish."

Lynaelle smiled to herself. Ambriel was always one to point out the good side of any problem that might arise, and his counsel to the people of Galen's Ford was no exception. Although the logging might be slim this winter, if they planned ahead, there would be plenty of other goods available to send down river to Quaervarr and Silverymoon next spring. Another bout of murmuring rose up from the small crowd, only this time it carried a tone of positive excitement.

"You know," Ambriel interrupted, glancing around, "this reminds me of a story that took place one winter we had back when I was with the Spellguard." A hush fell over the crowd. "But—" he paused dramatically, "I think it will go over much better after a nice hot slice of sourberry pie." Laughter sprang up all around and many heads nodded in agreement.

Very quickly, people sprang up to collect the dishes, cut the pie, or stoke the fire. Everyone loved it when Ambriel told a story, always a long, drawn out, embellished affair, and finishing the chores was a must before settling down for an evening of his tales. Lynaelle smiled as she gathered both of their bowls and hurried toward the cookfire, where a large kettle of water had been put on for washing. She did not want to lose her seat next to her elderly friend, who was now quite entrenched as the center of attention. She set the bowls down on the hearth near the fire and turned to head back to her seat when a hand grabbed her wrist.

"Since you got to spend the afternoon daydreaming by the river instead of helping with the chores, you can wash the dishes." It was Mavin Holcott, her words mocking, a scrub brush in her other hand. Lynaelle started to protest, but Teress Turlgoode was there too, nodding her head in agreement, although the look on her face was much kinder than Mavin's. Lynaelle knew they expected to be obeyed. The girl's mouth snapped shut and she reluctantly accepted the scrub brush from the hateful woman. With a smug look of satisfaction on her face, Mavin turned and stalked off to join the crowd gathering around Ambriel, Teress close behind her. Lynaelle sighed and tested the water in the kettle. It wasn't quite hot enough, yet, so she sat down to wait. She looked forlornly toward the gathering crowd, knowing full well that she would not be able to hear Ambriel's story.

Ambriel had finished his pie and was now in the process of lighting a pipe, his feet stretched out before him. She watched the elderly man as he savored the taste of his pipe for a moment longer, then began to blow the smoke into dancing shapes, a trick that delighted the small children in the group and made them squeal and clap their hands. Lynaelle smiled, familiar with this particular cantrip; it was one of the first bits of magic Ambriel had taught her. As he began his tale, Lynaelle reluctantly turned away, pushed the sleeves of her blouse up to her elbows, and tested the water once more. Satisfied with the temperature, she took up a bowl and the scrub brush and went to work.

Lynaelle felt movement at her back suddenly, but before she could turn around Daleon was seated next to her, that familiar mischievous smile on his face.

"Need some help?" he asked, reaching for a bowl.

"Sure," she whispered back, "but you don't have to. This is my penance for 'daydreaming' all day, according to Mavin Holcott."

Daleon snorted in derision. "That cranky old dame isn't happy unless she's making everyone else miserable," he said out loud, drawing a few irritated stares from people sitting at the back, closest to the two of them.

"Shh!" Lynaelle urged, not wanting to rile the woman any more than necessary. "It's all right. I can manage the dishes. Go enjoy yourself with the rest of them." She turned back to scrubbing.

Daleon, however, made no move to depart. "So?" he asked, still holding the bowl.

"So, what?" the girl replied, getting a tingle in her

stomach. She sensed what he was about to ask her. She found herself imagining what it would feel like to kiss him, and wished she hadn't, for that made the knots in her stomach even worse.

"So, do you want me to bring some firewood over to your cottage tonight?"

Lynaelle swallowed nervously, thankful it had grown dark enough by this time that the young man couldn't see. "Uh, um, yes, okay." Stop acting like a thimblehead, you foolish girl! She took a deep breath. "Yes, I would like that. After I get Ambriel home."

Daleon arose, setting the still unwashed bowl down next to the rest of the pile. "All right, then. I'm going to have another slice of pie and go listen to the story." He smiled that smile once more, and Lynaelle felt goose bumps and shivered. "Don't make me wait too long, though." He spun on his heel, a pie plate in his hand with a full quarter of a pie still in it, and went to join the rest of the crowd.

Lynaelle stared after the handsome young man as he departed, both thrilled and worried. Then she turned her attention back to the dishes and sighed, staring at the dirty bowl. Typical, she grimaced, flinging it into the water and attacking it vigorously with the brush. Their idea of helping is to keep you company while you do the work. And I, of course, was swooning with delight the whole time, like some addlebrained maiden. Humans may understand the ways of love, but I sure don't.

Ambriel finished his story, and as the gathering began to break up, Lynaelle hurriedly finished the dishes and went to escort her mentor home. It had begun to rain, as she had expected, but under the protection of the forest it was really little more than a light drizzle. Nonetheless, the two pulled the hoods of their cloaks up to protect them from the dampness. Lynaelle fetched and carried a lantern for them as they walked along the path toward Ambriel's cottage at the edge of the hamlet, her other hand on his arm.

"I missed your story tonight," she lamented. "You must promise to tell it to me tomorrow. Mavin and Teress ordered me to do the dishes."

"Did you get them nice and clean?" Ambriel teased.

"I did," Lynaelle said indignantly. "Daleon came over and offered to help, but he just ended up talking my ear off."

Ambriel chuckled. "I think he's sweet on you, Lynnie."

Lynaelle stammered, "I—he—I—I find him interesting, I suppose." She hoped she sounded noncommittal. "He seems like such a scoundrel, though. Don't you ever get a sense that he's up to no good?"

"Of course. All the time," Ambriel replied, a chuckle in his voice. "Especially where your virtue is concerned."

Lynaelle made a strangled noise and sputtered "Ambriel! That's not what I meant, and you know it!"

"What's wrong, Lynnie? Worried that you'll no longer have my undying love?" he teased. "Don't worry, I promise not to be too jealous."

Lynaelle rolled her eyes. "You're terrible!"

Ambriel laughed at her reaction and continued, "As for the dish duty, well, I suppose it's only fair, seeing as how I keep you busy with other things most of the day. There are some who feel we don't do our share. Mavin more strongly than most."

"Oh, I don't mind the work," Lynaelle replied, grateful for a change of subject. "It's just the way she delights in glaring at me. What did I ever do to make her hate me?"

Ambriel grew quiet for a time before answering the girl. "This world holds many wonders, for those who have the gumption to go find them. But some folk can't seem to see past the differences between themselves and everyone else.

"I will tell you this, though, child. For every cold and unhappy person like Mavin, there is a person who cares not one wit about your heritage, only that you are warm and kind and trustworthy. Those kinds of people you can be proud to call 'friend.' Like Daleon, for instance."

Lynaelle groaned, realizing Ambriel had found a way to bring the fellow up again. "He's convinced you to help him charm me. You're conspiring together!"

Ambriel chuckled. "Don't disparage his kindness too quickly, child. He seems to find you interesting enough." They had reached Ambriel's cottage.

"Yes, I know. He's coming over tonight to talk for a while." The girl admitted, her tone warning Ambriel against further quips at her expense.

The pair entered into the cottage, and Lynaelle began to light the various candles and lamps while Ambriel took his book of spells over to a trunk at the foot of his bed. He uttered a few phrases, softly enough that Lynaelle could not make them out, and then lifted the lid. He deposited the book atop a folded section of royal blue canvas adorned with a silver crescent moon sheltering a single silver star.

Ambriel had once shown Lynaelle some of the various items he kept stored here, mostly old books written by some of the most powerful sages and wizards of Silverymoon. There were a few other things there, too, pieces of memorabilia from his younger days such as the scrap of canvas. It was the flag of Silverymoon, and when pressed on its origins Ambriel claimed it had been given to him by Alustriel Silverhand herself a number of years ago. Whenever Lynaelle asked him why, he refused to say. She liked to imagine that it must have been to honor him for some great deed.

The elderly man firmly shut the lid and softly recited a few new words, then turned to face the girl. "I know I've told you this over and over, but—"

" 'Promise me you won't ever try to open this yourself,' " Lynaelle said in unison with her mentor. "I know, I know. And, like always, I promise."

Ambriel smiled, but it was sort of a sad smile. "I just don't want anything to happen to you, Lynnie."

Lynaelle went to Ambriel then and gave him a hug. "Don't worry. I will never open your chest. Besides, I don't really want any of your smelly old books, anyway."

Ambriel laughed at this and turned to hang up his cloak. "Get out of here, you insolent child. Go have fun with Daleon."

Lynaelle hesitated, wanting to make certain Ambriel was settled in for the night. "Are you sure? Do you want me to brew you some tea?"

"No, no. I'm fine. Go and let an old man rest. I'm going to read for a bit. You can make up for it tomorrow."

Lynaelle nodded then, and turned to go. "See you in the morning," she called over her shoulder as she once again pulled the hood up on her cloak and headed out the door. She saw Ambriel wave absently to her, already flipping open a musty tome that had been resting on the table by his bed.

Lynaelle ducked out into the evening, taking a moment to let her keen night vision adjust to the darkness, then trotted home along the path that led through the hamlet. Warm amber light seeped from the windows of the various dwellings, and she could hear soft voices from within as everyone settled in for the evening. She made her way through the center of the hamlet and on to her own small cottage. It was really little more than a hut, one small room nestled at the base of one of the great pines, but it was off by itself, as Ambriel's had been, and it was more than enough to suit her needs.

When she arrived, Lynaelle could see Daleon perched on her doorstep, a lit lantern by his side. She waved to him before she realized he probably could not see her in the evening gloom. She made a point of snapping a few twigs as she approached so as not to startle him.

"Hi," he said uncertainly, peering in her direction.

"Hi, yourself. I tried to hurry," she lied, looking the young man up and down from the darkness for a moment before stepping fully into the light of his lantern. She realized that she truly liked what she saw. She opened the door and moved inside as he jumped up and stepped to one side. "I thought you were going to bring me some wood for a fire tonight," she flirted.

"Oh," he said a bit sheepishly. "I added an armload to your woodpile, but it was too dark to drive my wagon over tonight. I'll bring more tomorrow."

"Uh huh," Lynaelle replied doubtfully. She suspected Daleon would use that same excuse to come visit every night if she allowed him to. Perhaps that wouldn't be such a bad thing, she mused for a moment, blushing slightly.

"So, you get the old man tucked in?" He asked, a chuckle in his voice.

She turned and noticed that he still stood outside. "Oh, hush. He was happily reading a book when I left him." She turned away again and pretended to busy herself getting a fire started, trembling a little at the implications of what she was about to ask. "So, would you like to come in?" she inquired, her voice softer and a little breathless.

Daleon paused a long moment before answering, and Lynaelle's heart began to pound as her words hung in the air. Finally he spoke, his voice slightly husky. "I wondered if you would ever extend that invitation." Lynaelle turned to look at him, a nervous smile on her lips. He continued. "As much as I would enjoy your company this evening, I should go. It's late, and I have to be up early tomorrow. Tomas said we're going to put in extra time for the next few weeks to try to get more timber in before the snows come."

Lynaelle blinked in surprise, both at his words and at the level of her own disappointment. She shrugged her shoulders, feigning indifference. "Suit yourself." She turned back to her fledgling fire, her lips pursed in a frown. What's he up to? she puzzled.

"So, anyway, I guess I'll see you tomorrow." Daleon said uncertainly.

"I guess." Lynaelle didn't want to look at him. "Goodnight."

"Goodnight." Daleon pulled shut Lynaelle's front door

and was gone.

Lynaelle stared at the door. *One minute he won't leave me alone, the next, he's all proper and decent; quite the gentle lord. And me playing the shameless wench! He must think I offer my bed to anyone who knocks on my door.* Her cheeks flushed with embarrassment as she blew onto her fire, trying to get the first log to catch.

Lynaelle stripped to her shift, climbed into bed, and lay there in the dark for a bit, running her fingers over the amulet around her neck and listening to the distant roar of the stream and the hooting of an owl. When sleep finally came, it remained untroubled until Hurlonn woke her with a crossbow in her face.

* * * * *

"I am innocent," Lynaelle said. Her voice cracked, but she forced the words anyway. "I would never . . . could never kill him." Tears threatened to flow again, but she cleared her mind of everything but the words. "I am innocent, and I want the chance to prove it."

"You'll get that chance soon enough, half-breed," Hurlonn said. "Shastin, ride for Quaervarr. Get the cleric." Teress's husband hurried off to fetch a horse as Hurlonn spun back around to face Lynaelle. "You can tell the cleric your lies, if you want, but the gods will seal your fate." With that, the enraged man stomped out of Lynaelle's house.

Gorlin began to steer Lynaelle toward the door, but Teress Turlgoode stopped him. "You are not taking that child out in the cold dressed like that. She'll freeze to death before her trial even starts."

The woman took a blanket from Lynaelle's bed and held it up as though to wrap it around the girl's shoulders. Gorlin merely shrugged and made room for the woman.

"Thank you," Lynaelle said quietly.

Gorlin took hold of her once again and directed her out the door. Lynaelle's breath was visible, and the tears on her cheeks were cold. A crowd had gathered, almost every-one in the hamlet, Lynaelle suspected. She looked for Daleon, hoping perhaps he would step forward and stop this madness, but he was not there. He and Tomas must have left before sunrise, she realized.

Lynaelle turned to Gorlin as they stepped forth. "Why do you think I did it?" she asked. She shifted her arms under the blanket as they progressed, for the ropes were tight and cutting into her skin.

Gorlin continued to guide Lynaelle up the path, toward the center of the hamlet. "I saw you head up there last night," he said.

Lynaelle gaped at the hunter. "But I go up there every night with him! You know that! Last night, I left him read-ing a book and came home. I met Daleon here."

"No, this was later. Several people saw you walk him home after dinner, but that was when it had barely started raining. I saw you again, after it had begun to rain pretty hard. Your footprints are even in the mud leading up to his cottage."

Lynaelle was stunned. "How do you know they were my footprints? What if someone was dressed to look like me?"

Gorlin looked at her levelly. "Girl, I think I would recog-nize your footprints when I saw them."

Lynaelle knew he was right, of course. He had spent his whole life tracking. Think! "It must have been magic, then," she stated firmly. "Someone impersonated me using magic."

Gorlin looked doubtful. "I don't think that's going to cut it, girl. It seems a whole lot more reasonable that you went up there."

Lynaelle felt panic rising. "I know, but give me a chance to prove otherwise. Let me go see for myself." She wasn't sure if she could bear the sight of Ambriel's dead body, but she had to try.

Gorlin had led her to the smokehouse. Lynaelle knew he intended to lock her inside until the cleric came to sort out matters. They stopped at the door, and Gorlin began to slide the heavy timber aside.

"Please, Gorlin. Give me a chance." Lynaelle pleaded. "Let me go up there and see for myself."

"I can't do that. The cleric is coming, and if you really are innocent, she'll find out from you soon enough."

"But that might be a day or two from now. Don't you want to know the truth? What if I'm not the one, and the real murderer is escaping?" Lynaelle was trying desperately to stay clear and focused, but she felt the panic rising again.

Gorlin considered for a moment. "All right. If you can prove your own innocence, I suppose we should give you the chance to do so. No use letting the real murderer get a big head start, if you're telling the truth." He led Lynaelle to Ambriel's cottage. When they got there, Gorlin showed her what looked like several of her own footprints leading to the door, plainly visible in the mud next to the path.

Lynaelle frowned at this. Why walk in the mud to the side, if the path itself has plenty of pine needles? She bit her lip, thinking. Suddenly, she had an idea. "Gorlin, I know someone was trying to impersonate me. You got a very clear look at me last night, didn't you?"

"Yes, your face was plain in the light of your lantern."

"Gorlin, I don't carry a lantern at night. I can see in the dark, remember?"

Realization began to dawn on Gorlin's face.

"If I had wanted to get away with this crime, don't you think I would have gone out of my way not to be seen? And why would I walk through the mud if the path is over here?" Lynaelle asked, nodding her head at the path. "Have you checked my boots for mud?"

"I can't argue with that, girl, but that's not enough. I'm going to let you go inside and see if we can't build you a better case," he said honestly. "But if you try anything, I will not think twice. Do you understand me?" Lynaelle nodded solemnly. "Good. Now, are you sure you want to do this?" She nodded again. "Then let's go."

The hunter pushed the door to Ambriel's cottage open and stepped inside. Lynaelle steeled herself to face her mentor's body and followed. The place was a mess. More muddy footprints led inside, still appearing to be made by Lynaelle's own boots. The table had been overturned, the bed clothes were flung about, and books and papers were strewn everywhere. Ambriel's trunk was open, the spell-book still where he had left it the previous evening. The elderly man himself was sprawled on his back, his feet pointing toward the trunk.

Lynaelle swallowed back the tears and bent down to get a closer look. Ambriel's chest was blackened, as though he had been hit by a searing flame. His lifeless eyes were still open, staring darkly at the ceiling. She stood again, unnerved by the elderly man's cold stare. She could not help crying softly then, her grief gripping her. She had no notion of what the future held, and he would no longer be a part of it. Stop it! There will be time to grieve later!

Lynaelle moved to the other side of the bed to inspect some more and spotted blood stains on the floor. She frowned, bending down for a closer look. Half hidden under the bed, she found a sheet of parchment, bloody stains on it as well. Lynaelle turned to the hunter, who was examining the muddy prints in the doorway. "Gorlin, come see this. I can't pick it up." Gorlin walked over to where the girl was standing. She pointed with one bare foot to the scrap of parchment. Gorlin very carefully pushed it out with the toe of his boot. It was blank, but one edge was rough and jagged, as though a part had been torn away.

Lynaelle recognized it instantly. "He was trying to escape. He tore a piece off that sheet of parchment in order to cast a spell he's been teaching me, but it seems he didn't have time to finish."

The girl walked back over to Ambriel's body and inspected it again. She frowned, not finding what she was looking for at first, then her heart began to pound. Is it possible? she thought, not daring to hope. "Gorlin! Why isn't there any blood on his body?" She was nearly frantic with excitement. "If he was bleeding over there, then there should be a wound somewhere. And blood on his hands that got on the piece of parchment!"

Gorlin walked over to the body once more. "Maybe it's not his blood," he offered.

Lynaelle immediately shrugged off the blanket, letting it drop to the floor, and stood before the hunter in her thin shift. "Then it would have to be his attacker's." Slowly, she turned completely around. "No wounds, Gorlin. Still think I did it?"

The hunter looked at her thoughtfully and shook his head.

"I think that's enough to prove my . . ." Lynaelle's words drifted off as she peered closely into Ambriel's face once more and saw at last what had troubled her before. The dark eyes, staring upward. The dark eyes!

"It's not him! Gorlin, this is not Ambriel!" She nearly laughed out loud. "Look at his eyes! Ambriel's are blue, the same color as his cloak!" Lynaelle wanted to jump for joy.

"If this is not Ambriel, then where is he?" Gorlin asked, looking around again.

Lynaelle had to force herself not to shout. "He did it! He cast the spell! He's somewhere right in this room!" She began to look around frantically. He can't have much time left, she thought. Where would it be? "Gorlin, his spell will run out very soon. We have to be ready when it does. Please, untie my hands." The hunter looked at her, unsure. "Please, Gorlin, he might be bleeding to death right now. I won't run away. Look at the proof! That body is not him! Someone used magic to fool us all. I can find where Ambriel is. Please!"

Finally, Gorlin nodded and took out his knife. He spun Lynaelle around and sliced through the ropes binding her hands. She gasped as blood began to flow again and rubbed her chaffed wrists. Then she began searching the floor of the room. She stopped when she found a fine white grit on the floorboards in one corner. Cornstarch!

"Gorlin, we need to move his bed over here. He's going to appear out of thin air and fall, and we want him to land on the bed. Okay? The hunter nodded and sheathed the dagger. Together, they pushed the featherbed toward the corner, positioning it so that it was directly over the residue of the cornstarch. They didn't have long to wait.

A shimmering black opening appeared for an instant in the air itself and through it dropped Ambriel. He landed on the bed with a soft thump, not quite square to the feather mattress, and nearly rolled off before Gorlin, gawking in amazement, caught him and settled him properly onto the pillows. The old man lay still, unconscious but breathing. He had a nasty gash in his shoulder, and his arm was soaked with blood.

Lynaelle sobbed tears of joy. "He's bleeding."

Lynaelle immediately began tending his wound. Gorlin went to fetch Teress Turlgoode, whose stitchery was just as useful on wounds as cloth. When the hunter returned, Ambriel was awake and smiling weakly.

"You found me, Lynnie. I knew you would." Ambriel breathed as Teress began to sew him up. Lynaelle merely hugged her mentor until he grunted in pain. She pulled back, then looked at the body on the floor.

"What happened?" she asked softly.

Ambriel reached his good hand out toward Lynaelle. "I think he was looking for this—" he said and pulled the stone amulet from under her shift, holding it up for her to see.

Lynaelle looked at her mentor, confused. "I don't understand. Why in Faerûn would he—?"

Ambriel released the amulet and settled back into his pillow. "It's my ward token from Silverymoon, child. From my days in the Spellguard. He—" Ambriel motioned weakly to the dead figure on the floor. "—apparently wanted it."

"A ward token? Why would he want that?" Lynaelle

asked. "And who is he?"

"Let me start at the beginning," Ambriel began, content to settle into a good story. "Not long after you left last night—I assume it wasn't long, it certainly didn't seem like very long, even though I always lose track of time when I read—you showed up again. Well, of course, it wasn't you, but I didn't know that at the time. I thought you were acting strangely, but I didn't really think much of it until you attacked me with a knife and demanded that I give you my ward token." Ambriel chuckled. "Of course, I knew that the real you would never demand it, since you wouldn't know what one is, and even if you did somehow know, you would have realized you already had it, anyway."

"Why didn't you just blast him with a spell?" Lynaelle prompted. "The gods know you have enough of them."

"Ha!" Ambriel snorted. "Lynnie, I was lucky to be able to cast the rope trick as it was. Since you and I have been practicing that one so much, I just happened to have the components close at hand. Now, are you going to let me tell my story?" he demanded, pretending to be indignant.

Lynaelle giggled. "I wouldn't want to ruin one of your best tales. Go on."

"Well, I managed to cast the spell, as you so cleverly figured out, and from there I watched 'you' transform into 'me.' This other me began looking around the place. I figure he must have wanted to throw off suspicion in case anyone else came to visit. The blast from the fire trap spell on my trunk killed him instantly, I guess."

"So who is this, then?" Gorlin asked, beginning to search the body.

Ambriel tried to sit up. "No spell I know of holds an illusion like that after death," he said. "But I once met a man who had a magical hat that allowed him to change forms at will. He always had to wear the hat, but he could incorporate it into the disguise. Lynnie, see if there is something magical on the body, especially around the head."

Lynaelle nodded and stood up. She cast a familiar spell and began to scan the body. The glow of magic surrounded a tiny clasp woven into the hair of the fake Ambriel. When she retrieved it the body transformed and she gasped. It was Daleon.

"Well, that tells us who," Gorlin remarked dryly. "And perhaps these will answer why," He said, producing some sheets of parchment from a hidden pocket on Daleon's belt.

Lynaelle looked at Daleon's corpse, barely hearing Gorlin's words. Why, indeed? she asked herself bitterly, hating the hurt she felt. "I told you he was up to no good, Ambriel," she said quietly, but there was no satisfaction in her voice.

"Aye, that you did. I'm sorry, child."

Lynaelle nodded solemnly. "So what is a ward token, Ambriel?"

Ambriel shrugged. "A ward token allows the bearer access to parts of Silverymoon where few are allowed to go, and even to cast magic that is otherwise restricted by the wards. I suspect he was trying to get somewhere he shouldn't have been."

Lynaelle gasped. "Why in the world did you give such a thing to me, then?"

Ambriel smiled. "I knew it would be safe with you. Anyone who knew of its existence would come to me looking for it, not you. Besides," he added, a warm smile in his eyes. "I hoped someday you might wear it as a member of the Spellguard."

Lynaelle smiled and hugged her teacher.

"By the gods," Gorlin muttered quietly. "Three different contracts, all offering him handsome sums to retrieve that token and use it to get to Queen Alustriel." The hunter's face was ashen. "He meant to assassinate the High Lady herself. . . ."

The Grinning Ghost of Taverton Hall

Ed Greenwood

"The ghost is one of the family, you see. The Doom of the Paertrovers. We couldn't banish him if we wanted to."

The young lord was in full fettle, his voice as polished as that of any master bard. Immult Greiryn, the seneschal of Taverton Hall, ran an irritated hand through his steel-gray hair and turned away, melting into the deep underbrush with practiced ease and silence. Not for him the fripperies of the high and mighty, nor was it his station to be seen listening or intruding when they were at play. Bad enough that he had to step around their bodyguards behind every second tree and bush. . . .

It was late in the warm summer of the Year of the Banner . . . and a busy summer it'd been, to be sure. All sun-dappled season long three ambitious noble lords of rising power had dragged their beautiful daughters the length and breadth of the realm, seeking suitable—that would mean rich, Greiryn reflected with a sour smile— husbands for their precious Flowers of Northbank. Farrowbrace, Huntingdown, and Battlebar. Oh, the three ladies were a delight to look upon, even for an old soldier, and well-educated to boot, but their whole journeying was so . . . calculated. Did these noble lords have iced wine in their veins, instead of blood?

Immult spat thoughtfully onto a fern, and traded cold and level gazes with yet another bodyguard whose gloved fingers were fondling the hilt of his belt dagger. Arrogant lapdogs, lording it over him in a garden that was his to defend!

Arrogant? Aye, and their masters were worse. In their foray up and down the realm, presenting their young ladies to the eligible young noblemen of Cormyr, they'd passed the gates of Taverton Hall thrice at least—more times, perhaps. Oldest and smallest of the great estates in Northbank this might be, but these three oh-so-noble lords must have been saving it for last, like a favored food at a feast. Taverton Hall was the seat of Lord Eskult Paertrover, Baron of Starwater and Horse Marshal to the Crown of Cormyr, bluest of the old blood houses to currently hold important court rank. Any lass who wed his son and heir, young Lord Crimmon, would gain her father an important ear at court.

Oh, yes, a very important ear. Doddering and lost in nostalgic glories Lord Eskult might well be, but his hand wrote the orders that conferred court ranks—and moneys and powers with them—upon nobles, and assigned other nobles standing garrisons of Purple Dragons. Soldiers that one had to feed, and that were always, so the suspicions went, in your home to keep an eye on you for the throne. So one lot of nobles gained wealth and power, and another saw their purses go flat under the weight of a lot of hungry, swaggering soldiers. Yes, there were many nobles who made a point of being "old friends" of Lord Eskult. Many a case of fine wine came in through the gates at feast days . . . Immult licked his lips at the memory of a particularly fiery sherry from a Rowanmantle wine-hall.

Another guard glared at him suspiciously, but the seneschal swept past him, pretending not to notice. Bah! Let

these dogs snarl. They'd all be gone from here soon
enough.

* * * * *

"Yet," Lord Crimmon said earnestly, knowing he had
their breathless attention, "the ghost always reappears."
He gave them a suitably ghostly half-smile, and broke his
pose to gesture grandly at a rather crumbling expanse of
old, close-fitted stones. The rings on his fingers sparkled
like miniature stars as the warm light of morning caught
them and set them afire.

"Here, 'tis seen as a shape on the wall, no matter how
often Paertrovers tear down these stones and rebuild
with new ones." He waved his glittering hand again, in a
wide circle above his head, three pairs of beautiful eyes
following his every move. "Everywhere else on the estate,
folk see a floating, grinning face in a long-plumed helm."
He gave them the smile again, knowing just how dash-
ingly handsome—and rich—he looked. "It quite put my
father off courting in these gardens."

"And has it had the same effect on you, Lord Crimmon?" Lady Shamril Farrowbrace's voice was a low,
throaty purr, almost a challenge. Her large, dark eyes
held his with a look that was more promise than challenge, as one of her slim hands played in apparent idle-
ness with the glistening string of silver-set pearls that
adorned her open bodice.

"Lady," the young lord told her in mock reproof, "that
would be telling rather more than it is good for the nobly
bred to know."

One elegant eyebrow arched, on the brow of another of
the three Flowers. "Because it ruins the game, Lord?" the
Lady Lathdue Huntingdown asked. "Do you seek to
slight our sport, or just that of our over-reaching sires?"

Lady Chalass Battlebar stiffened, eyes flashing for a
moment as she gathered herself to take proper offense.
Her head snapped around to see just where her father

was—and found that he and the other elder lords had strolled out of sight, their bodyguards drifting off in their wake. The remaining guards had carefully situated themselves just out of earshot of normal converse, but quite within hailing distance. She relaxed, turned back to face Lord Crimmon—he was an engaging rogue, not the thickskull or dribblechin one might expect to find as heir of an old-blood house—and smiled.

"For my part," she told them all lightly, "I care not if my lord father dies of old age snooping behind every stone in Cormyr for a 'suitable' mate for me. I have no interest in courtship at all this fine summer. Dalliance, now . . ." She lowered her lashes delicately as she put the tip of one slender, long-nailed finger to her lips, and licked it with slow languor.

"Oh, Chalass, a little subtlety, please," the Lady Shamril sighed. "There'll be plenty of time for thrusting ourselves at our gracious host here—and his father or yours, for that matter—when the dancing begins. I was enjoying the tale; 'tis a change from gallant young lords showing us their prized stallions and making clumsy, leering jokes about riding, and wanting to see our saddles, and all the rest of it."

She waved a disgusted hand, and all three Flowers tittered together at shared memories that were obviously strong enough to dash away the irritation that had flashed across the face of Lady Chalass under Shamril's chiding.

"Yes," Lady Lathdue Huntingdown agreed, leaning forward in real eagerness, rather than with the slower flourish she'd performed earlier to best display her jeweled pectoral. "Our fathers may be after an ear at court and the warehouses of Paertrover gold, but we—I think I can safely speak for all of us in this—are not hunting husbands. Yet."

She caught the eyes of both other ladies, saw their agreement and confirmed it with a nod that set her splendid fall of hair rippling along her shoulders—and then abruptly dropped courtly manners to address Lord Crimmon plainly. "Crimmon, tell us more of your 'grinning ghost.' I love a good scare."

The young lord shrugged, suddenly weary of showing off the family haunting like some sort of trophy of the Hall. "There's little more to tell; I don't make up stories about him just to impress."

"We've come a long way, Lord," the Lady Shamril purred. "Impress us just a little . . . please?"

"Will we see the Grinning Ghost?" Lady Lathdue asked directly, her eyes very large and dark. She leaned forward even farther, so like a hound eager for the hunt that Lord Crimmon had to smile.

Into the spirit of it once more—if that was not too dangerous an expression, given the subject—he leaned forward to almost touch noses with her, the sparkle back in his eyes, and half whispered, "So if you're anywhere about our grounds, and feel a gaze upon you, turn around. As like as not, you'll be staring into the twinkling eyes of the ghost, who's been floating along right behind you!"

Two of the Flowers gave little embarrassed cries of fright. The third—Lathdue—uttered not a sound, but Crimmon saw a shiver travel the length of her shapely shoulders and arms. Her dark eyes never left his as he lowered his voice again, and went on.

"He never says a word, and does nothing but follow folk who scream and flee." The young noble made a grand gesture, as if thrusting desperately with a sword. "Some have dared to attack him or charge straight through him. All such say they felt a terrible chill . . . and got a true fright when the smile ran off the ghost's face like a cloak falling from someone's shoulders."

Lord Crimmon left time for another chorus of delicious moans of fear, and added more soberly, "When he's watching you but not grinning, they say, 'tis a sign you stand in mortal danger."

The three ladies laughed lightly in dismissal of such a ridiculous notion—how could a spirit know the fates and troubles of the living?—but their host did not join in their mirth, and it died away weakly as they looked into his face.

The gray Paertrover eyes that had seemed so dancing but a moment before, were dark and level as they stared past the Flowers at something that was making the color slowly drain out of Lord Crimmon's face. The three ladies spun around . . . and joined in the deepening silence.

Floating behind them, perhaps three paces away, was a disembodied head, its face pinched and white, the plumes of the long helm that surrounded it playing about slightly in the breeze. Its eyes were fixed on Lord Crimmon's, and its face was expressionless—and yet, for all that lack of expression, somehow sad and grim. All at once it began to fade away, becoming a faint part of the sun dappled light, and then a gentle radiance among shadows . . . and then nothing at all.

* * * * *

Silent servants deftly lit the lanterns as the evening shadows lengthened and the nobles rose from their joyous feast, goblets in hand, to stroll in the gardens. Lord Eskult was in rare good humor, his wit as sharp as it had been twenty years past, and so were his guests, brightened by good food, fine wine, and the success of their trade-talks. Even if their does ran with no Paertrover stag, it seemed they'd won a firm friend in the old Horse Marshal.

" 'Stroardinary!" Lord Belophar Battlebar boomed, the force of his breath blowing his great mustache out from his full lips. "A maze, but only knee-high . . . and sunken, too!"

"The pride of my dear departed wife," Lord Eskult said, striding forth down its grassy entrance path with a gesture that told all Cormyr that he was proud of it too. "She wanted a maze like—no, better–than one she saw at some merchant's house in Selgaunt, but she never wanted to get lost in it. One evening, the light fell fast, and she couldn't find her way out before it was full dark. Well, she had a proper fright, and when she found some of the lamp-lads she marched straight out to the garden sheds and took up a scythe, panting and blowing out her nostrils like a charger after a good gallop, and set to work hewing. She fell asleep sometime before dawn, and I carried her in, bidding the morning servants to continue what she'd begun: cutting the highthorn down to the height you see it now. No one will ever get lost in Maeraedithe's Maze again!"

"Gods above," Lord Hornsar Farrowbrace exclaimed admiringly, "what a tale! What a woman! I can just see her, eyes afire—"

"Yes," their host said, spinning around, "They were. They were indeed! Oh, she was splendid!"

Trailing along somewhere in the shadow of the tall and patrician Lord Corgrast Huntingdown, his daughter, the Lady Lathdue, rolled her eyes unto the darkening heavens. Lord Crimmon patted her arm and grinned. She realized who was reassuring her, and gasped in horror at having slighted his dead mother, even unintentionally— but he waved in merry dismissiveness as they all strolled on into the maze together.

The twisting coil of stunted highthorn entirely filled a sunken square of rich green turf surrounded on all sides by a rising slope of flowers crowned by fruit trees. Behind the trees was a stone wall, pierced in the center of each of its four runs by a stair leading down into the maze. Benches and statues stood here and there among the flowers, some of them already adorned with lamps, but there were none in the maze itself. "This is beautiful," Lady Chalass Battlebar murmured. "Did you ever play here, Crimmon?"

There was no reply. She turned to see what might be preventing him from speaking, only to see him a good twenty paces off, taking a goblet and decanter from a gleaming tray carried by a servant. "He moves swiftly when he wants to," Lady Shamril commented to Chalass.

"Hmmph," she replied, "not as swiftly as I want to." With a nod of her head she indicated the four older nobles in front of them.

"Well, if I ran Cormyr—" Lord Farrowbrace was saying, apparently unconscious of the fact that the nobility of the realm uttered that phrase even more often than the gently born, a rung down the social ladder, discussed the weather. Lord Huntingdown and their host were both interrupting him, gesturing airily with flagons almost as big as their heads, to illustrate how, begging his indulgence, they'd be like to run Cormyr just a tad differently, thus and so . . .

"Gods," Shamril muttered, "let's get gone! They'll start talking about which noble houses will rise and which will fall when a new king takes the throne, next—"

"That brings to mind the solemn question upon which the future of fair Cormyr stands," Lord Battlebar boomed. "Who among us shall rise, and who fall, if Azoun—gods preserve and keep our king—should die tomorrow?"

The three Flowers groaned in unison as Shamril spread her hands in a disgusted "I told you so" gesture. "Shall we be off after Crimmon?" she hissed. "They'll be at this all night, given wine enough! I—"

"No," Lady Lathdue said with a dangerous smile, laying a hand on Shamril's arm. "No running away now! We've a wager, remember? I want to see our fathers' faces when we make a play not for Crimmon, but for his father! Where will they look? After all, the Baron as son-in-law—albeit one old enough to sire them—gives them more power at court, and a shorter wait for the gold, if they can bend him into parting with coins before Crimmon does, or the grave takes him!"

"The wager was for the most daring way to steal a kiss from old Eskult," Chalass reminded her with a frown. "I don't want to cross my father! He'll half flail the flesh off my behind if I disgr—"

"In front of our fathers is the most daring way!" Shamril said with sudden enthusiasm. "Ladies, watch me!" She strode away through the maze, catching up her gown to unconcernedly step over walls of highthorn and catch up with the four lords. Chalass and Lathdue stared at her progress with mingled apprehension, awe, and delight.

"She's going to do it," Lathdue said in low tones, as if pronouncing doom fast coming down upon them all. "Oh, gods above."

It was coming down to full night now, but the lamps gave light enough to clearly show what befell at the heart of the maze. They saw Shamril glide past Battlebar and her own father, duck under Lord Huntingdown's arm—Lathdue erupted in swiftly-smothered giggles at the look of horrified astonishment on her father's face at the sudden, bobbing appearance of a young lady clad in a very scanty green silk gown from under his own languidly-waving arm—and come up to Lord Eskult Paertrover.

The Baron of Starwater chuckled at whatever Shamril said then, and proffered his arm with exaggerated gallantry. Rather than surrendering her own arm, the young Lady Shamril spun past the old lord's hand to press herself against him, lace-cloaked breast to medal-adorned chest, and thigh to thigh. Lord Eskult looked surprised, but pleasantly so. His teeth flashed in a smile as she raised her lips, obviously demanding a kiss, and he bent over her as if he was a young brightblade, and not an old and red-faced baron of the realm.

Chalass bit her knuckle to keep from screaming in delight as Shamril stretched her white throat a trembling inch or two farther, ignoring a sudden startled oath from her father. Lathdue shook her head, murmuring, "Crimmon should be watching this! His father's got more than a bit of the old fire in his veins yet, I—"

A sharp snapping sound echoed through the soft evening air, followed by the vicious hum of a crossbow bolt snarling through the air toward the two trembling bodies. It seemed to leap out of the gloomy air like a bolt of black lightning, stabbing between old lord and young, playful lady.

Blood burst forth in a sudden, wet torrent as the bolt took Shamril through the throat. Hair danced as her head spun around with a horrible loose wobble. The Flower of House Farrowbrace made a bubbling sound—the last sound she'd ever utter—as the bolt hummed on across the garden, plucking her out of the old lord's grasp to fall sprawled across the highthorn, a limp and bloody bundle.

Eskult stared at his own empty hands for an instant, blinded by the bright blood that was fountaining everywhere—and then clutched at his chest, made a sound that was half roar and half sob, and toppled slowly, like a felled tree, to crash down on his face in the highthorn.

There was an instant of shocked and disbelieving stillness before the shouts and screams began. With one accord, everyone present turned to stare at where the bolt must have been fired from—and the shouts were cut off as if by a sword. Stunned silence returned.

A head could be seen above the weaponless, otherwise deserted stretch of garden wall they were all staring at. It looked for all the world as if it had just risen up from behind the wall to peer at the carnage below in grinning satisfaction. Teeth flashed white and fierce in its chalk-white face, luminous beneath the dark helm it wore. The Grinning Ghost of Taverton Hall was smiling again.

It grinned at them over the garden wall for the space of two of Lathdue's long and quivering breaths before it abruptly sank from view behind the wall. As if that had been a signal, folk stirred all around the sunken garden. There was a ragged roar, and then servants and bodyguards were sprinting toward the wall, swords and belt knives out. Even Lord Battlebar, down in the maze, plucked at his own knife and crashed across the highthorn in a lumbering run.

Chalass and Lathdue, white-faced, could only stare in silent horror. However fierce and grim the pursuit was now, as men converged on the garden wall in a frantic rush, it was too late for Shamril. Her daring was stilled forever. It might well also be too late for Lord Eskult Paertrover.

Chalass sagged soundlessly to her knees, staring at the two bodies as servants hurried to kneel over them, but Lathdue sobbed suddenly and loudly, and spun around to sprint after the rushing bodyguards. That crossbow had been fired from just where they'd seen the ghost, and—

Panting, she charged up the stair from the sunken garden and turned at its head, almost falling in her haste. A hand in livery caught her arm to steady her, and she swallowed, gasped for breath, and fell silent again.

There was no sign of the Grinning Ghost of Taverton Hall. A grim ring of men with drawn steel in their hands stood around the spot where the crossbow had been fired from. It dangled, string loose now, in the hands of Lord Crimmon Paertrover. His sword glittered in his other hand, beneath a face that was white and empty. His eyes stared past Lathdue, unseeing.

"Everyone I love . . . taken from me," he blurted—and fell forward on his face, even faster than the rough hands that snatched away his blade and caught at his arms. As half Faerûn rushed down on the young lord, Lathdue felt a deeper darkness than night rise up around her, and close its merciful grasp over her eyes.

* * * * *

"Any man may say he has business with Lord Paertrover. To gain entry here, many a beggar and old soldier has said as much. His friend and secret business partner you may be, too—but I know you not."

The old seneschal's voice was cold, his stare as wintry as a blizzard howling across the Stonelands, but the man across the table from him smiled with easy affability and replied, "Neither do I know you, goodman, but has that ever been a barrier between men of goodwill? You have the look of a retired Purple Dragon, and I respect all who've fought to keep our fair land safe. Might I know your name?"

"Greiryn," the bristle-browed man on the far side of the table said shortly. "Seneschal of Taverton Hall."

The stout man with the shaggy sideburns bounded from his seat to stretch a welcoming hand across the tabletop, for all the world as if he were the host, and not the visitor. "Glarasteer Rhauligan, dealer in turret tops and spires," he boomed. "No embattlement too small, no embrasure too large, no crenellation too eccentric. If you can draw it, I can build it! I've come from bustling Suzail herself, turning my back on insistent barons and eager knights alike, to keep my appointment with the Lord Eskult Paertrover." He gestured imperiously with the hand that Greiryn had been ignoring, and added firmly, "I do have an appointment."

"Saw you the black banner?" the seneschal asked, in grim and reluctant tones. Rhauligan shrugged in a "no, but what of it?" gesture, and Greiryn said icily, "My Lord lies dead in the family crypt, of heartstop, and won't be seeing anyone. Good day to you, merchant."

The fat man in silks and furs made another imperious gesture, more hastily this time. "His son, then," Rhauligan said eagerly, "the young blade who makes half the ladies in Cormyr swoon, and the rest sigh! He'll be Lord Paertrover now, right?"

"If he lives to take any title," Greiryn replied in tones of doom that were almost drowned out by the sudden blare of a hunting horn sounding from the gates.

He rose at the sound, reaching for his cloak. "You must excuse me—that will be a Wizard of War, sent from Suzail to see to Lord Crimmon's fate."

* * * * *

The royal arms gleamed on the door of the coach even through the swirling road-dust. Rhauligan counted no less than sixteen black horses in its harness, stamping and tossing their heads impatiently as that regal door opened, and a man in stylish robes of lush purple alighted.

The servant with the hunting horn blew a too-loud, wandering-note flourish, and the newcomer didn't trouble to hide his wince and frown. He extended his left hand in a fist, displaying a ring to the already-bowing seneschal, and snapped his fingers.

In answer to this signal, a servant still hastening out of the coach declaimed grandly, "All hail and make welcome Lord Jalanus Westerbotham, Scepter of Justice, Dragonfang Lord Investigator for Northbank, Starwater, and the Western Coast!"

The figure in purple inclined his head in coldly distant greeting to the three noble lords, swept past them and their daughters, ignored Rhauligan and a hastily-arrayed lineup of household servants, and strode toward the pillared entry of Taverton Hall. The seneschal practically sprinted to catch up with him, holding his ceremonial sword at one hip. Rhauligan gave Greiryn a cheerful grin as he puffed past, and was rewarded with a fierce scowl.

"Lord Jalanus!" the seneschal gasped, trying to smile, "be welcome indeed in Taverton Hall. A sad occasion calls you here, but I'm sure that your stay nee—"

"Where, man, are my quarters?" the war wizard demanded, in tones that Rhauligan promptly (and privately) dubbed "coldly patrician."

"Ah, we've prepared the Ducal Suite for you, milord," Greiryn said, waving a hand down the central hallway. "It's just ahead there; that door where the servants are waiting."

"I must see to its suitability, and theirs," Lord Jalanus said in a voice that managed to combine equal parts irritation at having to deal with dunderheads and gloomy anticipation of personal hardship and disappointment to come. He drew a slim, shiny black wand from his belt with a flourish, and marched off down the hall.

His servants streamed after him, pushing past Glarasteer Rhauligan on both sides. The merchant staggered first to the left and then to the right under their bruising impacts, and then shrugged and thrust out his foot, sending a heavily-laden servant crashing onto his face. Deftly he snatched up two carrychests from the chaos that had been the servant's high-stacked load, and joined the general rush down the hall. A ragged shout followed him, and as he turned to enter the Ducal Suite, an angry hand plucked at his sleeve.

"Hey, now, you—"

"Come, come, man," Rhauligan said grandly, "make yourself useful. Lord Wetterbottom seems to have brought no end of clobber with him up the short road from Suzail. Stir yourself to carry some of it, as I have!"

"You—"

Greiryn's face swung into view, lit with fury, and over his shoulder looked Lord Jalanus, boredom and withering scorn now vying for supremacy on his features.

"Merchant!" the seneschal snapped, "surrender those chests at once! I'll have you thrown out of the Hall—with coach whips!—if you aren't gone by the time our esteemed guest is settled! Do you hear?"

"Along with everyone in southern Cormyr," Rhauligan murmured mildly, extending his arms and dropping both chests on the highly-polished toes of Greiryn's best boots. "But to hear, I fear, is not always to obey."

"It is, among servants at court," the war wizard sneered as Immult Greiryn uttered a strangled shriek, bending over to clutch at his toes.

Rhauligan gave him a broad smile. "That's not what Vangey—oh, the Lord Vangerdahast to you, no doubt—is always complaining to me. Why, j—"

"Guards!" roared the seneschal. "Arrest this man! He—"

"Will go quite quietly, once this is all settled and I can keep my appointment with the surviving Lord Paertrover," Rhauligan said, stepping swiftly back against a wall as the heavy clump of hastening boots rang down the hallway. "I must be present when Wetterbottom here listens to all the evidence, and goes with his spells to interro—er, interview my future client."

"Oh?" The war wizard put out an imperious hand to silence Greiryn and push him aside, and his tones were silky as he advanced to face the stout merchant nose to nose, bringing his other hand up with slow menace to show the entire hallway of staring guards and servants the ornate and heavy rings that gleamed and glittered on his fingers. "By what bold right, man, do you make such insistence?"

Glarasteer Rhauligan smiled easily and reached into the open front of his loose shirt.

"Before you do anything rash," Lord Jalanus added quickly, "I must remind you that there are laws in fair Cormyr, and I, 'Wetterbottom' or not, am sworn to uphold them. I need no court to mete out final—fatal—justice." One of the rings he wore flashed once, warningly.

"Your slumbers must be troubled," Rhauligan replied in tones of gentle pity, as he slowly drew forth something small and silver on a chain, holding it cupped in his hand for only the wizard and Greiryn to see. It was a rounded silver harp: the badge of a Harper. "I have also come here from Suzail," the merchant told them softly, and leaned forward to add in a very loud whisper, "and I was sent by someone *very* highly placed in court."

The war wizard's eyes flickered, and he spun around with an angry flourish. "Admit him to my investigations," he snapped at the seneschal—and then wheeled around again to add curtly to Rhauligan, "Cross not my authority in the smallest way. Your presence I'll grant, but you are to be silent and refrain from meddling. Understand?"

Rhauligan spread his hands. "Your words are clarity and simplicity itself."

Lord Jalanus glared at him for a long moment, sensed nothing more was forthcoming, and turned on his heel again without another word. The merchant favored his retreating back with a florid court bow that made one of the servants snigger. Greiryn's head snapped up to glare—but the culprit, whoever it was, lurked somewhere in the stone faced ranks of the wizard's own servants, not the folk of the Hall.

Rhauligan smiled fondly at him. "As Lord Wetterbottom seems to need the entire Ducal Suite, could you open the Royal Rooms for me? Hmmm?"

The seneschal's hands came up like trembling claws, reaching for Rhauligan's throat, before more prudent thought stilled them. More anonymous titters were heard—and this time, some of them came from the servants of the Hall.

"The day," Rhauligan remarked to the world at large, as he strode off down the hallway, "does not seem to be proceeding well for seneschals, does it?"

* * * * *

"But he must have done it!" Greiryn protested. "We all saw him holding the bow! T-the string was still quivering!"

"My spells," Lord Jalanus said icily, "do not lie. Lord Crimmon is innocent."

"I-I quite understand," the seneschal said hastily. "I didn't mean to doubt you! It's just so . . . so bewildering. Who can have done it, then?"

"Bolyth," the war wizard snapped, turning to the mountainous Purple Dragon who always lurked at his elbow, "have the gates closed immediately. Post guards; I want this estate sealed. Seneschal, reveal unto me, as soon as your wits allow, who—if anyone—has left this house since the deaths." He rose in a swirl of cloth-of-gold and claret-hued velvet oversleeves, his third change of garments in as many hours.

"I—but of course," Greiryn agreed, almost babbling. "There can't be all that many. We're not like the Dales here, with Elminster flitting in and out like some great nightbat!"

Behind them both, a suit of armor in the corner blurred momentarily. Rhauligan saw it become a white-bearded man in robes, wink at him, and wave cheerily. He winked back, just before the armor became simply armor again.

Oblivious to this visitation, the seneschal was babbling on, clearly shaken at the thought of his young lord master's innocence. Now that was interesting in itself. . . . "Uh, great Lord Justice," Greiryn interrupted himself, "where're you going now?"

"To question the bodies, of course," the war wizard snapped, drawing out a wand that was fully three feet long, and seemed to be made entirely of polished and fused human finger bones. "They rarely have much of value to impart, but—'tis procedure . . ."

". . . and we are all slaves to procedure," Rhauligan told the ceiling gently, completing the court saying. At the doorway, the striding war wizard stopped, stiffened, and then surged into motion again, sweeping out of the room without a word.

* * * * *

"I answer to my Lord Eskult," the old man said shortly, "not to you."

Lord Jalanus drew himself up, eyes glittering. His nose quivered with embottled fury, and he fairly spat out the words, "Do you know who I am, puling worm?"

The head gardener spat thoughtfully down into the rushes at their feet, shifted his chew to the other cheek, and said contemptuously, "Aye, the sort of miserable excuse for a war wizard that's all Cormyr can muster from the younglings these days. You'd not have been allowed across the threshold of the Royal Court in my day. I guarded those doors for the good of the realm—and turned back from them far, far better men than you." He turned on his heel and strode out of the room, leaving the Lord Justice snarling with incoherent rage in his wake.

"Clap that man in chains!" Jalanus Westerbotham howled, as soon as he could master words again. Two Purple Dragons started obediently away from their stations along the walls—only to come to uncertain halts as the stout merchant, moving with apparent laziness, somehow got to the doorway and filled it . . . with one hand on the hilt of a blade that looked well-used and sturdy, and which hadn't been in evidence before.

"The Lord spoke in empty hyperbole," Rhauligan told the armsmen, "not meaning you to take his words literally. He knows very well that imprisoning a veteran of the Purple Dragons—and a close friend of the king at that, from the days when Azoun was a boy prince— merely for insisting that he be questioned with due courtesy, would be excessive. When word of such a serious lack of judgment reached the ears of Vangerdahast, even a Scepter of Justice would have to be hasty in his explanations . . . and no such haste would save him, if the King learned of the matter. After all, what is more valuable to the realm than a loyal, long-serving Purple Dragon? You'd know that better than most, goodmen, eh?"

The two Purple Dragons nodded. One was almost smiling as they turned slowly to look back at their quivering superior. His hands were white as he gripped the back of the chair he was standing behind, and murmured in a voice as hard and cold as a drawn blade, "Goodman Rhauligan is correct. I spoke in hyperbole."

Wordlessly the guards nodded and returned to their places along the walls. The Lord Justice glared down at several sheets of parchment on the table for a moment, his gaze scorching, and then snapped, "Bring in the master cellarer. Alone." He lifted his head and favored Rhauligan with a look that promised the merchant a slow, lingering death, sometime soon.

The turret vendor gave him a cheery smile. "It takes a strong, exceptional man to endure the strain of keeping up these truth-reading spells. You do us all proud, Lord Jalanus. I can well see why Vangey named you a Scepter of Justice."

"Oh, be silent," the war wizard said in disgust. "Have done with this mockery."

"No, I mean what I say!" Rhauligan protested. "Have you not learned all you needed to from yon gardener, even though he thinks he told you nothing? Hard work, that is, and ably done. Vangey missed telling you just one thing: never use the commands 'Clap that man in chains!' or 'Flog that wench!' They don't work, d'you see? That failure goes a resounding double with the younger generation—you know, the one the gardener thinks you're part of!"

Jalanus waved a weary hand in acceptance and dismissal as a disturbance at the door heralded the arrival of the master cellarer. The man had the look of an old and scared rabbit. Four grinning guards towered around him, obviously enjoying the man's shrinking terror, and the war wizard looked at them and then at Rhauligan. The Lord Justice cleared his throat and asked in a gentle voice, "Renster, is it not? Please, sit down, and be at ease. No one is accusing you of any wrongdoing. . . ."

The stout merchant leaned back against the wall and nodded in satisfaction. Perhaps war wizards could learn things, after all.

* * * * *

Rhauligan slipped out of the interviewing chamber as the twelfth guest—the castellan of the vaults, a surly, stout little man—was being ushered in. The merchant could feel the satisfied glare of the Lord Justice between his shoulder blades as he slipped through the doorway, trotted past a suspicious guard, and fell into step beside the war wizard's eleventh "guest:" the clerk of the estate.

The clerk—young and sunken-eyed, his face etched with fear and utter weariness—spared his new escort one glance and muttered, "I suppose the real questions begin now, is that it? After that strutting peacock has worn me down?"

"It's our usual procedure," Rhauligan confided reassuringly, man to man. "We have to give wizards something to do, or they're apt to get up to mischief—creating new monsters, blowing up thrones; that sort of thing. The problem is, there isn't much they're fit to do, so. . . ." He gestured back down the passage; the clerk smiled thinly and turned away, down a side hall. Rhauligan hastened to follow. "Where are Lord Eskult's personal papers kept?"

"His will, d'you mean?" the clerk asked dismissively. "The seneschal fetched that even before Lord High-And-Mighty got here. The three visiting lords wanted to l—"

"Yes, yes," Rhauligan agreed, "but where did he fetch it *from*?"

The clerk stopped and gave the turret vendor a curious look. "If it's all that gold you're after," he said, "forget about it. The castellan has it hid down in the vaults, somehow so arcane that to reach it three guards all have to attend him, each carrying some secret part of a key or other."

"It's not the gold," Rhauligan said. "It's the trading agreements, the ledgers, the tax scrolls—all that. Your work."

The clerk gave him a hard stare, and then shrugged. "Too dry for most to care about, but as you seem to be one of those touched-wits exceptions, they're all in an office just along here."

"You have a key, of course. Who else does?"

"Why, the Lord—or did; 'twas around his neck when I saw him laid out. Then, look, so does the head maid, the seneschal of course, the back chambermaid—'twas hers to clean, y'see—and the Crown has a key that the tax scrutineers use when they come."

"I," Rhauligan told him, "am a tax scrutineer. Here, I carry a royal writ; examine it, pray." Reaching into his shirtfront, he drew forth a rather crumpled parchment, from which a heavy royal seal dangled. The clerk rolled his eyes and waved it away—even before the three platinum pieces folded into it slid out, falling straight into the man's palm.

"I've come to Taverton Hall," Rhauligan said smoothly, as the man juggled the coins in astonishment, "without that key. I need to see those papers—now—in utmost secrecy." The clerk came to a stop in the corridor and squinted at the merchant, almost seeming excited.

"That meaning if I tell no one I let you in here, you'll say the same?" he asked, peering up and down the passage as if he expected masked men with swirling cloaks and daggers to bound out of every door and corner in an instant.

"Precisely," Rhauligan murmured. No masked men appeared. Satisfied, the clerk flashed a smile, shook a ring of keys out of his sleeve, and unlocked the nearest door with only the faintest of rattles. Then he was off down the corridor, strolling along in an apparent half-doze as if strange merchants and unlocking doors were far from his mind.

Rhauligan eased the door wide, held up a coin, and muttered a word over it. A soft glow was born along its edges, brightening into a little blue-white beam, like errant moonlight. The merchant turned the coin to light up the tiny office beyond, seeking traps.

After a long scrutiny, Rhauligan was satisfied no lurking slayer or death-trap awaited him. There was, however, a full oil-lamp, a striker, and a bolt on the inside of the door. Perfect.

The door closed behind the merchant, its bolt sliding solidly into place, a few breaths before the tramp of heavy boots in the corridor heralded the approach of a half-dozen guards, sent to find and bring back "that dangerous Harper." They thundered right past the closed, featureless door.

Rhauligan peered and thumbed scrolls and ledgers, and flipped pages. It wasn't long before something became obvious through all the scrawled signatures and expense entries and reassignments of funds. The Paertrover coffers were well-nigh empty. He sat back thoughtfully, stroking his chin, and only gradually became aware that the room behind him seemed brighter than before.

He turned with smooth swiftness, hand going to the hilt of the throwing knife strapped to his left forearm, but nothing met his eye save a fading, swirling area of radiance, like a scattering of misplaced moonlight. He blinked once and it was gone. Gone—but had definitely been there.

After a brief tour of that end of the room, poking and tapping in search of secret doors and passages, Rhauligan shrugged and began the quick process of returning the room to exactly how he'd found it. When he was done, he blew out the lamp and slipped out the door again.

Alone in the darkness, the radiance silently returned, and with it what Rhauligan had been too slow to turn and see: a disembodied head, its face pinched and white, the plumes of the long helm it wore dancing gently in an unseen breeze. It was smiling broadly as it looked at the closed door—and abruptly started to fade away. A breath later, the room was dark and empty once more.

* * * * *

Guards hunted Glarasteer Rhauligan around Taverton Hall for a good hour, shouting and clumping up stairs and down passages, but found no sign of the merchant. Their failure came as no surprise to their quarry, who spent the afternoon in happy slumber deep in the shade of an overhang high up on the roof. If Rhauligan was right, things would happen at the Hall soon, in the dark hours, and he had to be awake, aware, and in the right spot then. Unless, of course, he wanted to see more murders done.

* * * * *

Guards are notoriously lazy and unobservant after a heavy meal and a bottle of fine vintage each (contributed by the seneschal with a rather morose shrug and the words, "You may as well. My master, who gathered these, is a little too dead to miss them now."), and it was at that time, with sunset looming, that a certain much-sought-after dealer in fine turrets slid down a pillar and sprang away into the trees. He left in his wake only dancing, disturbed bushes for a bored guard to glance at, peer hard, shrug, and return his attention to a hard-plied toothpick.

Rhauligan circled the Hall like a silent shadow, keeping among the trees and shrubbery as he sought other sentinels. Armsmen guarded the gates and the grand front entrance of the Hall, but none stood like ridiculous statues in gardens or wooded glades any longer, to feed the biting bugs.

Not far from the closed and little-used cart-gate around the back of the Hall, however, something was stamping on the moss. It was a saddled horse, hampered in its cropping of grass by four heavy saddlebags. Rhauligan checked their contents and its tether, smiled grimly, and noted that the horse was just out of sight of the Hall windows. A little path wandered off from where he stood to the back doors. The merchant looked up, found a bough that was big enough, and swung himself aloft to wait.

It did not take all that long. The last golden light soon faded and the crickets began their songs. Night gloom stole through the trees, dew glistened as servants lit lamps, and the dark shadow on the branch shifted his position with infinite care to keep his feet from going numb.

The first sharp whiff of smoke came a breath before a long tongue of flame flared up, like an catching candle, inside a nearby window. There followed a sudden, rising roar, and then a dull gasp as flames were born around something very flammable; draperies or clothes well-soaked in lamp oil, no doubt. Then came the shouts, the shattering of glass, and men pounding here and there in the sudden, hot brightness with buckets and valuables and much cursing. The shadow never moved from its perch. All was unfolding as foreseen. Taverton Hall was afire.

The roaring became a steady din, and sparks spat forth into the night in a glittering rain. Draperies at one window erupted in a flame so bright that Rhauligan could clearly see the faces of the hurrying, jostling men. Lord Jalanus was among them, bent over an open book that an anxious-looking guard was holding open and up to him.

There was a crash and fresh flames as part of the roof fell in, and flaming embers rained down around the war wizard. Jalanus staggered back, snarling something. Then he snatched at a spark in the air, caught it, stammered something hasty—and all over the Hall the flames seemed to freeze for a moment, falling silent and turning green.

A breath later, they started to move again, crawling towards the stars with lessened hunger. The war wizard shook his head, slammed the book shut, and sent the armsman to join the bucket-runners. Then he raised his hands as if about to conduct a choir, and cast quite a different spell.

Several rooms suddenly vanished, fire and all, leaving a gaping hole in the darkness. The flames that remained were in two places, lesser remnants small enough that stable-buckets of hurled water might tame them. Every hand would be needed, however, and the night would be a long and sweat-soaked struggle. The shadow on the branch stirred, but did not move. It was waiting for something else.

The war wizard opened his book again and strode to where a lamp afforded better light. That was what someone had been waiting for . . . someone who slipped out of a window not far along from the flames, crossing the ember-strewn lawn to the trees in a few darting strides.

The tether was undone and hand-coiled, and then saddle-leather creaked just beneath Rhauligan, who flexed his fingers, waited a moment more, and then made his move.

The saddle had a high crupper. He lowered himself gently down onto it with one hand, steadying himself against the branch with the other. The faint whisper of his movements was cloaked by the roar of the fire and the sounds made by the unwitting man in front of him, leaning forward to shake out the reins. Rhauligan delicately plucked a dagger from its sheath on the back of the man's belt and threw it away into the night.

That slight sound made the man turn in his saddle and reach for his sword. Rhauligan turned with him, placing one firm hand on the man's sword-wrist, and snaking the other around his throat. "Warm evening we're having," he murmured politely, as the man in front of him stiffened.

His next few breaths were spent in frantic twisting and straining as the two men struggled together. Rhauligan hooked his boots around those of his foe to keep from being shoved off the snorting, bucking horse, and the night became a confusion of elbows and sudden jerks and grunts of effort. The merchant kept the man's throat in the vise of his tightening elbow, and frantic fingers clawed at his arm once they found the dagger-sheath empty—clawed, but found no freedom.

The man kicked and snarled, and abruptly the horse burst into motion, crashing through rose-bushes with a fearful, sobbing cry of its own. Trees plunged up to meet them in the night, with an open garden beyond. Rhauligan grimly set about kicking at one flank of the mount, to turn it back toward the flames.

He was failing, and taking some vicious bites from the man in the saddle in front of him, when firelight gleamed on a helm as a guard rose suddenly into view almost under the hooves of the galloping horse. It reared, bugling in real fear, and when it came down, running hard, the blazing wing of the Hall was suddenly dead ahead and approaching fast.

The man in the saddle twisted and ducked frantically, almost hauling Rhauligan off into thin air, but the merchant clung to him with fingers of iron as they burst through a closed gate, wood flying in splinters around their ears, plunged down a lane, and charged into a knot of men dipping buckets in a garden pond.

Someone screamed, and for a moment there was something yielding beneath the mount's pounding hooves. Rhauligan had a brief glimpse of the war wizard standing calmly in their path, casting another firequench spell at the Hall with careful concentration.

The horse veered to avoid this unmoving obstacle, slipped in ferns and loose earth, and caught its hooves on a low stone wall. Bone shattered with a sharp crack. Their mount screamed like a child in agony, kicked wildly at the sky, and fell over on its side, twisting and arching. It landed on a row of stone flower urns that shattered into dagger-like shards—and ended its keening abruptly.

An instant later, a flying Rhauligan fetched up hard against an unbroken urn. Its shattering made his shoulder erupt in searing pain.

As he rolled unsteadily to his feet, gasping, he saw drawn swords on all sides, the furious face of Lord Jalanus glaring down—and then a sudden, blindingly-bright white light as the war wizard unhooded a wand.

"You set this fire, thief!"

The shout was close at hand; Rhauligan flung himself forward into a frantic roll away from it without looking back to see how close the blade seeking his blood was.

Sharp steel whistled through empty air, very close by. Rhauligan came to his feet, sprang onto the ornamental wall, and spun around to face his foe. The man who'd been in the saddle lurched toward him, hacking at the air like a madman.

"You set this fire!" Immult Greiryn shouted again, missing Rhauligan with a tremendous slash, so forceful that it almost made the seneschal fall over. "Slay him, one of you! Cut him down!"

"No," said the Lord Justice, in a cold, crisp voice that seemed to still the sound of the fire itself, and made men freeze all around. "Do no such thing. This man lies. The merchant is innocent."

Wild-eyed, the seneschal whirled and charged at the

war wizard, his blade flashing up. Jalanus Westerbotham stepped back in alarm, opening his mouth to call for aid—but bright steel flashed out of the night, spinning end over end in a hungry blur that struck blood from Greiryn's sword hand, rang off the seneschal's blade like a hammer striking a gong, and was gone into the flowers in a trice.

Lord Jalanus muttered something and lunged forward with sudden, supple speed, thrusting his empty hand at Greiryn as if it was a blade. The blow he landed seemed little more than a shove, but the seneschal staggered, doubled up as if a sword had pierced him through the guts, and crumpled onto his side, unconscious.

The war wizard bent over the man to be sure he was asleep. Satisfied, he looked up, snapped, "Bolyth! The wire—this man's thumbs, little fingers, and big toes bound together. Then stop his bleeding, and watch over him yourself."

As his ever-present, most trusted guard lumbered obediently forward, Jalanus Westerbotham turned his head, found Rhauligan, and said shortly, "A good throw. My thanks."

The merchant sketched him a florid bow. The lips of the Lord Justice twisted into a rueful smile.

Guards were crowding in around them all now, pushing past the servants and noble guests. "Lord," one of them asked hesitantly, waving a gauntleted hand at Rhauligan, "shouldn't we be arresting this one too?"

The war wizard raised one cold eyebrow. "When, Brussgurt, did you adopt the habit of deciding for me who is guilty, and who innocent? I've had a wizard eye on this man for most of the evening—he's most certainly innocent of the charge of fire-setting. I suspect his only crime was learning too much . . . for the seneschal to want him to go on living."

"So who slew my daughter?" a darkly furious voice demanded. Its owner came shouldering through the last rushing smokes of the dying fire, with the other two noble lords and their white-faced, staring daughters in tow. Lord Hornsar Farrowbrace's eyes were like two chips of bright steel, and his hand was on the hilt of a heavy war sword that had not been on his hip before.

"Master Rhauligan?" the war wizard asked. "You tell him."

The merchant met the eyes of the Scepter of Justice for a long, sober moment, nodded, and then turned to the angry noble.

"The seneschal," he said simply, pointing down at the helpless, waking man who was being securely bound with wire, under the knees of three burly guards.

"The Paertrover gold is almost all gone, and Greiryn was the only longtime family servant with access to it. Lord, I fear your daughter lies dead this night solely because Greiryn's a poor shot. He'd accounted for the coins flowing out with bills and ledger entries that only one man could be certain were false: his lord and master. He meant to slay Lord Eskult while Shamril's attentions kept him standing more or less in one place, a clear target that an old veteran missed."

Lord Farrowbrace growled wordlessly as he looked down at Immult Greiryn, who cowered away despite the burly guards between them.

"But what of the ghost?" Lady Lathdue Huntingdown protested. "It's not just some tall tale from Crimmon! The servants have all been saying . . ."

Rhauligan held up a hand to stop her speaking, went to where the horse lay, and tore open the laces of a saddlebag.

Gold coins glittered in the hand he held out to her. "The last of Lord Eskult's wealth," he explained. "This wretch at our feet has already spent or stolen the rest. He had help from at least one man, the castellan of the vault—whose bones are no doubt yonder in the heart of the blaze, wearing the seneschal's armor or chain of office or something to make us think the flames have claimed poor, *faithful* old Greiryn."

Coins clinked as he tossed a second saddlebag down beside the first, and then a third. The last yielded up a plumed helm and a jar of white powder.

"The grinning ghost of Taverton Hall," Rhauligan announced to the gathered, peering folk, holding them up. "You were all supposed to flee, you see, not rush to see who'd fired the—"

Someone screamed. Someone else cursed . . . slowly, and in trembling tones. Folk were backing away, their faces pale and their fearful stares directed past Rhauligan's shoulder.

The turret merchant turned slowly, already knowing what he'd see. He swallowed, just once, when he found that he'd been dead right.

A breeze he did not feel was stirring the plumes of the helm worn by the grinning face of the head that was floating almost nose to nose with him. Lord Farrowbrace started calling hoarsely on god after god and Rhauligan could hear the sounds of boots whose owners were running away.

The dark eyes of the Grinning Ghost of Taverton Hall were like endless, lightless pits, but somehow they were meeting his own gaze with an approving look. Rhauligan stood his ground when ghostly shadows spilled out from the helm, flickered bone-white, and seemed to struggle and convulse. After long moments, some of those shifting shadows became a ghostly hand, reaching out for the Harper.

Scalp crawling, Glarasteer Rhauligan did the bravest, and possibly the most foolhardy thing in his life. He stood his ground as that spectral arm clapped his own arm firmly.

The cold was instant, and bone-chilling. Rhauligan grunted and staggered back involuntarily, his face going gray. There was a loud, solid thump beside him, and when he looked down he discovered that it was Lord Justice Jalanus Westerbotham, sprawled on his back in the mud, fallen in a dead faint.

Trembling just a trifle, Rhauligan looked back at the ghost—but it was gone. Empty air swirled and flickered in front of him; he was standing alone in the moonlight.

The Lady Lathdue and the Lady Chalass were approaching him hesitantly, their eyes dark and apprehensive, their blades borne by their fathers thrusting out protectively between their slim arms. Lord Farrowbrace, his eyes haunted with wonder, stood a little apart, his own sword dangling toward the trampled ground.

"Sir? Are you well?" the Lady Lathdue asked.

As she spoke, a throng of ghostly figures in finery and armor seemed to melt into solidity all around the nobles, all of them nodding approvingly or sketching salutes with spectral hands or blades. Rhauligan blinked, staggering under the sheer weight of so much ghostly regard—and when he could see again, they were all gone.

Wondering, the turret merchant looked down at his arm, which still felt encased in bone-searing ice. His leather jerkin had melted away in three deep gouges, where three bone-white marks were burned into his bronzed skin. Like old scars they seemed; the parallel stripes of three gripping fingers.

Glarasteer Rhauligan looked up at them all, drew in a deep breath, and said in a voice that was almost steady, "I'll live, but smoke can kill those who can't move out of it. We must find and free Lord Crimmon Paertrover. Let us be about it."

And from that night until the day he died, those three white marks never left Rhauligan's arm.

R.A. Salvatore

The *New York Times* best-selling author of the Dark Elf saga returns to the FORGOTTEN REALMS® with an all new novel of high adventure and intrigue!

the
SILENT
BLADE

Wulfgar's world is crumbling around him while the assassin Entreri and the drow mercenary Jarlaxle are gaining power in Calimport. But Entreri isn't interested in power—all he wants is a final showdown with the dark elf known as Drizzt. . . . An all new hardcover, available October 1998.

the SILENT BLADE

R.A. Salvatore

An Excerpt

Available in Hardcover
October 1998

"Do not come here," LaValle cried, and then he added, softly, "I beg."

Entreri merely continued to stare at the man, his expression unreadable.

"You wounded Kadran Gordeon," LaValle went on. "In pride more than in body, and that, I warn you, is more dangerous by far."

"Gordeon is a fool," Entreri retorted.

"A fool with an army," LaValle quipped. "No guild is more entrenched in the streets than the Basadonis. None have more resources and all of those resources, I assure you, have been turned upon Artemis Entreri."

"And upon LaValle, perhaps?" Entreri replied with a grin. "For speaking with the hunted man?"

LaValle didn't answer the obvious question, other than to continue to stare hard at Artemis Entreri, the man whose mere presence in his room this night might have just condemned him.

"Tell them everything they ask of you," Entreri instructed. "Honestly. Do not try to deceive them for my sake. Tell them that I came here, uninvited, to speak with you, and that I show no wounds for all their efforts."

"You would taunt them so?"

Entreri shrugged and asked, "Does it matter?"

LaValle had no answer to that, and so the assassin,

with a bow, moved to the window. Defeating one trap with a flick of the wrist and carefully manipulating his body to avoid the others, he slipped out to the wall and dropped silently to the street. He dared to go by the Copper Ante that night, though only quickly and with no effort to actually enter the place. Still, he did make himself known to the door-halflings and to his surprise, a short way down the alley at the side of the building, Dwahvel Tiggerwillies came out a secret door to speak with him.

"A battle mage," she warned. "Merle Pariso. With a reputation unparalleled in Calimport. Fear him, Artemis Entreri. Run from him. Flee the city and all the southlands." And with that, she slipped through another barely detectable crack in the wall and was gone.

The gravity of her words and tone were not lost on the assassin. The mere fact that Dwahvel had come out to him, with nothing to gain and everything to lose tipped him off that she had been instructed to so inform him, or at least, that this battle-mage was making no secret of the hunt. How could he repay the favor, after all, if he took her advice and fled Calimshan?

So perhaps the wizard was a bit too cocksure, he told himself, but that, too, proved of little comfort. A battle-mage. A wizard trained specifically in the art of magical warfare. Cocksure, and with a right to be. Entreri had fought and killed many wizards, but he understood the truth of the situation. A wizard was not so difficult an enemy for a seasoned warrior, as long as the warrior was able to prepare the battlefield favorably. That was usually not difficult, since wizards were, by nature, easily distracted and often unprepared. Typically a wizard had to anticipate battle far in advance, at the beginning of the day, that he might prepare the appropriate spells.

But when a wizard was the hunter and not the hunted, he would not be caught off guard. Preparing the battlefield against the mage would be no easy task.

Entreri knew that he was in trouble, and seriously considered taking Dwahvel's advice. For the first time since he had returned to Calimport, the assassin truly appreciated the danger of being without allies. He considered that in light of his experiences in Menzoberranzan, where unallied rogues could not survive for long.

Perhaps Calimport wasn't so different.

He started for his new room, an empty hovel at the back of an alleyway, but stopped and reconsidered. It wasn't likely that the wizard, with such a reputation as a combat spellcaster, would be overly skilled in divination spells as well, but that hardly mattered. It all came down to connections, and Merle Pariso was acting on behalf of the Basadoni guild. If he wanted to magically locate Entreri, the guild would grant him the resources of their diviners.

Where to go? He didn't want to remain on the open street, where a wizard could strike from a long distance, could even, perhaps, levitate high above and rain destructive magic upon him. He searched the buildings, looking for a place to hide, knowing all the while that magical eyes might be upon him.

With that rather disturbing thought in mind, Entreri wasn't overly surprised when he slipped quietly into the supposedly empty back room of a darkened warehouse, and a robed figure appeared right before him with a puff of orange smoke, and the door blew closed behind him.

Entreri glanced all around, noting the lack of exits in the room, cursing his foul luck in finding this place. Again, when he considered it, it came down to his lack of allies and lack of knowledge with present-day Calimport. They were waiting for him, wherever he might go. They were ahead of him, watching his every move and, obviously, taking a prepared battlefield right with them. Entreri felt foolish for even coming back to this inhospitable city without first probing, without learning all that he would need to survive.

Enough of the doubts and second-guesses, he pointedly reminded himself, drawing out his dagger and setting himself low in a crouch, concentrating on the situation at hand. He thought of turning back for the door, but knew without doubt that it would be magically sealed.

"Behold the Merle!" the wizard said with a laugh, waving his arms out wide, the voluminous sleeves of his robes floating behind his lifting limbs and throwing a rainbow of multicolored lights. A second wave and his arms came forward, hurling a blast of lightning at the assassin.

But Entreri was already moving, rolling to the side out of harm's way. He glanced back, hoping the bolt might have blown through the door, but it was still closed and seemed solid enough.

"Oh, well dodged!" Merle Pariso congratulated. "But really, pitiful assassin, do you desire to make this last longer? Why not stand still and be done with it, quickly and mercifully?"

He stopped his taunting and launched into another spellcasting as Entreri charged in, jeweled dagger flashing. Merle made no move to defend against the attack, just calmly went on with his casting as Entreri came in hard, stabbing for the mage's face.

The dagger stopped as surely as if it had struck a stone wall. Entreri wasn't really surprised—any wise wizard would have prepared such a defense—but what amazed him, even as he went flying back, hit by a burst of magical missiles, was Pariso's concentration, his unflinching spellcasting even as the deadly dagger came at his face, unblinking even as the blade flashed right before his eyes.

Entreri staggered to the side, went into another dive and roll, anticipating another attack. But now Merle Pariso, supremely confident, merely laughed at him. "Where will you run?" the mage taunted. "How many times will you find the energy to dodge?"

Indeed, if he allowed the wizard's taunts to sink in, Entreri would have found it hard to hold his heart; many lesser warriors might have simply taken the wizard's advice and surrendered to the seemingly inevitable.

But not Entreri. His lethargy fell away, all the doubts of his life and his purpose flew away at that moment, with his very life on the line. Now he lived completely in the moment, adrenaline pumping. One step at a time, and the first of those steps was to defeat the stoneskin, the magical defense that could turn any blade—but only a certain number of blows.

Spinning and rolling, the assassin, took up a chair and broke free a leg, then rolled about and launched it at the wizard, scoring an ineffective hit.

Another burst of magical missiles slammed into him, following him unerringly in his roll and stinging him. He shrugged through it, though, and came up throwing, a second and then a third chair leg, scoring two more hits.

The fourth followed in rapid succession and then the base of the chair, a meager missile that would hardly have hurt the wizard even without the magical defense, but one that took yet another layer off the stoneskin.

He paid for the offensive flurry, though, as Merle Pariso's next lightning bolt caught him hard. The bolt launched him spinning sidelong, his shoulder burned, his hair dancing on end, his heart fluttering.

Now, desperate and hurt, the assassin went in hard, dagger slashing. "How many more can you defeat?" he roared, stabbing hard again and again.

His answer came in the form of flames, a shroud of dancing fire covering, but hardly consuming, Merle Pariso. Entreri noted them too late to stop short his last attack and the dagger went through, again hitting harmlessly against the stoneskin. Harmlessly to Pariso, but not to Entreri, for the newest spell, the flame shield, replicated the intended bite of that dagger back at Entreri, drawing a deep gash along the already-battered man's ribs.

With a howl, the assassin fell back, purposely turning himself in line with the door, then dodging deftly as the predictable lightning bolt came after him.

The rolling assassin looked back as he came around,

pleased to see that this time the wooden door had indeed splintered. He grabbed another chair and threw it at the wizard, turning for the door even as he released it.

Merle Pariso's groan stopped him dead and turned him back around, thinking the stoneskin expired.

But then it was Entreri's turn to groan. "Oh, clever," he congratulated, realizing the wizard's groan to be no more than a ruse, buying the man time to cast his next spell.

The assassin turned back for the door, but hadn't gone a step before he was forced back, as a wall of huge flames erupted along that wall, blocking Entreri's escape.

"Well fought, assassin," Merle Pariso said honestly. "I expected as much from Artemis Entreri. But now, alas, you die."

The battle-mage drew a wand, pointed it at the floor at his feet, and fired a burning seed.

Entreri fell flat, pulling what remained of his cloak over his head as the seed exploded into a fireball, filling all the room, burning his hair and scorching his lungs, but harming Pariso not at all, the wizard secure within his fiery shield.

Entreri came up dazed, eyes filled with heat and smoke as all the building around him burned. Merle Pariso stood there, laughing wildly.

He had to get out. He couldn't possibly defeat the mage, and wouldn't survive for much longer against Pariso's potent magic. He turned for the door, thinking to dive right through the wall of fire, but then a glowing sword appeared in midair before him, slashing hard, and he had to dodge aside and get his dagger up against the blade to turn it. The invisible opponent—Entreri knew it to be Merle Pariso's will acting through the magical dweomer—came on hard, forcing him to retreat, and with the sword always staying between him and the door.

On his balance now Entreri was more than a match for the slicing weapon, easily dodging and striking back hard. He knew that no hand guided the blade, that the only way to defeat it was to strike at the sword itself.

That posed no great problem for the warrior assassin, until another glowing sword appeared. Entreri had never seen this before, had never even heard of a wizard who could control two such magical creations at the same time.

He dived and rolled, and the swords pursued. He tried to dart around them for the doorway, but found that they were too quick. He glanced back at Pariso, to see the wizard (though barely through the growing smoke), still shrouded in defensive flames, tapping his fireball wand against his cheek.

And the heat nearly overwhelmed him. And the flames were all about, on the walls, the floor, and the ceiling. Wood crackled in protest, beams collapsed.

"I will not leave," he heard Merle Pariso say. "I will watch until the life is gone from you, Artemis Entreri."

On came the glowing swords, slashing in perfect coordination, and Entreri knew that the wizard almost got what he wanted, the assassin barely, barely avoiding the hits, diving forward, under the blades, coming up in a run for the door. Shielding his face with his arms, he leaped into the fire, thinking to break through the battered door.

He hit as solid a barrier as he had ever felt, a magical wall, he knew, and then he was scrambling back out of the flames, into the burning room where two swords were waiting for him. Merle Pariso stood calmly, pointing the dreaded wand.

But then, to the side of the wizard, a green-gloved, seemingly disembodied hand appeared, sliding out of nowhere and holding what appeared to be a large egg.

Merle Pariso's eyes widened in horror. "Who?" he stuttered. "What?"

The hand tossed the egg to the floor, where it exploded into a huge ball of powdery dust, rolling into the air, then shimmering into a multicolored cloud. Entreri heard music then, even above the roar of the conflagration, many different notes climbing the scale, then dropping low and ending in a long, monotone humming.

The glowing swords disappeared. So did the wall of magical flames blocking the door, though the normal fires still burned brightly along door and wall. So did Merle Pariso's defensive fire shield.

The wizard cried out and waved his arms frantically, trying to cast another spell—some magical escape, Entreri realized, for now he was obviously feeling the heat as intensely as was Entreri.

The assassin realized that the magical barrier was likely gone as well, and he could have turned and run from the room. But he couldn't tear his eyes from the spectacle of Pariso, backpedaling, so obviously distressed. To the amazement of both, many of the smaller fires near the wizard then changed shape, appearing as little humanoid creatures, circling Pariso in a strange dance.

The wizard skipped backward, tripped over a loose board, and went down on his back. The little fire humanoids, like a pack of hunting wolves, leaped upon him, lighting his robes and burning his skin. Pariso opened wide his mouth to scream, and one of the fiery animations raced right down his throat, stealing his voice, burning him inside.

The green-gloved hand beckoned to Entreri.

The wall behind him collapsed, sparks and embers flying everywhere, stealing his easy escape.

Moving cautiously, but quickly, the assassin circled wide of the hand, gaining a better angle, and realizing that it was not a disembodied hand at all, but merely one poking through a dimensional gate of some sort.

Entreri's knees went weak at the sight. He nearly bolted back for the blazing door, but a sound from above told him that the ceiling was falling in. Purely on survival instinct, for if he had thought about it he likely would have chosen death, Entreri leaped through the dimensional door.

Into the arms of his saviors. . . .